POLI SCI FI

Poli Sci Fi: An Introduction to Political Science through Science Fiction allows readers, students, and instructors to explore the multiple worlds of science fiction while gaining a firm grasp of core political science concepts. This carefully composed text is comprised of sixteen brief chapters, each of which takes a prominent science fiction film or television episode and uses it to explore fundamental components of political science. The book is designed to serve as a supplemental text for undergraduate political science courses, especially Introduction to Political Science. The structure and content of the volume is shaped around the organization and coverage of several leading texts in this area, and includes major parts devoted to theory and epistemology, political behavior, institutions, identity, states, and inter-state relations. Its emphasis on science fiction – and particularly on popular movies and television programs – speaks to the popularity of the genre as well as the growing understanding that popular culture can be an extraordinarily successful vehicle for communicating difficult yet foundational concepts, especially to introductory level college students.

Michael A. Allen is Assistant Professor of Political Science at Boise State University.

Justin S. Vaughn is Associate Professor of Political Science at Boise State University.

Poli Sci Fi: An Introduction to Political Science through Science Fiction is destined to become a classic. The authors artfully present complex political science concepts, such as theory, epistemology and inter-state relations, through a science fiction lens that is sure to generate high student interest and lively class discussion. This novel book covers the core concepts of an introductory course – the perfect way to breathe new life into Politics 101.

Caroline Heldman, Occidental College

Poli Sci Fi is a fun and entertaining book to help students find political meaning in entertainment. The chapters are crisply written and provide provocative questions to stimulate thought and discussion. Students and instructors alike will find it fascinating!

Todd L. Belt, University of Hawai'i-Hilo

Thoughtful and thorough, this text proves that learning about politics through science fiction represents the best of what our discipline offers students and citizens alike. *Poli Sci Fi* is engaging, practical, and fun. It will be a must-read in courses across the American, comparative, IR and political theory subfields.

Brian Robert Calfano, Missouri State University

A very helpful supplementary text for introducing undergraduates to political science. Its leveraging of the implied or overt politics in well-known science fiction works will help students to see and understand important concepts and issues in familiar contexts while at the same time avoiding the informational biases and ideological baggage that tend to be tied to specific real-world cases.

William B. Heller, Binghamton University

POLI SCI FI

An Introduction to Political Science through Science Fiction

Edited by
Michael A. Allen and Justin S. Vaughn

NEW YORK AND LONDON

First published 2016
by Routledge
711 Third Avenue, New York, NY 10017

and by Routledge
2 Park Square, Milton Park, Abingdon, Oxon OX14 4RN

Routledge is an imprint of the Taylor & Francis Group, an informa business

British Library Cataloguing in Publication Data
A catalogue record for this book is available from the British Library

Library of Congress Cataloging in Publication Data
Names: Allen, Michael A., editor. | Vaughn, Justin S., 1978- editor.
Title: Poli sci fi : an introduction to political science through science fiction / [edited by] Michael A. Allen, Justin S. Vaughn.
Description: New York : Routledge, 2016. | Includes bibliographical references and index.
Identifiers: LCCN 2015036328| ISBN 9781138639768 (hardback) | ISBN 9781138639775 (pbk.) | ISBN 9781315637013 (ebook)
Subjects: LCSH: Science fiction--History and criticism. | Politics in literature. | Politics and literature.
Classification: LCC PN3433.6 .P65 2016 | DDC 809.3/8762--dc23
LC record available at http://lccn.loc.gov/2015036328

ISBN: 978-1-138-63976-8 (hbk)
ISBN: 978-1-138-63977-5 (pbk)
ISBN: 978-1-315-63701-3 (ebk)

Typeset in Bembo
by Integra Software Services Pvt. Ltd.

CONTENTS

PART VI
Inter-state Relations 197

FIGURES

INTRODUCTION

Science Fiction as a Tool of Political Science

Michael A. Allen

BOISE STATE UNIVERSITY

Justin S. Vaughn

BOISE STATE UNIVERSITY

Arthur Dent, waking up hung-over from overindulging in a party the previous night, walks downstairs to complete his morning routine just as his entire house begins to rumble. Unbeknownst to him, the city has planned to demolish his house in order to build a highway bypass. The plans had been on display in the cellar of the bureaucratic office for the past year. Troubling as this might sound, the razing of Dent's home soon becomes trivial compared to the imminent destruction of the Earth, as it too has been planned for demolition in order to build an intergalactic bypass. The citizens of Earth could have filed a complaint at any point prior to the planet's destruction, although as Earthlings had yet to develop the technology required for intergalactic travel, they, like Dent, did not know about the planned demolition.

The opaque bureaucracies of *The Hitchhikers Guide to the Galaxy* offer a parody that is not far from many of our own experiences with these government institutions. For example, the alien bureaucrats are so formalistic and droning that their poetry, which is considered nearly the worst in the universe, drives people mad. Is there a reason why bureaucracies are complex and difficult for outsiders to understand? Many of us do not enjoy dealing with the Department of Motor Vehicles or the Internal Revenue Service; is there a better alternative? Why is putting up the plans in the cellar of the local planning office fair to Arthur Dent or anyone else? Why does policy implementation sometimes look different than what we expect from legislation? These are the kinds of questions that fiction like *The Hitchhiker's Guide to the Galaxy* provoke and allows us to explore in a way that resembles but is still divorced from the reality in which we live our daily existence. This happens to be a humorous and satirical example; others strike far different emotional chords.

A more somber film opens up to a scene of huddled people, walking through the rain in 1944 Poland. These men and women shuffle into a concentration camp signifying to the audience the inevitable fate that awaits this newly arriving group of Jews, who we recognize by the gold stars they wear on their clothing. We see a child separate from his mother and, in his anguish as soldiers restrain him from going to his parents, the boy seems able to manipulate metal with his mind. This harrowing scene allows us to begin to understand the world Magneto, the arch-villain of the X-Men, grew up in, a world where humans exterminate his people along ethnic lines. Decades later, Magneto sees the beginnings of a second genocide as a different government, this time the United States, targets a different group of people he belongs to: Mutants.

The *X-Men* trilogy, and the second trilogy starting with *X-Men: Origins*, poses challenges for us to think critically about, especially concerning the struggles of a people as they deal with persecution, assimilation, and try to find the best course to deal with a hostile society. Can an event like the Holocaust happen again? Are Professor Xavier and Magneto (with his Brotherhood of Mutants) representations of Dr. Martin Luther King, Jr.'s non-violence path and Malcolm X's (with the Nation of Islam) more radical alternative during the civil rights movement of the 1960s? Are the movies simply entertainment, retellings of our past, warnings of our future, or parallels to ongoing struggles such as the LGBT movement's crusade for equal civil rights?

These difficult questions are not unique to the *X-Men* movies or *The Hitchhikers Guide to the Galaxy*. Much of science fiction examines, interprets, reflects, and exaggerates the world around us. Science fiction can explore serious social, cultural, and political questions through humor and parody or with gravity and drama. It is with such an understanding that we present this volume that uses science fiction to illustrate the key terms and ideas of political science. By doing so, we can figure out what science fiction can illuminate about what we know about the political world while also using political science to delve deeper into the realm of science fiction.

One of the biggest challenges in political science is that our research is, with the exception of laboratory experiments, historical in nature. This is true whether we are engaged in theory building, qualitative analysis, single case studies, comparative case studies, or quantitative analysis. This focus on the history of the political world leaves some level of emptiness in our research as we cannot manipulate time (or space), alter a few variables, and see what happens under different circumstances. Science fiction, on the other hand, gives us the space we need to explore the counter-factual – that is, we can explore things that did not actually happen.

Why Science Fiction?

Science fiction – or, as it is more commonly known, sci fi – typically focuses on worlds well beyond our own, offering opportunities for students and faculty alike to conceive important ideas in ways outside the typical constraints of our normal frames of reference. By using salient examples from the world of science fiction, we can use what happened in galaxies far, far away to better understand social scientific ways of thinking about what is happening now, just as observing the causes and consequences of fictional characters boldly going where others have not yet been can enable us to better understand the determinants and dynamics of political actions here on Earth. The authors of the essays in this volume use science fiction examples many students will already be well familiar with to communicate lessons from political science in a way that will stimulate interest, facilitate conversation, and underscore often complex concepts in fun and understandable ways.

Although science fiction engages in both the "what-if" of possible and impossible outcomes, it often remains firmly rooted in the period in which an author creates it. Many of the television shows and movies in this volume were adapted from written works whereas others were original screenplays. Regardless of their origin, the works we examine within this volume reflect upon the current political, social, cultural, and religious environment that an author resides in; whereas the technology may seem to be from a distant future, the struggles the characters face find their roots in the last few centuries of human existence.

Star Wars, a series of foundational movies that we turn to three times in this volume, certainly reflects the political considerations of George Lucas and the directors of the movies. This, perhaps, is most telling when the dialogue of the prequel movies parallels the ongoing debates in the United States about terrorism, domestic security, and increasing United States involvement in conflicts in Afghanistan and Iraq. *Idiocracy*, which Conor Dowling discusses in Chapter 4, reflects perennial concerns in democracies about the intelligence of the average voter and whether the masses are fit to participate in politics. Mary Beth Sullivan's discussion of *Ender's Game* in Chapter 15 takes on the task of war and the delicate balance between conducting a just war versus an unjust one. Orson Scott Card's original short story from 1977 – which led to a book in 1985 and a movie in 2013 – reflects the increasing tools of destruction states have as they engage in wars and intervention during and after the Cold War.

Even though political scientists are limited in how much predictive power we have in thinking about counter-factual cases, we do employ them in our analysis. We carefully create theories, models, and test our hypotheses on cases and make causal claims about the relationships between some event and some outcome. However, despite our careful attention to detail and specification, we are limited in our ability to fully imagine alternative scenarios with confidence. Science fiction has more freedom in this because, after all, it is fictional. By carefully constructing alternative realities where some facts are different, some variables change their values, some governments are less (or more) democratic, and some technologies are more (or less) deadly, the authors and filmmakers allow us to glimpse this world and imagine with them how everything plays out. We may, ultimately, disagree with how we expect particular actors or characters ought to behave, but this is not too far akin from adjusting preference parameters in a formal model and solving the equation a second time. Science fiction enables us not only to imagine a world of different possibilities, but also to examine our theories in a different world and see if they hold up. If they do not, then we can ascertain whether our theories are wrong, or perhaps the science fiction is missing something fundamental.

The films and television episodes discussed in this volume are ones that readers can watch alongside the material. Together, this should yield some engaging conversations about important and sometimes difficult topics. We think the chapters presented here engage the movies and TV shows on both science fiction and political science terms and illustrate how each genre of human understanding informs each other. Taken together, the chapters in this volume and the science fiction they engage offer a novel contribution to any introductory course on political science while also exploring some classic and important works in science fiction.

Plan of the Book

We organized the volume around six sections, which span the breadth of the discipline and mirror the coverage found in leading core texts on this topic. These sections include theory and epistemology, political behavior, political institutions, identity, states, and inter-state relations. Our section on Theory and Epistemology includes two essays that use a pair of recent successful films to underscore the central approach and assumption in the formation of political science knowledge. In the first substantive essay of this volume, Jennifer Kelkres Emery uses *Minority Report* – the Tom Cruise feature about law enforcement arresting "criminals" before they were able to commit their intended crime – to present the importance of measurement and prediction, key hallmarks of empirical research in political science. Additionally, while engaging in the construction and use of quantitative research in political science, Emery discusses at length the numerous problems with measurement in political science research, tying them to plot points in the film.

In Chapter 2, Benjamin Farrer uses the film *Equilibrium*'s plot about a totalitarian society where feelings have been banned to discuss rational choice, a central assumption in much political science research. This chapter helps to establish the foundations of rational actor models, game theory, predictions about human behavior, and the limits of such assumptions. Providing a basic introduction to the underlying ideas of rational choice and game theory, Farrer then links this new knowledge to everything from fight scenes to important personal choices made in the 2002 action-packed Christian Bale/Taye Diggs vehicle.

The second set of essays comprises our Political Behavior section, and accordingly focus on key dimensions of individual actions and attitudes relevant to political life and systems of governance. The three chapters in this section concern ideas of citizenship, voting and political participation, and political culture and ideology. In Chapter 3, Ted Brown and Christie Maloyed investigate notions of citizenship through its depiction in the 1996 cult classic, *Starship Troopers*. The authors investigate what it means to be a citizen in both democratic and non-democratic societies as well as understanding what the ideal of being a "citizen" means. *Starship Troopers* provides an excellent point of discussion, given the film's distinction between citizens and civilians, the different benefits provided to each group, and the path one must travel to leave one and ascend to another. They contrast the model presented in *Starship Troopers* with others, including those of ancient Greece and Rome as well as the United States, and elaborate on the advantages of citizen-based governance, especially when it comes to matters such as war and peace.

For Chapter 4, Conor Dowling uses another cult favorite, *Idiocracy*, to ponder the role of information and knowledge in elections. Taking the brainless dystopia from that 2006 movie as his point of departure, Dowling answers important questions such as: Do we need an informed citizenry to have a functioning democracy? How do voters make shortcuts that approximate their political interests? What role can the media play and how important is the media in shaping public perception?

The final chapter in this section focuses on two essential yet complex concepts in political science: political ideology and political culture. Using the 2014 film *Divergent* as the lens through which to view these concepts, Jocelyn Evans shows how the attitudinal and behavioral differences in the five factions of that film can help students understand the impact ideology and culture have on the different groups in contemporary society and the systems that govern those groups. Through an examination of the manifestos that provide each faction their mission and meaning, Evans shows how each group represents separate cultural entities that are also motivated by their own disparate ideologies. Evans shows how these two dimensions are simultaneously distinct and interwoven.

Our third section, Political Institutions, includes five essays, each of which engages one of the most important formal institutions in the study of political science. The first of these essays, Chapter 6, deals with executives, as Joseph Uscinski uses the range of portrayals of executive power and leadership across the *Star Wars* universe to explore questions of how much power is appropriate and the consequences of more or less executive power, subjects that are at the forefront of politics and political science alike today. Uscinski uses the creation and evolution of the American presidency as his central example, and between his discussions of that position and those found in the *Star Wars* series, covers significant theoretical and empirical ground.

In Chapter 7, Zachary Callen stays within the *Star Wars* universe, but emphasizes the insights the series provides into several foundational legislative politics concepts, including representation, deliberation, and interest group influence. In an excellent pairing with Uscinski's essay, Callen shows how it is not just the skills or preferences that legislators and those who seek to influence them have, but rather it is the manner in which the institutions are designed that structures the opportunity for leadership and representation.

Chapter 8 sees a return to *Divergent*, as Steve Lem distills lessons about party politics from observations about the factions at the heart of that film's narrative. Taking the reader through the steps from attitude formation to party affiliation, Lem shows how the process young people in *Divergent* go through is similar, if more permanent and fateful. In doing so, Lem distinguishes between factions and political parties before moving to a final question, one which matters equally to contemporary democracy as it does to the plot of *Divergent*: is independence dangerous or desirable?

In the next chapter, Ray Carman uses a landmark episode from the 1993–1999 television series *Star Trek: Deep Space Nine* ("Tribunal") to discuss central ideas in the study of judicial politics, such as judicial independence, separation of powers, and legitimacy. Carman's essay is particularly concerned with civil liberties, and contrasts a judicial system – in this case, that of Cardassia – where they are utterly absent with today's American system, where they are protected, if frequently contested. At each stage of the criminal justice process, we see not only the differences between what we are used to and how it could be different, but also the possible consequences of those potential differences.

In the last essay in this section, Scott Robinson and Justin Vaughn use *Futurama* as a lens through which to view bureaucratic politics. Focusing on Hermes Conrad, a character who embodies nearly every stereotype imaginable about bureaucrats, Robinson and Vaughn assess three separate episodes of the long-running animated sci-fi sitcom. In their observations they show that whereas *Futurama* is humorous, its depiction of the roles and responsibilities bureaucrats hold, as well as the ethical dilemmas they face, is spot on whether we are talking about the twenty-first century or the thirty-first.

The fourth section, Identity, emphasizes key groups and issues involved in the political decisions and developments of the day. The chapters in this section examine two major categories: gender and race. Lilly Goren uses the rebooted *Battlestar Galactica* franchise to explore gender dynamics, using the struggles of a small fugitive fleet seeking the safety of a fabled Earth to comment upon the multiple ways notions of gender affect and are affected by politics and contests for power. Goren identifies three central characters – fighter pilot Kara "Starbuck" Thrace, President Laura Roslin, and Number Six, the Cylon infiltrator – from the 2004–2009 SyFy network program that manifest qualities relevant to Goren's discussion of the categories and waves of feminism.

In Chapter 12, Jennifer Kelkres Emery and Jocelyn Evans use the experience of District 11 – one of thirteen districts comprising Panem, the nation-state portrayed in *The Hunger Games* trilogy – as a cultural entry point to discuss the relationship between race and politics. Distinguishing between the largely white, Appalachian residents of District 12 and the people of color who reside in the agrarian District 11, Emery and Evans show how different groups in different places can be marginalized in different ways based on their identities. They also use these identities as a way of exploring representation theory and how someone such as

Katniss, the trilogy's protagonist, can credibly claim to represent not only her own district, populated as it is by people with so much in common with her, but also other districts who are filled with people who are very different.

The fifth section, States, emphasizes the types of states studied by political scientists and two related problems states face: the breakdown of democracy and civil war. Julie VanDusky-Allen's Chapter 13 analyzes how democratic regimes break down, using *V for Vendetta* as a fictional example before expanding the observations there to explain similar devolutions in several European and African states. In it, VanDusky-Allen shows how only a few short steps separate the United Kingdom of today from that which is portrayed in *V for Vendetta*'s near future. By detailing these steps, VanDusky-Allen also reveals the cornerstone institutions and practices of contemporary democracy and shows what must be protected if we want to retain it.

Michael Allen then analyzes the ultimate form of government change – civil war – by returning to the *Star Wars* universe and showing how the breakdown of the Republic into warfare between the Empire and the Rebellion reflects what scholars know about the root causes of intra-state wars as well as how those conflicts typically end. Allen's essay shows that civil wars depend on getting a meaningfully resourced group to rebel, something a state may thwart through a variety of tactics. Once a civil war starts, however, Allen shows they tend not to end in negotiated peace, which is exactly what we observe in the *Star Wars* series.

Finally, our sixth section concerns the interactions between states. The two essays in our Inter-state Relations section concern different expressions of this phenomenon: war and foreign policy. In Chapter 15, Mary Elizabeth Sullivan probes notions of ethics, security, and warfare via her analysis of *Ender's Game*, comparing tactics and decision making in that fictional setting to real-life moral reasoning about warfare and violence. Focusing primarily on the 2013 film, but with references to the 1985 novel, Sullivan provides an introduction to just war theory, and applies the tenets of that theory to the events surrounding Ender Wiggins, including Earth's decision to go to war and how that war would be waged.

In the last chapter of this book, Michael Flynn returns to *Battlestar Galactica* as he focuses on foreign policy, with a particular emphasis on who makes policy decisions and how those decisions are made. Flynn is particularly concerned with one aspect of foreign policy decision making: civilian control of the military. Flynn's distinction here is institutional, and the chapter goes into valuable detail as it shows how institutions identify both the rules structuring available options and the individuals who have a role in choosing these options. Flynn's discussion shows how even in the chaos surrounding the denizens of *Battlestar Galactica* as they seek to escape the sneak attack and subsequent pursuit of their enemy, the Cylons, it is essential to maintain civilian control over military affairs.

Chapter Discussion Questions

1. How can science fiction be a helpful way of understanding political science concepts? What do you think might be the limits of how helpful science fiction can be? Why?
2. What do you think the authors mean by "counter-factual" and how do you think this would be helpful in wrestling with concepts we cannot otherwise manipulate in a laboratory-like setting?
3. What are some science fiction examples not brought up in this book that you think apply to key aspects of politics today? Why?

PART I

Theory and Epistemology

1

IMPROVING PUBLIC POLICY

Measurement and Prediction in *Minority Report*

Jennifer Kelkres Emery

THE WASHINGTON CENTER

An early scene in *Minority Report* shows a television ad encouraging voters to vote "yes" on National PreCrime Initiative. The advertisement states that the District of Columbia has had the PreCrime policy for six years and has eliminated murder in the district. Should the voters support the expansion of this program across the nation? One way to answer that question is to consider whether it supports American values. A politician onscreen is ready with the answer: "We want…to ensure that what keeps us safe will also keep us free." Those are fundamental values in America: freedom and the value of human life. A second way for voters to consider the policy is to consider whether the policy is effective. A chorus of voices in the advertisement agrees, "It works." The ad makes an effective case for the two key questions in evaluating public policy: "*Will it work?*" and "*Should we do this? Is it morally right?*"

This fictional advertisement provides a succinct look at the theme of *Minority Report*, which is the use of analysis to improve public policy decisions. The film contrasts two approaches, examining both facts and moral values to make the best policy decisions. Political debates often become confusing for voters in part because these two approaches to decision making are so different. Politicians can argue without addressing their opponent's point, by responding to moral claims with a factual argument, or vice versa. Understanding the difference between factual and moral queries can simplify politics for voters, which is a worthy goal and essential to a functioning democracy.

Governments have the power to control most aspects of life within their borders, from the roads we drive on to the quality of water that comes out of the tap. A government can maintain defenses, build infrastructure, regulate the products we buy, and through tax incentives control which industries provide job opportunities. All of these are the sum result of many decisions concerning the level of taxation, and the ways the government invests our tax dollars. These political decisions are mostly discussed in the US in terms of liberalism and conservatism, that is, what are our priorities to invest in? However, this chapter addresses a more fundamental question: How do we know which policies work? Which policy option will provide the greatest return on the investment?

This chapter will address three topics. First, the chapter will present two types of analysis and point out the strengths and weaknesses of each approach. Second, we will delve deeper into the scientific process used to make predictions. Third, the chapter details problems an analyst could encounter with measurement. Not everyone understands the best practices of the scientific approach. The goal of this chapter is to illuminate the predictive power of the scientific approach. Using measurement and prediction is an effective way to make political decisions. The movie, *Minority Report*, is based on a short story by an author, Philip K. Dick, and seems to have had the intention to use this story as a way to teach about the scientific method. The story of *Minority Report* illuminates obvious pitfalls of the method, but it also demonstrates the tremendous possibilities and power of social science to solve problems.

Solving Societal Problems: Morals versus Science

The purpose of this section is to clarify the difference between moral arguments and arguments based on scientific analysis. The story presents the two types of analysis, both moral ("Should PreCrime be the policy choice for the nation?") and empirical ("Does PreCrime work?"). The purpose of this paper is not to suggest that one is more valuable than the other, but rather, the two complement one another, but cannot be used to refute each other. They are both essential to decision making and solving problems in the world.

A foundational concept in political science is political analysis, meaning, the method used to solve a puzzle. Public policy offers many puzzles worthy of study, for example: Does government surveillance make America safer? Is a fence or deportation the most efficient way to limit illegal immigration? Does increasing free trade create more jobs in America? Does raising the minimum wage help or hurt the economy? As voters, we are often confused about how to answer these difficult questions. There are two main approaches, which are usually referred to as positivism and normativism.

Normativism approaches the world in terms of "What ought to be happening in the world?" whereas positivism asks "What is happening in the world?" Both questions are necessary to direct public policy. The story of *Minority Report* contrasts these two questions. As head of the PreCrime Unit, Anderton is responsible for making the unit's operations effective – a positivist endeavor. As the story unfolds, he also ponders whether their work is justified. He is predicted to become a murderer, but does not commit the crime. Knowing that some of those prisoners could have been innocent, Anderton questions whether he ought to have jailed so many people. He says to Dr. Iris Hineman, cofounder of PreCrime, "What about those people I put away with alternate futures? My God, if the country knew there was a chance they might not. . . [support the policy of PreCrime]." Iris replies, "The system would collapse." Although PreCrime was found to be efficient, it was ultimately demolished because decision makers decided that justice was more important than safety – a normative decision. As Dr. Iris Hineman said to Chief John Anderton, "Who wants a justice system that instills doubt?"

That conversation in the greenhouse is a key example of normative thinking because it prioritizes the way people ought to be treated. The efforts to colonize the moon, to conduct stem cell research, to build nuclear bombs, and to intervene in foreign wars are all policies in which there is a clear contrast between positivist and normative decision making. The fact that the government is able to accomplish a task does not make it something the government ought to do.

Normativist work is interested in prescribing optimal solutions to political, social, and economic problems. Depending on your values, the definition of the "best" outcome could be quite different. Consider that someone who values equality may prefer affirmative action policies, but someone who values freedom may not. However, most policy solutions typically cannot maximize several values at once, so our policy choices require some compromise. Usually, some freedom is sacrificed when we prioritize equality or efficiency, and vice versa. Determining which values should guide these choices is the essence of normative analysis, "an approach to the study of politics that is based on examining fundamental and enduring questions."[1] Political philosophy and political theory use normative analysis.

In contrast, positivism is a term used to refer to the philosophy of seeking facts to make decisions. The facts of the situation determine what outcomes are possible. The facts inform the analyst about whether the economy is growing or is in decline; whether illegal immigration is increasing or decreasing; or whether there is a tax surplus or deficit. This is empirical analysis, an approach that "seeks to identify observable phenomena in the real world with a view toward establishing what is, rather than what ought to be."[2]

The tension between the two approaches can be felt in the film. At the outset of *Minority Report*, a federal agent, Ed Witwer, arrives at the D.C. PreCrime unit ready to investigate the system for any weaknesses. As the police chief of the unit, Anderton is responsible for convincing Witwer that the unit's processes are flawless and ready to be duplicated across the nation. Although the department seemed to be performing perfectly – capturing all murderers – several flaws in the system become apparent as the story plays out. Anderton is accused of a future murder, and he goes on the run to clear his name and investigate this apparent flaw in the PreCrime system. He ultimately discovers that the founders of PreCrime, Iris Hineman and Lamar Burgess, kept secrets about the program to ensure its popularity.

The secrets kept by the two cofounders mirror the theme. Burgess concealed information about how PreCrime could not exist, and Hineman's secret concerned why PreCrime should not exist. Burgess murdered the mother of Agatha, the most valuable of the PreCognitive agents (known as "PreCogs"), because she wanted to withdraw Agatha from her captive life as a PreCog. Losing Agatha would have doomed the program. Hineman hid the fact that occasionally one of the PreCogs would see a different future from the other two PreCogs. This knowledge would have undermined support for the program given that the future is not predetermined and that PreCrime is fallible. This potential of a different future – the "minority report" – is where the movie derives its name. While acknowledging the importance of moral guidance, the rest of this chapter focuses on highlighting the advantages, disadvantages, and complexity of scientific research.

Normative analysis examines whether or not a policy supports our fundamental beliefs, but does not offer the ability to make predictions. Positive analysis does.

Prediction is important for practical reasons as well as emotional ones. Humans seem to have a fascination with predicting the future. Religion and mythology represent our desire to know what the future holds; so does science. The story of *Minority Report* illustrates the importance of prediction in several ways.

Eyesight is woven into the story as a metaphor for the guiding role of empirical analysis. Without his sight, John Anderton makes several mistakes. While his eyesight recovers, he attempts to find food in the refrigerator. There is a deli sandwich, and some mysterious, slimy dinner plate. There is a bottle of milk, and another full of green sludge. Blind, he chooses the wrong one of each pair, and washes them down by drinking from a box marked as a biological hazard. This represents how observing the world around us is essential to making good decisions.

The movie serves to present our desire to know the future as a fundamentally human desire, on par with religious beliefs. The PreCrime building is referred to as a temple, and the PreCogs are treated as holy figures. One character compares religion and science saying, "Science has stolen all our miracles." The delineation, however, is not as stark as it seems. Science has harnessed the Pre-Cognitives' abilities, but not explained them. Religious predictions about the end of the world typically rely on the process of empirical observation, e.g., the end times appear near because certain events are similar to those described in a religious text.

Prediction is also important for practical reasons. Both individuals and organizations make long-term investments. Your retirement investment is made using predictions about the future stock and bond market. The Congressional Budget Office makes predictions about the future of America for the purposes of advising Congress about how to write legislation. Industries sometimes lobby for regulation, because regulation makes the future easier to predict, and corporations have to make long-term investments in building factories and power plants up to the regulated standards. Surprises can be economically disastrous, which is why the insurance industry exists. Despite its flaws, prediction is an essential part of life and an instinctual part of being human.

The Scientific Method and the Process of Measurement

The scientific method gives us tremendous leverage in answering questions of political importance. The scientific method is to observe, hypothesize, test, and draw conclusions from the test results. You may already be familiar with the way this process is applied in the natural sciences, for example physics and chemistry. The scientific process looks quite different when political scientists pursue this method. Not only does the process of quantitative research look different, but political science also frequently engages in another approach that is also scientific qualitative research. Each approach has benefits and drawbacks.

Both approaches begin with observation of the world around us, and then developing a hypothesis. Speculating about the world to develop a hypothesis clearly requires some arrogance to believe that you might know something about the way the world works. Yet, it also requires the humble presumption that you might be wrong. A proper hypothesis is falsifiable.[3] That means that it is possible to prove your claim incorrect. Here is a falsifiable statement: It is raining in your neighborhood while you read this chapter. By contrast, the claim that unicorns exist is unfalsifiable. It can be proven true if a unicorn is located, but it cannot be proven false. The lack of unicorns does not prove their non-existence. Therefore, the claim that unicorns exist is not a falsifiable claim and therefore not a scientific hypothesis.

The search for unicorns can be approached using science. A fitting hypothesis might be "The newly discovered species uncovered in this archeological dig is the remains of what we now call a unicorn." This hypothesis can then be tested against a set of characteristics that the scientist asserts are a part of our popular conception of unicorns. Clearly, a hypothesis concerning vampires or zombies would be more difficult to test because the definition of those creatures has many variations and those assertions would be controversial

Quantitative research focuses on finding a way to measure concepts on a scale where each value can be easily compared to another. A scale has measurements that are evenly spaced, and can be interpreted as having more or less of the concept being measured. For example, political leanings are usually quantified into a seven-point scale using a survey question, where the survey respondent is told to classify themselves assuming that zero means "very liberal" and seven means "very conservative."

In contrast, when we classify concepts, this is called qualitative research. Qualitative research is often a necessary precursor to quantitative research. Examples of qualitative research are focus groups, interviews, and reading archived materials. These are open-ended analyses, and the results can suggest certain types of quantitative data that would be useful to pursue further. Think of the challenges posed by studying corruption; corrupt officials tend to hide their behavior. Qualitative interviews with current and former elected officials might reveal previously unsuspected methods for corruption, and the use of those methods can then be measured quantitatively. Qualitative analysis opens up new areas of research whereas quantitative analysis provides defined, numerical prediction. When considering a policy proposal, qualitative evidence might support the proposal by providing case studies and personal testimony about its success. However, quantitative evidence could provide a specific percentage chance that the policy will achieve the goal.

Although quantitative measurement has endless potential to provide us with information, it must be developed correctly. The measurements are the building blocks of the research process. Measurement is the process of observing changes in phenomena, for the purpose of predicting what makes them change and how they will change in the future. The first step in the process is to decide which particular aspect of the concept should be measured. Many people find value in knowing the weight of the food they eat in a meal; others are interested in measuring the meal's nutritional value, or cost. When it is time to vote, voters might pick the most experienced candidate, the most moral candidate, or the best-looking: that step relies on a normative analysis about what is good for society.

The second step is to choose the scale used to measure this aspect. This is also called quantifying or classifying concepts – that is, attaching a number or classification to the concept. If you measure out cereal for your breakfast, you could measure it by volume (a cup) or by weight (in grams) using a food scale. If measuring another aspect of the cereal, such as nutrition, this could be quantified using calories or grams of sugar. Looking at political candidates, one might classify them as having a left or right political ideology. In order to assign a particular number to their ideology, organizations like Americans for Democratic Action (ADA) and the American Conservative Union (ACU) examine each politician's Congressional voting record. The organizations use a similar method to create something called an index – a weighted combination of measures. The ADA describes their method thus: "Each year, ADA's Legislative Committee selects 20 votes it considers the most important during that session. ADA's National Board and/or National Executive Committee approves those votes. Each member receives 5 points if he/she voted with ADA, and does not receive 5 points if he/she voted against us or was absent. The total possible is 100."[4] Both the ADA and the ACU index are used in presidential election years to label the candidates as moderate or extreme, depending on their rating.

In the social sciences (e.g., political science, international studies, psychology, economics, sociology, and others) there are more often measurement choices than in the natural sciences. In the film, for example, the government could track the movement of its citizens using a tracker implanted underneath our skin, or a tattooed bar code, but here the choice was to use eye scanners. The choice is significant. Consider the question "Which is the most violent nation in the world?" As with the example of the cereal, the amount is the aspect scholars choose to measure. However, the amount of violence could be measured as the amount of money spent on the military; the number of wars fought; the number of bombing campaigns; or the number of people killed by its military. In addition, one could exclude the number of citizens killed within the nation's borders, which would exclude violence caused by civil war or repression. Based on the intentional murder rate, the answer might be Honduras.[5] Using the number of refugees, Sudan might be the answer, or Syria if studying violent repression.[6]

The second step is to quantify or classify the concept. In some cases, the work is already done and your only task is to locate the data. For example, in the film, the PreCogs produce the killer's identification. The definition used by the PreCrime unit is the killer identified by the majority of the PreCogs, two out of the three. However, a more accurate definition would be to use one PreCog's identification whenever it differs from the group, as Agatha has been shown to be the most accurate of the three. In the political world, quantification is sometimes simple but often difficult. If you are interested in the most productive economies of the world, you can easily find measurements for the GDP of most nations. On the other hand, if you want to know how much political corruption exists in these nations, you may have to create the data yourself. Let's say in the first step you have defined corruption as bribes exchanged for legislation. You will not find a dataset measuring this, provided by the governments themselves. Scholars have already studied this issue in the US and Europe. If you would like this data on Africa, you would read about the process others used to create the measurement in other nations, and repeat their process. As a researcher, you may even find improvements on the measurement process and share those suggestions by publishing them for other scholars to use. Those improvements often come about because researchers discover problems with previously published work. For example, a scholar who defined corruption as bribery might have mistakenly labeled some nations as free of corruption, but in reality nepotism and drug trafficking are common among government officials.

Problems with Measurement

Research is not easy; analysis is a complex process that is constantly evolving. We struggle to develop new methods to accomplish major goals. Mankind has worked toward many noble goals in the natural sciences: plotting the movement of the planets; landing men on the moon; and sending robots to Mars. It is no less amazing that we have developed the ability to predict when the country is slipping into economic recession, or who will win the presidency based on polls of only 1,000 voters. The process of empirical analysis has given us these gifts. In *Minority Report*, the gift is a city that has been free of murder for several years – and yet, viewers know that was a lie. The problems caused by inaccurate measurement become clear in *Minority Report* as the system struggles to identify and capture the correct criminal.

The PreCrime methodology has several components that make it what Anderton calls a "perfect" system. Three people called "PreCognitives" are kept in a pool connected to a system that projects the visions they have of future crimes. From the visions, the agents extrapolate the place and time of the murder, and meet the killer prior to the murder. However, empirical measurement can fail in several ways. The story demonstrates several ways that measurement is vulnerable to mistakes.

First, the paradox: The ultimate flaw in prediction is that free will can still influence what happens. Does prediction still represent prediction if you act to avert the future? Anderton poses this question to Witwer during his first visit to the PreCrime unit. Anderton rolls a ball down a chute, and Witwer catches it before it falls to the ground. Witwer caught the ball because it was going to fall, just as PreCrime jails citizens because they were going to commit a crime. But would they commit the crime if they knew their fate? Anderton finds out during the course of the film that he is predicted to commit a murder, and because of that knowledge he does not commit the crime.

In political science, this same issue complicates our experiments. In the social sciences, experiments usually involve human subjects. If a person suspects the hypothesis behind a survey, the person is likely to provide incorrect answers in an attempt to give the researcher what they want to hear. It is human nature to be suggestible, to want to please, and to give answers that represent oneself in the best possible light. For example, survey respondents lie about having voted, or having voted for the winner of an election, because it makes a person feel good to be right or have done the right thing. Therefore, researchers often try to hide the purpose of the experiment from the participants. Another technique is to tell the participants that the survey serves a different purpose to distract them from suspecting the truth. However, this type of deception can be unkind to the participants and is therefore carefully monitored by the institutions that fund and govern research.

Second, one of the common flaws in measurement is incomplete measurement. This refers to a situation where data is available only for part of the object being measured. For example, if we collect data on the literacy rate in countries around the world and cannot get information on countries with an active civil war or especially secretive governments, the missing nations would be missing data. The term missing data is most often used to refer to incomplete measurement but is misleading because missing data does not refer to cases where data is not yet measured or appears impossible to measure.

The movie includes several examples of "missing data" or incomplete measurement. In the case of the PreCognitives, they provide images from the murder, but not a complete picture. The agents have to imagine how the images relate to each other; sometimes they guess at the temporal order of the images and the layout of the crime scene. Making these assumptions about missing data is called interpolation, and it is also common in the social sciences. For example, in the United States, the Census Bureau counts the number of citizens every decade. Population change is continual, so analysts assume changes are taking place within the decade even though those changes are not measured. Most economic data is only reported quarterly, and again daily, weekly, and monthly change is assumed based on the quarterly trends.

Third, the title itself – *Minority Report* – puts the focus on the flaws within the existing data. In the story, two PreCognitives tend to provide similar reports and the third, Agatha, often provides a slightly different and fuller vision. Her vision is sometimes discarded as the "minority report", thought to be less accurate because the other two do not share the same vision. This type of process is often modeled in the real world. In predicting who will win a presidential election, analysts will use at least three measures to understand public opinion, for example, comparing three polls conducted in the same week by different organizations. If two polls suggest the Republican will win, the third poll predicting the Democratic win will be discounted. However, the discarded data may contain clues to the bigger picture. It is the responsibility of the analyst to learn whether the results differed because of a mistake or random chance. Polls, like all research, can only predict accurately if the entire research process was managed with care. A poll conducted with 1,000 voters in Ohio might be representative of the nation – but it would not be representative if Ohio voters are seeing different campaign commercials. Similarly, handlers knew Agatha to be the most accurate PreCog and so her reports became more respected and valued, even when in the minority.

Fourth, transparency in the method of data collection is important so that data cannot be faked. An agent monitors the visions alongside two official observers who keep the process transparent. The record of the criminal's name cannot be forged, because it is etched into wood, which has a unique grain difficult to recreate. Witnesses are sworn in to monitor the agents.

However, when Anderton finds that he is identified as a murderer, he is able to grab the evidence of his name and convince the other agent to leave for a snack break. He is able to turn off the monitors so the official observers are cut out of the process. The PreCognitive's caretaker is the only person who sees the vision immediately – and because they are friendly, he offers Anderton two minutes before he pulls the alarm. These weaknesses in the system give John the chance to escape.

Fifth, validity is the extent to which data measures what it claims to measure. In the film, there are some concerns about validity. For one, the images produced by the PreCognitives are sometimes misleading. The image of the murder supposedly committed by John Anderton showed a man in sunglasses outside the window. When he arrives at the scene, John comes to understand that there is no man – only a billboard in a nearby building. Second, eye scans are used to identify people for security and for advertising. Unsurprisingly, the criminal element has devised a means to outsmart the eye scans surgically replacing your eyeballs. Anderton has the surgery and is therefore able to break into the PreCrime headquarters and steal their most valuable asset, Agatha, the PreCog with the most complete visions.

A sixth concern is the accuracy of the system. PreCrime appears to be reliably predicting and preventing all murders in D.C. with no error. However, policies without error are impossible, just as it is impossible to arrive for an appointment exactly on time – you must choose a course of action that biases you either towards arriving slightly early or slightly late. A justice system serves as a good example because it will inevitably make mistakes; the choice is to determine what type of mistakes should be made. The United States justice system is constructed to lean towards something called "false negatives" or a "Type 2" error. Using the rule of "innocent until proven guilty," the system is biased toward letting the accused go as long as there is reasonable doubt. This is a false negative because when the system lets an accused criminal free, the jury searched for guilt and found none (the negative). Some of the accused criminals who win their case and are set free may really be criminals, in which case they would be a false negative – no guilt was found, but it exists. Put another way, a false negative error is when the researcher does not find evidence to support their hypothesis, but the hypothesis is actually true.

The major claim about PreCrime – "It works!" – is justified by the fact that PreCrime is not making any Type 2 errors, or "false negatives." No killers have been set loose, clearly, because no murders have been documented. The PreCogs are stable and consistent – they regularly produce new visions, and often the killers are found close to the murder with their intentions made clear. The policy is celebrated for the security it provides.

However, it is unknown how many Type 1 errors are made by the system. In a justice system, setting the guilty free constitutes a Type 2 error, and jailing the innocent constitutes a Type 1 error. A Type 1 error, or "false positive," is when the researcher is fooled by evidence to believe their hypothesis is confirmed when it is not. Anderton is in denial that he has arrested anyone who was innocent. He expresses shock, and sorrow, at the idea: "You're saying that I've halo'd innocent people? …What about those people I put away with alternate futures? My God, if the country knew…"[7] Anderton's experience proves that Type 1 errors are possible, and ultimately leads to PreCrime being abandoned at the end of the film.

Type 1 errors are considered dangerous to a justice system that is based on a normative decision to value freedom over security. Type 1 errors are also dangerous in scientific research because future research efforts will be based on those false findings. Therefore, research is constructed to purposely bias against Type 1 errors by starting with the assumption that the hypothesis is wrong and looking for evidence that it is correct. The way to guard against Type 1 errors is by creating falsifiable theories.

As discussed at the start of this section, falsifiability means there has to be evidence out there that can be collected that could prove the hypothesis wrong. Normative claims can never be proven wrong (e.g., freedom is more important than security), whereas scientific hypotheses always have that possibility. Scientists and justice systems lean towards Type 2 errors to guard against falsehoods. However, politicians and corporations have strong incentive to lean toward Type 1 errors because the appearance of success and infallibility is key to their success.

Conclusion

Dr. Hineman ordered Anderton to, "Find the minority report!"[8] This statement metaphorically represents the main pursuit of academic scholars: to look critically at observations already made, to improve upon existing forms of measurement, with valid, reliable, and complete measures that can fully represent the concepts we seek to understand. This is an essential part of the academic pursuit.

Yet, science is not only academic – it is so much more. It is useful for future endeavors in each of our lives. Humanity has developed a tremendous tool that cannot be ignored: the ability to make predictions about the future using the scientific process. Learning about the process is pertinent to the reader because in a democratic society each person has the right and responsibility to get involved in making decisions about government action. Government actions affect almost every detail of our lives, and often rely on scientific predictions to act.

This chapter has presented the reasons we pursue scientific analysis, the process by which it is pursued, the danger of making mistakes in the process and ways to ward against those dangers. There are huge errors that are made – for example, jailing the innocent – that pose moral questions for society. As long as science is used, there is a chance of errors being made, but the system can be biased toward either "false positive" or "false negative" errors. To select the best type of error, it requires scientists to have a conversation with normative analysts about the risks we are willing to take. These two types of analysis – moral and scientific – are opposed in many ways, but uniting them is the best way forward.

Chapter Discussion Questions

1. What are the two main approaches to analysis outlined in the chapter? Give an example of each approach in the movie *Minority Report.*
2. What are the two steps in measurement outlined in the chapter? Give an example of each approach in the movie *Minority Report.*
3. What are two ways in which measurement is vulnerable to failure? Give an example of each approach in the movie *Minority Report.*

Notes

1 Magstadt, Thomas M. 2015. *Understanding politics: Ideas, institutions, and issues.* Stamford, CT: Cengage Learning.
2 Garner, Robert, Peter Ferdinand, and Stephanie Lawson. 2012. *Introduction to politics.* Oxford: Oxford University Press.
3 Popper, Karl. 2002. *The logic of scientific discovery.* New York: Routledge.

4 "Voting Records," Americans for Democratic Action, http://www.adaction.org/pages/publications/voting-records.php, accessed May 11, 2015.
5 "Global Study on Homicide," *United Nations Office on Drugs and Crime*, 2015, http://www.unodc.org/gsh, accessed May 11, 2015.
6 "Global Peace Index: 2014," *Institute for Economics & Peace*, http://www.visionofhumanity.org/sites/default/files/2014%20Global%20Peace%20Index%20REPORT_0.pdf, accessed May 11, 2015; Shavin, Naomi 2014. "The most and least peaceful countries ranked as the global impact of violence reaches $9.8 trillion," *Forbes*, June 18, http://www.forbes.com/sites/naomishavin/2014/06/18/the-most-and-least-peaceful-countries-ranked-as-the-global-impact-of-violence-reaches-9-8-trillion, accessed May 11, 2015.
7 Spielberg, Steven. 2002. *Minority Report*, Los Angeles, California: Twentieth Century Fox Film Corporation.
8 Ibid.

2

EQUILIBRIUM

If Game Theorists Ruled the World?

Benjamin Farrer

KNOX COLLEGE

Preston is alone in what looks like a religious building, practicing a complicated martial arts routine, when he hears a voice: "Always practicing, Cleric… I guess that's why you're the best." Brandt interrupts him and they begin to spar, with Brandt continuing to taunt Preston, whom he suspects of being a traitor and of having murdered a group of soldiers the previous night. Without proof, all Brandt can do is drop hints that the authorities know that Preston is guilty "There are theories… I have one or two of my own… Whoever did it, all they accomplished was a quicker end to the resistance." The sparring goes on, until they simultaneously find an opening and reach what would be the point of mutual destruction. They both know the training routine so well that there are no unforeseen consequences. They each know the optimal counter-move to everything their partner throws at them, and finally arrive at a stalemate. In the larger game, though, Preston is dealing with a multitude of unforeseen consequences. He must find the optimal counter-move to continue his work with the resistance, but he is far less practiced at being a subversive agent than he is at martial arts. He wants to make the "right" decision, which is easy when you know what the future holds and what your opponent is likely to do – but far harder when the future is uncertain and you have no idea how to predict your opponent's move. How can people make the "right" decisions in those situations?

In this chapter I explore one of the most misunderstood concepts in political science – the idea of "rational choice." It is a way of understanding human choice based on personal consequences and so the basic definition of a rational choice is a choice that makes you better off. After someone has made a choice, we aim to understand why they thought that choice would make them better off: how did they "rationalize" that choice? Arguments that use a rational choice framework will focus on explaining why people made the choices they did, or will make predictions about what choices people are likely to make in the future. But rational choice arguments differ wildly in what they place under the umbrella of "choices that make you better off." After all, everyone has different definitions of "better off." As rational choice theorists, we strive to understand which definition of "better off" the people we study are using. As such, "rational choice" is a tool for communicating your arguments about the political world, rather than being a tool for explaining the political world. On its own, rational choice does not explain anything. The argument, the real explanatory power, needs to come from your idea about what "better off" means for the people in question, and only once this idea is in place can rational choice be useful for communicating that idea. This is what leads to the misunderstandings. It is easy to see rational choice as a trivial concept because at heart it is only a communication tool, similar to drawing a graph or a flowchart to explain a process. But rational choice can be a uniquely powerful way to communicate your argument, ideas, or theories. It helps you check the internal logic of your argument, convey your ideas in a parsimonious (that is, brief and to the point, thus reaching your audience as quickly as possible) but rigorous way, and in the hands of an expert, it can even help us deconstruct the most fundamental assumptions behind our arguments and reconstruct new hypothetical worlds based on different assumptions.

We start by looking at the most straightforward way to use rational choice: as a way to formalize and communicate an existing argument. *Equilibrium* is a useful movie to watch when discussing this topic, for a couple of reasons. First, it portrays a society controlled by a faction of individuals who are guided by a twisted version of "rationality." Looking at their vision of "rationality" not only helps us understand what rational choice is in political science, but also helps us understand the difference between using this communication tool wisely and using it unwisely. We will bring out these parts of the movie towards the end of the chapter. The second and more important reason why *Equilibrium* is a good companion movie is that at several points it highlights the two key things you need to understand in order to use rational choice yourself: utility and expectation.

Together, these two concepts constitute the central idea of rational choice: when individuals are confronted with a choice, they choose whatever option they believe will make them better off. This simple sentence actually conveys a very controversial idea and makes some complicated assumptions. But in essence, rational choice really is as simple as it sounds. When faced with a choice, individuals choose the option that gives them the highest expected utility. *Equilibrium* gives several important examples of how people do this, and it also puts these choices in a context that helps highlight the broader significance of these choices. So what is going on in *Equilibrium*?

Equilibrium is a 2002 science fiction film, directed by Kurt Wimmer, and starring Christian Bale, Sean Bean, Taye Diggs, Sean Pertwee, and Emily Watson. The film portrays the futuristic, dystopian human society of "Libria," which is rigid, authoritarian, and controlled by a shadowy organization called the Tetragrammaton. This organization communicates mostly through ubiquitous public video screens and is also in control of a large standing army that helps keep the population under control. The population is largely peaceful, however, and seems content to live under the Tetragrammaton. This manufactured consent exists because citizens must take mandatory pills called "Prozium" that suppress their emotions. This suffocation of human nature keeps the regime intact and has prevented most crimes of passion, has ended war and conflict, and has rendered society extremely docile – albeit at the cost of robbing it of almost all culture. To some, this society is a welcome respite from millennia of human conflict. But to others, it is a prison.

Enforcing the rules of this society is Preston, played by Christian Bale. He is a "Cleric," one of several heavily armed police officers who operate outside and above the standing army and who arrest citizens if they stop taking their pills (if they commit "sense-offenses," in the parlance of the film). If they are off their medication, these sense-offenders begin reciting romantic poetry, hoarding colorful trinkets, and generally being emotional. This behavior is viewed by the Clerics as a menace to society, and so the Clerics hunt them and confiscate their possessions. The film begins with a scene depicting a raid on a sense-offender hideout and the inevitable death of Sean Bean's character Partridge (Sean Bean seems to have cornered the market in playing science fiction and fantasy characters who come to untimely ends), but then it continues with Preston gradually wondering if those sense-offenders were not actually onto something after all.

A Basic Introduction to Expected Utility

So what does this movie have to do with political science? Well, let us return to the idea of expected utility. John Von Neumann and Oskar Morgenstern introduced this term in their 1944 classic, *A Theory of Games and Economic Behaviour*,[1] as a way of thinking about how humans make decisions when they are uncertain of the outcomes of those decisions. They introduce this framework in a simple way: imagining two games of chance, two lotteries, and then asking how to choose between multiple lotteries. Lotteries are simple games of chance that are simple to think about, but they can be used as a template for studying decision making in any situation where multiple outcomes are possible. So how do we choose between lotteries? If there are two different games in the casino, which one gives you the best odds of winning the most money? There is a mathematical answer to that question. The expected utility of a lottery is defined as: the probability of an outcome, multiplied by the benefits/costs of the outcome, summed over all possible outcomes. In mathematical terms, the definition is as follows:

$$EU(1) = \sum_{i=1}^{n} p_i b_i$$

Where *I* is a lottery situation which has *n* possible outcomes, labeled 1, 2, 3 …, all the way up to *n*, and for any given outcome *i* there is an associated probability and an associated benefit. So if one of the casino games was flipping a fair coin, such that if it comes up heads you get $1 and if it comes up tails you lose $5, then Von Neumann and Morgenstern would say that the expected utility of that lottery is –$2. Why? Well, you have a 50% chance of getting $1, so the probability of the outcome is 0.5 and the benefit of the outcome is 1. We multiply those two numbers and get 0.5. The other possible outcome of the lottery is that you will lose $5, and that outcome will occur with probability 0.5 too. We multiply those two numbers and get −2.5. Finally, we sum the expected utility over all possible outcomes (either heads or tails) to get an overall expected utility of –$2.

Conceptually, this represents your best guess as to what will happen if you decide to play this lottery. You can think of it as an average, a sort of balancing between the two possible parallel universes that you could end up in if you play. In one parallel universe, you will lose $5, and in the other, you win $1. Because you have a 50/50 of ending up in either of those hypothetical scenarios, your expected utility is an average between them. To take another example, imagine rolling a six-sided die, such that you win a number of dollars equal to the number displayed. So if the die comes up 6, you win $6, etc. The expected utility of that lottery is a positive $3.50 if there is not a cost to play it. Knowing that, we can say it is a rational choice to pay $3.49 for a ticket to play that game. It would also be rational to choose the dice game over the coin game, if you had a choice between the two lotteries, because the expected utility of the dice game is higher than the expected utility of the coin game.

The concept of expected utility is intuitive and straightforward. It helps us understand how people make choices, even when they are not entirely sure what the consequences of those choices will be. The rational choice school of political science argues that this basic model can be used to understand human decisions. Your decision to read this line of writing is an example. You have calculated (presumably unconsciously) that there is at least some probability that reading this will lead to a good outcome. Perhaps the good outcome is some knowledge you hope to acquire, some conceptual problem you hope to solve, or some grade you hope to earn. You might value that good outcome very highly, or not very highly at all. But that good outcome is only one possible outcome. The other possible outcome is that you learn nothing and have wasted your time. You have (again presumably unconsciously) estimated the probability of the good outcome occurring versus the probability of the bad outcome occurring: you might think you are extremely likely to receive the benefit if you keep reading, or you might think it is a long shot and you are probably wasting your time. But if you are still reading, then expected utility must be the explanation: the expected utility of the "reading the book" lottery must be higher than the expected utility of the other lotteries you could be playing right now. Note what the implication is here: if you have the opportunity to play a different and more valuable lottery, then the "reading a book" lottery seems unappealing. But if you are locked in a cell and given no alternative opportunities to pursue, then reading a book might suddenly appear worthwhile. Economists would distinguish between the first scenario, where there are "high opportunity costs" to reading, and the second scenario, where there are "low opportunity costs" to reading.

Of course, the paragraph above is not a great explanation for your behavior. A real explanation would have to include a more precise argument about exactly what you think the supposed "good outcome" is, and about how you estimated the probability that reading these words is an activity likely to bring you the good outcome. It would include the negative utility of not doing the reading for a class (if you are reading this for a class), and it would specify what your other lotteries are. If this were a busy week for you with lots of other activities that you would rather be doing, then we would need to specify that there are other attractive lotteries out there that you could be playing.

Two points are important here. The first is that hypothetically a true equation does exist that fully specifies all the potential costs and benefits of your decision, and all the potential costs and benefits of every other choice you could have made. You can imagine that this is essentially an infinite equation, because it would have to specify every possible consequence of every possible decision. Even the simplest decision, such as deciding whether to read a book or to go outside, could have a potentially infinite web of consequences, and those consequences would be impossible to fully list in an equation. But we will assume that this equation exists. The second point is that, fortunately, we do not need this infinite equation. We only want the simplified version that includes the most significant consequences. So if we are explaining your behavior, we do not include every potential benefit you might conceivably receive from reading this book, and we do not attempt to specify the probabilities you associate with this potentially infinite set of outcomes. Nor do we try to list every other possible decision you might have made (it is clear that even for a trivially simple choice, this would be impossible). Instead, we just talk about what we think the main benefits are. Trying to learn something. Trying to pass a class. We give our "best guess" as to what we think your estimated probability of this occurring is. Perhaps 50/50. Then we come up with what we think your best alternative lottery is. Once we have done that, we have a relatively parsimonious model that still retains explanatory power and communicates our main argument about what we think the primary factors driving your choices are.

Expected Utility in *Equilibrium*

Equilibrium gives us an interesting perspective on this idea, because it imagines a world where it is possible to construct simplified models of very complicated situations. In the world the Clerics inhabit, all of their martial arts training ("Gun Kata") is supposed to be based explicitly on expected utility. Their individual fighting decisions – whether to punch or kick, whether to duck or jump, whether to fight or flee – are all based on their ability to consciously assess the expected utility of the various lotteries they must choose between. So if a Cleric is facing three opponents in an alley, they might be choosing between a dozen or so lotteries. The first lottery is if you choose to punch the first opponent. In that lottery, you have a 50 percent chance of connecting with your first punch and knocking them out, a 25 percent chance of missing and doing no damage… and so on and so forth. The second lottery would be to kick the first opponent. In this lottery, you have a 25 percent chance of hitting and a 75 percent chance of missing. The idea of Gun Kata is that Clerics are explicitly trained to know what the best possible lottery is in all possible fight situations. They can look at an opponent, or a group of opponents, and immediately make a decision about how those opponents are likely to behave and what strategy is likely to be most effective against them. They can tell you that a punch has 75.42989238 percent of connecting, and they can tell you the exact amount of damage that will be done by it. You can imagine their martial arts training as a sort of manual, telling you in any situation what the expected utility of each potential option is.

Gun Kata therefore makes explicit what most of the time remains unconscious. Our decisions are often made in a millisecond, and if we were asked to explain those decisions later, we probably would not put it in terms of "evaluating the expected utility." But according to rational choice theorists, we make all of our decisions in a way very similar to how Clerics make their fighting decisions. Importantly, in the movie, Preston has a conversation with another Cleric where they reveal that Gun Kata evolved out of studying thousands of hours of footage of fights, and using that footage to estimate the probabilities that a given human will behave in a given way. So if you have witnessed a million fights, you probably have a pretty good idea of how people will react to a particular martial arts move. But *Equilibrium* also asks the bigger question: can people really be that predictable?

Rational choice theory classifies every situation as a lottery, with clear probabilities. If we have no idea what the relevant probabilities are, then we cannot calculate expected utility. If we are seeing a coin flip for the first time, and have no idea whether it is a 50/50 lottery or not, then it will be impossible for us to make a decision. If you are fighting a type of person you have never encountered before, and that there was no footage of, you would not be able to accurately estimate how they will behave. We would say that rational choice could still apply in that situation. If someone were forcing you into a choice between heads and tails, you would just have to make an uninformed guess as to what the probabilities were. And if you encounter a new type of person, you could just guess that they are probably going to be similar to the average person. But in these unforeseen situations, like the one Preston confronts when he joins the resistance and acts as a subversive agent within the Tetragrammaton, rational choice is not as useful an analytical tool as it would be in a situation with more explicit probabilities. Maybe martial arts *is* an area where people are predictable. Maybe you believe that if someone throws a punch at your face, then 99 times out of 100, you duck. That is certainly the logic of Gun Kata in *Equilibrium*.

A famous application of precisely this framework to political science is the "calculus of voting."[2] Voting is not fun, in and of itself. People do not usually volunteer to walk to an arbitrary location on a random Tuesday in November, stand in line for a while, and then tick a box, just for the sake of doing it. So why do so many people bother to do these activities on Election Day? Riker and Ordeshook argue that it is possible to understand this using rational choice.[3] We will walk through a simplified presentation here of whether an imaginary voter will vote, or not, in a two-candidate election similar to a United States presidential election. First, we specify the two main outcomes of voting. Once you've chosen to cast a ballot, two possible things can happen:

- Your preferred candidate wins the election.[4]
- Your preferred candidate does not win the election.

It should be relatively obvious which of these outcomes is the "good" outcome we want from the lottery, but we need to take both possible outcomes, and we need to formulate the *benefit* of each outcome and the *probability* of each outcome, for an imaginary "average" voter. To take the benefits of each possible outcome first:

- If your preferred candidate wins, the government will go in a direction you prefer. This will make your life better in many ways, for example lower taxes, or better public services. The only bad thing about this outcome is that you will still have paid the costs of voting, i.e., giving up some time and effort in order to vote.
- If your less-preferred candidate wins, the government will go in a direction you prefer less. This means you do not get any of the benefits in the first possibility. But again you will have paid the costs of voting, i.e., giving up some time and effort in order to vote.

Riker and Ordeshook therefore essentially say that the benefits of voting are dependent on how you evaluate the difference between the two directions in which the government could go.[5] In other words, if both candidates are identical, then they will both take the government in the same direction and the voter does not care who wins, and so voting has no benefits. But if the two candidates are not identical, then suddenly voting has benefits. One outcome of the lottery could be very desirable and the other could be highly unattractive. If one candidate is very similar to our imaginary voter, in terms of their political beliefs, and if at the same time the other candidate is the polar opposite of our imaginary voter, then there is a stark difference between the two directions in which the candidates would take the government, and the voter will clearly prefer the first candidate. To the voter, then, the first outcome (preferred candidate wins) has a bigger benefit, and the second outcome (less-preferred candidate wins) has a lower and perhaps even negative benefit. Thus voting will appear more consequential.

Riker and Ordeshook use the algebraic term B as a placeholder representing the extent to which your preferred candidate is better than your less-preferred candidate.[6] So if the candidates were identical, $B = 0$, and the more we make your preferred candidate's beliefs similar to you and make your less-preferred candidate's beliefs different from your own, the larger we can imagine B becoming. Note that we think of B as the difference between the candidates, regardless of the absolute levels of "utility" associated with the candidates. That is, our imaginary voter might hate both candidates, rating the first at a −100, and the other (the lesser of the two evils) at −99. So B here would be 1. Alternatively, the two candidates might both be wonderful, rated at +100 and +99, but B would still be 1. This way of thinking about it helps simplify the expected utility equation. Rather than writing a +100 and a +99, we just deal with a single parameter, B. Finally, we imagine the costs of voting as C, which refers to the time and effort you have to give up in order to vote (as mentioned earlier) and this can be assumed to be the same regardless of who wins. So, we can therefore take the first step in constructing a basic expected utility equation for voting, by writing the utility of each outcome. The utility of our preferred outcome is $(B - C)$ and the utility of our less-preferred outcome is $(-C)$, so the overall utility of voting is as follows:

$$(B - C) + (- C)$$

We have two sets of parentheses, each representing one potential outcome. In the first, our preferred candidate wins, so we get B but we pay C, and in the second, we do not get B but we still pay C. So far, so good. But we are only halfway there. We need to add the probabilities associated with each outcome. This is where Riker and Ordeshook have an important insight: the probabilities here are tiny.[7] It is very unlikely that your vote will make the difference in the election. In a United States presidential election for example, millions upon millions of people vote. No such election has ever been decided by a single vote. Our imaginary voter might decide to vote in the hope that the government goes in their preferred direction, but their decision to vote does not really have a huge probability of making much of an impact on the direction that the government takes. Riker and Ordeshook think that in any election of decent size, your probability of casting the deciding vote is very close to 0.[8] Now, our imaginary voter might acknowledge this but still think to themselves, "Well, what if everyone assumes that their vote will not be the deciding factor? Then, nobody will vote… and so, my vote actually could be decisive." Unfortunately, such a scenario is extremely unlikely because it leads to infinite regress: if everyone thinks that nobody is voting, then everyone might vote. But everyone can see that logic… and so everyone knows that everyone will vote… and so they know their vote will not be decisive… and so they might not vote… and we are back to the beginning again. Riker and Ordeshook convincingly argue that the probability that your individual vote will make the difference between obtaining *B* and not obtaining *B* is vanishingly small. We call this tiny probability *p*.[9] But Riker and Ordeshook also note that this probability really only applies to *B*, not to *C*.[10] The "*C*" parameter represents costs that you have to pay, whether or not you affect the outcome. The *C* parameter occurs with probability = 1. They add this into the equation and produce the following:

$$EU(v) = p(B) - C$$

Where *p* is effectively 0. Because even if *B* is huge (so if you were deciding between the worst possible candidate and the best possible candidate) this 0 will still wash *B* out, this equation means that there are always alternative lotteries that carry higher expected utility than voting does. If voting were a casino game, nobody would want to play it, because you have such a tiny probability of winning that even though the prize is worthwhile, you are so unlikely to receive it that there is no point in going to the effort of playing. So why does anyone vote?

Riker and Ordeshook try to solve this mystery by adding a "*D*" term[11] representing civic duty:

$$EU(v) = p(B) - C + D$$

Where did that term come from? They argue that we vote not because we expect to influence the outcome, or even because we prefer one candidate to the other, but simply because we think it is our civic duty to vote. This *D* term is unconditional – there is no *p* associated with it. We obtain the psychological "warm glow" of having done our duty by voting whether or not our preferred candidate wins. This is similar to arguing that people do not buy lottery tickets because they expect or even hope to win: they buy tickets because they enjoy the thrill of playing.

This rational choice model of voting has been critiqued[12] and expanded[13] but is still very influential despite its simplicity. The idea that expected utility is a good way of understanding all human decisions is a key component of the rational choice school of political science. Take any political phenomenon you are interested in. Pick anything. Then, figure out who the human actors are in that phenomenon. If you can write an expected utility equation for those actors, then congratulations: you are on your way to constructing a rational choice model. Rational choice has been used to understand decisions about whether or not a country will go to war, whether a federal country will stay together or collapse, how the United States President will negotiate with Congress, how party leaders in a coalition government will divide up ministerial portfolios, and whether activists will form political parties or interest groups to achieve their goals. And that is just a few.

There are plenty of examples of models you could imagine drawing out after watching *Equilibrium*. Before each of the major fight scenes, Preston falls silent and stares into the middle distance for a few seconds, calculating the expected utility of different strategies. In one scene six masked assailants confront him. He jumps into the middle of them, and then strikes one strange pose after another whilst firing his weapons. He is striking those poses so as to avoid the most likely lines of fire between six opponents of that height and weight, using those weapons, trained in the methods used by that group.

Outside the fight scenes, *Equilibrium* is full of interesting choices. What is the expected utility of trying to hide some contraband cultural artifact on your own versus telling a trusted friend or family member and hoping they will help? What is the expected utility of killing an opponent if you know they are taking a pill that suppresses their emotions, versus killing the same opponent if you know they are not taking that pill?

The Broader Environment of Rationality in *Equilibrium*

That question hints at another interesting point about *Equilibrium*. Is "rational choice" – the assumption that every choice is based on expected utility – a reasonable way of thinking about the world? It has certainly proved to be a controversial tool in political science,[14] with many objecting to its simplifying (almost trivializing) approach to human choices. It is easy to imagine why people would feel uncomfortable or even hostile toward academics making assumptions about their motivations. Even with the relatively mild voting example, it is not unreasonable to expect that people who have just overthrown an autocratic government and held their first democratic elections would be insulted by the implication that their desire to vote was somehow "irrational." Without question, rational choice models do a great deal of violence to individual narratives by extracting only what the modeler perceives as the key points. The question before us, though, is whether the benefits of doing so are greater than the costs of doing so. In essence, what is the expected utility of using expected utility models?

Even framing the question like that obviously betrays where I personally stand on this issue. I think rational choice can be useful for checking the internal logic of your argument. It encourages you to think in terms of actors, and their agency, and figuring out what people in the political world want. Note that "figuring out what people want" is not the same as assuming that everyone is acting selfishly. Acting selfishly is different than acting in your self-interest, because rational choice assumes the latter but not the former, and furthermore it makes no assumptions about how self-interest is constructed for different people. The parameters in your expected utility equation do not have to be selfish. For example, you can strive to make your friends and family better off because you have internalized their well-being as part of your own well-being. Because you feel their pain, working to make them better off is "'self-interested" from a rational choice perspective, but it is not "selfish" in the colloquial sense. Civic duty is conceptualized as a psychological benefit, and you could extend this and come up with a rational choice model of a completely selfless human being. You simply need to argue that it is in their self-interest to be selfless. They prefer being selfless to being selfish – being selfless gives them a psychological benefit, or put differently, they enjoy making other people happy more than they enjoy making themselves happy.

Rational choice not only encourages you to formalize the logic of your argument and therefore check its internal consistency, but it also allows you to make parsimonious arguments. If you can "do more with less" – that is, if you can construct a model that only has one or two parameters in it, and it still explains a lot of political behavior – then that is a valuable and probably generalizable model. Of course, it is easy to become too parsimonious, and a common critique of rational choice is that it relies on tautologies (i.e., circular reasoning: does a theory really have much traction if it simply states that "people vote because they enjoy voting"?). This is a valid critique – it is simply up to you to introduce arguments that make those tautologies interesting.

Equilibrium portrays a world of parsimonious explanations. A world where people think that war has only one cause – emotions. Is this the world that rational choice theorists want to live in, or think we already live in? Not really. Rational choice theorists assume that any individual has the right to estimate probabilities and evaluate outcomes any way they want. The cult that runs the dystopian world of *Equilibrium* has instead decided that they know best about what constitutes "utility," and which are good and bad outcomes for people. This cult can certainly be imagined as a group of rational choice theorists who have gotten carried away with making their equations simpler and who are prepared to suppress those individuals whose equations are complicated or unusual. But most rational choice theorists are self-critical, and know that their models cannot possibly explain all human behavior. People have so many diverse ideas about what is likely and unlikely, and what outcomes are defined as "good" and what outcomes are defined as "bad." If we construct a general model of behavior, we will undoubtedly be wrong in our predictions for some people who define their own utility is different ways. The best we can hope for is to provide a model that makes it clear what we think the main factors are. A common refrain among rational choice theorists is that all models are wrong, but some are useful. Many rational choice theorists, but not all, would agree that a useful model uses a parsimonious specification to create a generalizable and testable prediction. Voting is one area where people have made such models, but with a little imagination, it is straightforward to create your own.

Chapter Discussion Questions

1. Of all the characters in *Equilibrium*, whose version of "rationality" is easiest for you to understand? Whose motivations are most straightforward?

2. What does Prozium eliminate from the list of possible motivations for a character?
3. Does Preston act selfishly in this film, or does he internalize the well-being of others?

Notes

1 Von Neumann, John and Oscar Morgenstern. 1944. *Theory of games and economic behavior.* Princeton, NJ: Princeton University Press, 24–28.
2 Downs, Anthony. 1957. *An economic theory of democracy.* New York: Harper and Row, 36–45.
3 Riker, William H. and P. C. Ordeshook. 1968. "A theory of the calculus of voting," *American Political Science Review,* 62(1): 25–42; 25.
4 Note that we are introducing our own theory about what is important. Rational choice tells us how to present this theory; it does not tell us how to formulate it. Our idea that people have preferred candidates, and they want those preferred candidates to win, came from our own understanding of the political world.
5 Riker and Ordeshook, "A theory of the calculus of voting," 27.
6 Ibid., 26–28.
7 Ibid., 29.
8 Ibid., 39.
9 Ibid., 28.
10 Ibid., 25–28.
11 Ibid., 27.
12 Schuessler, A. A. 2000. *A logic of expressive choice.* Princeton, NJ: Princeton University Press, 30–38.
13 Brennan, G. and L. Lomasky. 1993. *Democracy and decision: The pure theory of electoral preference.* Cambridge: Cambridge University Press, 55–73.
14 Green, Donald and Ian Shapiro. 1994. *Pathologies of rational choice theory.* New Haven, CT: Yale University Press, 1–10.

PART II

Political Behavior

3

SERVICE GUARANTEES CITIZENSHIP

Starship Troopers and Democracy

Ted Henry Brown

SOUTHWESTERN OKLAHOMA STATE UNIVERSITY

Christie L. Maloyed

UNIVERSITY OF LOUISIANA AT LAFAYETTE

Most people living in modern democratic governments take for granted that citizenship is a birthright. Simply by being born in a country, an individual expects to have the liberty to speak and act freely, to have equal protection under the law, and to be able to participate in government. In the world of *Starship Troopers*, though, citizenship must be earned. In order to vote, run for political office, or even have children freely, individuals must serve a complete term of service to the government. When an alien bug species attacks the city of Buenos Aires, the earthly government, known as the Terran Federation, is caught off guard. The Federation ramps up recruitment efforts, especially for the Mobile Infantry unit, which will be the front line of defense in the bug war. One such recruitment ad opens the film: "Young people from all over the globe are joining up to fight for the future…They're doing their part. Are you? Join the Mobile Infantry and save the world – Service Guarantees Citizenship. To ensure the safety of our solar system, Klendathu must be eliminated!"[1] The Terran Federation uses the promise of citizenship to entice graduating high school seniors to join the war effort. As is the case in the audience's own world, the choice to enlist in the military during an active conflict is dangerous. In the United States, recent graduates may consider the risk of joining the military during an active conflict worthwhile given the promise of educational opportunities, job training, health care benefits, and the potential for a lifetime career. In *Starship Troopers*, however, enlisting and risking life and limb in battle against the bugs is the only way to gain the liberties of citizenship.

Starship Troopers offers insight into two related concepts in political science: citizenship and democracy. Today, most modern democracies grant citizenship status to anyone born in that country. Some democracies also offer the opportunity for foreigners to earn citizenship through military service, such as France through service in the Foreign Legion. Historically, however, most participatory and representative forms of government had highly regulated requirements for citizenship status that included restrictions on age, gender, property ownership, religion, military service, and lineage. *Starship Troopers* gives us a window into the ways society, religion, and culture influence ideas about who should be able to participate and the qualities that define good citizenship.

In addition to challenging our contemporary understanding of citizenship, the film also confronts a long-standing assumption in political science, that there is a clear relationship between military rule and regime type. Historically, military governments have been viewed as authoritarian regimes with power vested in the hands of a small number of military leaders. By contrast, the Terran Federation is governed democratically while also having strong military rule. Although only those who have completed government (typically military) service may participate as citizens, the process for choosing representatives and passing laws allows full participation for all those who have earned citizenship. Moreover, *Starship Troopers* challenges the idea that democratic governments are more likely to observe the rule of law and are less violent. Under Terran rule, Earth has been a very lawful place with extremely low crime rates and little conflict. Despite, or even because of the military rule, domestic peace has been easy to maintain and is only broken by the external attacks by the bugs.

Based loosely on Robert Heinlein's novel of the same name, the film offers the opportunity to question whether there might be advantages to military rule and a more restrictive form of citizenship.[2] Despite winning the 1959 Hugo Award for best science fiction novel, Heinlein's book received much criticism for its political ideas. Some critics claimed the novel glorified war and even promoted fascism, an authoritarian system of government that encourages extreme national loyalty.[3] Director Paul Verhoeven's film adaptation of the book mostly retains the same political structure outlined by Heinlein, but Verhoeven offers a far more critical examination of that system. Although a campy satire that lampoons the overconfident Terran government and its propaganda machine, the film raises serious political questions about citizenship and democracy.

The Moral Difference between the Citizen and Civilian

Starship Troopers makes clear early in the film that citizens have a different role to play in the Terran Federation than regular civilians do. Most of the students at Buenos Aires High School are sitting in their History and Moral Philosophy class, goofing off and seemingly unwilling to engage in the class discussion on what it means to be a citizen in the Terran Federation. Mr. Rasczak puts his student Johnny Rico on the spot and asks him to explain "what is the moral difference, if any, between the citizen and the civilian?" Johnny responds authoritatively: "The difference lies in the field of civic virtue. A citizen accepts personal responsibility for the safety of the body politic, of which he is a member, defending it, if need be, with his life. The civilian does not." Despite being correct, Rasczak derides Johnny for simply regurgitating the answer from the textbook: "But do you understand it? Do you believe it? Of course you don't. I doubt if any of you here would recognize 'civic virtue' if it bit you in the ass."[2] When Mr. Rasczak refers to civic virtue, he is invoking the ancient Roman idea that a citizen should be willing to sacrifice his own private interests for the sake of the common good. In this sense, virtue had less to do with religion, as we often think of it today, and far more to do with politics. Civic virtue might require a person to spend less time with their own family or business in order to attend public meetings, serve in a public office, or even join a military campaign. Even though Mr. Rasczak's students are on the brink of coming of age, most exhibit a lax attitude and are uninterested in the sacrifices necessary to become a citizen.

Under the Terran government, upon turning eighteen a person may volunteer for governmental service. Applicants are evaluated by a number of aptitude tests that measure everything from their math skills to their physical capabilities. After the completion of these tests, the volunteer is assigned a job. Although preferences may be specified and are sometimes honored, a person may be placed in any field or position based on the current needs of the government. That position may be in any number of different offices but it is understood that military service is a possibility. No volunteer is turned away regardless of race, gender, religion, handicap, or skills. Everyone who is willing is offered a position, even if it is simple manual or clerical labor. Moreover, anyone who has volunteered is free to quit at any time. However, that decision is final, as the person can never again volunteer. A term of service is typically two years but the government may extend terms as needed. Upon completion of a term, the volunteer is granted full citizenship rights, which include the right to vote, run for political office, financial support for pursuing degrees in higher education, and an increased likelihood of being granted a license to have children. Not all civilians are lucky enough to have the right to have children; Rico's parents are a rare example of civilians who are granted this privilege by the Federation. Despite being granted this right, his parents hold the government in contempt, which emphasizes the tension between the full citizens and civilians in the Terran Federation.

Citizenship has always implied that some people are full members of a society and that others are not. *Starship Troopers* is not new in suggesting that an individual should have to qualify for citizenship. However, those qualifications have varied widely across history and cultures, as have the rights and responsibilities associated with citizenship. Three historical examples from the ancient Western world offer different perspectives on what it means to be a citizen, both throughout history and also today: Athens, Sparta, and Rome.

Ancient Athens provides one of the oldest known examples of a democratic government. The term democracy comes from two Greek words *demos* (people) and *kratos* (rule). Although today we associate democracy with expansive citizenship rights, the Athenian democracy referred more to the process for making decisions, not who made those decisions. Only men of Athenian ancestry were eligible to qualify as citizens. At the age of eighteen, a free man could apply for citizenship with his local government, which would verify his eligibility. He would serve a short term of service, one to two years, where he would be trained to guard the city. At the age of twenty he would be eligible to attend the Assembly, which was responsible for all the major political decisions for the city. At the age of thirty he could apply to serve jury duty and he would be eligible for political office, both of which were selected by lottery. This model of citizenship has exclusive membership rights. Most estimates suggest only 30,000 people were full citizens of the 100,000 residents of Athens.[5] Citizens enjoyed many rights, including the right to speak freely at the Assembly and directly vote on laws. Moreover, participation was expected of citizens, especially if their name was drawn by the lottery to serve as a political officer.

By contrast, the city of Sparta operated under a form of participatory military rule. As with Athens, only free men were eligible for citizenship. However, the requirements were more stringent and tied to military service. In Sparta, male children were raised in common from the age of seven until twenty and underwent an extensive physical and mental education in the military arts. At the age of twenty, men began service in the military. Subsequently, a man could pursue membership in a "mess," a group of men who ate meals in common and maintained their military camaraderie. The current members of the mess needed to vote unanimously for a new member to be admitted, and he would need to pay monthly dues to the mess. He would earn the needed money from land given to him and worked by slaves. Members of the mess were eligible and expected to participate in the Assembly, one of Sparta's governing bodies. Failure to uphold laws, evidence of cowardice in battle, or failure to pay mess dues would all lead to the revocation of citizenship.[6] This model of citizenship made eligibility highly exclusive based on age, property ownership, military service, and personal conduct. The rights of citizenship allowed one to participate in the governing process, alongside the Council of Elders and the Spartan kings, but it also required a high level of responsibility in terms of participation.

The imperial Roman government offers a third model of citizenship. In the city of Rome, citizens could participate in their government in limited ways through popular assemblies or by being elected as a magistrate or tribune, a representative for the common people. However, most of the real political power was controlled by the Roman Senate, which was dominated by the patricians, members of the elite class. Unlike Athens and Sparta, Rome covered a vast geographic space. Although under the Roman Republic citizenship had been limited to free men of Roman birth, qualifications were eased as the empire expanded. As new territories were conquered, residents of those cities were offered dual citizenship. So long as they paid their taxes and did not violate Roman laws, they could retain their local governmental structures. Although they did not have the right to vote in Roman elections, they were given legal protection as citizens, such as the right to a trial and the right to sue.[7] By altering the membership requirements for citizenship, the expectations for citizens were dramatically lowered. Neither civic virtue nor participation was expected. Citizenship was redefined from a political concept that carried both rights and responsibilities to a legal classification that simply ensured legal protection.[8]

In the early modern era, the concept of citizenship was reinvigorated by a number of political revolutions. In the English Civil War (1641–1649), the leaders of the rebel movement, known as the Levellers, wanted the political distinctions between the highest and lowest classes to be removed and demanded that the franchise be extended to all free men. Similar demands were made during the French Revolution (1789–1799). Following the American Revolution, issues of citizenship were left for each state to decide. At the adoption of the U.S. Constitution in 1787, it was common for citizenship status to be reserved to free, white men who were at least twenty-one years of age and were either property owners or taxpayers. Suffrage, which is the right to vote, was only formally guaranteed to black men with the passage of the Fifteenth Amendment in 1869. This right was continually denied, however, especially in the South. Literacy tests with difficult questions about history and politics were given to African Americans as a means to disqualify them from registering to vote. Similarly, many counties required voters to pay a poll tax to discourage poor African Americans and whites from voting. Although some Western states granted women suffrage in the late nineteenth century, women were denied the right to vote in most states until the passage of the Nineteenth Amendment in 1920. Property requirements were eased in the 1820s but re-emerged following the Civil War as a way to prevent African Americans and poor whites from voting.[9] Even today, many states continue to bar convicted felons and individuals found mentally incompetent from voting. Although suffrage has been widely expanded from its earliest conception, it is still far from universal.

Citizenship in the United States today is closest to the imperial Roman model. Citizens are guaranteed equal rights under the law but participation is not required. For instance, take the issue of voting. In the United States voting is treated as a right and often many voters choose not to exercise that right. Typically only 60 percent or less of eligible voters participate in presidential elections, with much lower turnout in other years. By contrast, some democracies treat voting as a responsibility. Several democracies including Australia, Belgium, Brazil, Cyprus, Luxembourg, and Uruguay have passed compulsory voting laws where eligible voters who do not participate are subject to fines.[10] Much as there are differences surrounding expectations for voting, countries also differ in their treatment of military service. In the United States, all men between eighteen to twenty-five years of age are required to register for the Selective Service, although the U.S. has not held a military draft since the Vietnam War. Other modern democracies, however, treat military service as a requirement for citizenship including countries such as Austria, Greece, Israel, Poland, and South Korea.[11] By way of comparison, the model of citizenship under the Terran Federation draws elements from both the Spartan and Athenian models. The Federation requires government service in order to be eligible to vote or run for office. However, many of the ancient qualifications, including gender and property ownership, are dropped. Given that citizenship is more exclusive, there is a higher expectation regarding the responsibility of citizens to sacrifice for their country and participate politically.

Citizen Rule – People Making a Better Tomorrow

Although democracies guarantee rights and freedoms to citizens through birth and sometimes service, simply extending suffrage does not mean that a government is necessarily democratic. Is the Terran Federation a democracy, an authoritarian government, or some form of mixed regime? One way to think about how to characterize a government is by who exercises power. In democracies, as Abraham Lincoln famously put it in the Gettysburg address, government is "of the people, by the people, for the people." This definition has historical roots that stretch back to the ancient Greek philosopher Aristotle. He argued that three legitimate types of government exist and can be defined by who governs: only one person rules in a monarchy; in an aristocracy a few rule; and in a polity – or a mixed regime – many people rule. He also classified three corresponding illegitimate forms of government which he considered corrupt because they were ruled out of self-interest rather than for the common good: tyranny, oligarchy, and democracy. While it may seem odd to contemporary readers for democracy to be described as an inherently corrupt form of government, Aristotle's argument is that the best form of government is a mixed regime that is ruled with input from all classes of people and does not favor the interests of any one group. In his view a citizen is a person who "rules and is ruled in return" or put differently, one who can "participate in judicial functions and in office."[12] Being able to have a meaningful voice in government – whether through directly passing laws, being elected to office, or sitting on juries – is the hallmark of citizenship. In *Starship Troopers*, whereas citizenship is linked to the ability to exercise certain political privileges that civilians are precluded from, citizens and civilians are both guaranteed legal protections. Because citizens can participate in the rule of their government, by Aristotle's definition, the Terran Federation might reasonably qualify as democratic.

Although democracy for Aristotle centered on citizens having a meaningful role in government, approaches to democracy in the modern world emphasize both individual participation and choice. Economist and political scientist Joseph Schumpeter argued that democracy is best understood as a process for selecting leaders. The democratic method, in his view, provides "an institutional arrangement for arriving at political decisions in which individuals acquire the power to decide by means of a competitive struggle for the people's vote."[13] Schumpeter proposes an elitist view of democracy where the main role for citizens is to select leaders rather than make political decisions themselves. By contrast, political scientist Robert Dahl argues, a modern democracy requires that an election can only work properly if there are opponents that have a legitimate chance to win.[14] Elections without meaningful choices cannot be considered democratic in his view. Another critical element to Dahl's definition of democracy is that there are peaceful and smooth transitions between representatives following elections. Uncontested transitions of power are evident in the Terran Federation. After the failed invasion of Klendathu, Sky Marshal Dienes resigns and is immediately and peacefully replaced by Sky Marshal Meru. The incoming Sky Marshal outlines a new approach to the war against the Arachnids and the troops seamlessly undertake this change in leadership.

Despite the peaceful change in leadership, the ability of an opposition party to win an election in the Terran Federation is not readily apparent. *Starship Troopers* outlines a government that is seemingly based upon a democratic ideal where citizens have the ability to vote in elections and there are smooth transitions between incoming and outgoing leaders. However, there is very little discussion about whether there are opposition parties or if the government runs smoothly on its own. Without quite knowing these elements, it is difficult to establish whether the Terran Federation satisfies the requirements of Dahl's definition of a democracy.

Another alternative to Aristotle's classification scheme is offered by attempts to measure governments on a spectrum with highly democratic governments on one end of the scale and authoritarian regimes on the other. These measures focus upon quantifying elements of government such as the pervasiveness of free elections, suffrage being extended to minority groups, the ability of minority groups to win elections, and the extent to which the media is objective and free from government intrusion. Because the classification of democratic or autocratic government can be subjective, the Polity IV data set is one mainstream approach developed by scholars to measure objectively the institutional policies and procedures of governments. These measures include whether or not there are competitive elections, institutional restraint on the decision making of the executive, and the ability of all citizens conceivably to run for office.[15] If a country allows for all of these (as well as other factors), then it is generally considered to be democratic. The opposite scores on this index suggest that a country is autocratic. Applying these standards to the Terran Federation, the government would rank high on the ability of citizens to run for office but not necessarily high on competitive elections.

Where Polity IV measures regime type and the institutional approach of a government, an alternative way of measuring democracy has been developed by the group Freedom House. The Freedom House index focuses upon the liberties afforded to its citizens to determine the likelihood that free expression is accessible to the public. This scale accounts for the level of press freedoms as well as the legal restrictions for news organizations, the political considerations for reporters, and economic pressures that affect access to information in a target country.[16] These indicators are then summed, with the final score for a government being "free," "partly free," or "not free." Recall that *Starship Troopers* begins with a newscast that doubles as a recruitment tool. In this government, the press appears to be state-sanctioned and allows for very little dissenting opinion. Those that attempt to express dissatisfaction with the prevailing theory of the Arachnids as savage enemies that must be destroyed are quickly silenced and instead the Federation perpetuates itself by continuously running newscasts that call for solidarity and commitment to the cause.

The limitations placed on the press might also extend to the society as a whole, including limits on civil or human rights. One newscast advertises that a murderer was caught in the morning, tried, and would be executed on national television later that evening. Whereas the newscast openly reports the outcome of the trial, the fast-paced judicial process and lack of legal rights for the murderer suggest that Federal authority is absolute. If the media exists as an extension of the state, then this society would be classified as being "not free," even though the media openly reports on the state of affairs. Although the Polity IV and Freedom House data sets both provide a partial picture of whether a government should be classified as democratic, these measurements are more helpful when trying to compare governments with one another or governments over time. In this particular situation, we would need multiple snapshots of the Terran Federation to capture fully the political approach of the government.

Do You Want to Live Forever? Nationalism and War

In *Starship Troopers,* the world seems idyllic with grand high schools, a flourishing space program, including travel available to far-off planets, and general economic prosperity. This serene picture is so saccharine that it lacks substance and sustainability. For a society to function so well, we would expect it to be highly democratic. Under the Terran Federation, few people have full political rights and yet the citizens and civilians have an amicable relationship. Is this world merely a spectacle meant to amuse the audience or is there a possibility that such a world could actually exist?

Although the government has both democratic and authoritarian elements, the regime appears to be very closed with stilted communication and a lack of meaningful political choice. The philosophy underlying the Terran Federation is that only those who have been willing to undertake a term of governmental service, and possibly put their life on the line, are fit to participate in government. Echoing the concerns raised by Aristotle, by definition, those who become citizens have shown a commitment to putting the common interest before their own interest – and even self-preservation. Hence, the economic prosperity and general peace that we see as the movie opens may be attributable to the fact that only those who "take responsibility for the body politic" and are "willing to defend it with their life" qualify as citizens. But perhaps there are political and institutional factors that pressure democratic leaders into pursuing peace.

One possibility is that the citizens are able to pressure their political leaders from entering unnecessary conflicts. Given that the Sky Marshal can be replaced at any given time, as we witnessed after the failed invasion of Klendathu, this indicates that the Sky Marshal's decisions concerning warfare are almost the same as those made by democratically elected presidents. This replacement may indicate the government feared some level of backlash from the citizens. If this is the case, we can assume a degree of democratic accountability in the decision to go to war with the Arachnids.

One of the predominant theories associated with democratic countries and war is the belief that democracies rarely fight other democracies. A large scholarly literature argues that advanced democracies will choose to maintain a "Democratic Peace" because the population must bear the costs of war, and war is antithetical to commercial interests.[17] And although proponents of the Democratic Peace Theory argue democracies do not fight one another, several studies actually conclude democracies are not constrained through public opinion in their decision to go to war.[18] Instead, evidence suggests democracies can initiate war with one another but usually will not because of other considerations such as the perceived duration of the conflict, the costs, and the likelihood of success.[19] Because the Terran Federation has some democratic leanings, this theory about going to war with other democracies might explain the willingness or apprehension of the government to engage the Arachnids. Because the Arachnids are non-democratic aggressors, the democratic peace theory holds very little explanatory power in this situation.

Other research has suggested that the perceived cultural identity of a country also plays a key role in the decision to go to war. Countries with higher degrees of nationalism may tend toward violence regardless of their democratic underpinnings.[20] This may be the case for the Terran Federation. The individuals of Earth who have undergone a term of service to become citizens are clearly nationalistic and more than willing to sacrifice everything for their country. The same cannot necessarily be said of the civilians. In fact, some civilians, such as Johnny Rico's father, explicitly hold citizens in contempt as people who do short terms of service simply to mooch off the government. Nevertheless, there is no indication that the civilians are so upset as to stage protests or uprisings against the government. Hence, it is possible that the nationalism of the citizens may be enough to maintain internal peace but also support the interstellar war.

There is an altogether different possibility that this picturesque society is the result of another trend, which is the diversionary use of force. According to this theory leaders can use conflict to draw the attention of their populace away from any internal issues that may exist. The diversionary use of force suggests that leaders almost always have the ability to use policy alternatives rather than react aggressively to a situation.[21] In the case of *Starship Troopers*, the Terran Federation could have set limits on intergalactic colonization attempts in order to keep from provoking the Arachnids. A different policy would also be the "live and let live" approach that could possibly have led to an uneasy peace between the two species. Although both of these options were available, the Sky Marshal pursued going to war with the Arachnids. This course of action suggests that either the Sky Marshal or the population (or possibly both) wanted to go to war. Under the diversionary use of force theory, leaders are often able to quell domestic unrest by getting the population to focus upon a conflict. The Arachnids serve as the distraction that could lead to the internal cohesion and amicable relationship between citizens and civilians on Earth.

Do You Want to Know More?

Starship Troopers offers a critique of government that rang true both when the novel was originally published in 1959 and when the film was released in 1997. In each instance, the story criticizes the lack of interest and apathy exhibited by citizens in a well-functioning, economically successful democracy. In order for democracies to function well, it is hoped that citizens will not simply obey the laws and pay their taxes but be active and informed participants. However, numerous studies have shown that American citizens are often not well informed on political matters and have low participation rates. *Starship Troopers* offers a challenge to consider whether the ancient models of citizenship that emphasized civic duty and responsibilities are still workable today.

The film offers an incisive critique of the Terran government and its propaganda machine. One of the most common refrains heard is from the Terran government's advertisement campaign: "Do You Want to Know More?" The audience is offered a series of promotional materials that cover everything from the latest technology for killing the aliens to recruitment materials for the Mobile Infantry. Particularly telling are the images of young schoolchildren being taught how they can support the government's cause by killing bugs – not aliens, but literal insects crawling around the playground. In another advertisement soldiers hand children ammunition in a fashion reminiscent of American G.I.s handing out chocolate to children in World War II.

This type of indoctrination is linked to a form of uncritical patriotism whereby citizens are encouraged to support their own government regardless of whether that government behaves justly. This type of nationalism can give way to mindless violence towards those outside of one's own citizen group. Just as the children are encouraged to reflexively kill the playground insects, so too are citizens encouraged to support the eradication of the aliens. One news reporter suggests that the bugs were provoked to attack by Terran's efforts to colonize alien planets. However, the propaganda machine encourages citizens to treat the Arachnids as enemies and to view them simply as bugs despite their displays of intelligence. The possibility that the government may have behaved unjustly is never acknowledged.

As a work of satire, *Starship Troopers* urges the audience to question an unexamined trust in government especially in matters of war and about the role of citizens in shaping their own government. Most of the students depicted early in the film seem entirely uninterested in their History and Moral Philosophy class and are equally uninterested in becoming citizens. As we follow the escapades of the Mobile Infantry, it becomes obvious why so few students were interested in volunteering for service – the price of citizenship might be one's own life.

Johnny Rico confronts the high cost of war when his girlfriend Dizzy is killed in battle. In his eulogy at her funeral he reflects on what he has learned about the responsibilities of citizenship: "Once, somebody asked me if I knew the difference between a citizen and a civilian. I can tell you now. A citizen has the courage to make the safety of the human race their personal responsibility. Dizzy was my friend, she was a soldier, but more than that, she was a citizen of the Federation."[22] Johnny comes to endorse the vision of citizenship advocated by his teacher, Mr. Rasczak. Under this model, one similar to the ancient Athenian and Spartan approach, citizenship requires not only the protection of rights but also service, sacrifice, and civic virtue from its citizens.

Nevertheless, this film gives us reason to question whether this model of citizenship can work to hold the government accountable. The success of Johnny's schoolmate Carl, who is assigned a job in the Games and Theory Department working on military intelligence, provides an important counterpoint to the ancient ideals of citizenship. Carl is a conniving intelligence operative who is willing to sacrifice others in pursuit of his main goal – capturing a "brain bug." When Carmen and other members of the Mobile Infantry realize that they were sent on a death mission, they are shocked and appalled. Carl makes no apologies: "You disapprove? Well, too bad! We're in this war for the species, boys and girls. It's simple numbers. They have more. And every day I have to make decisions that send hundreds of people like you to their deaths."[23] Although no one would contest that difficult decisions need to be made during war, Carl takes an almost sadistic pleasure in killing the bugs and is willing to sacrifice even his closest friends in pursuit of his goal without regard for the necessity or justice of his actions.

Like lambs led to the slaughter, these future citizens are coaxed into supporting their government's actions based on propaganda and on their desire to pursue their own life goals (e.g., running for office, going to college, having children). On one hand, this model of citizenship seems to ensure that citizens would view their role not simply as an entitlement to political rights but also as a call to civic responsibility. On the other, political elites are able to manipulate the public through propaganda, a lack of political competition, and narrow political agendas to wage a potentially unjust war. *Starship Troopers* offers a view of citizenship that is far removed from the model of legal citizenship emphasized in the United States. In doing so, this film invites the audience to consider both the political costs and rewards of requiring a higher bar to be eligible for those legal rights.

Chapter Discussion Questions

1. What is the distinction between civilian and citizen in *Starship Troopers*? Do you think it would be a positive thing if we had these distinctions in American society today?

2. In what ways is citizenship in the United States today similar to the models of citizenship discussed in ancient Greece, Imperial Rome, early modern Great Britain, and revolutionary France? In what ways is it different? Are there any aspects of previous eras that you think we should import into contemporary understandings of citizenship?
3. What do you think of the Democratic Peace theory? Why do you think democracies tend not to fight other democracies? If the Arachnids were a democratic society, would the Terran Federation still have fought them? Why or why not?

Notes

1 Verhoeven, Paul. 2008. *Starship Troopers*. DVD. Culver City, CA: Sony Pictures Home Entertainment.
2 Heinlein, Robert. 1959. *Starship Troopers*. Reprint, New York: Ace.
3 Dolman, Everett Carl. 1997. "Military, democracy, and the state in Robert A. Heinlein's *Starship Troopers*," in *Political Science Fiction*, ed. Donald M. Hassler and Clyde Wilcox. Columbia, SC: University of South Carolina Press, 196–213; 196–197.
4 Verhoeven, *Starship Troopers*.
5 For information on Athenian democracy, see Dunn, John. 2005. *Democracy: A history*. New York: Atlantic Monthly Press, 23–39.
6 On the Spartan government, see Heater, Derek Benjamin. 2004. *A brief history of citizenship*. New York: New York University Press, 6–14.
7 Bellamy, Richard. 2008. *Citizenship: A very short introduction*. Oxford: Oxford University Press, 35–39.
8 For more on the tension between the political and legal models of citizenship, see Pocock, J. G. A. 1992. "The ideal of citizenship since classical times," *Queen's Quarterly*, 99 (Spring): 35–55.
9 For more on the evolution of voting rights in America see Keyssar, Alexander. 2009. *The right to vote: The contested history of democracy in the United States*. New York: Basic Books.
10 Massicotte, Louis, André Blais, and Antonie Yoshinaka. 2004. *Establishing the rules of the game: Election laws in democracies*. Toronto: University of Toronto Press, 36–37.
11 Watson, Cynthia Ann. 2007. *U.S. Military service: A reference handbook*. Santa Barbara, CA: ABC-CLIO, INC., 63–69.
12 Aristotle, *Politics*, 1275a.
13 Schumpeter, Joseph. 1943. *Capitalism, socialism, and democracy*. 1971 reprint. New York: Routledge, 269.
14 See Dahl, Robert A. 1971. *Polyarchy: Participation and opposition*. New Haven, CT: Yale University Press, 22–26.
15 For access to this data set or to more fully explore what is measured here, visit: http://www.systemicpeace.org/polityproject.html, accessed April 29, 2015.
16 For a more detailed explanation of this data set, go to: https://freedomhouse.org, accessed April 29, 2015.
17 For a more advanced discussion of the Democratic Peace Theory, see Doyle, Michael. W. 1983 "Kant, liberal legacies, and foreign affairs," *Philosophy & Public Affairs*, 12(3): 205–235.
18 For even more discussion of the Democratic Peace Theory, see Oneal, John and Bruce Russett. 1999. "Is the liberal peace just an artifact of Cold War interests? Assessing recent critiques," *International Interactions* 25(3): 213–241; Schultz, Kenneth. 1999. "Do

democratic institutions constrain or inform?" *International Organization*, 53(2): 233–266; and Maoz, Zeev and Bruce Russett. 1993. "Normative and structural causes of democratic peace, 1946–1986," *American Political Science Review*, 87(3): 624–638.

19 Bueno de Mesquita, Bruce, James D. Morrow, Randolph M. Siverson, and Alastair Smith. 1999. "An institutional explanation of the democratic peace," *American Political Science Review*, 93(4): 791–807.

20 Braumoeller, Bear F. 1997. "Deadly doves: Liberal nationalism and the democratic peace in the Soviet successor states," *International Studies Quarterly*, 41(3): 375–402.

21 See Miller, Ross A. "Domestic structures and the diversionary use of force," *American Journal of Political Science*, 39(3): 760–785 for a more detailed description of the diversionary use of force.

22 Verhoeven, *Starship Troopers*.

23 Ibid.

4

IDIOCRACY

Do you need to be informed to vote in a democracy?

Conor M. Dowling

UNIVERSITY OF MISSISSIPPI

"If you have one bucket that holds two gallons and another bucket that holds five gallons, how many buckets do you have?"[1] That, along with tasks such as putting appropriate shapes into the right holes, is one of the questions on the IQ test Joe Bowers is asked to complete after he wakes 500 years in the future in the year 2505. In *Idiocracy*, society has deteriorated to the point that a man who was completely average in every way (e.g., intelligence, blood pressure, heart rate, and overall health) 500 years earlier awakens from a government-sanctioned hibernation experiment that failed (it was only supposed to last one year) to find he is by far the smartest guy on the planet. According to the narrator, the future that Joe Bowers and his hibernation companion, Rita, wake up in has been dumbed down by mindless TV programming and mass commercialism.

Although the satire aimed at mass commercialism alone serves as important social commentary on the current state of the world and what it means for the future of the human race, *Idiocracy* also raises important questions about the ability of democracy to thrive under any conditions. For instance, if people are ill-informed, how can we expect them to select leaders who will work in society's best interest? Indeed, in addition to suffering from significantly reduced levels of intelligence, the citizens of *Idiocracy* appear to have made poor decisions in terms of selecting their leaders at least partially as a result of their lack of information, which came about as a consequence of an anti-intellectualism spirit that resulted in a dumbing down of the human race.

Thus, *Idiocracy* allows us to consider common concerns regarding the selection of leaders in democracies via voting. In this chapter, we will consider four: (1) the extent to which citizens need to be knowledgeable of candidates and issues to cast an "informed" ballot, (2) whether shortcuts such as party identification or incumbency are sufficient for voters to make decisions in their best interest, (3) whether the "wisdom of the crowd" can always be trusted, and (4) the extent to which the media can be relied upon to provide relevant information to citizens and the ability of citizens to then use this information to inform their voting decisions.

Is an Informed Citizenry Necessary in a Democracy?

The extent to which citizens should be well-informed about candidates and issues before casting a ballot is often debated. On the one hand, a common argument is that voters should be well-informed about political matters prior to casting a ballot because poor decisions are likely to be made when citizens are not informed.[2] On the other hand, a common counter-argument is that political shortcuts enable citizens to make voting decisions as if they were more informed.[3] In the next section we discuss the notion of political shortcuts and whether they are a saving grace for voters. Here, we focus on the lack of information and why and when it might pose a problem for voting and democracy.

The Framers of the Constitution were concerned about the dangers an ill-informed citizenry posed for democracy. Indeed, this is one of the reasons why many of the Framers, James Madison chief among them, favored a republican form of government, in which representatives selected by the people make decisions, over a pure democracy where the people have direct control over the government. To further combat against the dangers an ill-informed citizenry could pose, the Framers placed various intermediaries between citizens and the selection of their elected representatives. Most notably, although the citizens were permitted to directly elect their representative to the United States House of Representatives, state legislatures initially selected the two senators from each state (until the Seventeenth Amendment in 1913 enabled direct election of senators) and the Electoral College still stands between citizens and a direct election of the president. The events depicted in *Idiocracy* reflect these longstanding suspicions of the Framers about what would happen if the masses possessed total control of the government. For instance, the narrator introduces the nation's leader, President Camacho, as "five-time Ultimate Smackdown champion, porn superstar, and President of America." In addition, the House of Representatives is now called the "House of Representin'."

The movie certainly takes the lack of information on the part of citizens to the extreme for comedic effect. For example, Joe and Rita are only released from their hibernation chambers as a result of an inability of society to come up with a plan to take care of all the trash in the world, resulting in the Great Garbage Avalanche of 2505. The movie, however, does illustrate that a lack of information can pose serious problems for voting in at least three ways.

First, a general apathy on the part of the citizenry has resulted in little to no political efficacy, which refers to the extent to which citizens feel they can be effective when it comes to political affairs.[4] The citizens of *Idiocracy* are content to have decisions made for them and only seem to get involved in the theatrics of government; for example, court proceedings are televised, but do not get the ratings of the number one show on television, "Ow, My Balls!" (on the Violence Channel). In other words, the citizens of *Idiocracy* would be thought to have low levels of political efficacy – a general feeling that even if they tried, they probably could not affect change on the government. In Powell's foundational study, "American Voter Turnout in Comparative Perspective," he found that United States citizens tended to have higher levels of political efficacy compared to citizens of other democratic nations, so it is fair to say that political efficacy takes a steep decline 500 years in the future.[5]

Second, casting an informed vote typically means having an understanding of the important issues of the day – or at least of the issues important to you, as an individual voter – and where the candidates stand on those issues. In other words, informed voting is often associated with knowledge of *position* issues, rather than a reliance on *valence* issues. Position issues are generally defined as "issues on which the parties differ in their perspectives and proposed solutions," whereas valence issues are those on "which most voters and candidates share the same position."[6] For instance, a valence issue might be that terrorism is "bad." Nearly everyone agrees that to be the case. However, the best way to handle terrorists and terrorist threats is open for debate; hence, it is a position issue. In *Idiocracy*, it is abundantly clear that valence issues are all that the citizens care about. To be precise, the two things that everyone appears to care about are sex and money. For example, near the end of the film there was this exchange between Frito and a cameraman:

FRITO: I can't believe you like money too. We should hang out.
CAMERAMAN: Totally.

[A bit later]

FRITO: So, you like money and sex? You're tripping me out.

In short, everyone in *Idiocracy* agrees on two things: Money is good, and so is sex (i.e., they are valence issues). We return to this point later in the chapter.

Third, judging from the abundance of lounge chairs with attached toilets, the citizens of *Idiocracy* do not care to take time even to walk to another room to go to the bathroom. With apathy this extreme, it is safe to assume that paying attention to politics, let alone picking up a newspaper (if they even exist anymore), is something that is extremely unlikely to occur in this dystopian society. This nicely illustrates the concept of rational ignorance – "the state of being uninformed about politics because of the cost in time and energy."[7] Individuals who are rationally ignorant need not be ignorant. Rather, rationally ignorant individuals do not collect political information because they believe the benefits of doing so are outweighed by the time and effort it takes to gather the political information. Whether the citizens of *Idiocracy* are rationally ignorant or simply ignorant in the year 2505 is somewhat besides the point, as both pose problems for the ability and willingness of citizens to enact change through the machinery of government. In contemporary politics, many people are rationally ignorant, choosing to focus their time and energy on matters other than politics. Although this might seem undesirable, rational ignorance is only problematic for democracy if citizens are unable to use other less time- and energy-consumptive means to make decisions about whom to elect, a point we discuss in the next section.

Are Shortcuts Sufficient for Voters to Make Informed Decisions?

A growing body of evidence suggests citizens routinely use voting shortcuts (or, cues) – "pieces of information about a candidate that are readily available, are easy to interpret, and lead a citizen to decide to vote for a particular candidate"[8] – to help them decide how to vote. For instance, one such cue is party identification, which refers to a citizen's sense of loyalty to a specific political party.[9] By voting for the candidate whose party affiliation matches their own, citizens hope the candidate will share many of the same issue stances and policy goals that they do, and often they are correct. Other cues range from incumbency (whether the candidate is the current officeholder or not) and personal characteristics of the candidates (such as age, race, or gender) to whether a specific interest group backs the candidate or a cause. More often than not, using cues allows individuals to vote in the same way they would have if they had taken more time and effort to gather information about the candidates or issues.[10] For example, in Arthur Lupia's classic study of voting shortcuts, he found individuals who knew the insurance industry's position on California's 1988 ballot initiative on insurance policy were able to use that as a cue and act in the same way as someone who had "encyclopedic" knowledge of the ballot initiative.[11] That is, the cue of the insurance industry's position was enough for some individuals to cast a more informed vote on the initiative. Whether such cues are sufficient for *all* voters to make informed decisions in their best interest *at all times*, however, is an open question. Indeed,

> [s]tudies have found that citizens who use cues and are politically well informed are more likely to cast a reasonable vote (one that's consistent with their underlying policy preferences relative to candidates' positions), compared to those who use cues but are otherwise relatively politically ignorant.[12]

In other words, possessing some political information makes it more likely that a citizen will be able to select the cues that are most helpful in making a voting decision consistent with their underlying political preferences.[13]

It is quite clear that in *Idiocracy* people do not possess enough information to select the "correct" cues. Instead, the lack of information possessed by citizens results in a reliance on only three cues: money, sex, and strength. President Camacho is the quintessential example of this: the citizens view him as powerful because he is physically strong and communicates in a brash manner. Thus, *Idiocracy* serves as an example that cues can sometimes lead voters astray.

Although votes are certainly not based solely on such superficial characteristics today, there is evidence that they may at least in part be based on such considerations. Anecdotally, for instance, popular commentary during the 2004 presidential election between President George W. Bush (Republican) and his challenger, United States Senator John Kerry (Democrat), suggested that President Bush was winning the "who would you rather have a beer with" vote. Put differently, President Bush was seen as more likeable, whereas Senator Kerry was seen as more of a "snob," as former White House reporter Richard Benedetto put it at the time.[14] Indeed, a Pew Research Center Poll reported at the time that 56 percent of swing voters (those who had not already made a decision to vote for Bush or Kerry) thought Bush came off as more of a "real person," compared to only 38 percent for Kerry. Eight years later, the Republican Party faced the opposite problem in their 2012 presidential primary, as a *Washington Post* headline read: "GOP's primary problem: Would you want to have a beer with any of these guys?"[15]

More broadly, empirical studies have found that "candidate facial competence" (how "competent" a person looks based simply on being shown a picture of their face for one second) is associated with vote choice in elections even after controlling for partisanship and other electoral context factors.[16] Although candidate facial competence is not necessarily equivalent to candidate attractiveness, it is at the very least a judgment made with without any thought or information about the candidate's policy positions, partisanship, or other "relevant" information.[17] Further, these studies do not find that facial competence makes the difference between winning and losing an election in the contemporary political context, as it appears to in *Idiocracy*, but having a more competent-looking face appears to at least help politicians.[18] In short, using cues to make snap judgments can often lead to sound decisions, but perhaps not always, especially if the "wrong" cues are used.[19]

Can the Wisdom of the Crowd Always Be Trusted?

In *Idiocracy*, citizens are neither informed about political matters (or, really, any matters other than sex, money, and television) nor do they rely on reliable shortcuts for making political decisions. As the preceding section discussed, in contemporary politics many citizens are also relatively uninformed, but at least some can make up for this lack of information through a reliance on effective shortcuts (party identification, incumbency, etc.). Another way in which scholars often suggest uninformed individual citizens can save themselves from their own lack of information is through the "wisdom of the crowd" – the notion that the collective opinion of the group is wiser than that of any single individual.[20]

The idea that collective wisdom is greater than any individual's wisdom dates as far back as the ancient Greek philosopher Aristotle. A simple, non-political example of the benefits of collective wisdom would be asking a group of people to individually guess how many jelly beans are in a large jar without opening it. By chance, a single individual might guess the correct number, but the *average* guess of the entire group is probably more likely to be closer to the correct answer than any single estimate. In the political realm, the wisdom of the crowd is often referred to in reference to public opinion. In particular, there is an argument that even if individuals are rationally ignorant, the group's aggregate opinion might be real, meaningful, and informed. The events depicted in *Idiocracy*, however, point to the limits of such collective wisdom, particularly if the "wrong" shortcuts are used.

Specifically, although there is strong consensus around what is right and wrong in *Idiocracy*, this collective "wisdom" has been led astray through a focus on things that are not particularly relevant for politics and government. For instance, the legal system has gone off track. When Joe is arrested and put on trial for not paying his hospital bill, his court-appointed lawyer, Frito, states a case *against* him. Frito does so because Joe does not talk or look like everyone else, and Frito cannot imagine anyone doing anything other than what everyone else is doing. Indeed, there is almost no minority opinion in *Idiocracy*. In many ways, the movie illustrates how "tipping points" – the point at which some idea or trend becomes accepted by (nearly) everyone – can sometimes be adverse. Much like viruses spread, so too can ideas or trends.[21] In the case of *Idiocracy*, society has "tipped" in the direction of completely drowning out minority opinion, even if that opinion is well-informed (in the sense that it is grounded in science). For instance, when Joe attempts to convince the rest of President Camacho's Cabinet that the way to fix the dust bowl is by "watering" the plants with *water*, not Brawndo (a Gatorade-like liquid that effectively salts the earth), the rest of the Cabinet is utterly perplexed. Counter-arguments to Joe's claim that water would help the plants include simply repeating Brawndo's slogan: "Brawndo's got what plants crave… electrolytes." In essence, the idea that Brawndo should be used for everything, including "watering" plants, at some point became accepted by the majority, and once tipped in that direction any minority voices were not listened to. That is, not until Joe tried another tactic, and convinced the Cabinet that he could talk to plants and that the plants told him they wanted water

In sum, *Idiocracy* points out that the wisdom of the crowd cannot always be trusted, especially if the information used to create that wisdom is unhelpful and the majority is strong enough to silence (or effectively eliminate) the minority. Spirals of silence, a term that refers to situations where those holding a minority opinion do not feel comfortable challenging the opinion of the majority, also illustrate a potential downside to relying on the wisdom of the crowd. Again, *Idiocracy* certainly takes such concepts to the extreme for comedic effect, but a recent example of a spiral of silence in action comes from a 2014 report by the

Pew Research Center.[22] Pew surveyed individuals during the public debate surrounding Edward Snowden's revelations that there was widespread United States government surveillance of United States citizen phone and email records. Consistent with previous work, the report found that people were more likely to share their views on the matter if they thought their "audience" (for example, coworkers, Facebook or Twitter followers) agreed with them. When this occurs, people effectively block out any other opinions from their network. Indeed, a separate Pew Research Center report from 2014 found, compared to moderates, ideological conservative and liberal Facebook users were more likely to block, hide, defriend, or stop following other users because they disagreed with a post of theirs concerning politics, effectively silencing opinion that diverged from their own.[23]

The Media, Information, and Voting

In addition to being able to exercise the right to vote, a free press is also thought to be essential to any democracy.[24] As the United States Agency for International Development puts it:

> A free press plays a vital role in democratic societies, enabling the open exchange of information and opinions among ordinary citizens, businesses, citizen associations, political parties, and governments. Free and open media systems give voice to citizens, truth test candidates and political parties during elections, inform policy debates in legislatures, investigate corruption, hold public officials accountable, enable democratic governance and facilitate more effective development.[25]

In short, the media in democratic countries is responsible for transmitting an abundance of information to citizens.

In *Idiocracy*, however, the media clearly does not meet this responsibility. In addition to the number one show on television being "Ow, My Balls!", the number one movie in the country was "Ass" – as the narrator says, "and that's all it was for 90 minutes" [a picture of an ass] and "It won eight Oscars that year, including best screenplay." This, and the rest of the media content, represents an extreme view of the commercial bias – "the tendency of the media to make coverage and programming decisions based on what will attract a large audience and maximize profits"[26] – our own media often engages in today. In *Idiocracy*, even political information is conveyed via a shirtless, muscular man and a scantily clad woman. Examples of commercial bias today range from the tendency for stories about war and other conflicts to dwindle in number as the number of casualties decline, even if the conflict is very much ongoing,[27] to local news programs only spending on average six of 30 minutes on political news, focusing on weather, sports, and human interest stories instead.[28]

Moreover, the commercial bias evident in the media today is at least in part driven by the fact that only a few media conglomerates own the vast majority of news sources. More specifically, in the United States six corporations – CBS Corporation, Disney, General Electric, News Corporation Limited, Time-Warner, and Viacom – own well over half of the news sources available to people. This includes most of the major national newspapers and news magazines, as well as broadcast and cable television networks, movie studios, and publishing houses.[29] These entities compete over and are dependent on advertising dollars, which are in turn dependent on drawing an audience. This leads to news programs giving more time, and newspapers giving more space, to topics that are perhaps not "newsworthy" in the traditional journalistic sense, but entice and keep an audience. As a result, we learn far more about the latest political scandal, celebrity gossip, or (possibly) catastrophic weather event than we do about events that are less sensationalistic but far more important to our daily lives. As Will Ferrell's character from *Anchorman 2*, news anchor Ron Burgundy, put it as his news team was searching for ways to boost ratings, "Why do we have to tell people what they *need* to hear? Why don't we tell them what they *want* to hear?"[30] – the implication being people do not *want* to hear the nitty-gritty details of political and public affairs, even if that is what they *need* to hear in order to be informed citizens in a democracy.

The media clearly do convey some political information to citizens, though. Whether it is enough is a debatable matter, to which there is likely no definitive answer. No matter what political information is presented to citizens, however, there is still the question of how they choose to use it. In particular, what sort of information do people use to inform their voting decisions?

As the preceding sections have suggested, many voters rely on shortcuts to make their voting decisions. One theory of voter decision making, retrospective voting, is consistent with using shortcuts to make decisions based on (relatively) limited information. The theory of retrospective voting suggests that voters base their decisions about which political party or candidate to support based on their evaluation of how well they think the country, or even just the voter as an individual, is doing at the time of the election.[31] In essence, retrospective votes are those that signal a sign of approval (if for the incumbent) or disapproval (if for the challenger) with the current state of affairs. As Ronald Reagan put it to voters during his successful presidential election bid in 1980, "Are you better off than you were four years ago?" – the implication being that those citizens who felt they were better off than they were four years ago should vote for incumbent President Jimmy Carter, and those who did not should vote for Reagan.

An alternative theory of voter decision making is prospective voting. Prospective voting requires more information and effort on the part of citizens, as prospective votes are those that are based on "well-informed opinions and considerations of the future consequences of a given vote."[32] Voters in the 1980 presidential election who engaged in prospective voting would not have simply asked themselves if they were better off than they were in 1976, when Jimmy Carter became president, but instead would have attempted to make an informed decision about which candidate's policy proposals (Carter's or Reagan's) were more likely to be effective.

In *Idiocracy*, retrospective evaluations appear to be all that matter. For instance, a week is all that is given for water to grow some crops, and the decision to keep Joe around is based entirely on whether the crops grow. Decisions based on prospective concerns would weigh whether the desired outcome is more likely to occur with Joe around or not, and not be based on what he was able to do in the short time he was allotted. Indeed, when the crops have yet to grow, Joe is sent to "rehabilitation" (essentially death by monster truck) and gives an impassioned plea to the citizens of *Idiocracy*:

> Joe: If you put water on the crops it might actually… no, it will work. I promise you. You just have to believe me. I just wanted to help you. That's all. So, you can try and shoot me. You can try and run me over. Whatever! But I just want you to ask yourselves one question first: Do you really want to live in a world where you try to blow up the one person that's trying to help you?

Joe's (prospective) appeal, however, is ignored. It is only crops sprouting at the last possible second, and accidentally getting captured on film for all to see by a fallen camera, that saves Joe's life. In other words, it is still a retrospective decision that is made to keep Joe around and later make him president, not any good he was likely to do in the future.

In contemporary politics, anecdotal (see the 1980 presidential election) and empirical evidence suggests voters use a mixture of retrospective and prospective decision making, with more weight typically placed on retrospective factors.[33] Political elites understand this, and candidates tend to emphasize retrospective themes in their campaign messages.[34] Perhaps even more concerning for democracy, political scientist Gabriel Lenz shows that not only do voters tend to evaluate candidates based on past performance, but that the policy positions of voters can be influenced by those of the politicians.[35] That is, citizens often "follow the leader" and adopt the policy positions of the politician they have chosen to prefer for other reasons (past performance, appearance, etc.), something that almost certainly occurred in *Idiocracy* during the 500 years in which Joe and Rita were hibernating.

Conclusion

The futuristic landscape of the year 2505 painted by Mike Judge in the movie *Idiocracy* is not pretty, to say the least. Mountains of garbage line the skyline. Decrepit, falling buildings – and two buildings tied together with rope to help them stand up – can be seen everywhere. Cars drive off collapsed roadways. Most importantly, to the movie's plot line at least, there is a lack of plant life because people only drink and irrigate with Brawndo.

Society has deteriorated to this point for many reasons, but chief among them is a system of government that has ceased to function effectively. Voters do not seem to have held their elected officials accountable to a high standard or at the very least have chosen poor standards to hold them accountable to. *Idiocracy* therefore presents a unique setting to consider common concerns scholars have about the ability of democracy to function under any conditions, specifically with respect to the selection of leaders by the voters. In brief, considering the four questions that were laid out at the beginning of this chapter, no, citizens need not be exceptionally knowledgeable of candidates and issues to cast an "informed" vote, as there are shortcuts and cues they can rely on to do so. However, although many people effectively use shortcuts to make more informed decisions, not everyone is capable of doing so. And, yes, the collective wisdom of the group is often superior to that of any individual, but groups can be misinformed and when coupled with spirals of silence this can mean trouble for society. Finally, yes, the media does provide information to voters, but often it is not the most helpful information for citizens to figure out which candidate to vote for in terms of their policy positions.

Chapter Discussion Questions

1. What does it mean to be an "informed" citizen today? Should only those who are "informed" be allowed to vote?
2. To what extent are political shortcuts/cues helpful for voter decision making? Is it acceptable for voters to always/only rely on cues?
3. Discuss the difference between retrospective and prospective voting using examples from *Idiocracy* and contemporary politics.

Notes

1 Judge, Mike. 2006. *Idiocracy*. Los Angeles: Twentieth Century Fox.
2 Carpini, Michael X. Delli and Scott Keeter. 1996. *What Americans know about politics and why it matters*. New Haven, CT: Yale University Press.
3 Downs, Anthony. 1957. *An economic theory of democracy*. New York: Harper and Row; Campbell, Angus, Philip Converse, Warren Miller, and Donald Stokes. 1960. *The American voter*. Chicago: University of Chicago Press.
4 Barbour, Christine and Gerald C. Wright. 2015 *Keeping the Republic: Power and citizens in American politics: The essentials, Edition* 7. Thousand Oaks, CA: CQ Press, 516.
5 Powell, Jr., G. Bingham. 1986. "American voter turnout in comparative perspective," *American Political Science Review*, 80(1):17–43; Table 1.
6 Barbour and Wright, *Keeping the Republic*, 538.
7 Ibid., 426.
8 Bianco, William T. and David T. Canon. 2015 *American politics today, fourth essentials edition*. New York: W.W. Norton & Company, 241.

9 Green, Donald, Bradley Palmquist, and Eric Schickler. 2002. *Partisan hearts & minds: Political parties and the social identities of voters*. New Haven, CT: Yale University Press, ch. 2.
10 Popkin, Samuel L. 1991. *The reasoning voter: Communication and persuasion in presidential campaigns*. Chicago: University of Chicago Press.
11 Lupia, Arthur. 1994. "Shortcuts versus encyclopedias: Information and voting behavior in California insurance reform elections," *American Political Science Review*, 88(1), 63–76.
12 Bianco and Canon, *American politics today*, 242.
13 Lau, Richard R. and David P. Redlawsk. 2001. "Advantages and disadvantages of cognitive heuristics in political decision making," *American Journal of Political Science*, 45(4): 951–971.
14 Benedetto, Richard. 2004. "Who's more likeable, Bush or Kerry?" *USA Today*, September 17, http://usatoday30.usatoday.com/news/opinion/columnist/benedetto/2004-09-17-benedetto_x.htm, accessed May 13, 2015.
15 Fish, Sandra 2012. "GOP's primary problem: Would you want to have a beer with any of these guys?" *The Washington Post*, March 1, http://www.washingtonpost.com/blogs/she-the-people/post/gops-primary-problem-would-you-want-to-have-a-beer-with-any-of-these-guys/2012/03/01/gIQAg95wkR_blog.html, accessed May 13, 2015.
16 Atkinson, Matthew D., Ryan D. Enos, and Seth J. Hill. 2009. "Candidate faces and election outcomes: Is the face-vote correlation caused by candidate selection," *Quarterly Journal of Political Science*, 4(3): 229–249; Lenz, Gabriel S. and Chappell Lawson. 2011. "Looking the part: Television leads less informed citizens to vote based on candidates' appearance," *American Journal of Political Science*, 55(3): 574–589.
17 Todorov, Alexander et al. 2005. "Inferences of competence from faces predict election outcomes," *Science*, 308(5728): 1623–1626.
18 Lawson, Chappell et al. 2010. "Looking like a winner: Candidate appearance and electoral success in new democracies," *World Politics*, 63(4): 561–593.
19 Gladwell, Malcom. 2005. *Blink: The power of thinking without thinking*. New York: Little, Brown, and Company.
20 Surowiecki, James. 2005. *The wisdom of crowds*. New York: Anchor Books.
21 Gladwell, Malcom. 2000. *The tipping point: How little things can make a big difference*. New York: Little, Brown, and Company.
22 Hampton, Keith et al. 2014. "Social media and the 'spiral of silence'," Pew Research Center, August 26, http://www.pewinternet.org/2014/08/26/social-media-and-the-spiral-of-silence, accessed May 13, 2015.
23 Pew Research Center. 2014 "Political polarization and media habits," October 21, http://www.journalism.org/2014/10/21/political-polarization-media-habits, accessed May 13, 2015.
24 United Nations, "The Universal Declaration of Human Rights," Article 19, http://www.un.org/en/documents/udhr/index.shtml, accessed May 13, 2015.
25 Moss, Jill and Mark Koenig. 2013 "Free press: The cornerstone of democracy," USAID, May 3, http://blog.usaid.gov/2013/05/free-press-the-cornerstone-of-democracy, accessed May 13, 2015.
26 Barbour and Wright, *Keeping the Republic*, 565.
27 Pew Research Center. 2008. "Awareness of Iraq war fatalities plummets," March 12, http://www.people-press.org/2008/03/12/awareness-of-iraq-war-fatalities-plummets, accessed May 13, 2015.
28 Entman, Robert. 1989. *Democracy without citizens*. New York: Oxford University Press, 110–111.
29 Barbour and Wright, *Keeping the Republic*, 565.
30 McKay, Adam. 2013. *Anchorman 2: The Legend Continues*. Los Angeles: Paramount Pictures.

31 Fiorina, Morris P. 1981. *Retrospective voting in American national elections*. New Haven, CT: Yale University Press.

32 Barbour and Wright, *Keeping the Republic*, 526.

33 Lanoue, David. J. 1994. "Retrospective and prospective voting in presidential-year elections," *Political Research Quarterly*, 47(1): 193–205.

34 Benoit, William L. 2006. "Retrospective versus prospective statements and outcome of presidential elections," *Political Research Quarterly*, 56(2): 331–345.

35 Lenz, Gabriel S. 2012. *Follow the leader: How voters respond to politicians' policies and performance*. Chicago: University of Chicago Press.

5

ONE CHOICE CAN TRANSFORM YOU

Political Ideology and Culture in *Divergent*

Jocelyn Evans

UNIVERSITY OF WEST FLORIDA

In *Divergent,* Veronica Roth creates a post-apocalyptic world in which five factions live separately and semi-autonomously to promote peace and state stability. Children are born into a faction and raised by their parents to cherish the values of the faction. However, all must participate in a Choosing Ceremony at the age of sixteen. This event serves as a public rite of passage. Young adults must choose whether to stay with their family's faction or to leave everything they know and join a different faction. The society relies on aptitude testing to provide children with insight as to their natural propensities, but the final choice must be an exercise of their own free will. At the Choosing Ceremony, the entire society watches as each young person is called by name. The air is thick with anticipation as young adults make life-altering decisions, some choosing to stay with their parents and others choosing to leave home forever. Five bowls sit on the stage. To join a faction, each teen must drip blood drawn from the palm of the hand on the substance symbolically representing the faction of his or her choice. From that moment forward, they are joined to the faction. They then embark on an initiation process that serves to bring them more fully into the faction's fold. And so we come to understand the mantra of the society in *Divergent,* "Faction before blood."[1]

Each faction demonstrates a dominant value structure. Dauntless values fear-lessness and freedom; Abnegation values selflessness and dutiful behavior; Erudite values intelligence and elitism; Amity values peace, friendship, and collective decision making; and Candor values honesty. These values impact the political life of each community and ultimately shape the battles that ensue throughout the series. In this chapter, we explore the meaning of political ideology and political culture. We examine the dominant political ideologies and cultures present today and the value structures of these systems. The factions in *Divergent* each organize around distinct manifestos, utilize strong symbolism, and engage in meaningful ritual. *Divergent* provides a useful lens for understanding political ideology and culture in that Roth explores the complexity of human nature, the importance of political values, and the sources of group conflict grounded in belief structures.

Exploring Ideology and Political Culture

Ideology refers to an individual's set of beliefs about the role of government in society. Our beliefs about government shape our understanding of the political world. This shapes our preferences about what actions government should take to solve policy problems. This guides our partisanship, our political behavior, and our vote choices. We can express our political ideology through symbols that carry meaning about our relationship to the state. These symbols are in turn part of our political culture.

When we talk about political culture, we are referring to "a particular pattern of orientations to political action" in which "every political system is embedded," according to Gabriel Almond.[2]. Political culture involves shared social values, norms, and attitudes toward politics. The political culture of a community more broadly speaks to the collective makeup of the people. Stemming from a collective history, it includes the belief systems (or ideologies) as well as the cultural norms of the political community. It might involve traditions, rituals, and customs. Whereas political ideology refers to an individual's guiding principles about the role of government in society, political culture refers to the shared values as well as the practice of politics in a given place. Through political socialization we develop our own ideological understanding and absorb the political culture of the community. Some of the most powerful agents of political socialization include parents, teachers, peers, religious communities, and media. For example, in *Divergent*, parents seem to play a strong role in the political socialization of the young, even though teens have the opportunity to choose their own faction at the age of sixteen. The opening vignette of the book provides a window on this socialization process. Roth writes the series from the vantage point of the central character, Beatrice Prior. Her family's faction is Abnegation. Beatrice Prior's house only has one mirror. Those in Abnegation deride personal vanity. Beatrice is only allowed access to the mirror once every three months while her mother cuts her hair. It just so happens that this day coincides with the Choosing Ceremony at which Beatrice will choose for herself what faction she will call home for the rest of her life. Her mother finishes cutting and fixing her hair, and Beatrice steals a gaze at her own profile. She is surprised when her mother finds her staring at her appearance and doesn't reprimand her.[3]

Experts who study political culture come at the subject from a variety of lenses. Some choose to examine the use of symbol and ritual to shape political reality. For these scholars, symbols foster identification, reinforce national allegiances, and legitimize power.[4] Particularly important to our examination of political culture with reference to *Divergent* is the role of ritual. According to David Kertzer, ritual

> follows highly structured, standardized sequences and is often enacted at certain places and times that are themselves endowed with special symbolic meaning. Ritual action is repetitive and, therefore, often redundant, but these very factors serve as important means of channeling emotion, guiding cognition, and organizing social groups.[5]

Still others consider cultural identity and focus on those shared heritages that contribute to cultural identity. Samuel Huntington argues that differing cultural identities contribute to foreign conflict. His clash of civilizations thesis points us to factors such as "similar ancestry, religion, language, values, and institutions."[6] Among these, he finds shared religion to be the most important defining characteristic of a civilization. Those with different religions are most likely to clash. Even within a nation state, one can identify different political cultures. Robert Putnam, for example, observed different traditions of civic engagement in Italy and related these differences to the health of governing institutions.[7]

Others look at the impact of development on political culture. These scholars believe that political culture is somewhat a product of circumstance. Modernization, born from industrialization, brings several changes to a society. "Once set in motion, it tends to penetrate all aspects of life, bringing occupational specialization, urbanization, rising educational levels, rising life expectancy, and rapid economic growth."[8] Some suggest that these developments lead to major change in political institutions and participation. "[I]n the long run, modernization brings democracy."[9]

How does this process work? "Modernization brings rising educational levels, moving the work force into occupations that require independent thinking and making people more articulate and better equipped to intervene in politics."[10] Independent judgment leads to questioning of authority. With greater economic security, people begin to think beyond survival to self-expression. "People begin to place a growing emphasis on free choice in politics and begin to demand civil and political liberties and democratic institutions."[11]

Dominant Ideologies, Political Cultures, and *Divergent*

Several dominant ideologies define political debate today. It is helpful to think in terms of two dimensions when pinpointing ideologies across a spectrum of belief structures. One dimension involves the degree to which government should engage in economic regulation, and the other involves the degree to which it should engage in social regulation. Less government intervention might be considered individualist, whereas more government intervention might be considered collectivist. It is common to refer to the right and left ends of the spectrum as conservative and liberal, but this characterization oversimplifies the politics of contemporary conservatives and liberals in the United States. American conservatives today often prefer less government intervention in the economy (individualist) and more government intervention in society (collectivist), whereas liberals typically value more government intervention in the economy (collectivist) but less government intervention in society (individualist). Further complicating matters is the changing meaning of the term *liberal* over time. Classical liberalism emphasizes a free-market economy, whereas more modern notions of liberalism really refer to social liberalism with a mixed economy.

Although American political culture tends to center on liberalism and conservatism, a broader ideological spectrum would include anarchism, which is the lack of any state authority, and totalitarianism, which means complete state authority. Such a spectrum would also include socialism, where there is state ownership of the means of production and management of the economy, and fascism, or veneration of the nation and race and loyalty to a totalitarian leader. There are many other political ideologies as well. For purposes of this discussion, it is sufficient to observe that political ideology involves fundamental beliefs about the proper type and scope of government. Ideology colors the way we view the world in important ways.

It would, of course, be a stretch to draw a direct connection between the dominant ideologies in *Divergent* and the dominant political ideologies just outlined. Nonetheless, there are some strong beliefs we can identify and explore to understand the concept of political ideology and its role in structuring civic participation. Each faction prioritizes certain virtues over all others. For example, those in Erudite value intelligence, whereas those in Amity value sociability. Similarly, Dauntless values courage, those in Candor value honesty, and members of Abnegation value selflessness.

In *Divergent*, the people living in post-apocalyptic Chicago have a general political culture, and then each faction has a specific political culture unique to itself. The broader society adheres to the guiding principle of "faction before blood." To facilitate the transition from family to faction, the society observes certain traditions, including aptitude testing, choosing ceremonies, initiation, and indoctrination. These practices transcend individual factions and thus constitute an entire polity's political culture. Each faction, however, has its own set of shared values, norms, and attitudes that make it distinct from the others. Below we review the manifestos, symbols, and rituals for each of the factions, and then draw connections between these unique political cultures and our American heritage.

Abnegation: Service Above Self

The ruling body for this society is made up of representatives from Abnegation, due to the commitment of the faction to selfless behavior. As is the case with each of the factions, the central principles governing Abnegation are distilled in a manifesto.[12] The Abnegation Manifesto presents a pledge of selflessness, captures the idea that members are not to look at themselves, and the commitment to mutual dependency. There is an assumption in this creed concerning what leads to the good society. A life lived in service to others is best. A person chosen to rule must govern for the good of the community. Unsurprisingly, the faction's symbol is a set of helping hands, an image which reflects several philanthropic organizations in the real world that use the symbol of the hand to convey service to others, including United Way, Helping Hands, Both Hands, and Two Hands Project. In the Choosing Ceremony, gray stones represent the Abnegation faction. The color reflects the neutral palette of the faction's dress code. In this way, Abnegation shares certain values and character traits with the Amish. The Amish avoid trappings of vanity, choosing to wear muted colors, simple dress, and head coverings. They do not use full-length mirrors, but engage in rituals such as foot washing and barn raising, always serving each other in times of need. They are pacifists and refuse to serve in the armed forces. This is not a perfect comparison, however; one primary difference between Abnegation and the Amish is that members of Abnegation hold political power whereas the Amish eschew politics altogether.

Dauntless: Rebel Youth or Hitler Youth?

By contrast, responsibility for the protection of the community lies in the hands of Dauntless. They guard the borders of the community, borders demarcated by a chain-link fence topped with barbed wire that spans farther than the eye can see.[13] We learn the most about the Dauntless faction in *Divergent* because Beatrice, the protagonist, chooses to leave Abnegation and join Dauntless in the Choosing Ceremony. The plot develops from her vantage point as a Dauntless initiate. The early scenes of her adventure through Dauntless initiation include harrowing jumps from moving trains and tall buildings, a name change from Beatrice to Tris, a visit to the tattoo parlor, and a change into form-fitting black clothes. Dauntless seems fun, exciting, and free. But soon Tris must prove herself through bloody fistfights, weapons training, and "fearscapes" to be up to the task of Dauntless membership.

Dauntless breeds a militaristic culture through physical training, fighting, risk-taking, and displays of bravery. On the surface, the faction appears to value independence and freedom, but Tris's independent streak soon gets her in trouble with Dauntless trainers. As part of initiation, members of the faction must confront their worst fears and find ways to overcome them. Ultimately, all must traverse a drug-induced hallucination that presents them with a sequence of their worst fears. This is called a "fearscape." Only by successfully combatting these fears can an initiate end the hallucination and leave a fearscape. Four is one of the trainers and serves as a mentor and guide for Tris. The end of his unique fearscape never changes. He must shoot an innocent, his worst fear. This rite of passage speaks to a moral code that elevates resoluteness in action over all else. Obviously, when security for an entire community is on one's shoulders, resoluteness is a virtue; taken to extremes, as we shall see, it can turn into a vice.

In the first part of the *Divergent* saga, Jeanine Matthews, leader of the Erudite faction, heads a plot to inject all members of the Dauntless faction with a serum that makes them susceptible to command. Once injected, they march on Abnegation and begin to annihilate men, women, and children. This development shows us that although members of this faction express themselves and resist authority structures more than any other members of society, they also form a dangerous and mindless army under the right conditions. This transition and manipulation of Dauntless reminds us both of the anarchic conditions of reckless rebellion and the automaton attributes of the Hitler Youth. Leading up to World War II, the Nazi Party focused on building support and loyalty among the Aryan youth of Germany. The organization worked to indoctrinate all young men and women with Nazi values, including racism, and to strengthen them physically and mentally to act as paramilitary for Hitler's program of genocide and world domination.

Divergence uses symbols to reinforce Dauntless's emphasis on courage and physical conditioning. In terms of symbolism, the faction represents itself in the Choosing Ceremony with hot coals. The symbol of the faction is a burning fire. In Greek thought, fire is an element associated with energy and passion. In Hinduism, the Vedic god Agni is the god of fire. He is known for his energy and perpetual youth. The chakra associated with fire is Manipura, which is located above the navel – the gut. This chakra supports risk-taking, self-responsibility, self-esteem, and warrior energy.[14] In fact, blockages in this chakra produce fear.[15] In astrology, fire personalities are courageous, lively, self-sufficient, and spontaneous. However, they can also be selfish, forceful, and lacking in self-control.[16]

Amity: Democracy and Diplomacy

Those from Amity provide the society with "understanding counselors and care-takers."[17] The Amity Manifesto, titled "Conversations of Peace," is unique in that it is written as a series of dialogs or proverbs.[18] The Amity Manifesto is very similar to *The Analects* of Confucius and the oral traditions of the Native Americans. Through a series of proverbs about interpersonal conflict, we learn to prioritize trust, self-sufficiency, forgiveness, kindness, and involvement. These "Conversations of Peace" when taken together suggest a worldview that emphasizes diplomacy over all else.

In terms of governance, Amity is leaderless. Members of this faction participate in democratic deliberation, reaching unanimity whenever possible. They also prioritize neutrality in conflicts involving other factions but provide sanctuary when needed. Against this backdrop, it makes sense that the faction's symbol is a tree. Several real world cultures make or have made a great tree a gathering place for deliberation. For example, the Iroquois Confederacy began when the Great Peacemaker led five Native American tribes to create an alliance. A council governed this confederacy, and each representative on the council had an equal voice. "Before any action could be taken, all the chiefs who constituted the council of the League had to agree, had to be of 'one heart, one mind, one law.'"[19]

The founding of the confederacy, according to legend, included the planting of a tree. The Great Peacemaker said:

> I am Dekanawida and with the Five Nations' Confederate Lords I plant the Tree of the Great Peace. I plant it in your territory, Adodarhoh, and the Onondaga Nation, in the territory of you who are Firekeepers… .
>
> We place you upon those seats, spread soft with the feathery down of the globe thistle, there beneath the shade of the spreading branches of the Tree of Peace. There shall you sit and watch the Council Fire of the Confederacy of the Five Nations, and all the affairs of the Five Nations shall be transacted at this place before you, Adodarhoh, and your cousin Lords, by the Confederate Lords of the Five Nations… .
>
> If any man or any nation outside the Five Nations shall obey the laws of the Great Peace and make known their disposition to the Lords of the Confederacy, they may trace the Roots to the Tree and if their minds are clean and they are obedient and promise to obey the wishes of the Confederate Council, they shall be welcomed to take shelter beneath the Tree of the Long Leaves.[20]

The substance representing Amity in the Choosing Ceremony is soil. The faction farms for the society as a whole. The faction also serves as a safe harbor for those in need. It is interesting to note that the words of the Great Peacemaker at the founding of the Iroquois Confederation also included a promise of safety to those seeking shelter.

Candor: Transparency in Government

Known for their honesty, members of Candor provide society with "trustworthy and sound leaders in law."[21] Candor's manifesto reads much like an essay, but its guiding principles are clear.[22] It suggests that dishonesty is ubiquitous throughout society, is the foundation of evil, and is fleeting. Fundamentally, it causes mistrust and conflict between people and within society. The alternative, honesty, is the remedy.

The Candor faction prioritizes peace just as the other factions do, but the means of achieving peace are different still. For Candor, truth and transparency are required for the common good. It is curious that the symbol of Candor is the scales of justice. Could it be related to what we say when we are sworn under oath? – "I swear to tell the truth, the whole truth, and nothing but the truth."

Veronica Roth does not tell us much about Candor in *Divergent*, but she does describe some of their traditions, rituals, and customs. The customary dress in Candor is black and white. They are symbolically represented in the Choosing

Ceremony by glass. Both of these attributes reflect the faction's focus on transparency and truth as the essence of morality and the key to peace. It is interesting to note that the faction's symbol is the scales of justice, but these scales are tipped. As a legal symbol, scales of justice date to ancient Rome. Not only do they represent the weighing of two sides of a case: they also symbolize the balance between truth and fairness in reaching a just verdict. When used to represent the Candor faction, tipping the scales of justice could represent the faction's bias toward truth over fairness.

Erudite: A Meritocracy

The final faction is Erudite. Members of Erudite value intelligence and knowledge above all else. They provide society with scholars, both teachers and researchers.[23] Their manifesto reads like a formal proof of logic.[24] The beginning line of this manifesto – "We submit the following statements as truth" – reminds the reader of the Declaration of Independence. Written more as a declaration than as a proverb, a poem, or a piece of propaganda, Erudite's platform elevates knowledge above all else. Greater education or enlightenment will lead to agreement and quell conflict.

Erudite's color is blue, and it represents itself with water in the Choosing Ceremony. According to Chinese Taoist thought, water represents stillness, intelligence, and wisdom.[25] The symbol for the faction is an eye. When encircled, the eye looks as though it is peering through glass. In fact, many members of the faction wear glasses. As a symbol, the eye dates back to ancient civilizations, including the Egyptians. In the Western tradition, it is referred to as the Eye of Providence and appears throughout Christian iconography and Freemasonry. In Christian references, it symbolizes divine providence or the guiding hand of an Almighty God. Freemasons use the symbol to represent the all-seeing eye of God. Taken together, this image captures omniscience – Erudite is all-seeing and all-knowing, an observation underscored when it is revealed the faction's plot to overthrow the government is commanded from a room of monitors in its headquarters.

As a political culture, the Erudite believe in meritocracy. They elevate those with the highest IQs to positions of leadership. Consequently, they doubt that the Abnegation is well suited to govern. They believe leaders should be selected based on intelligence testing.[26] Throughout the book, Erudite plots to overthrow the government. In a climactic scene, Jeanine, the leader of Erudite, reveals to Tris and Four her faction's sentiment. She states, "We are tired of being dominated by a bunch of self-righteous idiots who reject wealth and advancement."[27]

Comparing *Divergent's* Society with the United States

Taken together, these factions shed light on the diversity present in political cultures around the world. Just as each faction prioritizes a single virtue over all others, some societies prioritize certain virtues. There are many competing assumptions about what leads to the good society. At different times in American history, we have valued different things. In general, we are very individualistic. We believe in limited government and popular consent to be governed. We protect individual rights, including the right to bear arms. However, the Framers worked into the United States Constitution a system of representative democracy built on elite governance. With limited suffrage and protection against majority faction, the system empowered the propertied, male minority. Yet, there was a cultural norm present at our Founding that public servants should hold political office. President George Washington served out of a sense of duty rather than desire for power and limited his terms in office, setting a precedent for those to follow.

Over time, we have demonstrated a commitment to participatory politics and transparency in government. We have expanded the right to vote to include women, African Americans, Native Americans, and eighteen to twenty-one-year-olds. A shift from party caucuses toward direct primaries also opened the door for greater participation in government. Politics in the United States is more participatory now than ever before. Finally, major scandals such as Watergate have made Americans wary of politicians and secrecy in government. We expect truth and transparency and devote time and resources to fact-checking and open records.

Generally speaking, American political culture emphasizes certain fundamental values. We embrace popular sovereignty, or the belief that power should be vested in the people, and hold that people should consent to be governed by exercising the right to vote. We believe in the rule of law, in justice, and in due process. We believe in freedom and civil liberty. We believe in the sanctity of the individual and the protection of private property. We believe in the idea of equality, although we debate whether that means equal opportunity or equal outcome in practice. More and more we value diversity and multiculturalism, although this represents a shift in values over our nation's history.

Broadly, this captures American political culture. However, just as there are factions within the broader society in *Divergent*, some political scientists argue that there are distinct political cultures within American society. Daniel Elazar, for example, has noted three political cultures in America: moral political culture, individual political culture, and traditional political culture. These "factions" might not be as distinct as those depicted in *Divergent*, but they demonstrate significantly different enough patterns of political behavior to warrant our attention.

The first political culture Elazar identifies is the moralistic political culture of parts of New England, the Midwest, and the West. This orientation to politics views society as more important than the individual. Politics is valued for its capacity to solve public problems and promote the public good. Government employees are considered public servants, and they are expected to prioritize the good of the community over private loyalties or personal gain.[28] By contrast, the individualistic political culture of Mid-Atlantic states and parts of the West holds government in low regard. Citizens are cynical over whether politicians act in the public's interest. They expect rampant corruption and consequently value limited government. Less government is more, as far as this culture is concerned.[29] Finally, the traditional political culture of the South demonstrates elitism uncharacteristic of the rest of the country. Politics is a family affair, with some well-established families holding office across the generations. It all depends on who you know in this political culture. Government is treated positively, but largely it serves to promote and maintain the existing social order. Rather than transparency in government, this culture expects backroom negotiations on behalf of the ruling elite.[30]

More recent work in this field points to a new cultural divide that accounts for differences across local communities. Given that those with high socioeconomic status often choose where to call home, there is a great deal of self-sorting across urban centers in contemporary American society. Some seek out social diversity in a community. They choose to live in places with more nontraditional families, atypical gender roles, or the presence and social acceptance of an LGTBQ community. This social diversity in turn shapes the political behavior of the city. We might consider San Francisco, Seattle, or Boston as examples of this type of political culture. Alternatively, some seek out more traditional urban environments to call home – places with high levels of religious involvement and low levels of social diversity. Birmingham, Atlanta, and Charlotte are good examples of this type of political culture.[31]

Conclusion

In *Divergent*, ritual and symbol are incorporated to develop a society with an overarching political culture and five clearly defined factions with unique cultural identities unto themselves. These post-apocalyptic Chicagoans value "Faction before blood."[32] Each faction holds strong assumptions about their chosen core virtue, each of which helps promote peace and leads to the good society. The respective systems they support value public service (Abnegation), individualism and self-protection (Dauntless), participatory government (Amity), transparency in government (Candor), and representative government by intelligent elites (Erudite). These factions help us see the role of both political culture and ideology in shaping civic participation, and better understand the dominant traditional, moralistic, and individualistic political cultures in America. Because it features such strong identities, *Divergent* provides a useful lens for understanding political ideology and culture. We see clear competing claims concerning the causes of conflict, and we understand the role of symbol and ritual in structuring reality in diverse political cultures.

Chapter Discussion Questions

1. Which faction in Roth's *Divergent* do you think best represents American political culture today? Why?

2. How would you describe the political culture of your region? What factors do you think influence that political culture? Does Elazar's depiction of political cultures in America still hold true today regarding your region? Why or why not?
3. Do you think segregating based on personality, interests, and behavior is good for society or bad? Why? At the end of the day, what is the best way to promote social order and peace?

Notes

1 Roth, Veronica. 2001. *Divergent*. New York: HarperCollins Publishers, 43.
2 Almond, Gabriel. 1956. "Comparative political systems," *Journal of Politics*, 18(3): 391–409; 396.
3 Roth, *Divergent*, 1–2.
4 Kertzer, David I. 1988. *Ritual, politics, and power*. New Haven, CT: Yale University Press.
5 Ibid., 9.
6 Huntington, Samuel P. 1996. *The clash of civilizations and the remaking of world order*. New York: Simon and Schuster, 126.
7 Putnam, Robert. 1994. *Making democracy work: Civic traditions in modern Italy*. Princeton, NJ: Princeton University Press.
8 Inglehart, Ronald and Christian Welzel. 2009. "How development leads to democracy: What we know about modernization," *Foreign Affairs*, 88(2) (March/April), http://www.foreignaffairs.com/articles/64821/ronald-inglehart-and-christian-welzel/how-development-leads-to-democracy, accessed May 18, 2015.
9 Ibid.
10 Ibid.
11 Ibid.
12 Roth, *Divergent*, 35; you can find the text of the Abnegation Manifesto on the Divergent wikia page at http://divergent.wikia.com/wiki/Abnegation, accessed May 18, 2015.
13 Roth, *Divergent*, 123; you can find the text of the Dauntless Manifesto on the Divergent wikia page at http://divergent.wikia.com/wiki/Dauntless, accessed May 18, 2015.
14 Herring, Barbara Kaplan. 2007. "Yoga poses for the Chakra system," *Yoga Journal*, http://www.yogajournal.com/article/beginners/asanas-for-the-chakra-system, accessed January 17, 2015.
15 "Manipura Chakra," *Chakras.net*, http://www.chakras.net/energy-centers/manipura, accessed January 17, 2015.
16 "Fire," *Astrology.com*, http://www.astrology.com/fire-0/2-d-d-67460, accessed January 17, 2015.
17 Roth, *Divergent*, 43.
18 You can find the text of the Amity Manifesto on the Divergent Wikia page at http://divergent.wikia.com/wiki/Amity, accessed May 18, 2015.
19 Tooker, Elisabeth, 1978. "The league of the Iroquois: Its history, politics, and ritual," in *Handbook of North American Indians*, ed. William C. Sturtevant. Washington, D.C.: Government Printing Office, 418–441; 422.
20 "Chapter 9: Dekanawida and Hiawatha," in *History of the Mohawk Valley: Gateway to the West 1614–1925*, http://www.schenectadyhistory.org/resources/mvgw/history/009.html, accessed January 17, 2015.
21 Roth, *Divergent*, 43.
22 You can find the text of the Candor Manifesto on the Divergent wikia page at http://divergent.wikia.com/wiki/Candor, accessed May 18, 2015.

23 Roth, *Divergent*, 43.
24 You can find the text of the Erudite Manifesto on the Divergent wikia page at http://divergent.wikia.com/wiki/Erudite, accessed May 18, 2015.
25 Schiesser, Michael. 2015. "The five elements," http://www.innerjourneyseminars.com/the-five-elements.html, accessed January 17, 2015.
26 Roth, *Divergent*, 45.
27 Ibid., 429.
28 Elazar, Thomas. 1972. *American Federalism: A view from the states.* 2nd edition. New York: Harper & Row. See also Elazar, Daniel. 1970. *Cities of the prairie: The metropolitan frontiers do American politics.* New York: Basic Books
29 Ibid.
30 Ibid.
31 DeLeon, Richard E. and Katherine C. Naff. 2004. "Identity politics and local political culture: Some comparative results from the social capital benchmark survey," *Urban Affairs Review*, 39(6): 689–719.
32 Roth, *Divergent*, 43.

PART III

Political Institutions

6

STAR WARS AND THE EXECUTIVE BRANCH

Joseph E. Uscinski

UNIVERSITY OF MIAMI

> In order to ensure our security and continuing stability, the Republic will be reorganized into the first Galactic Empire, for a safe and secure society which I assure you will last for ten thousand years. An empire that will continue to be ruled by this august body, and a sovereign ruler chosen for life …
>
> *Chancellor Palpatine*[1]

The six-part *Star Wars* saga, while adored by millions of fans, is often panned by science fiction buffs. One of the many criticisms aimed at the saga is that – unlike many other science fictions – it lacks a clear message about politics. This criticism does have some merit: the government in *Star Wars* is little more than a caricature, and there is little time spent in the films developing an overt statement about politics, power, and ideal political alternatives. (*Star Trek*, for example, explores such topics very explicitly.)

In *Star Wars* – it is said by critics – the good guys wear white and the bad guys wear black (and often look like Nazis).[2] Motives are clear, good and evil are easily differentiated, and there are few if any political moral dilemmas. There is something to these criticisms – *Star Wars* is at base as much fantasy and "space opera" as it is science fiction, and therefore lacks many of the overt political, social, and psychological messages one might find in other science-fiction franchises. For instance, many casual viewers might see *Star Wars* as a story about a father, Anakin Skywalker, who turns to evil despite his best intentions, and a son, Luke Skywalker, who redeems his father. But a look under the hood of the *Star Wars* saga shows that entire saga is driven by politics and the distribution of power.

The saga – currently divided into three films in the original trilogy and three films in the prequels – is entirely driven by political conflict and questions about the relative concentration of political power between political institutions and actors. In the original trilogy, the action is driven by a group of rebels who are attempting to overthrow a dictator – the Emperor – who has a monopoly on political and economic power. In the prequel films, the plot is driven by the disintegration of a democratic republic into a tyrannical dictatorship.

While many overlook the connection, dictatorship and high concentrations of power are repeatedly cast in the saga as undesirable, dangerous, and evil. The most evil character in the saga is the Emperor. This character controls all political and economic power in the universe. And whereas *Star Wars* audiences do not see much of the effects of this dictatorship, it is strongly implied that dictatorship is inherently evil and that the resultant policies are bad. In the abstract, the idea that dictatorship is bad may seem a rather banal statement about politics. Most people tend to oppose dictators and dictatorship in the abstract. But when it comes to specifically their own favored leader, people unfortunately tend to support giving that person more unilateral power to carry out their preferred policies without interference from people, leaders, and institutions who might disagree. For example, during President Obama's administration, many of his supporters urged him to sidestep Congress to more quickly and easily enact certain policies without having to negotiate with the other party or institutions.[3] What *Star Wars* suggests is that ceding power to an executive authority – in this case an executive leader – even if it is for a short period of time, or for an otherwise specific and noble purpose, can quickly slide down a slippery slope to tyranny.

This chapter examines the road to tyranny in the *Star Wars* universe, and how that road is paved by concentrating power in the hands of one person, an executive leader. George Lucas, the creator of *Star Wars*, much like the Constitutional Framers, knew that power was potentially dangerous. In this way, both seem to agree with the famous aphorism attributed to Lord Acton: "Power tends to corrupt, and absolute power corrupts absolutely." This chapter therefore examines perhaps the most important facet of executive leadership: how much power should they have? Using the *Star Wars* universe as an example of both what can happen when there is too little and too much power given to an executive, the chapter argues that given the dangers on both ends of the spectrum, a vigorous and empowered executive is necessary, but firm checks on that executive's power are desirable to prevent dictatorship and tyranny.

The Constitutional Framers and the Creation of the Executive

During the Constitutional Convention of 1787, one of the major issues confronted by the Framers was the question of executive power. Previously, under the Articles of Confederation, the national government had a very weak – almost non-existent – executive. This created several problems for the struggling republic, the most prominent being that laws could not be enforced and efficient unitary decisions could not be made. For example, if there was an insurrection, or an attack from a foreign country, the Articles provided no mechanism to address such pressing and urgent problems in a timely manner by a single person who could make spot decisions. This is, of course, something that Americans now take for granted given the powers given to the president in the Constitution.

The Framers, however, found themselves in a difficult spot. Having just waged and won the Revolutionary War against the British King, the former colonies were fearful of again living under the control of a distant and overly powerful government. Given the blood and resources the young nation had given to escape tyranny, there was a natural tendency for its leaders to be wary of government power. This tendency explains the weak governmental structure created by the Articles of Confederation, the weak super-majoritarian government created and instituted during the Revolutionary War.

The consequence of the weak executive branch was brewing rebellions and growing international threats. To address the dangers from within and without, the Framers met in Philadelphia to craft a solution. Their intent was to increase the power of the national government so it could address domestic and international crises, efficiently make and enforce laws, and provide sound governance.

Of all the issues to be resolved by the Constitutional Framers, the shape, scope, and power of the executive was perhaps the most contentious. Some argued that a powerful unitary executive would abuse its power and sink into despotism. Others argued that without a strong decisive leader, the states would fall victim to continued bloody revolution and foreign conquest. As it turns out, the Framers were well advised to meticulously debate the power of what would become the American Presidency. The results of the Constitutional Convention have been largely positive. Few governments experience the stability the United States has, and at the same time continue to expand and protect political rights. And few institutions in the history of the world have become as powerful without systematic abuses of power.

The six-movie *Star Wars* saga demonstrates the dangers of both having too little and having too much executive power. These films suggest why the Framers had such a difficult time designing the presidency and why it was so important for them to meticulously pore over Article II of the Constitution. In short, the Framers were tasked with finding a happy medium by giving the executive enough power to enforce laws and represent the nation, while at the same time, not so much power as to instill tyranny.

The Dangers of a Weak Executive

In *Star Wars Episode I: The Phantom Menace*, we are introduced to a galaxy far, far away. This galaxy is governed by a galactic democracy, called the Republic. The Republic is comprised of a long list of member planets that are represented in a legislative body referred to as the Senate. The Senate elects a chancellor who acts as the executive branch of the Republic, carrying out laws, ensuring tranquility, and providing for common defense. Although the chancellor's method of election makes him or her closer to a British prime minister, the duties of the chancellor are little different from those of an American President.

Episode I centers on a planet, Naboo, which has been blockaded by the Trade Federation, the space equivalent of the American Internal Revenue Service. The blockade is technically illegal and has been brought about by a secret agreement between the Trade Federation and a dark figure called Lord Sidious. The blockade has left the peaceful people of Naboo in a precarious situation because they lack the ability to defend themselves against the battle-hardened droid army of the Trade Federation.

Knowing that the Trade Federation's incursion into their system is both illegal and illegitimate, the Queen of Naboo appeals to the Chancellor to have him stop the blockade. The Chancellor secretly sends a pair of Jedi Knights – as negotiators – to convince the Trade Federation to abandon its blockade. That the Chancellor's first step to stop the incursion into Naboo is to take covert action is telling, and as we later find out, the Chancellor has little power to take more overt action to stop the Trade Federation.

When the Jedi Knights are unsuccessful in their attempts to stop the blockade, the Queen of Naboo heads to the Senate and pleads her case in front of that body and the Chancellor. The debate soon derails, and the inability of the Chancellor to take swift action is put on full display: the Chancellor, addressing objections from several senators to ending the blockade, asks if the Queen would defer her motion to allow a committee to investigate. The Queen's response to the Chancellor's inability to take swift action demonstrates why a weak executive poses a danger to society:

> I will not defer…I have come before you to resolve this attack on our sovereignty now. I was not elected to watch my people suffer and die while you discuss this invasion in a committee. If this body is not capable of action, I suggest new leadership is needed. I move for a "vote of no confidence"… in Chancellor Valorum's leadership.[4]

The Chancellor's inability to stop an obviously illegal and immoral move by the Trade Federation signals why a weak executive is undesirable. This echoes the trouble the United States faced before the passage of the Constitution: the weak national government could not address brewing rebellions and member states which would not abide by agreements or cooperate with other member states. The Queen's move to remove the Chancellor and replace him with a stronger leader shows how, in response, the pendulum could not only swing in the opposite direction, but swing perhaps too far, setting the stage for a leader who is *too* strong.

This episode not only uses the Chancellor to demonstrate why an executive constrained by a lack of official authority is undesirable, but also showcases how a decisive and unitary executive leader can do little good if they lack actual power. The Queen, while condemning the Trade Federation's attack on her people and sovereignty, vows to take judicious action. But she is hamstrung by the fact that she has little power to do so; her army is small and comprised solely of "security volunteers."

Taking the Chancellor's and the Queen's inability to thwart the attack on Naboo together, one can glean that a successful executive must have two attributes: (1) minimal constraints on their ability to make quick decisions and (2) the necessary tools to enforce those decisions. An executive leader without those attributes cannot protect their people from internal or external dangers. With this said, adding too much unitary decision making and too much enforcement power can lead to other, perhaps worse, problems. The next section of this chapter examines why.

The Dangers of a Strong Executive

Human history has witnessed over and over again the results of allowing one person to possess too much power. If initially starting with the best of intentions, leaders without checks in place will go far beyond acting in the common good. And even if supposedly acting in the common good (which is hard to define and open to interpretation as to what exactly that is), powerful leaders without institutional checks on that power will use terrible methods to achieve their ends. Several leaders of the twentieth and twenty-first centuries immediately come to mind: China's Mao, Russia's Stalin, Cuba's Castro, North Korea's Kim Jong-un. In addition, it would be easy to name many more examples of leaders who have denied basic rights, clung to power at the expense of the governed, slaughtered innocents, or starved people to death.

No one comes to power by saying outright that they will do horrible things or employ horrible methods. Even the worst dictators come to power declaring that they want to help people. The communist dictators of the twentieth century came to power declaring that they wanted a fairer economic system that would help the worse off in society. Of course, the result was close to a 100,000,000 dead at the hands of communist leaders.[5]

In *Episode II: Attack of the Clones,* we see the good intentions of a young Jedi named Anakin Skywalker. Despite his young age, he has already exhibited great physical strength and developed significant political power, given his relationship to the Chancellor. But, as the following exchange with his love interest, Padmé, suggests, Anakin is all too interested in using unrestrained force to achieve political ends:[6]

ANAKIN: We need a system where the politicians sit down and discuss the problems, agree what's in the best interests of all the people, and then do it.

PADMÉ: That is exactly what we do. The trouble is that people don't always agree. In fact, they hardly ever do.

ANAKIN: Then they should be made to.

PADMÉ: By whom? Who's going to make them?

ANAKIN: I don't know. Someone ... Someone wise.
PADMÉ: That sounds an awful lot like a dictatorship to me.
ANAKIN: Well, if it works ...

This is where good intentions go awry. One problem of government is that people often complain that government is too inefficient. The other problem of government is that efficient governments can do a lot of harm a lot faster. The reason for this is simple: without open debate, without checks and balances which tend to slow things down, government power can quickly run amok. The desire to limit debate, bickering, and negotiation in favor of more efficiency can not only lead directly to tyranny, but is tyranny in itself. The desire to limit debate and negotiation, and the desire to compel agreement – is a desire to use force and compulsion to change people's minds and/or lock them out of the political process. This is the very essence of tyranny. Moreover, this is exactly where the galaxy finds itself not too long after: Anakin and Chancellor Palpatine – a strong Chancellor – use their power to crush any opposition to their rule. They eventually even go so far as to liquidate the Senate so that there will be no official avenue for debate, and all power can flow directly from the Chancellor. Anakin continues this conversation with Padmé in *Episode III: Revenge of the Sith*:[7]

ANAKIN: I've become more powerful than any Jedi has ever dreamed of and I've done it for you. To protect you.
PADMÉ: Come away with me. Help me raise our child. Leave everything else behind while we still can.
ANAKIN: Don't you see, we don't have to run away anymore. I have brought peace to the Republic. I am more powerful than the Chancellor. I can overthrow him, and together you and I can rule the galaxy. Make things the way we want them to be.

This conversation reveals the desire of Anakin to rule with an iron fist. What began with seemingly good intentions has led Anakin to slaughter opponents and even children wholesale. The scales in this instance have now tipped too far in the other direction: the *Star Wars* saga began with an institutionally restrained and weak leader – by *Episode III*, the galaxy is headed into dictatorship.

The transition from good intentions to tyranny is perhaps most evident in the exchange below between Anakin and his former mentor Obi-Wan Kenobi. Obi-Wan has confronted Anakin about his turn towards tyranny and dictatorship:[8]

OBI-WAN: You have allowed this Dark Lord to twist your mind until now ... until now you have become the very thing you swore to destroy.
ANAKIN: Don't lecture me, Obi-Wan. I see through the lies of the Jedi. I do not fear the dark side as you do. I have brought peace, justice, freedom, and security to my new Empire.

OBI-WAN: Your new Empire?
ANAKIN: Don't make me kill you.
OBI-WAN: Anakin, my allegiance is to the Republic … to democracy.
ANAKIN: If you're not with me, you're my enemy.

Besides Anakin and his desire to see the government run more efficiently by a single ruler, the Emperor provides a great example of too much power in one person's hands. Starting his career as a senator under the name Palpatine, the future emperor connives his way into the position of Chancellor by offering strong leadership. He provides it. To enable himself to stay in office, he masterminds a galactic war. Palpatine uses the war to manipulate the Senate into allowing him to stay in office long after his term has expired. This rise to power is eerily reminiscent of that of Adolf Hitler, who rose to power in post–World War I Germany, only to consolidate power into his own hands without checks on his decision making.

After the war is over and Palpatine has consolidated his power in the Senate and in the military, he slaughters off his last remaining opponents, the Jedi. Upon doing so, he changes the government to allow him to stay in office forever and with greater power. It is for these reasons that some countries, including the United States, have term limits and institutional limitations on executive power. The United States, being particularly fearful of an overly powerful executive, has a two-term limit on the president, and leaves the president out of the constitutional amendment process – this way the president has little say in advancing his or her institutional powers.

But what is perhaps more interesting than the Emperor's seizure of dictatorial powers is the fanfare with which this move is met in the Senate. In *Star Wars*, the Senate appears to welcome the dictatorship, which by necessity leads their powers to circumscribed (and eventually lost). In *Episode III: Revenge of the Sith*, Palpatine announces his new powers to the Senate:[9]

PALPATINE: The war is over. [applause] The Separatists have been defeated, [applause] and the Jedi rebellion has been foiled. We stand on the threshold of a new beginning.

[There is a long period of applause.]

PADMÉ: Well, this is the moment we discover if he intends to return the Republic to a democracy.

Moments later, Palpatine declares the reorganization of the Republic into the First Galactic Empire, to a very supportive Senate.

PADMÉ: So this is how liberty dies, with thunderous applause.

As the opening quotation of this chapter shows, Palpatine does not return the Republic to democratic rule, but rather he changes it to an empire with himself as emperor chosen for life. With the Senate remaining intact for the time being, this acts as a check – even if weak – on the newly crowned emperor. Multiple institutions can divide power and make the execution of laws less swift, less decisive, and therefore less severe in their consequences. In this instance, the Emperor was wise to appoint himself for life – without election to check his actions or performance, he would be free to do whatever he wanted without reprisal or reprimand. And of course, he would be free to stay in office until death.

Padmé's horrified reaction to the Emperor's power grab becomes realized in *Episode IV: A New Hope*. As Governor Tarkin informs the Imperial leaders:[10]

TARKIN: The Imperial Senate will no longer be of any concern to us. I've just received word that the Emperor has dissolved the council permanently. The last remnants of the Old Republic have been swept away.

TAGGE: That's impossible! How will the Emperor maintain control without the bureaucracy?

TARKIN: The regional governors now have direct control over territories. Fear will keep the local systems in line. Fear of this battle station.

With this, the Emperor's vision is finally realized. He has consolidated all power into his hands. He controls all political and economic life, and he rules with an iron fist. He has slaughtered his enemies; he has regulated trade and production; and he enforces his will with fear and terror. By *Episode IV: A New Hope*, he has built a Death Star – a planet-sized space station that can destroy entire planets with one laser blast.

While more dramatic, this episode is eerily reminiscent of President Franklin Roosevelt's presidency. Having been elected to an unprecedented four terms, Roosevelt upon taking office quickly consolidated massive amounts of power into the federal government, specifically into the executive branch. Most of these policies were justified as being necessary to combat the Great Depression of the 1930s. Having been elected president in 1932 along with majorities from his party in both houses of Congress, Roosevelt had little opposition in government to combat him. Only the Supreme Court, which was a majority Republican appointed Court, stood to oppose Roosevelt and the Democrats. The Court overturned several of their policies as unconstitutional, and was able to act as a check. But, Roosevelt threatened to enlarge and then pack the Court with his own appointees – in a sense, he threatened to put the Court under his control and make it moot. The Court, under threat, ceded to Roosevelt's will and began to greenlight his policies. Without any institutional checks, Roosevelt was able to pass and implement many excessive parts of his "New Deal." This episode shows why having meaningful opposition is good.

Conclusion

The Framers of the American Constitution struggled over the design of the executive branch. They knew that too little power in the hands of the executive would leave the nation open to dangers from both within and without. Too much power in the executive would leave the country vulnerable to tyranny. The six episodes of the *Star Wars* saga demonstrate both ends of the spectrum and show why finding an appropriate balance is both difficult and desirable.

The American constitution attempts to find this delicate balance by putting executive power into the hands of one person, a president, who can make decisions and act efficiently. But the Constitution also limits the executive's power – through elections, through separation of powers, and by expressly prohibiting certain actions by the executive. Given a more than 200-year track record of success, I would suggest that the Framers succeeded in finding the most appropriate balance.

It is precisely times when executive power is needed that executive power is often extended, and sometimes in excess. For example, after 9/11, Congress gave President Bush a green light to pursue an unending "War on Terror" with little oversight. This included the passage of the PATRIOT Act, which allows for domestic spying and the wiretapping of American citizens without warrant or cause. What has made the American experiment work so well is that our other institutions have fought against executive encroachment and have from time to time limited executive power when it has been necessary to do so. For example, after abuses of power by the Nixon administration, Congress quickly pulled back some of that power and instituted stricter controls on the presidency.

While examining the portrayal of executive power in the *Star Wars* saga, a few other points of interest should be brought to light. First, intentions – particularly those of executives – do not always pan out. An old saying says that preparing for peace can sometimes bring war, and preparing for war can sometimes bring peace. We see this in *Star Wars* repeatedly. In *Episode I*, Queen Amidala states clearly that she will not condone a course of action that will lead to war. By the end of the movie, she is putting together an army to go to war. In the original trilogy, the Emperor puts numerous plans in place to stop the remaining rebel forces. His plans repeatedly fail. Often plans do not work and intentions fall flat, precisely because the future is so variable.

Second, perception matters – particularly perception of leaders. Take *Episode IV*, where we are first introduced to Luke's troubled lineage. Obi-Wan tells Luke that a young Jedi, Darth Vader, who turned to evil, killed Luke's father. In later films we learn that Darth Vader is in fact Luke's father, and Luke confronts Obi-Wan about this apparent lie.[11]

LUKE: Obi-Wan! Why didn't you tell me? You told me Vader betrayed and murdered my father.

OBI-WAN: You father was seduced by the dark side of the Force. He ceased to be Anakin Skywalker and became Darth Vader. When that happened, the good man who was your father was destroyed. So what I have told you was true… from a certain point of view.

LUKE: A certain point of view?

OBI-WAN: Luke, you're going to find that many of the truths we cling to depend greatly on our own point of view.

With this conversation, George Lucas – the creator of *Star Wars* – seems to signal that truth is subjective to the point of almost being non-existent. And this is an important point to make. Even though the Emperor was evil, he had many supporters, just as many evil leaders in history had many supporters. Their point of view led them to pay less attention to the evil acts and focus only on the "good" things. When *Star Wars* was originally conceived, for example, President Richard Nixon was being investigated for serious charges of corruption and for subverting the Constitution. But even when the evidence of his crimes became clear, he still had many supporters. This is not to say that George Lucas abandons the concept of truth: in *Episode III*, he uses the battle between Obi-Wan and a new evil Anakin to demonstrate that even though points of view may color how each of us views reality, there is truth at the end of the day.

OBI-WAN: I have failed you, Anakin. I was never able to teach you to think.

ANAKIN: I should have known the Jedi were plotting to take over …

OBI-WAN: From the Sith!!! Anakin, Chancellor Palpatine is evil.

ANAKIN: From the Jedi point of view! From my point of view, the Jedi are evil.

OBI-WAN: Well, then you are lost!

At some point, despite partisanship or ideology, democratic citizens must always be cognizant of encroachments on their rights, even if they agree with some of those policies. Giving too much power to an executive, whether we agree with their stated intentions or not, could have tragic consequences. Not just for the country, but for the whole galaxy.

Chapter Discussion Questions

1. Do you think the American President has too much or little power?
2. Which specific powers do you think the president should have more or less of?
3. How much power should an executive leader have? What are the dangers of giving the president too much power?

Notes

1 Lucas, George. 1999. *Star Wars episode I: The phantom menace*. May 19, San Francisco: LucasFilm. For clarity, the quotes provided in this chapter are from the original scripts and as such, the wording in the quotes may vary slightly from that heard in the final (and often changing) versions of the movies.

2 Brin, David and Matthew Woodring Stover. 2006. *Star Wars on trial*. Dallas: Benbella Books, Inc.

3 Epstein, Jennifer. 2014. "Obama points to 2014's pen-and-phone strategy," *Politico*, January 14, http://www.politico.com/story/2014/01/obama-state-of-the-union-2014-strategy-102151.html, accessed September 11, 2015.
4 Lucas, *Star Wars Episode I.*
5 Courtois, Stéphane, and Mark Kramer. 1999. *The black book of communism: Crimes, terror, repression.* Cambridge, MA: Harvard University Press.
6 Lucas, George. 2002. *Star Wars episode II: Attack of the clones.* May 16, San Francisco: LucasFilm.
7 Lucas, George. 2005. *Star Wars episode III: Revenge of the Sith.* May 19, San Francisco: LucasFilm.
8 Lucas, *Star Wars episode III.*
9 Ibid.
10 Lucas, George. 1977. *Star Wars episode IV: A new hope.* San Rafael, CA: LucasFilm.
11 Ibid.

7

STAR WARS AND LEGISLATURES

Zachary Callen

ALLEGHENY COLLEGE

At first glance, *Star Wars* does not seem to be as overtly political as other science fiction sagas of recent years. Despite its many pleasures, *Star Wars* lacks the optimism of human spirit found in *Star Trek*, the realpolitik of the rebooted *Battlestar Galactica*, the environmental undertones of Frank Herbert's *Dune*, or the post-human angst of films like *Blade Runner*. Due to its colorful characters and straightforward plot, when we first turn to analyze this space opera, our initial impulse is look at the six-movie saga as more tied to a classic "hero's journey" lens, where a young and inexperienced protagonist gains experience and wisdom through his travels.[1] When combined with the cultural mishmash that comprises the *Star Wars* universe – with George Lucas borrowing widely from other cultural tropes, including samurai films, Westerns, and World War II dogfights – the two sets of *Star Wars* trilogies appear to be more individualized and personal stories rather than overtly political narratives.

In many ways, the Prequel Trilogy of Episodes I–III (PT) and the classic Original Trilogy of Episodes IV–VI (OT) most obviously function together as inverse mirrors of the hero's journey. The OT tells the story of how Luke Skywalker left his backwater farming life on Tatooine, joined the Rebel Alliance, trained in the ways of the Force with Yoda, redeemed his father Darth Vader, and helped vanquish the Emperor, freeing the galaxy from fascist domination. The PT reveals how Luke's father, the Jedi Knight Anakin Skywalker, is rescued from slavery (also on Tatooine), trains with Obi-Wan Kenobi, fights in the Clone Wars, marries Senator Padmé Amidala, falls under the thrall of Chancellor Palpatine (who is secretly a Dark Jedi plotting against the Republic), and eventually falls to the Dark Side to become Darth Vader. Both stories, while telling a unified family saga, are also very much about personal choice and the way we grapple with our own psychological demons. On a more abstract level, the *Star Wars* saga is about the moment when a hero rises, or falls, and speaks to the struggles we all face as we grow into adulthood and must tackle difficult choices.

But, even given that first layer of subtext, it is hard to ignore the very real political implications of *Star Wars*. After all, the OT is a story of plucky rebels taking on an empire after the fall of a republic. Princess Leia is, in addition to being a rebel leader, also a member of the Imperial Senate when we first meet her in *Episode IV: A New Hope*. The political undertones of the *Star Wars* franchise are only heightened when we consider the context of the original film's release. The original *Star Wars* film was released in 1977, just a few years after the American withdrawal from Vietnam. Similarly, the second trilogy was released in the wake of 9/11 and the PATRIOT Act, and raised hard questions about how democracies trade freedom for security. Although it would be a stretch to equate the Empire with the post-war United States, and the North Vietnamese with the Rebellion, it is also hard to ignore that George Lucas wrote a movie where the main heroes are essentially guerilla fighters just a few years after the United States engaged in a protracted conflict with the North Vietnamese. Hence, it appears that there is, in fact, a larger, socially oriented narrative that comments on American political life lurking beneath the family drama of the *Star Wars* story.

However, the political aspects of *Star Wars* extend beyond metaphorical cultural critiques. Although the films are primarily concerned with the exciting adventure sequences, from pod races to lightsaber duels, the PT in particular reveals a fair amount about how the political world of the Republic operates. More specifically, *Episode II: Attack of the Clones* can act as a useful window into just how political decisions are made in the Republic. Further, when the Republican Senate is combined with real world examples from American politics, *Attack of the Clones* serves as a powerful tool to help discuss how legislatures in general function. Indeed, the Republic teaches a great many negative lessons of what not to do when designing a legislative branch. Beginning with a brief summary of the movie's plot as well as a discussion of just what a legislative body is, I will offer insight into a number of key features of how legislatures function. In particular, I will discuss issues of representation and deliberation, problems of centralization, and consider the role of interest groups in legislative politics. Out of each of these discussions, a common theme will arise: designing a legislature to truly represent any body politic is a difficult and fraught task, and a failure to do so well can produce a whole range of negative effects – from poor policy to outright state failure. Sadly, for the citizens of the Republic, its early institutional engineers made one too many mistakes, setting the stage for Sith Lords and Separatists to seize the government.

The Opening Crawl

All of the *Star Wars* films begin with the now iconic crawl, which serves to introduce characters, set up major conflicts, and reveal necessary pieces of world-building history. Consider this section my version of that famous text: a very quick introduction to the events and characters of *Star Wars*, as a way to set the stage for a conversation about legislative politics in a galaxy far, far away.

As mentioned above, the *Star Wars* film universe is comprised of two trilogies. The OT tells the story of how the Rebel Alliance challenged the Empire, and eventually defeated the Emperor. The OT focuses on Luke Skywalker learning to become a Jedi, and defeating the Empire. His primary antagonists are Emperor Palpatine and Darth Vader, who is also Luke's father. In the final film, Luke challenges Vader and the Emperor, eventually guiding his father to redemption, killing the Emperor, and destroying the Empire's secret weapon – a planet-destroying Death Star.

The OT introduces a number of powerful themes around destiny, family, freedom, and the pains of growing into adulthood. But, on a pure story level, it also teases the audience with a number of powerful questions. In particular, the OT makes us wonder: how did the Republic fall? Luckily, there is a balm for the nagging question of how the Republic fell from grace: George Lucas created a second series of films, the PT, that laid out the events that lead to the opening moments of the OT. The PT begins with growing unrest in the Republic, as the Republic government is in conflict with the Trade Federation. However, the evil Sith Palpatine is actually manipulating the Trade Federation. In the first film, we are introduced to key characters such as the Naboo's queen and future Senator Padmé Amidala, Anakin Skywalker (the future Darth Vader), and Sheev Palpatine (who will eventually become the Emperor).

As the second film opens, Anakin Skywalker is now apprenticed to Obi-Wan Kenobi, following Qui-Gon's death at the hands of the Sith villain Darth Maul. The galaxy is engaged in a major war at this point, with the Trade Federation having attracted the support of a number of Separatist planets that are dissatisfied with the Republic and seek to secede. At the same time, the Jedi continue their battle against the Sith, including against the Sith Palpatine – who, unbeknownst to the Jedi, is manipulating policy from within the Republic to ensure the downfall of the Republic, the end of the Jedi, and his own ascent to power. It is in *Attack of the Clones* that we get the most extended view of how the Republic works (or perhaps, *fails* to work). With this background of the basic players and conflicts laid out, we can now jump into a consideration of how governance occurred in the Galactic Republic.

The Great Debate

The primary political body in the Galactic Republic, as we are led to understand from what we observe in *Attack of the Clones*, is the Galactic Senate. The Senate is, obviously, a legislative body. Quickly defined, we would state that a legislature is the law-making apparatus of any government. But, more than just making rules, an ideal legislature incorporates the voices of numerous representatives along with deliberation in the rule-making process. In practice, a despot could be a source of law – but a despot would not be a legislature, as s/he would be a unitary and lack the diversity of opinion as well as the deliberative aspect that is so crucial to legislative politics.[2] In an ideal situation, a legislature works on the basis of selected representatives coming together at an appointed time to discuss policies and make decisions about what action to take. Both elements – a range of representatives and discussion – are critical to how a legislature works. As an institution, a legislature does not rely on the direct participation of citizens to make laws. Rather, legislatures function through citizens selecting, through some mechanism, a select few representatives to stand in for their own interests at the assembly. Thus, representatives are a kind of distillation of public opinion into a relatively few figures. The intention is that by removing direct citizen involvement, more productive conversations can take place. At the most idealistic, we might actually believe that representatives are nobler or possess greater wisdom than the average citizen.[3] Of course, realistically, we know that this probably is not the case. What is more likely to happen is that each representative comes to the assembly prepared to fight primarily for the interests of his or her constituents (or their own) and not to rise above the ideological fray. In addition to selecting a handful of representatives, a legislature is also marked by deliberation. Rather than just arriving at the assembly and voting, representatives are expected to engage in debate and discussion around political ideas. In this way, legislatures are actually in the business of sharing information and using the emergence of the ideas that come from sharing that information to craft better policies. The ideal of a legislature is to, through structured debate and law-making procedures, somehow transform general public will into specific policies and governmental acts.

Although this account describes the broad outlines of what a legislature is, it goes without saying that within that vague structure there are a multitude of legislative possibilities. The way that any legislature functions, and the policy outputs that it produces, are directly connected to its institutional design. The number of chambers, the process for debating and passing a law, and even the selection of members all exist in a wide array of permutations. For instance, in the American context we select our members for the House of Representatives by voting for members in single-member districts, each of which should contain the same number of citizens, be compact, contiguous, and not divide communities of interest. In these elections, we employ a first-past-the-post/winner-takes-all model, so that any candidate who wins the plurality of votes in their district wins the seat in that district. This means that someone with 50.1 percent of the vote will win the full seat for his or her district – potentially leaving over 49 percent of the population dissatisfied with their elected official in the House. If there are three candidates, it is possible for a candidate to win without the support of 66.6 percent of the population!

Connecting the definition of a legislature with the problem of how to best build a legislature, we have the tools to start asking real questions about how the

Galactic Senate functions. Beginning with the problem of representation, it is apparent from what we see in *Attack of the Clones* that the Galactic Senate is problematically designed to say the least. Specifically, it is designed poorly in terms of picking its representatives, both in terms of refining the number of representatives and in ensuring that all necessary voices are heard in the Senate. The first problem with the Senate that is immediately obvious when watching *Attack of the Clones* is that it is huge. Really, really huge. In fact, the Galactic Senate has over 2,000 members.[4] *Attack of the Clones* reveals that the Galactic Senate assembly chamber is a massive, multi-story cylinder, with levitating pods placed in the walls. Each pod docks in the side of the chamber and houses the representatives from one planetary system. When those members address the Senate, their pod detaches from the wall and floats to the vast space in the middle of the chamber. Through the use of holographic technology, an audio and video feed of each speaker is then projected to other pods. With this technological boost, the Galactic Senate attempts to conduct business with its hundreds and hundreds of members.

If we think about the design of the Galactic Senate for even the briefest moment, it is not a surprise that this system fell apart. In fact, it is actually a surprise it lasted as long as it did. This is, frankly, a terrible system for a representative government. There are simply too many representatives on the floor at any one time for effective conversation to take place. In this setting, it is hard to imagine that every member who has important information to share on a topic is allowed to speak. The fact that the Senate seemed largely unaware of the Trade Federation embargo on Naboo chronicled in *A Phantom Menace* serves to reinforce this point. The Senate clearly needs a system to further divide itself, and decentralize some of its decision-making power to regional clusters of planetary systems.

If we are staying with the American context as a comparison, the problem of institutional design faced by the Galactic Senate recalls the Great Compromise during the American founding. While writing the Constitution, the Framers faced the question of whether states would receive equal representation or be granted representation based on population. The solution was bicameral legislature, with the lower chamber, the House of Representatives, having state representation based on population, whereas the upper chamber, the Senate, gave each state two senators.[5] At the same time, the Constitution also delegated a great deal of authority to state governments, which possessed their own legislatures and executives to carry out laws.[6] In 1929, as the population grew, Congress decided to limit the number of representatives in the House to 435, rather than having the chamber grow with the nation's population, as a means to keep the House at a manageable size for debate and voting. This decision obviously comes with a cost: it makes the House less representative, as each member must now speak for more and more citizens. However, it also comes with the very real benefit of keeping the House at a manageable size, so that debate and personal connections can produce viable legislation. What the American case highlights is that the number of representatives we have, and the way we divide responsibilities among them, matters. If a legislature is intended to be a site of debate and discussion, there needs to be a mechanism to corral public opinion into a workable number of elected officials – otherwise the system is chaotic.

The other problem with the Galactic Senate is how representatives are selected. In many ways, this is a problem that is unique to each planetary system. Yet, if the Galactic Senate intends to function as a representative body, it should be able to ensure that all of its citizens have their voice heard – or at least have an equal chance. It is in this spirit, after all, that the Voting Rights Act in the United States worked to make sure that state and local elections were fair for African Americans during the Civil Rights era. In the case of Naboo, representation was obviously a critical problem. Naboo is divided into two discrete civilizations: a race of humans living on the surface as well as the Gungans, humanoid amphibians living below the surface of Naboo's many bodies of water. Yet, the Gungans – as observed in *Episode 1: The Phantom Menace* – are *not* part of Naboo's senate delegation. A legislature is only as legitimate as its selection of representatives, and overlooking an entire species/civilization – is problematic. The notion that only a Gungan can represent a Gungan, of course, suggests a very narrow view of representation, strongly tied to notions of identity politics. It seems very possible that non-Gungans could stand for Gungan issues. However, there is very little evidence that this was occurring before Jar Jar Binks was appointed to Naboo's Senate delegation as a junior senator. Certainly, not every planet necessarily suffers from this problem of under-representation of key species and ethnic groups. However, political exclusion of any kind – especially in an idealistic republic – certainly gives pause and reason to question the legitimacy of the Senate.

With these features in mind, some serious questions about how well the Senate handles representation start to arise. With its massive collection of voices and its apparent inability to include all voices, the Galactic Senate seems destined to fall apart as a representative body. The Senate requires a better institutional structure, notably better rules surrounding debate and political inclusion, in order to truly function as a representative body. Unfortunately, these are not the only structural problems the Senate faces. As we will see below, the Galactic Senate not only fails to represent its citizens, but it is also unable to carry out its own directives.

I Cannot Fight a War for You

The first of two factors that shape a legislature's power is the legal powers it is given as well as the actual resources it has to carry out those legal responsibilities. To expand on how legislative capacity hinges on both legal rules and administrative resources, it is useful to turn to the American example. Starting first with legislative reach, this is really a discussion of federalism, or how policymaking responsibilities will be divided between national and local legislative bodies. In practice, political power in a society exists along a continuum. At one extreme, political institutions can be organized in a unitary fashion, where a single actor at the national level holds all power. At the other end of this continuum is a confederal system, where most power is local and divided among many local political actors. In each of these systems, the reach of the legislature can vary wildly – from granting legislatures a great deal of power in the former to a more restricted set of powers and policy arenas in the latter.[7] The U.S. Constitution lays out a number of formal federal powers – including coining money, building post roads, and providing national defense – while turning all other powers over to the state governments. Of course, in practice, things are a bit more complicated, as certain aspects of the Constitution (such as the "necessary and proper" clause) grant the national state expanded, unstated powers that might be necessary for it to complete its primary tasks. This leads to a great deal of power sharing and cooperation between the various layers of American government. Although the details are muddled at times, there are certainly very clear federal powers – especially those related to commerce, international relations, and defense – that the Constitution provides to the national legislature.

But, to expand on this point, the issue at stake is not just whether the legislature has formal control over an issue, but also whether it has the capacity to enforce its decisions. American political history provides a complicated, useful view of this problem. In many ways, the classic story of the American federal government is that the Founders revolted against the domineering ways of the English Crown and built a very loose political system in its place – the Articles of Confederation. That system failed to pay debts and was too chaotic for effective governance, a reminder that poor legislative design has very real social and economic consequences. Given these limitations, the Articles of Confederation were replaced with a somewhat stronger central government in the current Constitution. Often, the early decades of the American republic are characterized as "stateless" – in other words, there was no strong central authority making choices, and local actors (such as state legislatures) had all the meaningful power and responsibility.[8] This view is complicated by the realization that the federal government has always had certain key powers, such as taxation and control over the military.[9] Furthermore, the federal state has been active – right from the beginning, even in areas where it had seemingly very little formal constitutional authority such as disaster relief, public health, and transportation infrastructure.[10] However, even if the state did have more formal power at its inception than we might normally assume, there is still the problem of whether the state had the capacity to enforce those decisions. Although the early American state certainly was proactive at times, it also lacked a large military, a dedicated bureaucratic corps, and a large pool of technical experts to call upon to turn its directions into action. Thus, legislative power has two elements: not only how much power the legislature is formally provided, but also the amount of administrative might that same legislature holds in order to actually carry out its decisions.

The second question of federalism that is tied to legislative power, beyond its power and capacity, is how unfettered legislative actions will be. It is possible to design a legislature that possesses all of the decision-making power in a government, with no other entity really designed to stop it. This is really a question about separation of powers, and what other actors will have a say in the law-making process. The United States is a clear example where power has been split among legislative, executive, and judicial branches. The passage of any law requires coordination across all three branches, and each branch can stymie the efforts of the others (for instance, the president can veto a bill passed by Congress). Other systems, such as the British parliamentary approach, have weaker courts and fold the executive into the legislature through a prime minister. The result is a much stronger legislative branch that is less subject to outside interference. Both of these aspects of legislative power and federalism are really, at their core, questions about political centralization and how concentrated power will be.

When designing a legislature, it is obviously necessary to put all of these pieces into balance with one another. Designing political institutions is not easy, and it is difficult to imagine recommending an ideal way to balance legislative reach, legislative power, and legislative checks that would work in all situations. After all, legislative bodies extend from Galactic Republics all the way down to small town councils, incorporating a wide range of cultures, species, and differing levels of technology. However, as a rule of thumb, I suggest it is necessary to provide a legislature with powers and resources commensurate with its level of prestige and oversight. In other words, a legislature that is making rules for a nation might need more leeway and administrative capacity than one working for a township. With this rough standard in mind, along with the above-mentioned considerations of legislative power, it quickly becomes clear that there are some real problems with the power balance in the Republic.

The most obvious problem faced by the Galactic Senate is that it seems to lack much administrative presence. In *The Phantom Menace*, the Senate seems wholly unaware of the seriousness of the Trade Federation blockade on Naboo. In fact, the Senate seems only roused to address the issue when the child-queen Amidala herself breaks the Trade Federation blockade line to come and speak before the Senate on Coruscant. In this same vein, the Republic also appears to lack the capacity to carry out its policies. The Senate does not seem even to have the typical powers or resources we would usually find in a governing body. In fact, the Senate does not even have control over any kind of military force.

To be clear, this is not because some other branch of government controls the military. The Senate does have a chancellor, who directs the legislative body. However, the chancellor does not appear to have any unique powers beyond convening and directing the legislature. In other words, the chancellor is not an executive with oversight over the military operation. Instead, the Republic simply lacks any kind of standing army. Outside of guards, policing responsibilities in the Republic fall to the Jedi, and although they are wise, well-trained warrior monks with mystical powers, they are a terrible police force and military. First, the Jedi are not numerous. Only a handful of citizens in the Republic are Force-sensitive, and even eligible to attempt to join the Jedi order. And, of those recruited, many fall during training. Further, the Jedi are individualistic and iconoclastic; in *Attack of the Clones* we rarely see them working in anything larger than small groups, outside their final assault on the Separatist government. In fact, in *The Phantom Menace* the Jedi Master Qui-Gon Jinn makes to Queen Amidala the statement that opens this section: "I cannot fight a war for you." On the one hand, this certainly speaks to the fact that there are only a few Jedi. But Jinn's comment also reminds us that the Jedi are highly ethical political actors, serving the Light Side of the Force. They do use violence and even kill, but do so sparingly, for the Jedi are reflective, contemplative, and would certainly resist Republican orders with which they disagreed. In fact, as the Jedi have their own discrete governing council, it is not clear the Senate even controls them. Instead, the Jedi and Senate merely seem to share overlapping goals and tend to cooperate, rather than there being a clear power relationship between the two bodies. Finally, it is worth noting: the Jedi of the *Attack of the Clones* era do not seem especially competent. During the entire PT, the Sith are maneuvering right under the Jedi's collective noses, as Palpatine is in actuality the Sith Lord Darth Sidious. The inability of the Jedi to ferret out their fierce nemesis, even when he is housed on the same planetary system as them, suggests that they are a less than effective policing body.

Of course, the Senate does attempt to solve this problem. As *Attack of the Clones* escalates, the Separatist movement threatens the Republic and secession seems more and more likely. In part, the Separatist movement is empowered by their droid army, which allows them to resist Republic demands, and a more centralized hierarchy, represented by the leadership of General Grievous and Count Dooku, a fallen Jedi, seduced away to the Dark Side by Darth Sidious. The Senate responds to this by granting Chancellor Palpatine emergency powers, essentially extreme and draconian powers to govern the Republic. In many ways, this expansion recalls the PATRIOT Act and other invasive policies put in place following the terrorist attacks of 9/11. Without an external executive or judicial system, there is no mechanism to challenge these potentially unjust laws (of course, the passage of the PATRIOT Act in the United States suggests that a strong system of checks and balances will not stop all problematic legislation, but it should at least make passing such laws harder and rarer). Seemingly, the Republic is poorly designed to handle times of crisis without extreme measures. In addition, the Senate turns to a clone army to carry out its plans, notably to fight a war to stop Separatists from leaving the Republic. The clone army itself is a fascinating turn for a government that seems to embody contemporary Western liberal, democratic ideals. Although the clones are based on the DNA of Jango Fett, a feared bounty hunter, they have no choice but to be conscripted into the Republic's war, and much of their free will is washed away. Yet, as indicated in the *Clone Wars* television show, the clones are individuals, with feelings, sentience, and individuality. What we see, then, is that the lack of power placed in the Senate in previous generations resulted in the Senate making rash choices during its darkest hours. Thus, whereas centralized power can be a dangerous thing, an inability to act can obviously produce just as problematic outcomes. Legislatures require formal legal power to act and the resources to back their decisions, but also external oversight to check their more dangerous impulses. The Galactic Senate, however, appears to possess neither the power to act nor a formal political adversary to temper its decisions. With this structure, it is not surprising that the Senate eventually falls prey to its own poor design.

Making the Law

Through now, our discussion has focused on the institutional structure of the Galactic Republic; that is, how much power does the Senate have and how does it accomplish the tricky task of representation? In thinking about these issues, we have seen that the Senate has some fairly serious design flaws. However, we have not discussed the actual work that the Senate does, which is making laws to govern the Republic. Unfortunately, a careful examination of the law-making process in *Attack of the Clones* reveals that the Galactic Senate is a poor locale for debate and, as a result, is easily dominated by special interests. The result is narrow policy that only benefits a few, and fails to serve the common good.

Interest groups, in particular, are a complicated part of democratic political life. Our most common knee-jerk reaction to interest groups is one of visceral distaste: interest groups are seen as powerful, resource-rich groups that interject themselves into the political process. At the very worst, interest groups are seen as perverting the political process.[11] However, whereas interest groups certainly are biased and certainly do attempt to shape public opinion, it is not clear that interest groups are always inherently undemocratic. After all, interest groups are associations of citizens, who certainly have a right to lobby for their interests before their elected representatives. In fact, interest groups can often be powerful sources of information for legislators, offering insight into citizen preferences as well as useful fonts of policy information.[12] Furthermore, whereas interest groups do work to turn out votes and provide money to campaigns, it is not clear that interest groups actually buy votes. Interest groups purchase time and access. Interest group support is often able to gain time with a legislator or secure more of that legislator's effort in support (or opposition) of a bill.[13] Thus, nothing quite so naked as vote buying typically happens.

However, our unease with interest groups is not wholly misplaced, either. Interest groups are self-interested actors, and they often possess sizable war chests with which to pursue their policy goals. In most cases, interest groups cannot generate wholesale support from a legislator for an issue which that member is not already interested in. This is, in part, because a legislator is generally deeply tied to the interests of his or her constituents, and the electoral incentive ensures that legislators will always put their constituents' concerns over anything else.[14] Thus, a donation from an interest group cannot make a legislator from Iowa suddenly uninterested in the new farm bill, or persuade a representative from Silicon Valley to impose a new tax on research and design departments. But, interest groups can certainly manipulate and shift public opinion. Interest groups excel at finding populations that are unhappy with a current policy, but often lack direction about what new policy they prefer. Stepping into this gap, interest groups supply a fully formed policy option that may or may not fully reflect what voters want, but is at least a raft to grab onto in a sea of political uncertainty. In this way, rather than fostering debate that leads citizens to their own answers, interest groups offer a pre-packaged political platform that also serves their own interests.[15] Thus, whereas interest groups are absolutely legal, possibly essential, and certainly reflective of our right to associate and engage in politics as a group, they also have a perverse effect on political life, tipping the direction of a democratic polity in disproportion to the actual number of people repressed by the interest groups.

This concern over interest group politics often leads to questions of how to curtail or contain interest group influence, including ideas like capping the amount of money one group can spend on the political process. In *Attack of the Clones*, the Republic has stumbled on a particularly original strategy for dealing with the problem of interest groups: making them part of the legislative process itself. The Trade Federation, the same group that is associated with the Separatists and led a blockade on Naboo, has an official seat in the Senate. The Trade Federation appears to be an actual economic organization, not a planet or civilization that has named itself in a particularly corporate manner. Instead, a presumably private, profit-making entity is granted free and open access to the legislature itself, with the capacity to engage in debate and potentially even vote on policy. In the PT, we see members of the Trade Federation called in and engaging in debate on the Senate floor, in an attempt to defend their actions. In effect, the Senate gives interest groups – at least some of them – a direct say in the legislative process. Structurally, this again should give us pause about the organization of the Senate and the nature of political representation in the Republic. More profoundly, it might also lead us to ask hard questions about the quality of policy in the Senate: if interest groups who are directly affected by a bill have a hands-on role in drafting, debating, and voting on the bill, how can that bill possibly speak to the common good and not simply reflect particular interests?

The inclusion of interest groups in the Senate simply reflects an overall problem with the nature of policymaking in the Senate. On the whole, the Senate is a body where deliberation does not seem to occur. Further, Senate debates are long and tedious, and rarely produce strong policy. Whereas it might seem like a cheap shot, the fact that Jar Jar Binks bears a heavy responsibility for bringing down the Republic is telling. Binks is appointed as Naboo's junior senator, which, while it does at least provide representation for the Gungans, seems problematic.

Presumably, after all, Gungans might want some say in their senator, rather than having him or her appointed by executive fiat. But that aside, Binks later – in response to Palpatine's suggestion as the Clone Wars begin and the Separatist threat intensifies – introduces the bill to give Palpatine extensive executive powers. It is from this base that Palpatine will take charge of the clone army, eliminate the Jedi, consolidate his power, and dissolve the Republican Senate. This occurs, in an obvious parallel to the PATRIOT Act and the immediate post-9/11 United States, with minimal debate in the Senate. For viewers, it is somewhat frightening that a clownish (and reviled by fans) junior senator from a backwater planet is able to plant the seed that undoes the Republic. But the fact that there is so little discussion over this suggests a real breakdown in the deliberative work of the Senate. Thus, the Senate engages in a great deal of discussion, but is ultimately unable to penetrate the more serious issues that come before it. These poor deliberative habits, when combined with the inclusion of interest groups in the chamber, considerably undermine the law-making ability of the Senate. It is simply not clear that this is a system that is given over to producing quality, strong, and well-considered policies.

The Path to the Dark Side

In many ways, this essay might read like more than a critique of the (admittedly, imaginary) Senate in the *Star Wars* universe. In some ways, this essay could be read as an indictment on legislative bodies in general. But that is not the intention. Instead, what I want to highlight here is both the possibility and pitfalls that come with democratic life, and that I think are perfectly captured by *Star Wars* and the Republican Senate.

There is something truly inspiring about the Republican Senate in *Star Wars*. In the United States, we struggle – as partisanship increases and polarization undermines the basic functioning of Congress – to have an effective deliberative body. Further, as one species on a single planet, we struggle to govern ourselves globally. Although organizations like the United Nations, the World Bank, and the World Health Organization might provide some forums for international discussion, they also lack the oversight and power to truly enforce meaningful policy. And that lack of power might be reasonable, given the range of challenges we face at the national and local level. Perhaps international governance would, at this stage in our social development, be more of an imposition than an expression of general will. However, in *Star Wars*, they have overcome this problem. In Star Wars, they have built a Senate that represents not only a range of worlds that cover a galaxy, but also a wide array of species with a bewildering number of forms of communication.

But there are also important lessons to be learned from the Republic, particularly concerning dangers to be avoided in the name of preserving democracy. Much as the Jedi strive to avoid anger and attachment in pursuit of a purer, higher truth, we need to ask hard questions about how we develop our legislative bodies. Seemingly innocuous rules about who is represented, and how decisions are made, produce tremendous effect in terms of both policy quality and the efficacy of citizens. Thus, poor choices about how we design our institutions can radically undermine their ability to actually represent us, much as a small choice about breaking the Jedi code can snowball into becoming the lackey of a fascist Emperor. Thus, whereas *Attack of the Clones* shows us what is grand about legislative bodies, it also very smartly reminds us of what we need to be careful of. The Galactic Senate suffers from poor design, problematic representation, and a dangerous reliance on interest groups – all flaws that hobble its ability to effectively govern over a massive territory and numerous cultures. In many ways, we can watch *Attack of the Clones* as a call to arms – as a challenge to do better in our institutions, to make sure they work and are actually representative. The film is not a case against democracy, but rather an advocate for better democracy.

Chapter Discussion Questions

1. Did the Galactic Senate fail because of its poor design, or because of outside pressures like war, economic conflict, and the Sith's manipulation? What does your answer suggest about why democracies in general might fail?
2. If you could design your own legislature, what kind of rules and systems would you include to make it work? Consider problems like efficiency, representation, and capacity to enforce rules versus concerns over liberty.
3. How should a legislature regulate its interaction with interest groups like the Trade Federation? How involved should interest groups be with policy-making? In a similar vein, how much independence should police units such as the Jedi have from the legislature? How much control should civilian legislators have over the military?

Notes

1 Campbell, Joseph. 2008. *The hero with a thousand faces: The collected works of Joseph Campbell.* Novato, CA: New World Library

2 Montesquieu, Charles de. 2002. *The spirit of the laws*, ed. A. M. Cohler, B. C. Miller, and H. S. Stone. New York: Cambridge University Press.

3 Hamilton, Alexander, James Madison, and John Jay. 2003. *The Federalist papers with letters from "Brutus,"* ed. T. Ball. Cambridge: Cambridge University Press, 2003. See also Montesquieu, *The spirit of the laws*.

4 The information on the size of the Galactic Senate was found on Wookiepedia at http://starwars.wikia.com/wiki/Galactic_Senate, accessed October 20, 2014. Wookiepedia is an online wiki that gathers any and all information relevant to *Star Wars*.

5 Walker, David B. 2000. *The rebirth of federalism: Slouching towards Washington.* 2nd Edition. New York: Chatham House.

6 Teaford, Jon C. 2002. *The rise of the states: Evolution of American state government.* Baltimore, MD: The Johns Hopkins University Press.

7 Rodden, Jonathan A. 2006. *Hamilton's paradox: The promise and peril of fiscal federalism*. Cambridge: Cambridge University Press. See also Walker, *The rebirth of federalism*.
8 Novak, William J. 1996. *The people's welfare: Law and regulation in nineteenth-century America*. Chapel Hill, NC: The University of North Carolina Press; Skowronek, Stephen. 1982. *Building a new American state: The expansion of national administrative capacities 1877–1920*. Cambridge: Cambridge University Press, 1982.
9 Edling, Max M. 2008. *A revolution in favor of government: Origins of the U.S. Constitution and the making of the American state*. Oxford: Oxford University Press.
10 Dauber, Michele Landis. 2013. *The sympathetic state: Disaster relief and the origins of the American welfare state*. Chicago: The University of Chicago Press; Larson, John Lauritz. 2001. *Internal improvement: National public works and the promise of popular government in the early United States*. Chapel Hill, NC: The University of North Carolina Press; Rao, Gautham. 2008. "Sailors' health and national wealth: Marine hospitals in the early Republic," *Common-Place* 9(1), http://www.common-place-archives.org/vol-09/no-01/rao, accessed October 12, 2014.
11 Hansen, John Mark. 1991 *Gaining access: Congress and the farm lobby 1919–1981*. Chicago: The University of Chicago Press.
12 Hansen, *Gaining access*.
13 Hall, Richard L. and Frank W. Wayman. 1990. "Buying time: Moneyed interests and the mobilization of bias in Congressional committees,' *The American Political Science Review*, 84(3): 797–820.
14 Mayhew, David R. 2004. *Congress: The electoral connection*. 2nd edition. New Haven, CT: Yale University Press.
15 Hansen, *Gaining access*.

8

ARE YOU DIVERGENT?

Political Factions and Personal Identity

Steve B. Lem

KUTZTOWN UNIVERSITY OF PENNSYLVANIA

> The faction system is a living being composed of cells: all of you. The only way it can survive and thrive is for each of you to claim your rightful place. The future belongs to those who know where they belong.

The words of Jeanine Matthews, leader of the Erudite faction, echo across the silent room at the Choosing Ceremony. Marcus Eaton, one of the city council leaders, follows: "When we leave this room you will no longer be dependents but full fledged members of our society. Factions before blood."

A nervous look comes over Beatrice's face as the first initiate is called. The choice she makes today will define the rest of her life. At age sixteen, each citizen must join one of society's five factions: Abnegation the selfless, Amity the peaceful, Candor the honest, Dauntless the brave, or Erudite the intelligent. The choice is permanent – once an initiate selects a faction, she must embrace their attributes and values. If she fails to do so, she cannot go back to her family or original faction. Rather, she would become one of the Factionless, society's outcasts, who are impoverished and unwelcome by the other factions.

For most members of society, it is an easy choice. Individuals with strong personal values easily identify their faction. Beatrice, however, is selfless, brave, *and* intelligent. As a result, she shares values with three factions: Abnegation, Dauntless, and Erudite, respectively. Individuals who share values with multiple factions are considered "Divergent" and pose the greatest threat to the established social order because their existence undermines the foundation of the faction system. Consequently, Beatrice must choose her faction wisely or risk being identified as Divergent and become a target of the government.

Although Beatrice's choice carries life-or-death consequences in a fictional, dystopian future, there are parallels to the political choices facing young citizens today in democratic nations around the world. In the United States, for example, at age eighteen each citizen is presented with the opportunity to join one of society's political factions. There are two dominant factions, the Democratic Party and the Republican Party, a handful of moderately sized ones (e.g., Libertarian Party, Green Party), and a plethora of minor parties (e.g., America First, Communist Party of the USA). Although each party has a specific outlook on many of society's issues, we often characterize parties by their general orientations. For instance, if we were to use *Divergent*-style phrasing, we might say Democrats the Liberals, Republicans the Conservatives, or Greens the Environmentalists.

Although tens of millions of Americans choose to join one of the political parties, many more do not formally affiliate with a faction. Approximately 50 million Americans do not register to vote, which represents nearly one in four people who are eligible to do so. Unregistered voters tend to be younger, from lower socioeconomic backgrounds, and from racial minority groups. Because voter registration is a prerequisite for participation in the political system, these members of society do not receive the full benefits of their citizenship and, in many ways, are analogous to the Factionless in *Divergent*, albeit without suffering the same institutionalized oppression.[1]

Citizens who wish to participate in the political process but are conflicted about which party to join may choose another option: identify as an Independent. The number of individuals in the United States doing just that has been on the rise since the 1960s and is becoming an increasingly sizable threat to the major parties. In the lead up to the 2012 presidential election, there were approximately 24 million registered Independents versus 30 million registered Republicans and 42 million Democrats.[2] Perhaps even more problematic for the major parties, Gallup polls indicated a record high of 42 percent of Americans self-identified as Independents in 2013. These data suggest that party identification among the major parties' registered members may be on the decline.[3]

Independents, like Divergents, threaten the established political system. In democratic societies, political parties gain control of government by competing for and acquiring votes. Because most party members vote for their party, each party has a strong incentive to maintain and increase its membership. In this regard, parties count on their core demographics for support. The Democratic Party, with its emphasis on social justice and equality, tends to recruit voters that are young, lower-income, and from racial minority groups. The Republican Party, on the other hand, emphasizes free market principles and conservative social policy. Consequently, their members tend to be older, higher-income, and white.

These patterns of support bring stability to the political system. Both parties have a good sense of the level of support they and their opposition have, where their supporters live, and where their campaign dollars will be most effective. For instance, both parties recognize that voters in the state of Texas overwhelmingly support the Republican Party. Thus, neither party spends much effort campaigning or recruiting there. Conversely, in swing states like Ohio, where partisan support is mixed, candidates campaign heavily for their citizens' votes.

Because Independents do not affiliate strongly with a party, they threaten the campaign and recruiting strategies of the major parties. If, say, Texas sees a drastic rise in Independents, it signals that the Democratic Party *may* be able to recruit new members and successfully campaign in the state. However, in the face of a rising number of Independent voters, it is not necessarily clear how to win the support of these voters. For instance, Independent voters may want free market principles combined with social equality – a combination neither the Democratic nor the Republican Party currently offers. The major parties could accommodate Independents by modifying their political agenda, but this strategy potentially alienates their existing core support base. If the parties do nothing, it could open the door for new parties to emerge that embrace the hybrid values of the Independents. In both instances, established parties risk losing members and voters.

Are you Divergent?

Before the Choosing Ceremony, Tris undergoes the Test, which uses a series of choices to narrow down potential factions until only one remains. During the Test, Tris must confront a vicious dog. She considers her options: run, but the dog would catch her, or fight, although the dog would probably win. Thinking back to her biology class, Tris recalls that dogs smell fear due to chemicals secreted from human glands during times of duress and staring a dog in the eye is a sign of aggression. Consequently, Tris steadies her breathing, closes her eyes, and sinks to her knees.

Moments later, Tris sees a gentler dog whimpering and panting at her. She hears a voice say, "puppy," and turns to see a young girl in the room. Before Tris can react, the dog has reverted back to its former self and attacks the young girl. Without thinking, Tris springs to her feet and tackles the dog to the ground. The Test is over, but the results are inconclusive.[4]

Why were the results inconclusive? Tackling the dog to save the little girl indicates selflessness, which suggests Abnegation. However, Tris did not run from the dog, a Dauntless response, and handled the situation by drawing on her knowledge of dogs and fear, which suggests intelligence – an Erudite response. Consequently, the Test administrator concludes that she shares traits from all three factions and the results point to Divergence.

In the real world, there are plenty of tests to help individuals identify their correspondence to a political party. Ahead of the 2012 United States Presidential Election, PBS NewsHour collaborated with the Pew Research Center to create, "Where Do You Fit? The Political Party Test."[5] Respondents were asked to rate whether they completely agree, mostly agree, mostly disagree, or completely disagree with twelve statements. For example, respondents evaluate whether, "One parent can bring up a child as well as two parents together," and "Poor people have become too dependent on government assistance programs."

The test produces one of three main results; individuals are identified either as a Democrat, Republican, or Independent. Like the Faction Test, each question or choice is tailored toward one of the major political parties. For instance, Democrats are expected to agree with the statement about parenting, whereas Republicans are expected to agree with the statement about government assistance. Thus, strong agreement with statements regarding progressive social policy (e.g., gay marriage) and government intervention in the economy to support equality yields a Democratic result, whereas strong agreement with conservative social policy and free market principles produces a Republican outcome.

Although each individual question is meant to affirm an individual's affinity with one of the political parties, it is possible – and often likely – that respondents will agree with both Democratic- and Republican-oriented statements. These responses are particularly problematic for the Political Party Test, as individuals who agree with both types of statements end up in the middle of the spectrum and cannot easily be linked to either party. As a result, the test labels individuals who provide mixed responses as Independents, which are the functional equivalent of Divergence because they share beliefs with more than one political group.

The Nature of Belief Systems

Whether we refer to them as Divergent or Independent, many citizens cannot be neatly characterized into one of society's existing political groups. Part of the classification problem stems from assumptions the tests make about the structure of people's belief systems. In both instances, the tests presume the majority of individual behavior is derived from a cognitive structuring principle. In the world of *Divergent*, individual behaviors are structured by one of five human virtues: selflessness, peacefulness, honesty, intelligence, or bravery. Individuals structured by selflessness, for instance, would be driven to sacrifice their own safety to save the girl from the dog during the Faction Test, help the elderly and disabled carry their bags, and give up some of their food to help feed the Factionless.

The factions in *Divergent* and political parties in the real world tend to embody these structuring principles. The problem for the average citizen, however, is that the structuring principles represent ideal cognitive patterns, which are often quite different from the way individuals actually see the world. That is, few people could be considered "perfectly brave" or "perfectly conservative" and would therefore not necessarily fit into the Dauntless or Republican archetype, respectively.

In his highly influential essay, "The Nature of Belief Systems in Mass Publics," Philip Converse argued that the disconnection between American voters and parties was because political ideology – as a relevant structuring principle – ceases to exist in any meaningful way for the average voter. Converse concluded:

> For the truly involved citizen, the development of political sophistication means the absorption of contextual information that makes it clear to him

> the connections of the policy area of his initial interest with policy differences in other areas; and that these broader configurations of policy positions are describable quite economically in the basic abstractions of ideology. Most members of the mass public, however, fail to proceed so far … A realistic picture of political belief systems in the mass public, then, is not one … that presumes widespread ideological coherence.[6]

Converse's claims caused a serious dilemma for political scientists and a great deal of controversy. In Converse's view, parties are organized around ideological principles, but average voters only possess random and often conflicting opinions, which are driven by idiosyncratic and subjective factors such as the "nature of the times" (e.g., voters in the 1950s disapproved of Democrats because of the Korean War rather than on ideological grounds) and "group interest" (i.e., voters oppose parties because of the groups they think they represent, such as Republicans representing big business or the wealthy). Under this framework, democratic representation breaks down, as ideologically driven parties are not representative of non-ideological voters.

In the decades following the publication of Converse's work, political psychologists rethought the relationship between ideology and voter attitudes. As one would expect, the current consensus falls between the two extremes. Contemporary studies indicate that voter attitudes are not necessarily random and unconnected as Converse proposed, but neither are they wholly produced by a coherent and well-articulated ideology. Rather, beliefs are structured hierarchically, which Russell Dalton eloquently summarizes in Figure 8.1.[7]

Under the revised model, specific opinions are derived from one or more general orientations rather than directly from a single, structuring principle. For

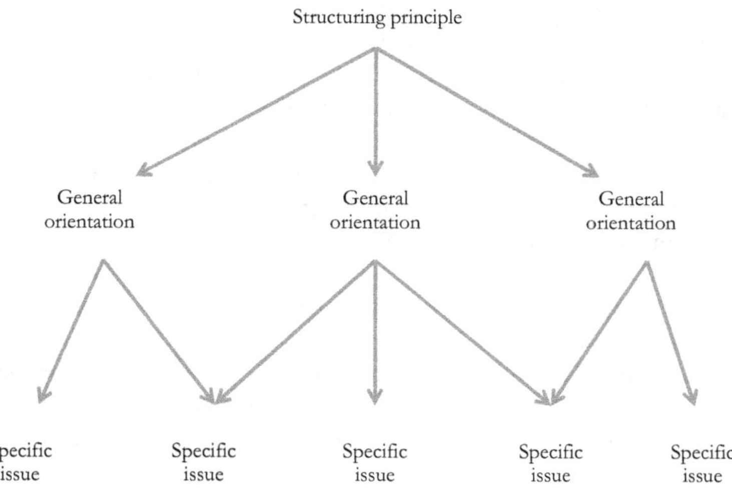

FIGURE 8.1 Hierarchical Model of Voter Attitudes

instance, some one's view on immigration policy may be influenced by her political orientation toward government's responsibility to provide national security, her general perspective on civil rights, and her attitudes toward immigrants. Even though these orientations may be connected to an even more general structuring principle, such as political ideology, they may not necessarily be well connected to each other. For instance, a generally conservative person may strongly believe that the government should protect the border from illegal immigration but also feel that the civil rights of current immigrants should not be violated in the pursuit of stricter border control.

We can easily adapt the model to explain many of the conflicting and often contradictory behaviors in *Divergent*. Arguably, although Tris's Divergence makes her equally suited for membership in Dauntless, Erudite, and Abnegation, bravery appears to be the structuring principle of her personality. It leads her to stand her ground against the dog during the Test, jump off the roof first following the faction transfer, and not flinch during the knife toss. However, bravery does not solely produce Tris's behaviors. During the Dauntless game of capture the flag, for instance, Tris climbs the Ferris wheel to gain a vantage point over the opposing team. She is able to do so because her bravery (structuring principle) makes her unafraid of heights (general orientation), but she chooses to do so because she was clever enough to deduce that the point of the game was to learn strategy and teamwork (reflecting an orientation more closely aligned with intelligence).

The hierarchical model of voter attitudes indicates that structuring principles, such as ideology, only indirectly affect an individual's specific opinions and beliefs. Rather, voters' specific opinions are derived from their general political orientations, which are influenced not only by ideology but also by individual life experiences. In this regard, political orientations are not static; they can and are regularly updated as voters incorporate new information into their understanding of the political world. People get new information from a variety of sources, including books, magazines, newspapers, and the Internet. Still, the two most prevalent sources of information are the media (television/radio news) and conversations with friends and colleagues. In addition to external information, voters often use their own life experience – for instance, how well they are doing economically – to evaluate government performance.

Which Faction Should You Choose?

It is important to note that possessing a plethora of opinions on specific policy issues does not necessarily mean Independence from the political system. Likewise, possessing more than one virtue, say honesty and peacefulness, does not inherently make one Divergent. Rather, in order to be Independent/Divergent, a second condition must be met: the absence of a party/faction that corresponds to one's specific mix of opinions and preferences.

For instance, there is nothing inherently contradictory about supporting tax reductions for businesses while also supporting progressive social policy. American voters who adopt these positions, however, are often ambivalent toward the political system and, therefore, identify as Independent because none of the major political parties advocate this combination of policy preferences. The Republican Party advocates tax reductions but generally opposes racial integration and diversity initiatives. Conversely, the Democratic Party tends to push for higher taxes to fund government programs and advocates for minority rights and social equity.

Interestingly, a similarly minded voter in Belgium would likely have a strong affinity with the Liberal Democratic Party, *Open VLD*. The party openly supports cultural diversity and integration but also adheres to free market principles by calling for eliminating tax barriers for businesses and entrepreneurs. In this regard, *Open VLD* offers a fundamentally different combination of policies than the United States Republican and Democratic Parties. Independence, therefore, not only depends on some one's political opinions but also on the party options that are available in her political system.

The same dynamics exist in the world of *Divergent*. If a sixth faction, perhaps named Exemplar, existed that recruited intelligent, selfless, and brave individuals such as Tris, she would cease to be Divergent. Exemplar might also have been the preferred faction for Tris's mother, Natalie Prior, who is also revealed to be Divergent when she dies a brave and selfless death to save Tris from the Dauntless attack against Abnegation.

Defining Factions and Political Parties

Thus far we have made a distinction between the factions in *Divergent* and political parties in the real world. We have also discussed how Independence/Divergence depends on the factions that exist in one's social or political system. Given the centrality of these groups to political identity, our discussion raises the question: How are factions and parties different? And, perhaps more importantly, how are factions and parties formed?

Factions are sub-groups that exist within a larger group and are largely built around a common interest or goal. Many people are familiar with the factions (commonly referred to as cliques) that exist in most high schools. Typical examples include jocks who rally around sports, thespians who share an interest in the performing arts, and hipsters who assemble vintage wardrobes and wear Buddy Holly glasses.[8] Importantly, members of factions self-identify and interact with other members of their group. This sets them apart from a grouping of individuals, who may be categorized by some shared characteristic but lack a collective identity.

The overlap between the shared interest and lifestyle of faction members is dramatically displayed in the opening scenes of *Divergent*. The Erudites are portrayed as scientists who spend their time in labs looking through microscopes. Their attire is professional and composed of dress shirts, slacks, skirts, and vests.

Amity the Peaceful is a farming faction. Its members wear attire and share a style aesthetic with the hippie culture of the 1960s and 1970s. The honesty of Candor puts them in charge of the justice system, where they are shown debating in the halls of justice wearing full suits.

Much of the film, however, is spent focusing on Abnegation and Dauntless. Tris's original faction, Abnegation the selfless, dress in near-identical gray attire in an effort to not call attention to any individual member. Their primary role in society is governance, although faction members spend their time helping others and feeding the Factionless (homeless). Dauntless are portrayed as a counter-culture warrior class. Members tend to be young, tattooed, and defiant, often shown climbing buildings and jumping off moving trains. Their aesthetic style borrows heavily from rock and punk subcultures in the contemporary real world. In this regard, the factions are the primary social and political structure; members live, work, and primarily socialize with other members of their group. Cross-faction interactions are largely discouraged.

A political faction is a sub-group of individuals who are bound by a common political interest or goal. In general, political factions in democracies can be categorized in one of two ways. An interest group is a political faction that seeks to *influence* public policy. Common examples include labor unions (such as the AFL-CIO) and civil rights groups (e.g., the NAACP). They pursue their political goals, such as a higher minimum wage, by pressuring government officials to enact their preferred policies.

Political parties, on the other hand, are factions that attempt to fulfill their policy goals through the acquisition of *power*. However, political parties often contain highly diverse membership because they are actually comprised of multiple factions. In democracies, parties acquire power through the electoral process; parties nominate and fund candidates to contest elections, mobilize voters, and guide policy once elected to office.[9] Because obtaining power is a necessary pre-condition for implementing policy, political parties must aggregate multiple smaller factions in the electorate under a common party banner to win enough electoral support to control government. The Democratic Party, for example, draws its support from highly distinct groups including labor unions, ethnic minorities, and city-dwellers. There is no a priori reason, however, that these groups be bound together other than that the Democratic Party advocates a policy package (labor-friendly economic policy, pro-civil rights, and progressive social issues) that happens to include all of their interests.[10]

The way parties pool smaller factions determines a society's party system. More specifically, the number of political parties that exist in a political system and who those parties represent depends greatly on how different political factions aggregate their interests in the electoral arena.[11] In the United States, the Democratic and Republican Parties tend to be catch-all parties; that is, the packages of the major parties recruit nearly all of the smaller factions. Outside of the US, party systems tend to more diverse and complex. In Belgium, for instance, there were around ten parties that effectively competed for votes in the 2014 election, and eight received meaningful representation in the legislature. One of the reasons for Belgium's comparatively high number of political parties is that the country is divided along linguistic lines: French and Dutch. As a result, two parties exist for each ideological group. The Parti Socialiste (PS) and Socialistische Partij Anders (SP.a), for example, both represent the working class and advocate for pro-labor policy. However, they maintain separate formal organizations (factions) for the French and Dutch members of society, respectively.

Given that parties pool multiple factions, large multiparty systems tend to emerge when small, homogeneous factions choose to pursue power alone. Conversely, small party systems emerge when several, smaller factions campaign under a single common banner. Although many citizens may conform to the faction archetypes that exist in small party systems, there are simply fewer combinations of policy preferences that can be represented. In the US, a wealthy African American who lives in the suburbs and supports progressive social policy, for instance, may be conflicted on which party to support. Should she vote along ethnic lines and support the Democratic Party? Or she should vote along the economic dimension and support the Republicans? The lack of options that reflect her structuring principles leads to ambivalence about the party system. Consequently, a combination of complex personal ideologies and the lack of corresponding political factions lead to the rise of Independents and Divergents.

Is Independence Dangerous?

During the film's climax, Jeanine Matthews says to Tris, "The brilliance of the faction system is that the conformity to the factions removes the threat of anyone exercising their independent will. Divergence threatens that system."[12] Why do the Erudites view Divergents as such a threat? What would the consequences be if Divergents were allowed to freely exist in the post-apocalyptic Chicago society? These questions are never fully answered in the film, but one might speculate given the disruption that occurred in many European party systems in the late twentieth and early twenty-first century.

Earlier we noted that stable faction systems are desirable by political leaders, because they provide predictable voting patterns and levels of support. Significant cultural, technological, and political changes, however, have eroded traditional patterns of party support in many established democracies. Increased global trade, particularly a shift of manufacturing to the Global South, for instance, eroded the traditional support base (i.e., unionized wage employees) for many social democratic parties.[13] The remarkable level of economic affluence achieved in the second half of the twentieth century also fundamentally changed mass ideology. As citizens' material needs (e.g., food, clothing, and shelter) were consistently met, voters' political preferences shifted toward post-materialist values, which include personal freedom, good democratic governance, and maintaining a clean and healthy environment.[14]

As voters developed these new combinations of political beliefs, the existing party systems, which had developed from the traditional economic cleavage structures, became insufficient for political representation.[15] In response, the once stable voting patterns that characterized European elections for nearly three decades became increasingly volatile. The alienation of modern voters, consequently, led to party system dealignment, which refers to the breakdown of the existing party system. In Denmark, for instance, the Social Democrats enjoyed roughly 40 percent of the electoral vote through the 1950s and 1960s but dropped significantly over the next three decades to a much lower average of 27 percent for elections between 2000 and 2009.

The secondary consequence of the weakened ties between voters and traditional parties is the rise of new political factions. As the existing parties lost votes, new parties emerged to represent modern voter interests. Green parties, for instance, experienced a dramatic increase in their vote share since they debuted in the late 1970s and early 1980s. For example, Alliance '90/The Greens in Germany received 1.5 percent of the vote in 1980, winning zero seats in the Bundestag. In comparison, they received 8.4 percent of the vote in 2014, which won them 63 (10 percent) of the seats in Parliament.

Several other types of parties have also emerged. On the left of the political spectrum, new parties have responded to the decline in social democratic and communist party votes. Labeled the "New Left," these parties attempt to appeal to the traditional working class and adopt several Communist Party positions such as opposition to market forces and a call for a controlled economy. However, they also advocate for freedom and democracy, which has historically been associated with the right. Consequently, scholars often refer to their position as "left-libertarian" to reflect their particular blend of policy preferences.

There has also been significant growth on the far right. Although these parties were non-existent in most European democracies in the 1950s and 1960s, they now seriously compete for votes and seats in many parliaments. Some of the more notable parties, the French National Front and the Belgian Vlaams Blok, are highly nationalist and xenophobic; they oppose immigration, European integration, and multicultural policies. Far right parties are generally considered anti-establishment, as they actively campaign against the established political system, often on platforms of anti-government corruption. Several countries have historically used electoral thresholds – minimum vote requirements (typically around 5 percent) to obtain representation in parliament – to prevent these types of parties from significantly disrupting the political system. However, as far right parties grew over the 1990s, some have managed to overcome these thresholds and, in some instances, been included in government.

This real-world evidence suggests that the Erudites' fear of Divergents may not be unfounded. If Divergents were allowed to swell the ranks of the existing factions, they would probably start opposing faction leaders' decisions and call for change. However, existing factions would most likely be both unable and unwilling to accommodate the diverse set of Divergent interests. Given the factions' inability to meet these demands, it would only be a matter of time before Divergents began forming their own groups that better reflect their particular combination of virtues. Finally, in the ensuing realignment of the faction system, the current factions would certainly see their membership and influence in society diminish.

Veronica Roth explores these possibilities in the subsequent books in the *Divergent* trilogy.[16] Interestingly, but unsurprisingly, the faction system starts to unravel following the events of *Divergent*. Without giving too much of the plot away, some faction leaders lose control of their factions and are replaced, and multiple factions begin competing for political power, including the previously ostracized Factionless.

With this in mind, despite their drastically different ideological principles, it makes sense that the one thing the Democratic and Republican parties generally agree on is this: they hate third parties. As we discussed above, Independents – individuals who do not feel strongly attached to any existing party – disrupt stable voting patterns and, in several other countries, have contributed to party dealignment and the birth and growth of new parties.

In the United States, a majority of Americans, as high as 60 percent, believe a third party is needed because the two major parties "do such a poor job" representing its citizens.[17] Despite public opinion, however, no third party has successfully managed to win enough votes to gain a significant number of seats in Congress. The discrepancy between public opinion and public votes in the United States is a result of several interrelated factors, including campaign finance, the role of the media, and how elections are conducted.[18] As a result, the major parties in the United States tend to be more resilient to the demands of party system change.

This should not imply that the Democratic and Republican parties are so entrenched in government that they can ignore the demands of the American citizen. Under the pressure of social change, the frozen party systems in Europe thawed and, over the past twenty years, old parties declined and new parties emerged to take their place. The drastic rise of self-declared Independents and the call for new parties in the United States are certainly a threat to the strength of the party duopoly. However, better representation in government can only occur if voters can coordinate their interests and overcome the constraints of the electoral system to force the party system to adapt to their policy preferences.

Conclusion

Tris Prior's evolution through *Divergent* illustrates several important points about individual identity, factions, and representation. When the film begins, Tris is desperate to fit into one of the existing factions, because factions structure identity. However, as Tris embraces her Divergence, she realizes that her values – selflessness, intelligence, and bravery – make her exceptional. As a result, her unique perspective allows her to succeed in several situations where the limits of one virtue would not allow her to see the best course of action.[19]

Although the factions are not political parties per se, the film also shows that the different factions, particularly Abnegation and Erudite, have different views on how government should operate. Abnegation, much like the social democrats, favor redistribution of wealth to the needy and the Factionless. Erudite, on the other hand, criticizes Abnegation for wasting resources.

Finally, Tris's journey implies that the people around her do not necessarily fit the ideal archetype established by their faction. Caleb's family life taught him Abnegation's values, so although his main attribute is intelligence, he is also capable of great selflessness. Tris's parents exhibit extraordinary bravery in their acts of selflessness to protect her despite being longtime members of Abnegation. Even the nameless Erudite goons at the end of the film exhibit their bravery by actively engaging in physical combat with Dauntless-trained Tris and Four.

In the real world, political parties are crucial vessels that help translate citizen preferences into public policy. However, this process requires that parties accurately represent the interests of their members and electoral supporters. To achieve accurate representation, citizens must possess informed policy preferences and be able to vote for the faction that best represents their particular combination of interests.

In many countries, existing party systems have sometimes failed to keep pace with the changing values and preferences of their citizens. In established European democracies, for example, this disconnect led to the erosion of old parties and the emergence of new ones. The United States party system has been comparatively more durable despite widespread voter dissatisfaction and low identification with the major political parties. This is not to say that the party system is necessarily bad or that change is not possible. Rather, if one wants to improve representation between parties and citizens, it will require the thoughtful consideration and coordination of voters.

As Jeanine Matthews stated in her opening remarks at the Choosing Ceremony, "the future belongs to those who know where they belong." This is just as true in the real world as it is in a future dystopian Chicago. For some citizens, they may be well represented by the existing party system, but the evidence suggests many more are not. Meaningful political change cannot be achieved, however, if citizens continue to vote for parties that do not represent their interests. Undoubtedly, the future will be decided by the next generation of voters who must evaluate whether the existing party system represents their interests or whether they are, in fact, Divergent.

Chapter Discussion Questions

1. The rise of Independents signals a decline in voter loyalty to a particular party. What could parties do to recruit new members and strengthen ties with existing members? How would these strategies enhance the representative function of the parties?

2. Third parties in the United States form for many reasons. Some exist to protest the existing parties whereas others form to capitalize on new combinations of interests. What types of third parties might emerge in the next few years? What types of protests or interests would they represent?
3. Outside of the United States, multiparty systems are common. Although these systems provide voters with more electoral options, it makes some parts of the democratic process more complicated. How would a multiparty system make it more difficult for parties to form majority governments and for voters to hold parties accountable for bad public policy?

Notes

1 Roth, Veronica. 2011. *Divergent.* New York: Katherine Tegen Books.
2 Wolf, Richard. 2011. "Voters leaving Republican, Democratic parties in droves." *USA Today*. December 22, http://usatoday30.usatoday.com/news/politics/story/2011-12-22/voters-political-parties/52171688/1, accessed October 18, 2014.
3 Jones, Jeffrey M. 2014. "Record-high 42% of Americans identify as independents." *Gallup*. January 8, http://www.gallup.com/poll/166763/record-high-americans-identify-independents.aspx, accessed October 18, 2014.
4 Because it is not clear from the film version of *Divergent*, the rationale for Tris sinking to her knees is adapted from the book in the discussion.
5 PBS News Hour. 2012. Political Party Quiz, http://www.pbs.org/newshour/spc/vote2012/quiz, accessed October 24, 2014.
6 Converse, Phillip E. 1964. "The nature of belief systems in mass publics." In *Ideology and Discontent*, ed. David E. Apter. New York: Free Press of Glencoe.
7 Dalton, Russell J. 2014. *Citizen politics: Public opinion and political parties in advanced industrial democracies*, 6th edition. Thousand Oaks, CA: Sage CQ Press.
8 For an interesting discussion of the social dynamics behind high school cliques, see McFarland, Daniel A., James Moody, David Diehl, Jeffrey A. Smith, and Reuben J. Thomas. 2014. "Network ecology and adolescent social structure," *American Sociological Review*, 79(6): 1088–1121.
9 See Key, V. O., Jr. 1942. *Political parties and pressure groups*. New York: Thomas Y. Crowell Company. See also Aldrich, John. 1995. *Why parties? The origin and transformation of party politics in America*. Chicago: University of Chicago Press; Katz, Richard S. and Peter Mair. 1994. *How parties organize: Change and adaptation in party organizations in Western democracies*. London: Sage.
10 For a discussion of how different divisions in society coalesce into political parties, see Lipset, Seymour and Stein Rokkan. 1967. *Party systems and voter alignments: Cross-national perspectives*. Toronto: The Free Press.
11 There are many ways to "count" the number of political parties in a country. A common approach is to weight the number of parties that receive representation in the legislature by the number of votes or seats they receive. Laakso, Markku and Rein Taagepera. 1979. "'Effective' number of parties: A measure with application to West Europe." *Comparative Political Studies*, 12 (1): 3–27.
12 Berge, Neil. *Divergent*. 2014. Production Co: Red Wagon Entertainment.
13 Kitschelt, Herber, Peter Lange, Gary Marks, and John D. Stephens. 1999. *Continuity and change in contemporary capitalism*. Cambridge: Cambridge University Press.
14 Post-materialism is largely attributed to Ronald Inglehart. For his earliest discussion, see Inglehart, Robert. 1971. "The silent revolution in Europe: Intergenerational change in post-industrial societies." *American Political Science Review*, 65(4): 991–1017.

15 For a discussion, see Best, Robin E. 2011. "The declining electoral relevance of traditional cleavage groups." *European Political Science Review*, 3(2): 279–300.
16 Roth, Veronica. 2012. *Insurgent*. New York: Katherine Tegen Books.
17 Jones, Jeffrey M. 2014. "Americans continue to say a third political party is needed." *Gallup*. September 24, http://www.gallup.com/poll/177284/americans-continue-say-third-political-party-needed.aspx.
18 Campaign spending (over $1.5 billion in 2014 for Federal races) has increased dramatically over the last twenty years. Additionally, single member district (SMD) elections tend to discourage third party participation (see Riker, William H. 1982. "The two-party system and Duverger's Law: An essay on the history of political science." *American Political Science Review*, 76(4): 753–766).
19 For instance, Tris's bravery and intelligence are both used to succeed against Jeanine Matthews in the film's climax. In particular, she is able to quickly deduce that the best course of action to stop Dauntless from killing Abnegation is to inject Jeanine with the mind control serum to force her to shut down the system.

9

YES... YES... ALL YOUR "RIGHTS" AS DEFINED BY THE CARDASSIAN ARTICLES OF JURISPRUDENCE WILL BE PROTECTED

Civil Liberties in *Star Trek: Deep Space Nine*

Raymond V. Carman, Jr.

STATE UNIVERSITY OF NEW YORK COLLEGE AT PLATTSBURGH

Chief Archon Makbar, looming from the viewscreen above, looks down at Commander Sisko, Constable Odo, and Mrs. O'Brien. "Mrs. O'Brien, there is nothing for you to prepare. Your husband's verdict has already been determined. He is guilty. The trial will reveal how this guilt was proven by the most efficient criminal investigation system in the quadrant. You may, if you desire, attend the trial, which begins in two days' time." Odo inquires, "What penalty does Mr. O'Brien face?" Makbar answers, "His execution is scheduled for next week." Horrified, Mrs. O'Brien asks, "How can you schedule an execution before the trial even begins?" Coldly, Makbar responds, "We believe in swift justice."

Constitutions are an exercise in institutional design. First, constitutions structure governments. The Constitution of the United States, for example, creates a government made up of three distinct branches. First, in Article I, it vests legislative power in the Congress of the United States. This body, a bicameral legislature with representatives of one chamber selected based upon state population and the other distributed evenly among the states, is charged with passing laws. Second, in Article II, the Constitution vests executive power in the president of the United States. This single executive is charged with executing the laws of the United States. Third, in Article III, it vests the judicial power in the Supreme Court of the United States and in such other courts as Congress shall create. The judicial power extends to all cases under the United States Constitution and the laws of the United States.

Constitutions also create tension among the branches of government by separating governmental powers among several branches of government in order to safeguard against tyranny. The United States Constitution provides that, for example, whereas Congress is charged with passing legislation, the president must sign legislation for it to become law. If the president declines to sign a piece of legislation and instead vetoes it, Congress can override his veto by a super-majority vote. Whereas the president is commander-in-chief of the military, only Congress may declare war. Whereas the courts can declare laws unconstitutional, Congress may amend the Constitution to overturn a court decision.[1] Whereas the courts can declare an executive action unconstitutional, the president is charged with appointing judges.

Finally, and arguably more importantly, constitutions enumerate and secure certain rights and liberties for their citizens. These rights and liberties protect individuals against government action. The First Amendment of the United States Constitution, for example, provides for freedom of speech, freedom to peaceably assemble, freedom of the press, freedom to practice one's religion, and freedom from the establishment of an official state religion. The Second Amendment, noting "A well regulated militia being necessary to the security of a free state," provides that "the right of the people to keep and bear arms shall not be infringed." The Third Amendment forbids the housing of soldiers in any home, without a homeowner's consent, in times of peace.

Courts are most often designed as those bodies charged with interpreting government action in light of the rights and liberties provided under their respective constitutions and with prohibiting the state from violating the constitutional rights and liberties of its citizens. Andrew Jackson wrote, "All the rights secured to the citizens under the Constitution are worth nothing, and a mere bubble, except guaranteed to them by an independent and virtuous Judiciary."[2] Just how important are these cherished rights and liberties? Why are certain rights and liberties provided? What might a civilization look like where they are not provided for? What if courts were not independent and virtuous, but instead tools of state persecution? The Cardassian Union of the *Star Trek* universe provides one such example.

First introduced in *Star Trek: The Next Generation* (and playing a very prominent role in *Star Trek: Deep Space Nine*) the Cardassians are "Tall, long-necked, humanoid in appearance, marked by several bony protrusions and ridges: one from the shoulder to under the ears, whose bottom lobes in turn are more pronounced forward to the jawline, and from above the eyes and back over the head to the rear base of the skull, showing through hair."[3] In its ancient history,

> The Cardassian society was known as the Hebitians. It was home to fine art and beautiful architecture. Once the Hebitian civilization fell into decay from lack of natural resources, millions of Cardassians were starving and the planet was subjected to utter chaos… In order to survive, Cardassian society embraced a totalitarian police state that would be strong enough to provide for the material needs of its citizens.[4]

In the Cardassian Union we come to know in *Star Trek: Deep Space Nine*, "The ideal Cardassian life was one of complete loyalty and servitude to the state and family. The Cardassian government was assumed to be omniscient, omnipotent, and benevolent."[5] Indeed, the state's importance was so great and its control so complete that, at age ten, Cardassian children give their first molar to the Bureau of Identification.[6] The Cardassian Union had the most rigid and unorthodox of all legal systems known in the twenty-fourth century.[7] Viewers get the most comprehensive view of the Cardassian legal system in the episode of *Star Trek: Deep Space Nine* entitled "Tribunal."

An Analysis of Civil Rights and Liberties

Arrest and Booking

In "Tribunal," Miles O'Brien, Federation of Planets citizen and Chief of Operations for Starfleet's Deep Space 9 starbase, is piloting a shuttlecraft on the way to a vacation with his wife. A Cardassian ship intercepts the shuttlecraft and orders the vessel to lower its shields to be boarded and inspected. After some protest, Chief O'Brien complies and the Cardassians board and inspect the vessel. After their inspection, a Cardassian commander states, "I have orders to arrest you, Mister O'Brien." Chief O'Brien asks what he is being charged with. The commander responds, "You have the right to refuse to answer questions, but such refusal might be construed as a sign of guilt." Chief O'Brien now forcefully demands to know the charges against him. "You deny all knowledge of this crime then?" the Cardassian commander replies. Chief O'Brien responds, "How the hell am I supposed to deny something when I don't even know what you're talking about…" Becoming upset, Mrs. O'Brien states, "We are Federation citizens and we have rights!" To which, the Cardassian commander responds, "Yes… yes… all your 'rights' as defined by the Cardassian Articles of Jurisprudence will be protected."

The Cardassian Articles of Jurisprudence clearly provide no right for the accused to be informed of the charges against him. In the United States, however, the Sixth Amendment provides that "In all criminal prosecutions, the accused shall enjoy the right… to be informed of the nature and cause of the accusation." This right enshrined by the United States Constitution, can, like many of its other rights, find its origins in English law. In 1164, King Henry II announced a "memorandum… of some part of the customs and liberties and dignities… which ought to be observed and kept in the kingdom."[8] Included among these "customs and liberties and dignities" was "Laymen ought not to be accused unless through reliable and legal accusers and witnesses."[9]

Building upon this pronouncement, the Magna Carta of 1215 provides, "No freemen shall be taken or imprisoned or disseised or exiled or in any way destroyed, nor will we go upon him nor send upon him, except by the lawful judgment of his peers or by the law of the land."[10] Parliament enacted subsequent legislation to further rein in the king, providing that "From henceforth none shall be taken by petition or suggestion made to our lord the King, or to his Council, unless it be by indictment or presentation of good and lawful people of the same neighborhood where such deeds be done, in due manner, or by process made by writ original at the common law."[11]

Despite these legal developments, however, English courts did not require the accused to be informed of the charges against them. Indeed, one of the charges leveled by the Declaration of Independence was an accusation that King George III "transport[ed] us beyond Seas to be tried for pretended offences." It should come as no surprise then that the Founders of the United States Constitution chose to include the notice of accusation requirement in the Sixth Amendment. This requirement "entitles the defendant to insist that the indictment apprise him of the crime charged with such reasonable certainty that he can make his defense and protect himself after judgment against another prosecution on the same charge."[12]

Processing

The next we see of Chief O'Brien is under a bright light in a darkened room. O'Brien is told twice by a Cardassian officer to remove his clothes. When he responds twice with his name, Starfleet rank, and citizenship, O'Brien is forced face-first against a wall where one of the guards uses a knife to rip his clothes off. O'Brien is then "processed" by the Cardassians, which involves taking an optical scan of his eyes, taking some of his hair, and forcibly removing a molar with a plier-like instrument. Following his processing, O'Brien is visited by the Chief Archon.[13] After apologizing for the way O'Brien has been treated, the Chief Archon says, "I want your stay here to be as comfortable as possible under the circumstances. I have scheduled your trial to begin in two days. You have been assigned the Venerable Kovat as Public Conservator." O'Brien asks what a Public Conservator is. "Your lawyer," the Chief Archon responds. "Many feel he's the best counsel in all Cardassia." O'Brien asks why he needs a lawyer: "What am I charged with, and who is accusing me?" The Chief Archon responds, "All in good time, Mister O'Brien. All in good time…"

We learn in a later scene, in which Chief O'Brien's commander is being informed about the arrest, just when the Cardassian legal system provides for the accused to be informed about the charges against them. "The charges will be announced when the trial begins. As is customary in Cardassian jurisprudence," the Chief Archon informs Commander Benjamin Sisko. To this, Mrs. O'Brien responds, "How are we supposed to prepare for the trial if we don't know the charges?" Coldly, the Chief Archon says, "Mrs. O'Brien, there is nothing for you to prepare. Your husband's verdict has already been determined. He is guilty. The trial will reveal how this guilt was proven by the most efficient criminal investigation system in the quadrant."

Here again, the rights and liberties provided by the United States Constitution would protect against such treatment. First, whereas taking an accused's fingerprints upon arrest is routine practice in the United States – and, indeed, one day similarly non-intrusive retinal scans might likewise be the norm – the removal of a tooth to identify the accused would clearly be illegal. In general, the United States Supreme Court considers challenges to prison conditions as a whole under the Cruel and Unusual Punishment Clause of the Eighth Amendment, which states: "Excessive bail shall not be required, nor excessive fines imposed, nor cruel and unusual punishments inflicted."[14]

Courts examine challenges to the conditions of pretrial confinement, however, in light of the Due Process Clause of the Fifth or Fourteenth Amendment.[15] In such challenges, the United States Supreme Court has held that, while the government may detain those accused upon finding probable cause, and the detention may subject the prisoner to the restrictions and conditions of the detention facility, the government may not punish the accused prior to a finding of guilt.[16] Certainly, the removal of a tooth would be considered punishment by the courts.

Connected to the notice of accusation required by the Sixth Amendment, and notably absent from the Cardassian legal system, is the right that "No person shall be held to answer for a capital, or otherwise infamous crime, unless on a presentment or indictment of a Grand Jury." As the Congressional Research Service notes, the right to an indictment by grand jury dates back even further than the right to notice of accusation: "The history of the grand jury is rooted in the common and civil law, extending back to Athens, pre-Norman England, and the Assize of Clarendon promulgated by Henry II."[17] The right to a grand jury indictment under the Fifth Amendment attaches to all "infamous" crimes. The United States Supreme Court has determined that infamous crimes are those in which the defendant may be subjected to one year or more in a state or federal prison or penitentiary.[18]

The right to an indictment by a grand jury is meant to provide a great check on the power of the state to seize its citizens. Arrests should only be effected and indictments should only be issued in cases where there is probable cause to believe that a crime has been committed and where there is probable cause to believe that the defendant committed said crime. Grand juries, "convened as a body of laymen, free from technical rules, acting in secret, pledged to indict no one because of prejudice and to free no one because of special favor," and operating "under the direction but not control of a prosecutor," ensure that the standard of probable cause has been met by the state.[19] Without the requirement for a grand jury indictment, officers of the state alone would be responsible for attesting to probable cause (the arresting officer) and for determining whether probable cause is met (the prosecutor).

As we learn, the Chief Archon has appointed a lawyer to represent Chief O'Brien; the Cardassian legal system seems to provide for the assistance of counsel, just as is asserted by the Sixth Amendment of the United States Constitution: "In all criminal prosecutions, the accused shall… have the assistance of counsel for his defense." Interestingly, the enunciation of this right, unlike many other rights adopted by the Founders, was an explicit rejection of English common law practice as "the development of the common-law principle in England had denied to anyone charged with a felony the right to retain counsel…"[20]

Connected to this right for the assistance of counsel, and also notably absent in the Cardassian legal system, is the requirement that the defendant be afforded sufficient time to prepare his legal defense. In *Powell v. Alabama*, the United States Supreme Court held, "The right of the accused, at least in a capital case, to have the aid of counsel for his defense, which includes the right to have sufficient time to advise with counsel and to prepare a defense, is one of the fundamental rights guaranteed by the Due Process Clause of the Fourteenth Amendment."[21] While the United States Supreme Court has not set a clear rule as to what constitutes "sufficient time" to prepare a defense, two days, as was provided O'Brien, would fall short.

Trial

The purpose of a trial in Cardassia differs dramatically from its purpose in the United States. As we learned in the exchange between Mrs. O'Brien and the Chief Archon when Chief O'Brien's commander was informed of his arrest, "[The] verdict has already been determined. He is guilty. The trial will reveal how this guilt was proven by the most efficient criminal investigation system in the quadrant." Chief O'Brien comes to learn this purpose of the trial in his meeting with his lawyer. When his lawyer introduces himself, O'Brien asks, "I've been told that I've already been charged, indicted, convicted and sentenced. What do I need with a lawyer?" The lawyer responds, "Mister O'Brien, if it seems immodest of me, I apologize, but the role of Public Conservator is key to the productive functioning of our courts. I am here to help you concede the wisdom of the state. To prepare you to accept the inevitable with equanimity." O'Brien asks, again, what he is being charged with. "No need to worry about that at this point," the lawyer responds:

> Whatever you've done, whatever the charges against you – none of that really matters in the long run… This trial is to demonstrate the futility of behavior contrary to good order… Once again, justice will prevail. Our lives will be reaffirmed safe and secure. Here on Cardassia, all crimes are solved. All criminals are punished. All endings are happy. Even the poorest of our citizens can walk the streets in the dead of night in perfect safety. You are only one man, but your conviction will be a salutary experience for millions.

And, indeed, the Chief Archon begins the trial by stating, matter-of-factly, "The offender, Miles O'Brien, human, officer of the Federation Starfleet, has been found guilty of aiding and abetting seditious acts against the state. The sentence is death. Let the trial begin."

In the United States, the purpose of a trial is to determine whether, beyond a reasonable doubt, a crime was committed and the defendant committed said crime. The Sixth Amendment provides: "In all criminal prosecutions, the accused shall enjoy the right to a speedy and public trial, by an impartial jury of the State and district wherein the crime shall have been committed." Whereas the foundations of a speedy and public trial can be traced back to the Magna Carta of 1215, the practice of juries being the triers of evidence did not become common until the reign of Henry VI (1422–1461).

During the seventeenth century the jury trial emerged as a true safeguard for the criminally accused, so much so that famed English legal commentator William Blackstone declared the institution part of a "strong and two-fold barrier… between the liberties of the people and the prerogative of the crown" because "the truth of every accusation… [must] be confirmed by the unanimous suffrage of twelve of his equals and neighbors indifferently chosen and superior to all suspicion."[22] This English right was so revered that trial by jury was guaranteed by the constitutions of the original thirteen states, was guaranteed in the body of the Constitution and in the Sixth Amendment, and was guaranteed by the constitution of every state entering the Union thereafter.[23]

In *Duncan v. Louisiana*, the United States Supreme Court made clear just how crucial the role that the right to a determination of guilt by a jury plays in the American legal system:

> The guarantees of jury trial in the Federal and State Constitutions reflect a profound judgment about the way in which law should be enforced and justice administered. A right to jury trial is granted to criminal defendants in order to prevent oppression by the Government. Those who wrote our constitutions knew from history and experience that it was necessary to protect against unfounded criminal charges brought to eliminate enemies and against judges too responsive to the voice of higher authority. The framers of the constitutions strove to create an independent judiciary but insisted upon further protection against arbitrary action. Providing an accused with the right to be tried by a jury of his peers gave him an inestimable safeguard against the corrupt or overzealous prosecutor and against the compliant, biased, or eccentric judge… [T]he jury trial provisions… reflect a fundamental decision about the exercise of official power – a reluctance to entrust plenary powers over the life and liberty of the citizen to one judge or to a group of judges. Fear of unchecked power… found expression in the criminal law in this insistence upon community participation in the determination of guilt or innocence.[24]

During O'Brien's trial, Deep Space Nine's Chief of Security, Odo, tries to get O'Brien's lawyer to introduce evidence of O'Brien's innocence. "If O'Brien is accused of stealing warheads from Deep Space Nine, we can prove he didn't do it." O'Brien's lawyer responds, "Of course he did it. He's been found guilty, hasn't he?" Odo retorts, "Someone manipulated a recording of his voice to gain entry. I can produce that recording here…" O'Brien's lawyer cuts him off. "No evidence can be submitted after the verdict has been reached." The Chief Archon stops the discussion. "As for new evidence, yes, I fully expected the Federation to come up with remarkable new evidence in an attempt to free Mister O'Brien. I'm sure your experts can create all sorts of interesting evidence to confuse the issues. That may work in your courts, but not here. There will be no new evidence considered."

Whereas this Cardassian prohibition on the defense offering evidence of innocence might seem unbelievable given the Sixth Amendment's provision that "In all criminal prosecutions, the accused shall enjoy the right to… have compulsory processing from obtaining witnesses in his favor," a similar situation existed under English common law. "For centuries, Britons had struggled against the common-law rule that forbade an accused from calling witnesses in his defense in cases of treason or felony… The common-law rule survived in the American colonies even after England had abolished it by statute."[25] After declaring independence from Britain, however, "a number of state constitutions established in one form or another the right to call defense witnesses. When the First Congress considered the Compulsory Process Clause, there was little debate over its value, and it became part of the Sixth Amendment without opposition."[26]

At the height of O'Brien's trial, the Chief Archon announces, "The offender will step forward to testify." Chief O'Brien responds that he has nothing to say. The Chief Archon then informs O'Brien that "Under Cardassian law, you are compelled to testify. Step forward." The Chief Archon then asks O'Brien, "Do you have a warm place in your heart for your Cardassian neighbors? … Or… do you not in fact hate Cardassians? Have you not on several occasions publicly stated your opposition to the treaty because, and I quote: 'The bloody Cardies can't be trusted?'" O'Brien declines to answer. The Chief Archon responds, "There are no grounds in Cardassian law which allow you to decline. Answer the question. Is it an accurate quote or not?" O'Brien responds that it is an accurate quote.

Whereas the Cardassian Articles of Jurisprudence allow the state to force a defendant to testify against his self interest, and there is a general obligation to provide testimony under oath when called upon in the United States, the people of the United States have a right against being forced to incriminate themselves. The Fifth Amendment provides "No person… shall be compelled in any criminal case to be a witness against himself." This right was another, which, like the Sixth Amendment's provision that the accused be informed of the nature of the accusations against them, the right to the assistance of counsel, and the right to obtain evidence, was a response to the English legal system rather than a tradition carried over from England. In the English ecclesiastic, or religious courts,

> a presiding official had the power to compel a witness to take an oath to tell the truth to the full extent of his knowledge as to all matters about which he would be questioned; before administration of the oath the person was not advised of the nature of the charges against him, or whether he was accused of crime, and was also not informed of the nature of the questions to be asked.[27]

The only restrictions on the right against self-incrimination are that the right must: (1) be asserted and (2) must be supported by a reasonable fear that a response will be incriminatory.[28]

An Analysis of the Role of Judge

The Cardassian Union was formed under a treaty that created a power-sharing agreement between the Cardassian Central Command and the Obsidian Order.[29] Although an elected civilian body serving as the chief governing body of Cardassia, the Detapa Council was virtually powerless.[30] During the time of "Tribunal," the Cardassian Union was, for all intents and purposes, a military state. It is unclear whether the Cardassian people ever had rights like those enjoyed in the United States, but it is clear that, by the time of "Tribunal," the Cardassian Articles of Jurisprudence provide no such rights. The Articles of Jurisprudence provide no right for a defendant to be informed of the charges against him, no right to be indicted by a grand jury, no right to time to prepare a defense, no right to a trial by jury, no right to obtain evidence in his favor, and no right against self-incrimination.

Even if the Cardassian Articles of Jurisprudence had provided for any of these rights, it is doubtful that the Cardassian judiciary was independent and virtuous enough to protect and defend these rights. The Cardassian court system described in "Tribunal" is one where guilt and sentence were predetermined, no evidence or defense could be raised, and all actors were controlled by the state. The Public Conservator does not act as a defense council, despite being likened to one by the Cardassians. Rather, the Public Conservator's job, as described to Chief O'Brien by his Public Conservator, is to "concede the wisdom of the state. To prepare you to accept the inevitable with equanimity." There is no prosecutor or jury in the Cardassian courtroom. Rather, the Chief Archon, the judge, serves as prosecutor, jury, and executioner. All act on behalf of, and all are controlled by, the state.

Contrast that with the purpose and operation of the United States court system. Although the shortest and vaguest of the three articles creating branches of the federal government, Article III of the United States Constitution provides that "The judicial Power... shall be vested in one supreme Court, and in such inferior Courts as the Congress may from time to time ordain and establish." Although none of the Founders debated creating a national judiciary, whether it should consist of "one high court at the apex of a federal judicial system or a high court exercising appellate jurisdiction over state courts that would initially hear all but a minor fraction of cases raising national issues was a matter of considerable controversy."[31] In the end, the Founders struck a compromise by creating the United States Supreme Court and empowering Congress to create lower federal courts at a later time. The Founders also provided mechanisms for federal judges to be independent from the other branches of government and, by extension, the people, because "a Judiciary free from control by the Executive and the Legislature is essential if there is a right to have claims decided by judges who are free from potential domination by other branches of government."[32]

The modes used by the Founders to secure judicial independence are twofold. First, they provided that judges serve in office "during good behavior." Life tenure was familiar to the Founders, as it was the system used for judges in England, although colonial judges were given no such protections. In fact, one of the charges leveled by the signers of the Declaration of Independence was that the king "has made Judges dependent on his Will alone, for the tenure of their offices." Wrote Alexander Hamilton in *Federalist*, No. 78:

> In a monarchy [the good behavior standard] is an excellent barrier to the despotism of the prince; in a republic it is a no less excellent barrier to the encroachments and oppressions of the representative body… It is the best expedient which can be devised in any government to secure a steady, upright, and impartial administration of the laws.

The requirement that judges be secured in office by life tenure excited no controversy during the Constitutional Convention of 1787.[33] To guard against a tyrannical judiciary, the Founders provided that judges could be impeached by the House of Representatives and removed from office by the Senate.

Second, conceptually and literally tied to life tenure, is the Constitution's provision that "Judges, both of the supreme and inferior Courts… shall, at stated Times, receive for their Services a Compensation, which shall not be diminished during their Continuance in Office." This provision was crucial to securing an independent judiciary because, as Alexander Hamilton wrote in *Federalist*, No. 79, "In the general course of human nature, a power over a man's subsistence amounts to a power over his will." Unlike the life tenure provision, however, there was some debate about this clause during the Constitutional Convention. James Madison's original draft of this clause provided that "no increase or diminution shall be made" to a judge's salary.

> On July 18, 1787, the issue came to a head when delegates argued for the prohibition on increases to be struck from the clause. Gouverneur Morris insisted that Congress should be given the ability to raise salaries "as circumstances might require." Other Framers, such as Benjamin Franklin, agreed with Morris, for the Framers had had intimate experience with the effects of inflation during and after the Revolution. Madison lost, and the Framers

> removed the language banning judicial salary increases. Unlike the President, whose salary under Article II, Section 1, Clause 7, could neither be decreased nor increased, judges had lifetime appointments and would have grievously suffered from inflation. Thus, it was resolved that Congress could not diminish judicial salaries, but could increase them.[34]

As Andrew Jackson wrote, "All the rights secured to the citizens under the Constitution are worth nothing, and a mere bubble, except guaranteed to them by an independent and virtuous Judiciary."[35] In the end, these two provisions guaranteeing life tenure and secure salary create a judiciary that is both independent and virtuous. Being independent and virtuous enables the United States court system to protect and guard the many civil rights and liberties, including those for the criminally accused, provided for by the United States Constitution.

Conclusion

In the final analysis, it might very well be that the intricacies of the Cardassian Articles of Jurisprudence and the Cardassian judiciary articulated by the authors of the *Star Trek: Deep Space Nine* episode "Tribunal" were meant to serve as a moralistic cautionary tale. *Star Trek*'s creator, Gene Roddenberry, once said, "I have no belief that *Star Trek* depicts the actual future. It depicts us. Now. Things we need to understand."[36] Indeed, the history of the Cardassian people – a society that was once peaceful and known for its fine art and beautiful architecture that, in desperation and out of the utter chaos of millions of Cardassians starving due to depleting natural resources, created a police state in the form of the Cardassian Union to provide for the people – is quite reminiscent of the society that Benjamin Franklin famously warned against: "Those who would give up essential Liberty, to purchase a little temporary Safety, deserve neither Liberty nor Safety."[37]

However, as demonstrated above, "Tribunal" does more than just serve as a moralistic cautionary tale. The Cardassian Articles of Jurisprudence are so inverted from the United States Constitution and the Cardassian judiciary is so opposite of the United States judiciary that they serve to exemplify the reasons behind and consequences of the institutional design choices that were made by the Founders during the Constitutional Convention. As discussed above, some rights announced by the United States Constitution were included because they were tradition under English common law, whereas others were included in response to treatment of the colonists by the British. In both cases, the decisions were consciously made. In the case of those rights provided for the criminally accused, they provide protection against abuse by the police, overzealous prosecution, and cruel and unusual punishment. Likewise, the Founders created an independent and virtuous judiciary capable of defending the rights provided by the Constitution through the choices they made in drafting Article III. The consequences of their absence are apparent in "Tribunal."

Chapter Discussion Questions

1. How are the rights and liberties provided for by the Cardassian Articles of Jurisprudence, as described in the *Star Trek: Deep Space Nine* episode "Tribunal," different than those provided for by the Constitution of the United States?
2. How does the role of judge in the Cardassian legal system differ from the role of judge in the United States' legal system?
3. What are the consequences of these differences? What are the implications of these differences for concepts such as fairness and justice?

Notes

1 In fact, five United States Constitutional Amendments were enacted to overturn United States Supreme Court decisions. The Eleventh Amendment overturned *Chisholm v. Georgia* (1793) to prohibit residents of one state from bringing suit against another state. The Thirteenth and Fourteenth Amendments overturned *Scott v. Sandford* (1857) to outlaw slavery and declare all those born in the United States to be citizens of the United States. The Sixteenth Amendment overturned *Pollock v. Farmer's Loan & Trust* (1895) to allow Congress to levy an income tax. The Twenty-Sixth Amendment overturned *Oregon v. Mitchell* (1970) to lower the voting age to eighteen. Epstein, Lee, Jeffrey A. Segal, Harold J. Spaeth, and Thomas G. Walker. 2012. *The Supreme Court compendium: Data, decisions, and developments*, 5th edition. Thousand Oaks, CA: CQ Press.

2 Jackson, Andrew to Andrew Jackson Donelson. 1996. 5 July 1822, in *The papers of Andrew Jackson, 1821–1824*, eds. Harold D. Moser, David R. Hoth, and George H. Hoemann. Knoxville, TN: University of Tennessee Press.

3 "Cardassians," *Star Trek*, http://www.startrek.com/database_article/cardassians, accessed January 6, 2015.

4 Ibid.

5 Ibid.

6 Ibid.

7 Ibid.

8 "Constitutions of Clarendon, 1164," Lillian Goldman Law Library, http://avalon.law.yale.edu/medieval/constcla.asp, accessed January 6, 2015.

9 Ibid.

10 "Magna Carta 1215," Lillian Goldman Law Library, http://avalon.law.yale.edu/medieval/magframe.asp, accessed January 6, 2015.

11 Benner, Laurence A. 1989. "Requiem for Miranda: The Rehnquist Court's voluntariness doctrine in historical perspective," *Washington University Law Review*, 67(1): 59–163; 73.

12 Congressional Research Service. 2014. *The Constitution of the United States of America: analysis and interpretation*, Centennial ed. Washington: U.S. Government Printing Office, 1634.

13 The Chief Archon is the Cardassian equivalent of a judge. "Cardassian," Memory Alpha, http://en.memory-alpha.org/wiki/cardassian, accessed January 6, 2015.

14 Congressional Research Service, 2014, 2031.

15 The former in cases involving federal prisons; the latter in cases involving state prisons.

16 Congressional Research Service, 2014, 2031.

17 Congressional Research Service, 2014, 1463.

18 Congressional Research Service, 2014, 1467.

19 Congressional Research Service, 2014, 1464.
20 Congressional Research Service, 2014, 1646.
21 *Powell v. Alabama*. 1932. 287 U.S. 45, 46.
22 Congressional Research Service, 2014, 1611.
23 Congressional Research Service, 2014, 1611–1612.
24 *Duncan v. Louisiana*. 1968. 391 U.S. 145, 157–158 (1968).
25 "Compulsory Process Clause," Heritage Foundation, http://www.heritage.org/constitution#!/amendments/6/essays/157/compulsory-process-clause, accessed January 11, 2015.
26 Ibid.
27 Congressional Research Service, 2014, 1496.
28 Congressional Research Service, 2014, 1498.
29 The Central Command is Cardassia's military authority, while the Obsidian Order is Cardassia's primary intelligence agency. "Cardassian Union." Memory Alpha, http://en.memory-alpha.org/wiki/Cardassian_Union, accessed April 30, 2015.
30 "Cardassian," Memory Alpha, http://en.memory-alpha.org/wiki/cardassian, accessed January 6, 2015.
31 Congressional Research Service, 2014, 637.
32 *United States v. Will*. 1980. 449 U.S. 200, 217–218.
33 Congressional Research Service, 2014, 638.
34 "Judicial Compensation Clause," Heritage Foundation, http://www.heritage.org/constitution#!/articles/3/essays/105/judicial-compensation-clause, accessed January 19, 2015.
35 Jackson, Andrew to Andrew Jackson Donelson, 1996.
36 Asherman, Allan. 1988. *The Star Trek Interview Book*. New York: Pocket Books.
37 Franklin, Benjamin. 1756. To Governor Richard Morris on Behalf of the Pennsylvania Assembly, 11 November 1755, in *Votes and proceedings of the House of Representatives, 1755–1756*. Philadelphia: New Printing Office.

10

THE BUREAUCRATIC MIND OF HERMES CONRAD

Administrative Behavior in *Futurama*

Scott E. Robinson

UNIVERSITY OF OKLAHOMA

Justin S. Vaughn

BOISE STATE UNIVERSITY

The first time viewers of *Futurama* meet Hermes Conrad, his employer, Professor Farnsworth, introduces him as the manager of Farnsworth's delivery business. Farnsworth explains to the other employees he is meeting with (as well as the viewers) that Hermes "pays the bills, notifies next of kin, what have you." Moments later, Conrad is seen going over the legal release with another character, called Leela, who has just been named captain of Farnsworth's delivery ship. In the next episode, Conrad is seen leading a staff meeting where he attempts to introduce a twelve-point agenda, and a few episodes later, we see him enforcing the company's vacation day policy as he requires another of the employees, a robot named Bender, to accompany the rest of the team on a delivery to a planet (which happens to be populated by human-hating robots). Still later in the first season, we see Bender sitting in Conrad's office – outside of which a "Chewing Out In Progress" button flashes and beeps – as the house bureaucrat berates him for a performance that does not merit what he is being paid in salary.

By the time viewers reach the ninth episode of the series, titled "Hell is Other Robots," we are unsurprised to see Conrad pointing out the company's rapidly rising electric bill and, later, discussing cost-saving measures he has implemented. We are unsurprised because over the course of these several episodes Hermes Conrad has given life to the title painted on his office door: bureaucrat. In doing so, he has both demonstrated the activities most closely related to bureaucracy (i.e., implementing policies and developing standard operating procedures designed to promote effective and efficient action) and conformed to our cultural expectations of the stereotypical bureaucrat by being inflexible and unsympathetic. The fact that bureaucrats receive this negative treatment is not surprising; indeed, scholars Mordecai Lee and Susan Paddock have noted that hostile portrayals of bureaucrats are actually quite common.[1] As the series evolves, Hermes Conrad the character becomes more complex and likeable, but even then what does not change is the valuable commentary his character provides on the key duties and dimensions of contemporary bureaucrats.

The television cartoon *Futurama* presents a vision of the world a thousand years in the future. Imagining the far future allows the writers to propose advanced technologies like easy space travel, advanced medicine, and ubiquitous robotics. At the same time, the ways in which the future resembles the present speak to the elements thought to be common to all humanity. The characters in *Futurama* face problems that are familiar to us all: personal relationships, aging, etc. A persistent theme in the show is the continued development and permanence of bureaucracy. While humanity may have colonized several planets and learned how to sustain the life of heads in jars, it is still plagued by the limitations and frustrations of bureaucratic processes. This chapter explores key characteristics of bureaucracy through the character of Hermes Conrad. First, we examine an episode from the show's second season – "How Hermes Requisitioned His Groove Back" – with an eye to the roles and responsibilities of a bureaucrat. Then, we discuss "The Six Million Dollar Mon," an episode from the seventh season that provides insight into the importance of measurement and efficiency in bureaucratic management. Finally, we will focus on bureaucratic ethics as we discuss "Lethal Inspection," an episode from *Futurama*'s sixth season that showcases the ethical dilemmas bureaucrats frequently must confront. Before doing so, however, an introduction to the world in which *Futurama* takes place is in order.

Welcome to the Thirty-First Century: A Brief Introduction to *Futurama*

Futurama centers on the experiences of Philip J. Fry, a pizza delivery boy from the twentieth century who was accidentally cryogenically frozen in 1999 and was only revived one thousand years later, into the world in which *Futurama* takes place. He takes a job doing deliveries for Planet Express, an interplanetary delivery service company formed by Professor Hubert J. Farnsworth (who happens to be a descendant of Fry). At Planet Express, Fry's main colleagues are Turanga Leela, a Cyclops-eyed pilot, and Bender Bending Rodriguez, an alcoholic ne'er-do-well who also happens to be a robot.

Although the series largely focuses on Fry, Leela, and Bender, several other recurring characters play major roles in the show, including the aforementioned Hermes Conrad. A proud bureaucrat, Hermes serves as Planet Express's accountant, although, as we will discuss, his role goes well beyond the traditional bean-counting activities we associate with accounting. A former professional limbo dancer, Conrad is now dedicated wholeheartedly to his bureaucratic career, despite being a relatively low-level bureaucrat (his rank fluctuates throughout the series, but his grade always hovers in the mid-thirties).

As a character, Conrad represents a popular cliché of modern bureaucracy and the types of people who work in such careers. For example, in "How Hermes Requisitioned His Groove Back," Conrad laments how he is only anal 78.36 percent of the time, the implication being that true bureaucrats would be far more punctilious and strict. This insufficiency has him convinced he is not only "not worthy to stamp a form" but unworthy of continuing to live, as well. Countless other bureaucracy-related jokes pepper the series, from fellow bureaucrats stamping one another's documents being considered "small talk" to an overweening emphasis on the banal and boring characteristics associated with bureaucracy, such as filing, stamping, and interminable wait times. Indeed, at a certain point, these jokes and tropes become consistent enough that they present a particular perspective about the institution of bureaucracy itself. In the next section, we will discuss the ideas of bureaucracy and bureaucrats in more depth before turning to the aforementioned three episodes and examining how *Futurama* depicts core components of it.

A Brief Refresher on Bureaucracy and Bureaucrats

Bureaucracy is, at bottom, a method of organizing work. When we talk about the role bureaucracy plays in society, we are referring to the now conventional practice of empowering non-elected managers, who are often but not always experts in a particular area, to implement policies and enforce rules and regulations within a certain sphere of public life. Examples range from police officers to courthouse clerks to the president of the United States of America. The term bureaucracy is most closely associated with the work of German social theorist Max Weber.[2] Weber argued that the end of the nineteenth century saw the emergence of a new form of authority. Where in previous times the traditional and personal authority of certain charismatic individuals dominated, in the new era Weber saw authority increasingly stemming from the rational design of organizations, with emphasis placed not on the person in charge, but rather on the expertise and efficiency provided by the bureaucratic organizations themselves. People began to obey these organizations because they provided goods and services efficiently rather than because obedience was required by their religion or they thought a particular individual was powerful.

To better illustrate the difference, consider the case of being pulled over by a traffic officer. If an officer pulled you over while you were driving, your reason for accepting her demand for you to pull over would tell you a great deal about the nature of her authority. If the authority were traditional in nature, you would pull over because your predecessors had always done so and had taught you to accept this authority. If the source of authority were related to a person's charisma, you would pull over only if the officer proved that she herself was either powerful or represented another powerful individual. Conversely, *bureaucratic* authority implies that you pull over because the officer represents a rational, legitimate police force. You pull over because of the authority of the rules that empower the police officer, not because of the officer's personal identity or something you were taught was a demand of tradition or religion.

This simple illustration highlights some of the most important aspects of a bureaucratic organization. The most important element of bureaucratic authority is the reliance on general rules. The police officer personifies the rules – but it is for the rules that you pull over. This central premise has several important implications. First, the identity of the bureaucrat does not affect the application of the rule. If one police officer or another pulls you over, it should not matter. They merely enforce the rules. Their interests should not influence their enforcement. Second, obedience to the orders of the police officer is actually obedience to the general system of rules. The basis for the authority of the general system of rules is the efficiency of the system as a whole – its ability to manage the matters of the state. One does not have to assess the characteristics of any individual bureaucrat to decide whether to obey his or her order. Third, the rules are intended to be general in nature. For the most part, just as the bureaucrat acts in a depersonalized manner (acting on behalf of the rule system, not themselves), the rules are supposed to apply to entire categories of people – not specific individuals. Although not all rules will apply to all people, they should apply to large classes of people. For instance, we can have different tax brackets but cannot have personalized tax statuses in a bureaucratized system.

Weber's analysis showed that the key question of legitimacy had moved from the individual enforcing the rules (as well as their characteristics, such as personal charisma, family connections, or religious certification) to the legitimacy of the system of rules itself. This raises a natural question: how does the entire system gain (or lose) this authority? For Weber, this is in the system's ability to provide a neutral administration of the tasks of the state in an efficient manner. It is this general role of administering the tasks of the state that is known as implementation. Whereas the legislative bodies of the state (like legislatures and parliaments) may write the laws, it is the bureaucracy that carries out, enforces, or implements these laws. Understanding how bureaucratic organizations operate to enforce laws is essential for understanding how political systems enact policy.

They can lose legitimacy if they are seen as favoring particular people (in violation of their principle of neutrality) or as failing to act efficiently (by wasting resources or failing to achieve theirs goals). If they do either, they stand to lose the moral high ground, the pragmatic advantage, or both. Indeed, implicit in our frequent complaints about the nature of bureaucracies and the individuals who staff them are fundamental critiques of how society should be administered. If the positive attributes of the bureaucratic approach to administering rules and order prove to be less than their negative attributes – or compare disfavorably with alternative models – then why should we continue to suffer through a dehumanized, nonresponsive mess?

These questions and ideas are not simply grist for academic exercises, of course. Rather, they are central to our ongoing experiences – as citizens and people – with the governments that structure our society. And, as we shall see in the next section, they are fodder for popular culture, which provides a powerful opportunity for reflecting (and shaping) the ways in which we relate to our own realities, including our political reality.[3]

Futurama and the Depiction of Bureaucracy

Now that we have discussed the nature of bureaucracy in general, we can turn to our discussion of how *Futurama* engages its key attributes. The next sections will illustrate the importance of a rule-based bureaucracy through the examination of Hermes Conrad, *Futurama*'s preeminent bureaucrat, in three episodes. The first discussion will focus on the nature of obedience to rules and the depersonalized nature of bureaucratic work. The second discussion will turn to questions of the legitimacy of the bureaucratic system and the importance of efficiency. Finally, the third discussion will discuss the role of moral judgment in bureaucratic decision making.

Hermes the Bureaucrat: Roles and Responsibilities

Hermes represents an idealized bureaucrat in *Futurama*. He is a bureaucrat in a bureaucracy that has been honed by another thousand years of development. The result is an organization that is so extreme in its obedience to rules that it leads to nonsensical behavior. Indeed, the extremity of the obedience to rules is a large part of what makes Hermes Conrad a comedic character. The role of obedience to rules becomes a central theme in the episode "How Hermes Requisitioned His Groove Back." The very title sets up the theme of runaway bureaucracy, because to speak of someone's "groove" is usually a reference to a natural state of mind. The title suggests that to Hermes it is natural to "requisition" (a formal term for ordering or acquiring) his state of mind. Bureaucratic processes, such as requisitioning materials for a business, are where Hermes feels comfortable.

As the episode opens, Hermes is singing while he is filling out a series of forms. This is an important place to start, given the role of forms in bureaucratic organizations. The nature of a form is to standardize how people qualify for services and the monitoring of the work done in organizations. Of course, as these forms accumulate, people working in the organization begin to complain of "red tape." Red tape is simply a complaint that the number and length of forms has begun to interfere with the ability of a worker to complete his or her actual work. The filling out of forms slowly takes over work time. Hermes represents the final evolution of the bureaucratic worker's relationship with forms: everything he does is through forms. Even when he considers suicide, he is told the act will require a form.

Hermes' threatened suicide is the result of a demotion from grade 35 to 36. In a bureaucracy, some one's authority stems from their position within the system of rules – not from any personal authority, social contact, etc. Hermes takes this a step further in that he has invested his own personal worth in his organizational rank. A demotion from rank 35 to 36 is such a slight that he considers his life not worth living. If it were not for the threat of further demotion for not filing a form to commit suicide, he would have killed himself rather than suffering the indignity of a demotion. This illustrates how, for Hermes, all value is in the rules of the organization, rather than in his humanity, his experience, or his social connections.

After deciding not to commit suicide after all, Hermes is dispatched to forced vacation at Spa 5, a destination that is supposed to be a luxury retreat but is really a forced labor camp. Meanwhile, his replacement at Planet Express is Morgan from the Central Bureaucracy, a higher-ranked bureaucrat who ordered his mandatory rest and relaxation. Morgan's ability to directly and immediately replace Hermes is an indication of how interchangeable the workers in a bureaucracy are. Morgan simply slides her ID into the nameplate on Hermes' desk and everything is re-oriented to her; she has instantly replaced Hermes. Because the authority of the bureaucrat stems from their position in a system of rules and ranks and not their personal identity, anyone can substitute for anyone else. It is atypical, though, for people of dramatically different ranks (again, Morgan possesses much higher rank than Hermes) to work in the same position.

Morgan quickly provides a new view of the rule-attentive bureaucrat. As a new (and temporary) character, the writers let her represent the overzealous enforcement of rules to a degree that even Hermes could not reach. Just as people complain about how bureaucrats ignore context and the needs of individuals to enforce rules, Morgan enforces rules even when they seem trivial. In an initial inspection of the locker room, she complains about Leela's jacket. Everything seems in order but the zipper is not zipped all the way down to the bottom of the jacket. Of course, this zipper presents no danger to anyone and does not even look messy. It is merely out of place in a trivial way that may technically violate a rule – but it is a rule that really has no point. Morgan's enforcement of the rule just illustrates how rule enforcement has a life of its own – regardless of any rational basis for the individual rule.

Ironically, in the end, inattention to these sorts of details undoes Morgan. After escaping his hellish vacation, Hermes returns and points out Morgan has not filed an appropriately stamped form to notify the Central Bureaucracy of a prior romantic entanglement, in this case concerning her high school prom date, which Morgan describes as a regulation date that ended in regulation disappointment. Morgan's belief in the system is so strong that although we might think it absurd that bureaucrats have to file forms concerning their high school dates, she shows that she has willingly done so. However, Hermes quickly points out that the form requires five stamps but she has only stamped it four times – an oversight

Morgan attempts (and fails) to explain by claiming she was young and reckless then. Why does having five stamps make the form more valid than if it has four stamps? It does not matter. The rule requires five and that is all that matters. This evidence of Morgan's bureaucratic imperfection nets Hermes a small promotion and sees Morgan dragged away by uniformed guards. Tellingly, however, even the powerful head bureaucrat (1.0) who orders the guards to take her away must fill out the appropriate paperwork necessary to have Morgan taken away.

This scenario is clearly a farce, yet we have all had moments where we wondered why seemingly excessive and redundant paperwork was required and bureaucrats appeared to be more focused on technicalities than the big picture. Where do the rules gain such importance that they matter even if they do not make sense? This is the topic of the next section.

Measurement and Efficiency

Bureaucrats typically enforce individual rules regardless of the rule's reasonableness. The legitimacy of the rules comes from the system rather than the person enforcing the rule. The authority of the system of rules itself is the efficiency with which the system of rules provides an orderly society. It is this basis of legitimacy that Hermes Conrad rediscovers on his visit to Spa 5. After his escape, he reflects that "Organizing that forced labor spa rekindled my lifelong love of bureaucracy." His wife, LaBarbara, concurs: "My Hermes got that hellhole running so efficiently that all the physical labor is now done by a single Australian man."[4]

The theme of the importance of efficiency is picked up in a later episode entitled "The Six Million Dollar Mon." Hermes has decided to conduct efficiency evaluations for all of the Planet Express employees. To do so, he has to assess the contribution of each employee to the operations of the organization. After donning his firing tie, he interviews each employee about his or her work. In the end, Hermes decides that he is the one that contributes the least to the organization – primarily because his oversight inhibits the team from performing, a common criticism of bureaucracy – and fires himself. Hermes is replaced by a robot, whose immunity from human weakness and imperfection evokes jealousy in Hermes that drives the self-sacrificing bureaucrat to extreme body modification.

This seeming paradox illustrates the importance of efficiency to bureaucratic organizations. Although they have the reputation of inefficiency, the levels of efficiency they can achieve legitimize this form of organization. The same bureaucrat that was ready to kill himself over a demotion is now firing himself in the name of efficiency. Hermes's critical self-assessment is itself a criticism of bureaucracy. Although we think the rule-based approach to organizations will result in stability and efficiency, the rules themselves can create inefficiency. Taken too far, the very pursuit of efficiency can even waste resources. The pursuit of efficiency can result in extra rules and monitoring activities that do not themselves actually improve efficiency.

An easy way to see the potential contradictions in hyper-optimization leading to inefficiency is in the current lifehacker movement.[5] The lifehacker movement involves sharing tips and tricks to improve a person's productivity. This ranges from personal finance tips to advice on how to manage one's time or relationships. Much of the advice involves the collection of data on how one lives (i.e., how much money one spends on food, how much time one spends commuting to work, etc.) and then applying rules to find a better way to organize the time. This movement applies the actions of a bureaucrat like Hermes Conrad to one's own self-improvement. In Hermes' case, in this episode, this takes the form of self-improvement by replacing his own organs with robot parts.

Of course, these efforts can themselves become counter-productive. You can spend so much time trying to figure out the most efficient way to get to work that you actually save less time than you invested in the optimization exercise. As Hermes found in his assessment of Planet Express, his efforts to improve performance actually caused more problems than they solved. Of course, he repeats this cycle at the personal level as he replaces parts of his body (read: improves) to the point that he eventually even seeks to replace his own brain.

In terms of bureaucratic organizations, calls to improve efficiency are constant reminders of the fundamental source of their authority. It is uncommon, though, for the improvement processes themselves to come under scrutiny. It is rare to see assessments of the specific efforts said to improve efficiency and productivity. The fear is that the measurement and improvement processes begin to waste time and take over the organization itself. A contemporary example could be the large proportion of time that students in American public elementary and high schools devote to testing. It is the case for some students that they spend almost as much time assessing their learning as they do actually learning. It is less common that the tests themselves are assessed or that the entire project of testing-based assessment is itself assessed for efficiency and productivity.[6] The rules of the organization – its method for ensuring the efficient administration of policy – may become the greatest threat to efficiency.

Ethical Dilemmas

Even so, the operation of rules and the pursuit of efficiency have helped spread the bureaucratic form of organization across various nations and times. The basic structure of the bureaucratic organization now dominates government at all levels, as well as large private sector and nonprofit organizations. As people have come to work with and for bureaucratic organizations, they have also become more familiar with the potential dangers of these forms of organizations.

The dangers of bureaucracy stem from unthinking emphasis on rules and the depersonalization of authority. Recall that, in bureaucracy, decisions are supposed to be made without reference to personal values or goals. Decisions are supposed to follow from rules – not individual, personal choices. When the rules lead to morally questionable decisions, however, people begin to wonder about the implications of this rule-based approach. In such situations, conscientious bureaucrats are faced with an age-old dilemma: what to do when the system of order depends on following rules, but a rule or set of rules is either immoral or yields immoral outcomes.

This basic ethical conundrum is illustrated in an episode from *Futurama*'s sixth season titled "Lethal Inspection." By this point in the series, it has been well established that Hermes Conrad is the consummate bureaucrat. After all he has been through with the Central Bureaucracy, he has cemented his place as the show's personification of bureaucracy in action. In this episode, Bender finds out that he lacks the capacity to resurrect his consciousness, as other robots can. He is, in fact, a broken robot. Bender finds out that he was passed by "Inspector 5" as fully functional despite this problem and wants to find out why the inspector would allow him to live with this flaw. Hermes agrees to help Bender find Inspector 5 and the two set off on an adventure that eventually reveals Bender's origin story. After several twists and turns, we learn (although Bender does not) that a much younger Hermes was actually Inspector 5, and the decision to spare Bender's "life" took place when Hermes was confronted with the choice of either "recycling" a toddler-esque Bender or overriding the alert that had identified the robot's defective backup unit. Hermes chooses to spare young Bender, and later is shown resigning from the robot-manufacturing corporation that employed him.

The decision of Inspector 5 stands for the common ethical dilemma of a bureaucrat. The bureaucrat is told to act by a set of rules. These rules are supposed to operate irrespective of the thoughts, feelings, or values of the bureaucrat. In this case, the rules dictated that the flawed robot must be destroyed. Inspector 5 decided to act against this rule (choosing to embrace his own values) and allow the flawed robot to live. He acted based on his own values, his own identity, rather than implementing the rules. After making this choice, the inspector quit his position. He no longer could accept a position where he was expected to enforce a rule with which he might disagree.

The basic dilemma of choosing between implementing a rule and taking an action that morality seems to demand is difficult for a bureaucrat. Choosing to enforce the rule allows a bureaucrat to remain consistent with her source of authority. The only reason she has the job – and the authority to act at all – is because of the system of rules. When she acts contrary to the system of rules, she is stepping outside the legitimacy afforded to the system. At that moment, it is not clear the bureaucrat has any more authority than anyone else to act. In the case of Inspector 5, his authority to certify robots depends on obedience to rules. Once he chooses not to enforce those rules, he has no more authority to inspect or certify robots than anyone else. This is why he must step down.

The illustration of this dilemma within *Futurama* may have been slanted (the viewers clearly support the decision to allow Bender to live) but it stands for a wider class of much more difficult moral decisions. Enforcing rules even when personal morality suggests a different action can take many forms. It could mean violating rules relating to hiring policies to hire a family member. In this case, the reason for the rules is clearer. If every bureaucrat could simply ignore these rules in the name of their own personal morality, hiring could become nepotistic and corrupt. Similarly, a police officer could violate rules of evidence – maybe up to the point of fabrication – to make absolutely sure that an accused criminal would be convicted. Of course, this could look moral to the police officer but a system that allows this to happen is terrifying.

There is no simple solution to the potential conflict between implementing rules and a bureaucrat's personal morality. There may be cases, like those described above, where trivial rules must make way for fundamental moral obligations. In other cases, the personal moral code seems like a flimsy excuse to ignore important and legitimate rules. The personal morality of the bureaucrat (firmly grounded in his or her personal identity) and the impersonal authority of the rule system are difficult to balance – but this is a situation that bureaucrats may face.

Conclusion: The Future of Bureaucracy

Since Max Weber first observed the evolution of how authority was administered more than a century ago, both bureaucracy and the study of it have evolved, becoming both more sophisticated and mainstream. Bureaucracy has gone from an emerging phenomenon to the dominant paradigm of public administration, and in doing so has become a source of consternation and critique. Each of us has experienced a range of frustrations with bureaucracy, from gripes about standardized testing to waiting in line for a driver's license and vehicle registration to the apparent inanities about documenting our income for the purposes of student financial aid and paying our taxes.

Unsurprisingly, the cultural representation we most frequently see of bureaucracies and bureaucrats alike is one that emphasizes making and following rules regardless of context, stodgy adherence to technicalities, and dedication to efficiency so absurd it yields the opposite. *Futurama*'s Hermes Conrad underscores and embodies these cultural stereotypes, reflecting what we think and feel about bureaucrats as well as the inescapable reality of bureaucracy. After all, a major premise of *Futurama* is that even a millennium into the future, bureaucracy is not only still relevant: it is omnipresent and omnipotent. Further, bureaucrats and citizens of this fictional future share the same frustrations and experiences, at least to a certain degree that we do today in the twenty-first century. As we have discussed, efficiency is still the ultimate goal, rules and standard operating procedures still govern bureaucratic action, and bureaucrats still wrestle with ethical dilemmas, even if the ones in *Futurama* involve toddler robots drinking beer out of a baby bottle.

Chapter Discussion Questions

1. In what ways are the stereotypes we have about bureaucrats and bureaucracies accurate, and in what ways are they false? What are some scenarios you have personally experienced that both reminded you of these stereotypes and defied them?
2. Why are rules and standard operating procedures so essential to modern bureaucracy? What are the negative consequences of this? What, on the other hand, are the positive consequences? How would you pursue being a bureaucrat differently and what would you keep the same?
3. The ethical dilemma every bureaucrat faces is when to enforce the rules and when to allow an exception without undermining the system of authority itself. If you were a bureaucrat, how would you balance this concern?

Notes

1 Lee, Mordecai and Susan C. Paddock. 2001. "Strange but true tales from Hollywood: The bureaucrat as movie hero." *Public Administration & Management*, 6(4): 166–194.
2 Weber, Max. 2009. *From Max Weber: Essays in sociology*, ed. H. H. Gerth and C. Wright Mills. Abingdon, Oxon: Routledge.
3 Delaney, Tim. 2007. "Pop culture: An overview." *Popular Culture and Philosophy*, 64 (December): 6–7.
4 *Futurama*, Season 2, Episode 14, "How Hermes Requisitioned His Groove Back."
5 For an interesting discussion of the lifehacker movement and its industrial roots, see Saval, Nikil. 2014. "The secret history of life-hacking." *Pacific Standard*, April 22, 2014, http://www.psmag.com/business-economics/the-secret-history-of-life-hacking-self-optimization-78748, accessed May 15, 2015.
6 For an overview of the arguments against standardized testing, see Kohn, Alfie. 2000. *The case against standardized testing: Raising the scores, ruining the schools*. Portsmouth, NH: Heinemann.

PART IV
Identity

11

THE POLITICS OF GENDER IN THE WORLD OF THE TWELVE COLONIES

Lilly J. Goren

CARROLL UNIVERSITY

About half way through the first season of *Battlestar Galactica*, Kara "Starbuck" Thrace, one of the fighter pilots from the battleship Galactica, is lost during a battle with the enemy's fighter jets. Her viper is disabled and she crash-lands on a desolate planet, having ejected from her jet, and finds herself low on oxygen and out of radio connection with the Galactica. The Galactica sends out search parties, even as their fuel reserves diminish and their enemy, the Cylons, pursues them. The episode, which is titled "You Can't Go Home Again," uses a classic narrative often seen in science fiction: the hero's fight against a number of constraints that will lead to certain death if a rescue is not made or some lucky break does not arrive. Starbuck eventually gets that lucky break in the form of a disabled Cylon fighter jet. As everyone on the Galactica keeps an eye on the clock monitoring the amount of oxygen Starbuck has left, tensions rise as members of the leadership disagree about the wisdom of pursuing the search-and-rescue mission as opposed to abandoning Starbuck for dead. Meanwhile, Starbuck, using the last dregs of her oxygen, cuts her way through the interior of the Cylon fighter, which is very much like human entrails.

Starbuck mucks her way through the innards of the Cylon fighter, cutting and chopping what seems like intestines and veins, all the while trying to figure out which part might hold some precious oxygen. She finally locates the oxygen vein, and continues to try to figure her way through the functioning of this cyborg fighter jet. The entire scenario of Starbuck, alone on the desolate planet, putting together her own rescue by reconfiguring the downed Cylon fighter, is a clear inversion of this narrative arc, however, because Starbuck is female, whereas the hero in such situations is typically a man.

Back at the Galactica, President Laura Roslin upbraids both Commander Adama and Captain Adama for being overwhelmed by their emotions, forgetting reason and strategy, and expending reserve fuel, which endangers not only the pilots, but the entire human civilization, just to look for Starbuck. We see a female president critique the male military commanders for giving in to excessive emotional connections to their ace fighter pilot. We can say that these accusations are inverted, because it is usually women who are accused by men of being overly emotional, attached to the individual or the particular and not the common good or the overall, and thought to be unable to take into consideration the broader requirements or demands of situations. These two separate instances of inversions highlight only some of the key ways in which the television program *Battlestar Galactica* subverted traditional presentations and integrated feminist and transgressive approaches to characters, narratives, and the overall show.

As many of the chapters in this text explain, science fiction as a genre often provides an opportunity to consider ideas and concepts from unexpected or unanticipated perspectives. This genre also has often been used to undermine the traditional roles and operations of gender and sexuality as contextualized within fictional universes created by writers, actors, and directors. Science fiction often provides a fertile arena in which to explore understandings of gender, especially in the context of society and politics. Because the framework is "sometime in the future," traditional gender constructs can be replaced by the unexpected or the non-traditional in terms of roles, relationships, or positions of power. This chapter examines the ways in which the second version of *Battlestar Galactica*, created in the early 2000s, used the medium of science fiction to reconsider expected sex and gender concepts. These reconsiderations transpire within a social, cultural, and political universe distinct from contemporary America, but not too far afield. Through its nuanced approach, *Battlestar Galactica* challenges viewers to consider some of their understandings of gender and sexuality, exploring our dominant perspectives and pushing the audience to think about different approaches or perspectives. For example, *Battlestar Galactica* takes the opportunity to speculate: what would it be like to have a woman president of what is left of the Twelve Colonies in the midst of a prolonged military engagement against a lethal and advanced enemy? What would it be like if the best fighter pilot was female – how does that change dynamics, power relationships, sexuality, and attraction? What would it be like if the highest-value captured enemy is both female and pregnant, and how would that impact generational considerations, treatment of enemy combatants, expectations around childbirth and motherhood? What would it be like if the voice of the enemy and apparently the voice of the monotheistic god are female, sexual, and always dressed seductively in red? What would it be like if the highest-ranking military commander is female? These are the considerations that are imagined over the course of the series in the context of perhaps unexpected or out of the norm portrayals of female power, position, and role within the *Battlestar* universe.

Battlestar Galactica and Ways of Thinking about Feminism

Ultimately, feminism is an articulation of the issue of equality – equality with regard to being a citizen in society, parity of rights, power, educational and career opportunities, choices and options, specifically in reference to discrimination based on gender. As a movement, either in the earliest incarnations in Western societies like the United States (or other Anglo-Western countries such as Great Britain, Australia, Canada, etc.) or in its more recent versions, feminism has been fragmented and sometimes at odds with itself. Robert Garner, Peter Ferdinand, and Stephanie Lawson explore liberal, radical, and socialist/Marxist feminism, as they define the different aims and functioning of feminisms.[1] Others approach some of the same points of distinction through the so-called "waves" or generational understandings of feminism, which is similar in some regards, but clearly delineates feminism in terms of chronological advances.[2] *Battlestar Galactica*, through a variety of different characters and plot developments, explores aspects of these distinctions and imagines potentially different and distinct ways of thinking about norms associated with gender, power, and women. This is the way in which feminism, as an ideological construct, is analyzed and, to a degree, embodied within a fictional, futuristic construction. The two approaches to considering different theoretical and time-bound understandings of feminism can be seen within either the categorical model (i.e., liberal, radical, Marxist) or the generational model (first wave, second wave, etc.). These two approaches take up substantively overlapping and connected ideas; for example, second wave feminism is the time period during which radical feminism took root and, to a degree, replaced liberal feminism as the dominant feminism paradigm.

Waves of Feminism

Historian Marlene LeGates explains that the initial form of contemporary feminism was liberal feminism, described as "a woman who sees her self-advancement as beneficial to all women."[3] Other scholars identify this version as the "first wave" within the longer and broader feminist movement. This first wave/initial form of feminism grew out of the advocacy for basic liberal political and legal rights for women: the right to vote, to hold public office, to buy or inherit property, etc. Although certain rights were attained through the suffrage movement in Western liberal democracies (specifically the right to vote), parity, especially within political office, remains absent. The second wave of feminism grew out of the advocacy for more general gender equality, or in the phrase that was used at the time, "equal rights." Both the first and second waves of feminism were dominated by privileged white women who were advocating, through mostly established political structures, for equality as they defined it.[4] The second wave, taking place in the late 1960s through the 1970s, drew women who were living mostly private lives into the public space and into political advocacy for any number of goals, among them reproductive rights, personal autonomy, and equal access to opportunities (i.e., work, education, recreation, sports, etc.). This was also known as the "women's liberation movement." Part of the critique by the second wave was of entrenched and structural patriarchy – the forms and institutions of society that have been created by and generally advantage men, often to the exclusion of women – which governs women's lives (personal and public) and limits their options and choices. Part of the advocacy was to free women from their position as "second class citizens" and to indicate that they were not alone, but that there was a community of support and of sharing.

One of the unifying points of this second wave movement was to explain that the "personal was political" – that choices one makes in the bedroom, or the kitchen, or anywhere, should not be circumscribed by accepted norms of patriarchy, male dominance, or simple tradition, and that these decisions are, by their nature, political decisions. Third wave feminism is often seen as both a movement that built upon the previous waves and one that made corrections to these movements because of absences within them.

All of feminism is dominated by both the ideas (or theory) of feminism itself (often explored by academics and philosophers) and the advocacy to change aspects of society that oppress or discriminate against individuals based on gender. Third wave feminism continued to operate along these same tracks but it corrected for absences of the previous feminist movements by opening up the dialogue, purposely including voices from under-represented groups, especially based on race, ethnicity, class, and sexuality and sexual orientation. This subsequent feminism movement also took on some of the dimensions of a woman's experience that had been dismissed by the second wave, most particularly exploring sexual pleasure, femininity, and the social demands around beauty and fashion.

In response to the theoretical basis of feminism, along with the activist dimensions of feminism, there have been a number of backlashes. For example, in 1991 Susan Faludi documented what she considered to be the adverse reaction to second wave, or radical feminism, in her bestseller, *Backlash: The undeclared war against American women*. Faludi categorized all the ways in which there were cultural, political, societal, and structural responses that grew up in reaction to the women's movements of the early 1970s, stymieing progress towards gender equality and equity. A more recent backlash comes in the form of what advocates call "post-feminism," or critiques made by women in the intellectual elite that there is no more need for feminism because all the goals of the feminist movements have been adequately achieved. Some aspects of the backlashes also tend to track along partisan political lines, especially in the United States, with advocates on the left highlighting the continued need for regulatory policy like Title IX and the Lilly Ledbetter Fair Pay Act, while advocates on the right argue such programs are detrimental and unnecessary.[5]

Categories of Feminism

As an ideology, feminism is demarcated into various categories: radical, liberal, Marxist, and post-feminism. All these categories, like the chronological waves, explore and often advocate for gender equality through different lenses (i.e., economics and class, abrogation of the state, political and legal, sexual, etc.) and are applied to different aspects of society and individual existence. *Battlestar Galactica,* while not arguing for one particular approach to feminism or understanding the issues around feminist advocacy, does explore a variety of considerations that come out of feminist thought and theory, as well as activism.

Radical feminism suggests that there is a general exploitation of women that is extensive and, to a degree, universal, even though this form of feminism, like the second wave, was critiqued for not paying sufficient attention to issues of race, class, and sexuality.[6] Radical feminism is philosophically parallel to second wave feminism, advocating for liberation from the oppressive patriarchal institutions that dominate Western societies. This movement came out of the political radicalization that had transpired in response to post–World War II imperialism, civil rights advocacy (in the United States, South Africa, etc.), and discriminatory treatment of minorities in a number of countries, as well as the tragic United States involvement in Southeast Asia. Radical feminism tracks along the same political lines that critiqued Western colonization, capitalism, dominant institutions, and oppressive tactics and policies.

Liberal feminism grew out of the demand that women should have the same rights and privileges of citizenship that men have – namely access to participate in civil society through the usual means of participation (i.e., voting, public advocacy, access to education, etc.). Traditional liberal theorists like John Stuart Mill[7] argued for the opportunity for women to participate in the public sphere, as citizens. Mill's work built upon Mary Wollstonecraft's articulation of these ideas in her 1792 treatise *A vindication of the rights of women.* [8] In the United States, these theorists influenced the women who would pen the 1848 *Declaration of sentiments* in Seneca Falls, New York as a complement to Thomas Jefferson's 1776 *Declaration of Independence.* The early feminists, such as Harriet Tubman and Elizabeth Cady Stanton, were active in the abolition movement in the United States and campaigned for the amendments that followed the Civil War that transformed former slaves into United States citizens with full rights. Their ultimate goal was similar: to constitutionally protect the right to vote for women. This eventually would be achieved by a subsequent generation when the Nineteenth Amendment passed in 1919 and was finally ratified in 1920.

These categories and waves highlight the many different iterations of feminism and the different approaches, goals, and advocates for feminism over hundreds of years. Different dimensions of feminism are explored throughout the entire *Battlestar Galactica* series. There are numerous representations of both men and women who are cast in what we would consider to be feminist contexts. Some of the characters are more transgressive in their embodiment of gender adaptation and operation according to gender norms. "Transgressive embodiments" are representations of inverted or unexpected behavior, defying general norms and traditions in action, demeanor, representation, conduct, or the like.[9] Thus characters act or are seen in a transgressive manner when they conduct themselves in an inverted or unexpected way, because the audience brings norms of behavior and expectation to whatever we might watch or observe. Within this narrative construction, this chapter examines the role and understandings of feminism, gender, and sexuality within the broader context of politics and power through the lens of *Battlestar Galactica* and documents how dominant assumptions or expectations are undermined, played with, or otherwise contested.

Battlestar Galactica, Take Two

Battlestar Galactica started out in the late 1970s as a short-lived television show designed to appeal to those clamoring for "more *Star Wars.*" It was canceled after just one season, occasionally reincarnating in a variety of forms until 2003, when SyFy produced a miniseries reboot, which the network ultimately extended through four seasons, airing the show from 2004 to 2009. The show drew on many contemporary themes as it unfolded over the course of the four seasons – including issues of the military state, the rise and threat of technology, questions of belief and faith, and, of most relevance to this chapter, issues surrounding gender, power, and responsibility.

Battlestar Galactica is a form of *the Odyssey*, set in space, some time in the future. Because the thrust of the story is about a "ragtag" band of warriors (for the most part, with some civilians as well) trying to find their way home, the show's arc fits within the traditional journey narrative. It also includes, alongside the narrative references to *the Odyssey*, reference as well to its prelude, *the Iliad*, where mighty armies fought over the idea of honor, the proper conduct of societies, and the value of female beauty. The humans aboard the Galactica, and the other ships within the fleet (again mimicking the classical military of ancient Greece), are locked in a battle that may destroy all of human civilization.

Prior to the events that take place in *Battlestar Galactica*, the Twelve Colonies (United Colonies) of Kobol were composed of humans. These humans had created artificial life forms that had evolved, over time, into independent beings known as Cylons. Eventually the Cylons chose to destroy their creators (in part because of the idiosyncrasies that make humans human, such as fallible reason and a tendency toward mistakes), and launched a prolonged war against the Colonies and all of human existence in the galaxy. *Battlestar Galactica* commences with the Cylons' nuclear destruction of most of the Colonies, and much of the subsequent narrative concerns their pursuit of those still alive to finish the job. The battleship Galactica becomes the essential leader of the fleet of starships that are looking for safe haven, a new home where they cannot be detected by Cylons and where they can live, farm, and re-establish the human race.

The next section explores three of the main female characters from *Battlestar Galactica*: Starbuck, President Roslin, and 6. These three characters – two human, one a Cylon – are the most important female characters that remain prominent throughout the entire series. There are a number of other women, specifically various versions of Sharon/Number 8 and Admiral Cain, who are distinct and interesting in context, and demonstrate some of the same feminist qualities that shape Starbuck, Roslin, and 6.

Starbuck: Not Exactly as Expected

For anyone who watched the original series from the 1970s, one of the first adaptations encountered in the reboot is that of Lt. Starbuck – the most skilled, intuitive, and fearless viper pilot on the Galactica (or any other Battlestar) – who is played by actress Katee Sackhoff. Starbuck, otherwise known as Kara Thrace, was a male character in the original series, played by Dirk Benedict. Both actors are blond and dashing, but casting Starbuck as a female was a transgressive choice because it immediately compelled the audience to think about the role of a fighter pilot from a much different and unexpected perspective. In fact, not only is Starbuck the best viper pilot, her dominance is overtly challenged by another female pilot, Louanne "Kat" Katraine, in the second season of the series.

The fact that not only are the best pilots women but that having a co-ed squad of fighter pilots goes without comment indicates that a woman in air combat in this imagined universe is normal. Thus, Starbuck fits in among the fighter pilots because she is one of many women we see helming vipers and engaging in risky combat missions with the enemy Cylons. The transgressive quality here is that we are bringing our political and cultural perspectives to the show, we see it through our expectations, and thus Starbuck – swaggering, daring, dogmatic, sexual, hard-drinking, and fearless – is unexpected. We are used to imagining and seeing men in these situations and exhibiting these characteristics, not women. And because Starbuck is such an integral part of the series and the narrative, we, as an audience, are constantly exploring our own expectations for this character and how those expectations are undermined by the gender switch.

Starbuck embodies the daredevil attitude and insubordinate approach that has been portrayed in other fictional artifacts about fighter pilots. Not only is the re-imagined Starbuck female, but she has as much swagger, ego, and bravado as does Tom Cruise's character "Maverick" in *Top Gun*. We also see her in contrast to Captain Lee Adama, otherwise known as "Apollo" – who is also considered to be one of the top fighter pilots, but lacks the intuitive finesse or grace that Starbuck brings to the cockpit. In casting a fit, fierce woman as Starbuck, the show imagines the results of feminism; In *Battlestar Galactica*, debates and controversies about women in combat, much less as fighter pilots, have been concluded and women are fully integrated into the military. What we do see, because Starbuck is not the only female viper pilot, is that the pilots all have certain qualities and characteristics, a toughness that they must hone, and an understanding of the enemy that must be integrated into how they think about combat and military missions. These qualities and skills contribute to the kind of individual who is very good at air combat, as those who are the very best, as in so many fields, exhibit the arrogance and superiority that comes with such refined and valuable skills. Starbuck is demonstrably proud and extremely sure of her skills. Again, this image tacks back to our cultural expectations of fighter pilots, although our expectations draw these pilots as men. And thus the images we encounter through the character of Starbuck track, in a certain sense, along the lines of post-feminism. Indeed, acknowledgment of gender is irrelevant here. Starbuck has proven over and over again to be the best viper pilot. No accommodation is made based on her gender, physical limitations, etc. Her superiority is rarely challenged; no one thinks that she has taken the place of a man who could do the job better; no one doubts her fearlessness, her commitment, or her skills. That all those qualities come in a female body is rendered irrelevant by the narrative.

Starbuck is also overtly sexual, again connecting to the expected stereotype of male fighter pilots. In this manner, she does what gives her pleasure, as we see her wanting and enjoying sex with various partners at different points. This sexualization is in keeping with third wave feminism, which highlighted the opportunity for women, freed from the constraints of the connection between sex and pregnancy given the advent of modern birth control, to pursue sex for pleasure outside of the confines of marriage without feeling guilty or ending up with a child. And so we see Starbuck, over the course of the series, with swaggering sexual bravado. She knows she is attractive and that men find her enticing because of her fiery fierceness and power. Starbuck's sexuality is another inversion of traditional gender norms that have been attacked by iterative waves and forms of feminism – the attempt is to provide women with the opportunity to want sex, pursue sex, enjoy sex, and not to be labeled or degraded because of this.

Laura Roslin: President or Kindergarten Teacher?

Not only is the most talented fighter pilot in the *Battlestar* universe a woman, so is the president who leads the surviving humans after the Cylon attack.[10] President Laura Roslin's character has been written about in a number of venues because she inhabits the role of an American-like president, but her experience as president is distinct from the typical American one for a variety of reasons, including her gender.[11] Equally important is that Roslin, played by Mary McDonnell, came to her position in the wake of the attack and through the line of succession, only after the deaths of forty-two higher-ranking officials. Prior to the attack, she had been the Secretary of Education, a female-gendered position.[12] Indeed, much is made of her moving from that position to the presidency; for example, Admiral Adama refers her to as a "kindergarten teacher" as she is in the midst of taking over the position of civilian leader of the remnants of the Twelve Colonies and the fleet of ships that survived the Cylon attack.[13]

Roslin is also ill, having recently learned that she has terminal cancer. We, the audience, know of her illness, which she keeps from others for a long stretch of the series. Roslin is thus presented, initially, in typically female ways: she is physically weak, she is an educator, she is uninterested in politics (she explains this in context of her position in the president's cabinet and her impending decision to resign). According to those around her, especially those in the military, she is in way over her head and she essentially is in the position only for symbolic purposes. In comparison with Starbuck, we first encounter someone from whom we do not expect much. Much of this initial context is soon undermined as Roslin comes into the leadership position and gets her bearings as president. Thus she herself operates in a kind of trangressive manner. Whereas we encountered Starbuck and knew exactly how that character was subverting gender expectations from the moment we met her (i.e., smoking cigars in a tank top, playing cards) because they were our own expectations, Roslin becomes a different individual than the one we first meet, and she comes to reify some gender expectations while transgressing or undermining others.

Roslin, as the civilian leader of what is left of the Twelve Colonies, is often at odds with William Adama, who is the military leader of the fleet (aside from a brief period when Admiral Hine is in charge.)[14] Their positions also contribute to some of our gender expectations: a man of war and veteran of battles against a former schoolteacher who is now an inexperienced civilian leader. Because of Roslin's initial physical fragility and her background, the audience expects her to defer to Adama, and so does Adama. We also expect her to "mother" others because she comes out of the teaching profession, because of her age and gender, and because of the level of concern and worry that she initially demonstrates for the rest of the fleet – and again, she starts off from this footing (although she herself is not a mother). The total human population is posted on a small whiteboard in her office, with additions and subtractions made as they occur. This number, those people, these are her children; she is responsible for their well being, for their survival. Thus, Roslin is cast in the role of mother but in a political context – she is like Franklin Roosevelt, or Winston Churchill, who were tasked with protecting their people, keeping them safe from enemies. Roslin's character is transgressive in this manner – she is given the job of mother, but in a public context, not in the private sphere. This redefinition of motherhood and mothering has been part of the discussions and advocacy within the later waves of feminism, and in the context of women's liberation and radical feminism. Motherhood is complicated!

President Roslin is transgressive physically as well as positionally and in her general demeanor. She adopts the position as protector of the species, and then has to conduct herself in that manner. At times that means taking a very hard, unrelenting position that may jeopardize the lives of some for the good of the many. She views Adama's previously discussed decision to expend so much time and fuel searching for Starbuck as wasteful and dangerous. She thought this effort to potentially save one individual was not appropriate in the assessment of risk and return in the middle of a war. In another episode, Roslin also chooses to execute a Cylon, Leoben Conoy, whom Starbuck had been interrogating – even after Starbuck suggests that he may not be a threat to the fleet – without hesitation. These kinds of decisions – quickly made, quickly executed – often define patriarchal expressions of power and show as she comes more fully into her position as president, that she becomes more decisive in her actions and decisions. This is another transgressive presentation, especially of a woman in executive power. And it is set in reflection of and, at times, in contrast to Adama's execution of power as a military commander.

Thus President Roslin adapts as she comes into her position as the civilian leader of the Colonies. She is initially more traditionally feminine and subsequently transcends both her own tendencies and those of the audience's expectations to become a decisive and politically adept executive. She integrates feminine qualities into her leadership capacity while taking on a more masculine approach. This highlights her acceptance and growing comfort with power and the need for decisive action in the face of uncertainty and threat. All of these qualities in the public sphere reflect second and third wave feminism, opening up public spaces for women to exercise political power while still embodying female qualities and characteristics.

Number 6: Madonna in a Red Dress

Number 6, played by actress Tricia Helfer, mostly haunts the consciousness of another character, Gaius Baltar. Number 6 is distinct from many of the other female characters throughout the series because she is most often seen in seductively revealing deep red dresses that expose as much of her skin as they tend to cover. She is beautiful, sexual, seductive (especially of Baltar), and appears very human indeed, except that she is a Cylon, and we see her reborn (in a rather baptismal-like manner) during the course of the series. She is also very concerned with the human–Cylon child that was being carried by the Cylon Sharon (Number 8). Thus, like President Roslin, Number 6 marries a very traditional feminine visage and a concern with motherhood and childbirth (all within the norms of expected female behavior) with her continual elaboration on God and love and belief in that love and monotheism.

This is yet another representation of transgressive expectations. We meet Number 6 in her interactions with Baltar, which are generally physical, sexual, and tempting. She has manipulated him into helping her and the Cylons get into the military defense system so that they can attack the Twelve Colonies. She is dressed in form-fitting clothing and initially seems to be a sexually promiscuous professional career woman. She has been using sexuality to seduce Baltar and get him to trust and work with her. He is clearly enchanted with her. Gaius Baltar is *Battlestar Galactica*'s resident intellectual and scientist – thus he is presented as embodying reason in its most advanced form, and yet he is quite susceptible to the feminine wiles of this red-dressed image of female sexuality who is, on some level, promoting a fairly Christian theology. Number 6, in her non-humanness, is thus transgressive in being (she is not an actual woman but a machine made to seem like a woman) and in presentation, because she is offering up a kind of purity of belief and religious love very much in keeping with Jesus's teaching about God and the role of Jesus on earth while dressed as a kind of sexual stereotyped temptress (i.e., blonde, sexy, sultry red dress, demure, passionate). This caricature of both Mary Magdalene and most high-priced prostitutes might well come off as Number 6 is presented, but this is combined with her role within the series as the most consistent witness to God's love and compassion, and her urging of Baltar, a man of reason, to embrace the faith and commitment of her theology. Number 6 is thus situated in some capacity in radical and third wave feminism – she is arguing for eliminating the structures and institutions that confine or limit (in this case, not in terms of gender discrimination but instead in terms of spiritual commitment), while embracing a vibrant and engaging sexuality that she never hides or elides.

As an audience, we are as transfixed by Number 6's sexual presentation as is Baltar, but her argument and her role among the Cylons shifts a bit during the course of the series, and she is sometimes uncomfortable among her own (the Cylons) but while she is not human, she can emotionally feel more than can most Cylons. Like Jesus, she is without a place in any of the societies she inhabits. Number 6's character, on some level, is more of a broad integration of basic stereotypes, such as the prostitute/whore, the religious evangelical, and the devout religious adherent. Thus, like Starbuck and Roslin, Number 6 inverts traditional gender norms and expectations in who she is and what she is representing within the narrative. She looks sexy and sexualized (aspects of the third wave and some forms of radical feminism), but she is also the voice of God, of belief. Taken together, she is yet another example of transgression within the *Galactica* universe.

Conclusion

This chapter has explored various modern approaches and understandings of feminism, both in theory and as presented in the narrative of the *Battlestar Galactica* narrative. Key characters Starbuck, Roslin, and Number 6 embody different feminist ideas and come from different theoretical perspectives. As consumers of *Battlestar Galactica*, we bring our gender norm expectations to what we see within this speculative universe and find ourselves having to confront those expectations as we encounter these multidimensional and unanticipated characters.

This is part of the teaching of feminism – to explore unacknowledged norms and seek to adjust them to be more egalitarian and inclusive. In each example here, we find ourselves faced with female characters who transgress our expectations. They are flawed, complex, and enticing; yet they do not conform to gender norms per se. The creators and writers of *Battlestar Galactica* wanted viewers to consider many themes from different and unanticipated understandings, gender and sexuality among them. In their crafting and writing of these important characters in ways that prod us to reconsider our understanding of power, religious witness, military strength, and sexuality, we confront many of the salient features of the various iterations and forms of contemporary feminism, all while enjoying a thoughtful and exciting television series.

Chapter Discussion Questions

1. What is inverted or transgressive in the three female characters at the center of *Battlestar Galactica*: Starbuck, President Roslin, and Number 6? How do these women embody different aspects of the waves or categories of feminism? What are the waves or categories of contemporary feminism?
2. What are the norms that we, as an audience, bring to our understandings of gender and sexuality, femininity, and motherhood, and how do these characters, in the context of the narrative, disrupt those norms?
3. What is feminism and how can we think about it as a political theory as seen within this example of speculative fiction?

Notes

1 Garner, Robert, Peter Ferdinand, and Stephanie Lawson. 2009. *Introduction to politics*, Oxford, UK: Oxford University Press.

2 Haywood, Leslie and Jennifer Drake, eds. 2003. *Third wave agenda: Being feminist, doing feminism*. Minneapolis, MN: University of Minnesota Press.

3 LeGates, Marlene. 2001. *In their time: A history of feminism in Western society*. New York: Routledge Press, 311.

4 Hernandez, Daisy and Bushra Rehman, eds. 2002. *Colonize this! Young women of color on today's feminism*. New York: Seal Press; Haywood and Drake, *Third wave agenda*; Aikau, Hokulani K., Karla A. Erickson, and Jennifer L. Pierce, eds. 2007. *Feminist waves, feminist generations*. Minneapolis, MN: University of Minnesota Press.

5 Secretary of State Condoleezza Rice noted in the film *Miss Representation* that she and George W. Bush advisor Karen Hughes made the case within the Bush Administration to not attempt to dismantle Title IX: "When there was an attempt to change Title IX and some pressure from Capitol Hill about that, I remember Karen Hughes and I going to the President and saying 'You can't do that. You don't remember what it was like to be a woman in college prior to Title IX when you had to have a bake sale to get your sports team to take a trip.'" Newsom, Jennifer Siebel and Kimberlee Acquaro. 2011. *Miss Representation*. San Francisco, CA: Girls' Club Entertainment.

6 See a number of the collections that focus on the third wave, including Gillis, Stacy, Gillian Howie, and Rebecca Munford. 2007. eds. *Third wave feminism: A Critical exploration*. New York: Palgrave MacMillan; Findlen, Barbara. 2001. *Listen up: Voices from the next feminist generation*, Emeryville, CA: Seal Press; Dicker, Rory and Alison Piepmeier, eds. 2003. *Catching a wave: Reclaiming feminism for the 21st century*, Boston, MA: Northeastern University Press; Walker, Rebecca. 1995. *To be real: Telling the truth and changing the face of feminism*. New York: Anchor Books; and Hernandez and Rehman, *Colonize this!*

7 Mill, John Stuart and Harriet Taylor Mill. 1970. *Essays on sex equality: John Stuart Mill and Harriet Taylor Mill*, ed. Alice Rossi. Chicago: University of Chicago Press.

8 Wollstonecraft, Mary. 1967. *A vindication of the rights of women*, New York: W. W. Norton.
9 Jack Migdalek explains distinctions between the way that transgressive embodiments are staged in performance as opposed to transgressions that occur in daily life. Migdalek, Jack. 2014. *The embodied performance of gender*, New York: Routledge Press, 173.
10 President Laura Roslin is another inversion from the original *Battlestar Galactica*, when the role was played by Lew Ayres, a film and television star from the 1940s. Ayres's character, President Adar, is not with the *Galactica* all that long in the original series.
11 Linda Horwitz and Holly Swyers assess President Roslin in contrast to male fictional presidents in their chapter "Why Are All the Presidents Men?: Televisual Presidents and Patriarchy," in Goren, Lilly J., ed. 2010. *You've come a long way, baby: Women, politics and popular culture*. Lexington, KY: University Press of Kentucky. I integrated President Roslin into my analysis of the evolution of televisual fictional female presidents in Vaughn, Justin and Lilly J. Goren, eds. 2012. *Women and the White House: Gender, popular culture and presidential politics*. Lexington, KY: University Press of Kentucky.
12 Borrelli, MaryAnne. 2002. *The President's cabinet: Gender, power, and representation*. Boulder, CO: Lynne Rienner.
13 Goren, Lilly J. 2012. "Fact or fiction: The reality of race and gender in reaching the White House," in Vaughn and Goren, *Women and the White House*, 97–120; 109.
14 Michael E. Flynn explores the issue of civil–military relations in much greater depth in Chapter 16.

12

"WE SHALL OVERCOME"

The Districts of Panem and Identity Politics in *The Hunger Games*

Jennifer Kelkres Emery

THE WASHINGTON CENTER

Jocelyn Evans

UNIVERSITY OF WEST FLORIDA

In *The Hunger Games* trilogy, author Suzanne Collins introduces a simple hand gesture to express complex emotions that include admiration, gratitude, and love shared between characters. In the books and film adaptations of the series, when Katniss offers to take the place of her younger sister Prim, the citizens of District 12 choose to recognize her with a district salute (three fingers touched to the lips and then held to the sky) rather than applause. When Rue, the youngest of the tributes dies in the arena, Katniss expresses her sorrow and respect to Rue's district using the same salute. And when Rue's District 11, the predominantly African-American district of Panem, meets Katniss and Peeta on their Victory Tour, the citizens respond to the victors' speeches with the same salute. In this series, Collins uses this highly symbolic gesture to establish identification between Katniss and the people she represents.

The study of identity politics involves examination of the social organization and political behavior of people based upon shared characteristics such as race, ethnicity, class, religion, gender, and sexual orientation. In this way, it is the study of the political experience of diverse groups. In American history, racial identity has shaped African-American social and political experience. From the colonial period and the slave trade, the abolitionist movement and the Civil War, to the civil rights struggle of the twentieth century, American history has a racial legacy. This historical and cultural heritage not only sustains identity politics but also shapes African-American representation in politics today. We explore the relationship between the representative and the represented through the lens of identity and oppression in the *Hunger Games* trilogy. *The Hunger Games* sheds light on the meaning of marginalization and representation in American political history through the story of Panem's diverse districts. District 11 represents the American South in the age of slavery, while District 12 represents white poverty during the Great Depression. Taken together, these districts illustrate the intersection of racial and class-based politics. Katniss proves to be District 11's strongest advocate against an oppressive regime, serves as a protector for Rue in the Games, recognizing the plight of District 11 after her death, and provides hope to those left behind.

Marginalized Places in Panem

Political scientists have been interested in studying groups in society for a long time. One of Madison's primary arguments for creating a Union in *Federalist 10* was its ability to break and control the violence of faction. He clarified that by faction he meant "a number of citizens, whether amounting to a majority or a minority of the whole, who are united and actuated by some common impulse of passion, or of interest, adversed to the rights of other citizens, or to the permanent and aggregate interests of the community."[1] In other words, factions are interest groups – groups that share common goals that might or might not be shared with the larger political body. With the advent of polling technology, twentieth-century scholars developed means of scientifically identifying such groups and tracking their political behavior.[2] Today, scholars study the groups we form for all types of identities, including religious affiliation, class identity, marriage, and even fleeting constructs like the 1990s' "soccer mom," who was thought to be decisive in determining political elections, or today's "millennial," who someday might be decisive.

Race and ethnicity strongly influence group identity. In fact, race and ethnicity have played a defining role in American history. Further, identity politics have shaped the African-American political experience. In the twentieth century, the civil rights movement, involving pushes for desegregation, greater enfranchisement, antidiscrimination, and affirmative action, continued this legacy. Today, attention to racial profiling and police brutality continues to bring identity politics to the forefront of national policy debate.

This legacy means that Americans have a rich backdrop of racialized politics from which to contextualize *The Hunger Games*. Although Panem, the nation at the heart of the trilogy, is depicted as a fictional future of Earth, it contains many remnants of Americans' racial past, our racial present, and potentially our future. First, the geography of Panem reflects the racial mapping of the United States today. Many fans have spent time digging into the text of Collins's books to pull out clues about the geography of the districts: their racial makeup and where they sit in relation to one another. Some speculate that Panem's 11th district is located in the southern region of the United States. Collins portrays District 11 as a majority black district with many characteristics of the pre–Civil War South, where slavery reigned. In the south, the District would include Atlanta, a major population center for blacks today, and cover vast expanses of rural farmland.

Second, in addition to the geographic similarities between District 11 and the American South, there are other cultural practices in District 11 that hearken to historic African-American experience, particularly in the antebellum South. The heritage of working the fields, displaying peaceful protest, and suffering public police brutality all remind the reader of the vestiges of slavery and the civil rights movement. "Perhaps the clearest connection between District 11 and African-American cultural history is in the oppression perpetrated on District 11's citizens by the Capitol and Peacekeepers, especially the violent response to their peaceful protest."[3]

The Hunger Games reflects our present racial politics as well, and what might be our future. There is a debate about whether racial politics matters in the United States today. In 2014, the shooting by a white policeman of Michael Brown, an unarmed African American, in Ferguson, Missouri, prompted massive protests all over the country. The subsequent decision of the grand jury not to indict the officer in question drew even more attention to racism, police brutality, and criminal justice as ongoing issues in American society. Among white Americans, 9 percent thought "race relations" or "racism" was the most important problem facing the country in the days following the decision not to indict. However, more than twice as many non-whites felt the same way, at 22 percent.[4]

In the aftermath of Ferguson, a CNN poll revealed that America is quite split over whether or not race relations as a problem will ever be worked out. Nearly half of whites (46 percent) and non-whites (48 percent) suggested that race would always be a problem in the United States.[5] However, a much wider gap in public opinion exists when evaluating whether the death of Michael Brown was related to race. In answering the question, "Do you think race was a major factor, a minor factor or not a factor in the death of Michael Brown?" only 22 percent of whites believed it was a major factor, while 75 percent of blacks believed it was a major factor.[6] More broadly, Gallup found that while 68 percent of blacks think the American justice system is biased against black people, only 25 percent of whites think the same.[7] This demonstrates that one of the racial problems facing America today is the lack of agreement about whether or not we have a "race problem."

The Role of Oppression in Identity Politics, Districts 11 and 12

In Panem, the Games epitomize the heinous brutality sanctioned by the state to maintain order in the districts. To fully appreciate the meaning and violent potential of the Games in Panem, and particularly Districts 11 and 12, we have to understand the role of oppression in identity politics. The games are a grotesque ritual that pits drafted children against each other in a fight to the death for survival. The system is unjust. There is no freedom. It is an extreme form of oppression. Contrasting the world of the arena with the districts from which contestants originate, we see varying degrees of difference. For children from District 4, this world stands in stark contrast to their relatively privileged home life. They see the

Games as a challenge – an Olympics of sorts. For children from Districts 11 and 12, this world is just more oppressive. It drags them from poverty and surveillance into involuntary brutality.

The theme of oppression dominates both the story of District 11 in general and Katniss's experience in District 12 more specifically, just as it has the narrative of African-American history. Where District 11 represents the agrarian South, District 12 represents contemporary Appalachia. Food is scarcest in District 12. District 12 is a white district, and thus it illustrates that identity might extend beyond race to issues of socioeconomic status. Jennifer Lawrence, a Kentucky native, played Ree Dolly in *Winter's Bone* before being cast as Katniss Everdeen in *The Hunger Games*. Set in the Ozarks, this film depicted the harsh realities of life in rural, poverty-stricken American communities. Both the Ozarks of *Winter's Bone* and District 12 of *The Hunger Games* lack strong colorization. This is a very subtle but powerful message about the dreariness and hopelessness of the settings. District 12 almost looks black and white, to the point that the pastel blue of Prim's dress at the reaping stands out. Note that in other districts, the Capitol, and even District 11, color dyes are widely available. The author and the director of *The Hunger Games* used visual cues to depict District 12 as poverty-stricken. In summary, District 11 represents the American South in the age of slavery, while District12 represents white poverty in Appalachia.

Taken together, these districts illustrate the shared oppression of race-based and class-based identity politics. These stories are different, but they illustrate the role that group identity, or an "us" vs. "them" mentality plays in politics. Social identity takes on many forms, and any group, if sufficiently marginalized, can create a political movement born out of shared experience. In District 11, defiance can mean death, either through starvation or brutality at the hands of Peacekeepers. From this perspective, it is easily understood why District 11 is the first to rebel and take back its resources during the Second Rebellion.[8]

The lyrics of "The Hanging Tree," sung by Katniss in the book and throughout the movie speak to this shared experience of oppression. In fact, the song is forbidden in Panem, according to Katniss. She sings it to her sister Prim before the Reaping, and she sings it over Rue at her death. The folksy tune to which the song is set is "a recognizable riff on the genre" of Appalachian ballads.[9] This makes sense because Katniss comes from District 12, a district described by Collins to reflect the coal-mining, poverty-stricken region of the Appalachian Mountains. The song masterfully weaves together a story of punishment and symbols of injustice relevant to both race-based and class-based identities. Amelia Mason reveals some of the varied subtexts of the song. "It expresses a yearning for freedom. It contains an invitation – to death, perhaps, or more specifically to martyrdom. As a cultural artifact co-opted and imbued with coded significance by the rebellion, it is a very plausible rallying cry."[10] She further explains its relationship and relevance to District 11. We might link the song with black identity because the subject reminds us of lynchings and the music reminds us of black spirituals. And just as civil rights leaders co-opted the spiritual "I Shall Overcome" to be more universal in "We Shall Overcome," so rebel leaders co-opt the lyrics of "The Hanging Tree" to suit their purposes later in *The Hunger Games.* [11]

Throughout, *The Hunger Games* grapples chiefly with two forms of identity politics (race and class), but the story speaks to an even larger theme. Political movements are fueled by feelings of oppression and inequality. The Games are a brutal venue that demonstrates how it feels to be without consent. Oppression has many definitions, for example, the suffering endured by "economically and culturally marginalized groups."[12] A general definition of oppression is the lack of political power to exercise your will, and that is the essence of the Hunger Games. It is possible that Collins wanted to teach the reader about oppression in a relatable way by showing an experience of white suffering as part of a window into the African-American experience.

Katniss represents abolitionists who created the Underground Railroad. Katniss proves to be District 11's strongest advocate against an oppressive regime, serving as a protector for Rue in the Games, recognizing the plight of District 11 after her death, and providing hope to those left behind. Katniss has a special place in her heart for District 11, certainly after Rue's death, if not before. Katniss demonstrates an interest in the plight of others and wants to help them personally, even though she is not interested in being the symbol of protest that she ultimately becomes. Collins intentionally articulates the purpose of hope and has Katniss play this crucial role of delivering hope with Rue's death (hand sign meaning respect). Her death causes Katniss to respect District 11, to give its citizens hope, and to empower them to riot and rebel against the Capitol. In return, the overwhelming response of District 11wakes something up in Katniss and causes her to stand up to the President and pose a serious threat to his regime.

Part of the oppressiveness of the ruling regime in Panem is the stark contrast between life in the Capitol and life in the districts. This mirrors the historical example of life in ancient Rome. Capitol residents live a life of excessive opulence. For example, they can afford to buy enough food to eat, regurgitate their meal, and eat again to enjoy the pleasure of tasting food as often as possible. The parallel with ancient Rome is not lost on the author, as the characters living in the Capitol are given Roman names, suggesting the elitism of the ruling class. The Hunger Games can be compared to gladiators fighting in the Coliseum, who were killed for the mob's entertainment. The government does not value the lives of people outside of their realm. This serves several purposes for the government: the entertainment pleases Capitol residents, reinforces the sense of entitlement for Capitol citizens, and distracts citizens from any discontent with the system. The Games also provide a compelling demonstration of the government's strength.

Through this literary lens, Collins asks us to reflect on the character of our own capital. If we understand the Capitol to represent the hub of power, then a lack of racial and economic diversity speaks volumes about the value system undergirding the politics of the place. To what extent are our governing bodies representative of the nation as a whole? With a Congress that is only 20 percent female and 18 percent racial minority,[13] it is hard to say that we value diversity and inclusiveness in deliberative politics. In this section, we reviewed the role of oppression in cementing group politics. In the next, we review why representation matters to marginalized populations and think through the kind of representation Katniss provides to the citizens of District 11.

Representation Theory and the Relationship Between Katniss and District 11

In *The Hunger Games*, we see representation in two separate dimensions. First, the people of the districts put forward tributes from among their children to represent them in the Hunger Games. Second, the victors develop popular followings and give voice to the people of Panem in dealing with the Capitol regime. Katniss takes on a special role in representing the people of District 11. This district is notable as the only district in Panem with a concentrated minority population. In the film adaptation, this population is cast as African American. One of the two tributes selected to represent District 11 in the 74th Hunger Games is Rue. Katniss describes seeing Rue for the first time. "And most hauntingly, a twelve-year-old girl from District 11. She has dark skin and eyes, but other than that she's very like Prim in size and demeanor."[14] She is the youngest tribute in the games, and Katniss develops a special relationship with her. In fact, the reader gets the sense that Katniss wants to protect Rue because of her age and vulnerability. Much as she protected Prim, her younger sister, from participation in the Games, she attempts to protect Rue from danger in the arena.

As Rue dies, Katniss sings to her. After she dies, Katniss surrounds her with flowers. Her care of Rue even in death endears her to the citizens of District 11 and forms the basis of the representational relationship she has with them throughout the series. She communicates her loyalty to Rue and her district by raising a three-fingered salute to the sky as Rue's body is removed from the arena. The district shows its appreciation to Katniss during the Games by sending a sponsor gift of bread. Later, we see further evidence of this representational relationship when Katniss recounts her time with Rue (as well as Thresh) while on the Victory Tour after the 74th Hunger Games. In fact, it is Katniss's recounting that spurs the Second Rebellion.

Just as Katniss acts as a surrogate mother for Rue in the Games, so she acts as a surrogate representative for the citizens of District 11. In American politics, our elected officials often represent ideological movements, industries, or interests without much voice in their home districts. When political elites share unique personal attributes or experiences with groups under-represented in the governing body, they sometimes feel a sense of responsibility to represent these perspectives in office. As Jane Mansbridge summarizes:

> Representatives who are female, African American, or of Polish ancestry, who have a child with a disability, or who have grown up on a farm, in a mining community, or in a working-class neighborhood, often feel not only a particular sensitivity to issues relating to these experiences but also a particular responsibility for representing the interests and perspectives of these groups, even when members of these groups do not constitute a large fraction of their constituents. Feelings of responsibility for constituents outside one's district grow even stronger when the legislature includes few, or disproportionately few, representatives of the group in question.[15]

Mansbridge helps us to understand representation as more than a simple delegation of authority by a district to a representative to make decisions that reflect majority preferences. Political actors can act as surrogates. As she explains, "Surrogate representation occurs when legislators represent constituents outside their own districts."[16]

We see this dynamic at work in Panem as well. It is important to recognize that Katniss, who is Caucasian, is not the same ethnicity as the predominant population in District 11, which is African American. When a representative shares a demographic characteristic with the population he or she represents, we call it descriptive representation. A woman is a descriptive representative of other women, for example. Often districts with very large minority populations, termed majority–minority districts, elect descriptive representatives to office. African-American Members of Congress frequently represent predominantly black districts. Scholars argue that "[p]referable descriptive representatives have strong *mutual* relationships with *dispossessed* subgroups."[17] They should not merely look like those they represent, but they should have relationships involving mutual recognition, identification, and common understanding with the represented. In short, the marginalized group members should see the representative as "one of us."[18] Ideally, these representatives work to "mobilize a historically disadvantaged group, encouraging the active engagement of that group."[19]

It is important to have representatives who look like us. Anne Phillips provides us with four reasons why descriptively representative politics is important. Representatives who look like us provide us with role models. For those who have been marginalized, having representatives who look like them can compensate for previous (and continuing) injustices. These representatives can also bring perspectives to the table of those who are often overlooked. Finally, their presence can encourage political participation among the electorate if voters perceive their government as more diverse and thus more legitimate as a reflection of the population as a whole.[20]

Representation involves more than appearances, however. It also involves activity. Hanna Pitkin argues that we should pay attention to what our representatives do on our behalf, the activity in which they engage. She suggests that representation means "the making present *in some sense* of something which is nevertheless *not* present literally or in fact."[21] It is to make present something that is not present. In *The Hunger Games*, Katniss makes present Rue even after her death in the arena. She makes present District 11 in that she *re-presents* the tragedy of Rue's death and challenges the oppressive conditions that led to it. In this way, she goes beyond the "looking like" of descriptive representation to the "acting like" of substantive representation.

In the case of Katniss as a representative of District 11, a majority–minority district, we are faced with the idea that descriptive representation can be based on group membership beyond race. That is, although Katniss is not black, she does substantively share in the concerns of the citizens of District 11. According to Mansbridge, group membership might involve shared visible characteristics and/or shared experiences. Although Katniss might not be black, she *is* from District 12, which is the poorest of the districts in Panem. She understands the impoverishment experienced by the citizens of District 11, and she understands the oppression experienced under the Capitol's authoritarian regime.[22]

Economic disparity in America continues to fall along racial lines. African Americans are disadvantaged in terms of earnings, wealth, and relative economic gains. Michael Dawson finds that African Americans share a sense of "linked fate," perceiving that their individual fates are linked to the group's fate. For this reason, it makes rational sense to align as a political voting bloc to "speak with one voice" to protect racial group interests that include issues of economic marginalization.[23]

Suzanne Dovi further suggests that descriptive representation is important when dealing with a dispossessed subgroup. Those who have been "unjustly excluded from and/or stigmatized by the political process and consequently lack the political and economic resources necessary for effective representation" particularly need descriptive representation in government.[24] When it comes to the politics of race and representation, it is important to recognize the distinction between an African American who has a mutual relationship with the black voters in the district and one who has a mutual relationship with the black impoverished voters in the district. Dovi argues that "when one has the choice between two descriptive representatives, one who has strong mutual relationships to dispossessed subgroups and another who does not, one should … prefer the former."[25] Katniss understands the oppression experienced by District 11. She has a strong mutual relationship with this district. It is a complex dynamic at work in the representation provided by Katniss for Rue's memory and the people of District 11.

In the end, District 11 identifies with Katniss because she conveys through her friendship to Rue that she is one of them and through her shared experience of poverty that she is dispossessed as well. As a surrogate representative of Rue and District 11, she becomes the mouthpiece of the movement. She serves as a role model to others, shares their perspective, and inspires them to mobilize and rebel.

The Relevance of Race and Representation Today

When *The Hunger Games* appeared in theaters, some fans criticized the casting of an African-American actress to play Rue.[26] Though Collins depicted Rue in the novels as a twelve-year-old girl with dark skin, some fans were "'shocked,' or confused, or just plain angry." Dodai Stewart, a journalist writing in *Jezebel*, presented some of the Tweets (140 character messages on the social network Twitter) fans posted after the movie's release:

> "I was pumped about the Hunger Games. Until I learned that a black girl was playing Rue."
>
> "I know, rue is too black for what I pictured…"
>
> "After watching the hunger games preview 6 times in a row, I realized Rue is black. whaaaaat?!" #shocked
>
> "HOW IN THE WORLD ARE THEY GOING TO MAKE RUE A FREAKIN BLACK BITCH IN THE MOVIE?!?!?!?!??! lolol not to be racist buuuut…. I'm angry now ;o"
>
> "I just pictured darker skin, didn't really take it all the way to black."
>
> "Sense when has Rue been a nigger."[27]

This reaction to the casting of Rue reinforces that race plays a major role in shaping American identity politics. The marginalization of an actress based on the color of her skin reflects the marginalization of District 11 based on the race of its residents. With strained race relations in major United States cities due to charges of racial profiling and police brutality by law enforcement, it is not difficult to understand the world Suzanne Collins has created in District 11. The dynamic between this district and the Capitol and the employment of Katniss as a spokesperson for these dispossessed citizens resonates with us because we are familiar with the identity politics and the representation that accompanies it. We see blacks representing blacks descriptively and substantively in public and in government. We also see the backlash to these figures and the politics they represent.

In *the New Yorker*, Anna Holmes asks a provocative question concerning this backlash to Rue's casting:.

> If the stories we tell ourselves about the future, however disturbing, don't include black people; if readers of "The Hunger Games" are so blind as to skip over the author's specific details and themes of appearance, race, and class, then what does it say about the stories we tell ourselves regarding the present?[28]

Identity politics continues, descriptive representation continues, because identity matters. Race is relevant whether we like it or not.

Conclusion

The Hunger Games presents a rich story of identity politics, one that includes oppression along racial and economic lines. Collins's depiction of District 11 and District 12 reminds the reader of the American South and rural Appalachia. Through song, dress, ritual, symbol, and imagery, the books and films capture the spirit of oppression and the hope of protest movements. Further, the relationship of Katniss and Rue, and later Katniss and District 11, helps us understand the relevance of representation to identity politics. Through Katniss we come to appreciate the difference between descriptive and substantive representation and the role of surrogate representatives in speaking for under-represented groups. Finally, we appreciate the importance of identity to politics today.

In June of 2014, reports surfaced of youth in Thailand using the three-fingered salute invented by Katniss in *The Hunger Games* to express solidarity and protest against the military. The salute carried symbolic weight in *The Hunger Games* as "a way for the downtrodden people of Panem to mutely register their defiance of the government."[29] Military rulers saw this expression as defiance, "a new form of silent resistance to the coup," and threatened arrest for those using the salute. In commenting on behalf of the coup's leaders, Colonel Weerachon Sukhondhapatipak said, "If it is an obvious form of resistance, then we have to control it so it doesn't cause any disorder in the country."[30] One online photo montage labeled the fingers of the salute "1. No Coup, 2. Liberty, 3. Democracy."[31] Identity politics and the fight against oppression speak to our humanity; in *The Hunger Games*, it is spoken in the universal language of hope and freedom.

Chapter Discussion Questions

1. In *The Hunger Games*, Katniss uses a three-fingered salute to identify with the citizens of District 11. Do we have any symbols in American culture that represent oppression and identification? Who uses them and to what effect?
2. Why do you think District 11 in *The Hunger Games* is portrayed as African American rather than Hispanic or Native American? Is there something about the experience of African Americans that makes this reference particularly meaningful?
3. Does Collins's story of race, class, and oppression in *The Hunger Games* carry a message for us today when confronted with headlines of race-based police brutality? How do we respond in a constructive way?

Notes

1 Madison, James. "*Federalist* 10." The Avalon Project (187). http://avalon.law.yale.edu/18th_century/fed10.asp, accessed April 30, 2015.

2 Campbell, Angus, Philip Converse, Warren Miller, and Donald Stokes. 1960. *The American voter.* Chicago: University of Chicago Press; Lazarfeld, P. F., B. Berelson, and H. Gaudet. 1948. *The people's choice: How the voter makes up his mind in a presidential campaign.* New York: Columbia University Press.
3 Arrow, V. 2012. *The Panem companion: From Mellark Bakery to Mockingjays.* Dallas: Ben Bella Books.
4 McCarty, Justin. "As a major US problem, race relations sharply rises," *Gallup,*http://www.gallup.com/poll/180257/major-problem-race-relations-sharply-rises.aspx, accessed April 27, 2015.
5 "Race and ethnicity," *PollingReport.com,* http://www.pollingreport.com/race.htm. accessed January 16, 2015.
6 Ibid.
7 "Race relations." *Gallup,* http://www.gallup.com/poll/1687/race-relations.aspx, accessed January 16, 2015.
8 Arrow, *The Panem companion,* 140.
9 Mason, Amelia. 2014. "The hidden roots of 'Hunger Games' hit song? Murder ballads, civil rights hymns." *The Artery,* http://artery.wbur.org/2014/12/10/hunger-games-mockingjay, accessed January 15, 2015.
10 Ibid.
11 Ibid.
12 Prilleltensky, Isaac and Lev Gonick. 1996. "Polities change, oppression remains: On the psychology and politics of oppression," *Political Psychology,* 17(1): 127–148.
13 *Associated Press.* 2015. "New Congress includes more women, minorities." *The New York Times,* http://www.nytimes.com/aponline/2015/01/04/us/politics/ap-us-congress- by-the-numbers.html?_r=0, accessed January 15, 2015.
14 Collins, Suzanne. 2008. *The Hunger Games.* New York: Scholastic Press, 45.
15 Mansbridge, Jane. 2003. "Rethinking representation," *American Political Science Review* 97(4): 515–528; 523.
16 Ibid., 515.
17 Dovi, Suzanne, 2002. "Preferable descriptive representatives: Will just any woman, black, or Latino do?" *The American Political Science Review,* 96(4): 729–743; 729.
18 Ibid., 736.
19 Ibid.
20 Phillips, Anne. 1998. "Democracy and representation: Or, why should it matter who our representatives are?" In Anne Phillips, ed., *Feminism and Politics.* Oxford: Oxford University Press, 224–241.
21 Pitkin, Hanna Fenichel. 1967. *The concept of representation.* Berkeley, CA: University of California Press, 8–9.
22 Mansbridge, Jane. 1999. "Should blacks represent blacks and women represent women? A contingent 'yes,'" *Journal of Politics,* 61(3): 628–657.
23 Dawson, Michael C. 1995. *Behind the mule: Race and class in African-American politics.* Princeton, NJ: Princeton University Press.
24 Dovi, "Preferable descriptive representatives," 738.
25 Ibid., 741.
26 Rosen, Christopher. 2012. "Hunger Games' racist tweets: Fans upset because of Rue's race." *Huffington Post,* http://www.huffingtonpost.com/2012/03/26/hunger-games-racist-tweets-rue_n_1380377.html, accessed January 12, 2015.
27 Stewart, Dodai. 2012. "Racist *Hunger Games* fans are very disappointed." *Jezebel,* http://jezebel.com/5896408/racist-hunger-games-fans-dont-care-how-much-money-the-movie-made, accessed April 30, 2015.

28 Holmes, Anna. 2012. "White until proven black: Imagining race in Hunger Games." *The New Yorker*, http://www.newyorker.com/books/page-turner/white-until-proven-black-imagining-race-in-hunger-games, accessed January 12, 2015.
29 Gilbey, Ryan. 2014. "How the Hunger Games salute is fighting oppression in Thailand." *The Guardian*, http://www.theguardian.com/film/shortcuts/2014/jun/02/hunger-games-salute-fighting-oppression-thailand-panem, accessed January 15, 2015.
30 Associated Press. 2014. "Hunger Games salute banned by Thai military." *The Guardian*, http://www.theguardian.com/world/2014/jun/03/hunger-games-salute-banned-thailand, accessed January 15, 2015.
31 Ibid.

PART V
States

13

DEMOCRATIC BREAKDOWN IN *V FOR VENDETTA*

Julie VanDusky-Allen

BOISE STATE UNIVERSITY

> I suddenly had this feeling that everything was connected. Like I could see the whole thing, one long chain of events that stretched all the way back before Larkhill. I felt like I could see everything that happened, and everything that is going to happen. It was like a perfect pattern, laid out in front of me. And I realized we're all part of it… and all trapped by it.
>
> – Inspector Eric Finch, *V for Vendetta*

V for Vendetta is set in the United Kingdom during the late 2020s. Democracy no longer exists; instead, the Norsefire Party rules the country through a party dictatorship. It is an extremist conservative party that espouses British nationalism and radical religious values. High Chancellor Adam Sutler, the party's leader, keeps tight control over what party members and British citizens can say and do. Consequently, government officials arrest, torture, and execute anyone who disagrees with the party or its leaders. In addition, the party determines who holds government positions and what types of policies the government pursues.

How does *V for Vendetta* explain the United Kingdom going from being one of the oldest fully institutionalized democracies in the world to a totalitarian party dictatorship in a span of less than twenty years? According to the film, it happened in part because the United Kingdom faced a series of crises its democratically elected government could not resolve. It all began when the United States started a war that devastated the world's political and economic systems. During this same period, a series of new diseases and viruses spread throughout the United Kingdom. Then, the chaos came to a climax when terrorists staged three biological attacks that killed thousands of people. Throughout all of these events, it seemed as if the government was becoming incapable of combating the myriad problems associated with these crises. Slowly, a new political party, the Norsefire Party, rose to power. It promised voters that if it took complete control over the British government, it could solve all of the problems facing the United Kingdom. Eventually, the party won 87 percent of the votes in a nationwide election. Once in power, the party took advantage of majoritarian political institutions (which gives majority parties a great deal of power) in the United Kingdom legally to suspend democracy, appoint Adam Sutler as High Chancellor, and abolish political opposition in the country.

The British political system in *V for Vendetta* is so far removed from the democratic system of government in the United Kingdom today that it seems almost impossible for a similar situation to occur in the real world. This is especially the case because democratic breakdown is a rare event. However, whereas it is unlikely for democracy to fail in the United Kingdom, it is still possible as long as certain conditions are met. Throughout the rest of this chapter, I am going to discuss democratic breakdown in depth and focus on how a political party could undermine democracy in a country like the United Kingdom. I will use the case of democratic breakdown in the movie *V for Vendetta* as an illustration of how this could occur.

This chapter proceeds as follows: First, I will discuss the basic characteristics of democracy and discuss how rare it is for democratic breakdown to occur. Then I will discuss how democracy could break down in the United Kingdom in a similar fashion to how it occurred in *V for Vendetta*. I argue that majoritarian political institutions in the United Kingdom could allow a democratically elected political party to slowly increase its power and take over as a party dictatorship (where a single party controls all aspects of government activity) if the right conditions are present. Specifically, a major crisis must exist and British elites and citizens must allow the party to concentrate power to solve the crisis.

Democratic Breakdown: An Overview

Before I discuss how a democracy breaks down into a dictatorship, I am going to define what the terms democracy and dictatorship mean. We must know what these terms mean in order to properly determine whether a country is a democracy or a dictatorship. In general, four characteristics must exist for a country to be considered democratic. First, the country must have free and fair elections. "Free elections" mean that anyone can run for office. "Fair elections" mean that the rules that determine who wins do not favor one party or individual over anyone else; the elections are up to the voters. Next, there needs to be a shift in power between political factions from time to time. A single individual or party cannot hold onto power indefinitely. In addition, election losers must accept their losses and not try to undermine elected officials using non-democratic means. And last, election winners should not have the incentive to use their power to take over government using non-democratic means.[1]

In contrast, three conditions must be met in order for a country to be considered a dictatorship. First, only a small group of people gets to select the executive. Usually there is an unspoken but generally accepted process by which these officials are selected, although this process can be ignored from time to time. In addition, political, economic, and military elites in the country have to provide some support for these officials' rule; otherwise, these elites would try to take over government themselves. Last, there can only be limited constraints on executive power.[2]

Based on the above criteria, we know that, up until recently, most countries in the world have not been considered democratic. In order to demonstrate how uncommon it was for a country to be democratic in the world throughout history, I gathered data from the POLITY IV dataset.[3] The POLITY IV dataset classifies countries throughout the world from 1800 to 2013 as democratic, anocratic (or mixed-system), or autocratic (or dictatorial). Based on this data, throughout most of modern history, most of the countries in the world have either been autocratic or anocratic, not democratic. In 1800, at the start of the dataset, 0 percent of countries in the world were democracies. It was not until 1809 that the dataset included one democracy (the United States),[4] but even this was not fully democratic. In addition, it was not until 2001 that more than half the countries in the world were democracies. Hence, as demonstrated in Figure 13.1, throughout most of modern history, it was uncommon for a country to be democratic.

Although it was uncommon for a country to be considered democratic throughout the modern period, it was even more uncommon for a democratic

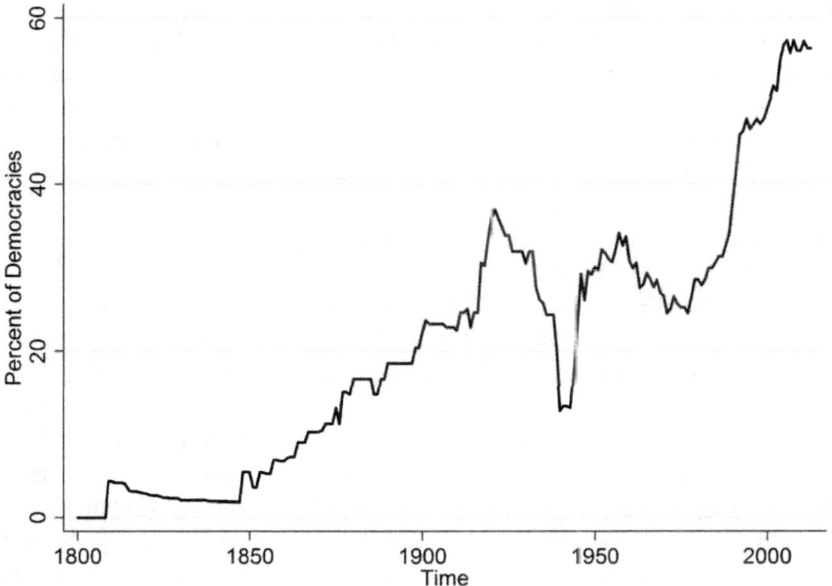

FIGURE 13.1 The Percent of Countries that Were Democracies in the World (1800-2013)

country to break down and regress back into a mixed system or dictatorship.[5] By examining democratic countries in the POLITY IV dataset,[6] I measured 4,656 years where democracies were stable in the dataset and only 86 cases where democracy broke down (or only 1.8 percent of the time). Hence, this data tells us that it is rare for a country to go from having a system where voters select political officials to having a system where only a small group of people selects political officials.

Given that democratic breakdown is a rare event, it is somewhat difficult to pinpoint the exact conditions under which it occurs. The existing literature on democratic breakdown suggests that several conditions must be met for a democracy to fail. According to Paul Brooker's framework, three general conditions must be met for a dictatorship to emerge: the dictators that take over government (be it the military elites, a political party, or an individual) must have the (1) means, (2) motive, and (3) opportunity to take over government.

First, in order for the potential dictators to take over a democratically elected government, they have to *be able to* take over government. There are several methods by which they can accomplish this task. They can use force, or the threat of force, to take over. They can also take over through legal means by being elected and rewriting the rules to keep themselves in power. Rewriting the rules could include eliminating elections or having elections but only allowing one party to run candidates.

Next, in order for the potential dictators to take over, they must also want to take over government. There are several reasons why a group would want to take over government. Democratically elected officials may be deeply divided over policy issues, meaning that they are incapable of passing legislation and running the day-to-day functions of government. In such cases, a small group of people may take over government for the good of the nation, so that it can ensure that the basic functions of government are met.[7] Of course, groups may take over government for nefarious reasons as well. These groups may have a radical policy agenda[8] (such as creating a socialist or communist economy, or repressing a religious or ethnic minority), and the only way that agenda will be established is if they take over government and eliminate all opposition to their cause.

Last, in order for the potential dictators to take over, they must also have the opportunity to take over government. More specifically, other elites and citizens in the country must generally agree that they would rather have the potential dictators rule the country than have a democratically elected government rule the country. This could happen in several ways. A crisis may occur, like an economic depression or a major corruption scandal, and the government may not be able to agree on how to handle the crisis. Then a group of potential dictators can try to convince the public and other elites that they are better capable of addressing the crisis than the democratically elected government.[9] Alternatively, the military may become weakened due to a war, which could make it easier for other types of elites to take over government, as the military would be incapable of preventing the potential dictators from taking over.[10]

Brooker's argument provides a basic framework to explain how dictators take over democracies, but it cannot tell us how dictators take over *specific types* of democracies. Although all democracies share similar characteristics (i.e., free and fair elections and respect for the rule of law), there is a great deal of variation in democratic institutions from country to country. Generally speaking, there are two types of democracies: majoritarian democracies and consensus democracies. Majoritarian democracies are designed to encourage two political parties to compete for control over government, whereas consensus democracies encourage multiple parties to work together to control government.[11] As a result, the specific factors that give potential dictators the means, motive, and opportunity to take over government in majoritarian democracies differ from the factors that give groups the means, motive, and opportunity to take over government in consensus democracies. In the rest of this chapter, I will focus specifically on how a certain type of dictator, a dictatorial political party, is able to take over a majoritarian democracy.

Means to Take Over Democracy: Majoritarian Democratic Institutions

The Norsefire Party in *V for Vendetta* took advantage of the majoritarian democratic political process in the United Kingdom in order to misappropriate power, suspend democracy, and take over the government. Although the United Kingdom is one of the oldest democracies in the world, there are several characteristics about the democratic system in the United Kingdom that may create the conditions for a single party to take over government. The United Kingdom is a majoritarian, parliamentary democracy, which gives a majority party a great deal of power over the policymaking process. In addition, the political system severely limits the power of opposition parties from checking the power of the party in power. Below I discuss the specific aspects of democracy in the United Kingdom that may give a single political party the means to take over democracy: (1) the executive is chosen from and can be removed by the legislature, (2) there are only two major political parties, (3) executive power is concentrated within one party, (4) the executive dominates the policymaking process, (5) there is constitutional flexibility, (6) judicial review does not exist, and (7) there is a unitary and centralized government.

Two-Party Parliamentary Systems and Executive Dominance

In order to understand how a single party could take the political system in a parliamentary system, first you have to understand how parliamentary systems work.

In a parliamentary system, the executive and legislative branches are fused in the national legislature (known in the United Kingdom as Parliament). Voters vote for legislators (or Members of Parliament or MPs) in a national election.

Then legislators choose the executive (or prime minister who leads the Cabinet) from the legislators themselves. Throughout their term, the prime minister and members of the Cabinet get to set the policy agenda, giving them a great deal of influence over the policymaking process.[12]

Next, MPs, including the prime minister, can hold office for a fixed period of time (five years maximum in the United Kingdom). However, MPs can also remove the executive through a no-confidence vote. With a no-confidence vote, the prime minister introduces a piece of legislation with a no-confidence vote attached to it. The prime minister wants the MPs to support the bill, but if they vote against it, they vote no-confidence in the government. As a result, Parliament dissolves and new parliamentary elections are held.[13]

Next, because the United Kingdom is a majoritarian parliamentary system, there are only two major political parties (usually split over socioeconomic lines), meaning that a single party controls at least 50% + 1 of the seats in parliament at any given time. As a result, the majority party gets to choose the prime minister. This gives the prime minister a great deal of power. MPs from the majority party are highly unlikely to vote against the prime minister's bills because they generally agree with the prime minister's policy positions and they want to maintain their seats in Parliament. The prime minister knows this, and thus can introduce a piece of legislation that some of the MPs in his party may disagree with, but they will vote in favor of the legislation to avoid a no-confidence vote.

Although a prime minister in a single-party, majority system has a great deal of influence over policymaking, this does not necessarily give the prime minister the means to take over government. A prime minister would need a great deal of support in parliament to convince MPs to suspend democracy and keep the ruling party in power indefinitely. Many MPs may support democratic principles, and may not want to stay in power indefinitely. Hence, the prime minister's party would have to control more than just 50% + 1 of the seats in parliament. Ideally, the party should control a supermajority of seats, so that the prime minister could garner enough votes to change the rules to stay in power.

In *V for Vendetta*, the Norsefire Party gets elected to parliament with 87 percent of the vote in a national election (whereas the Conservative and Labour Parties share the other 13 percent of the vote). This gave the party the supermajority it needed to not only select the prime minister, but also rewrite the rules to keep themselves in power. Almost immediately after taking office, the Norsefire Party suspended democracy, abolished the prime minister's position, and appointed Adam Sutler to a new position of High Chancellor. They also eliminated any opposition. The party arrested, tortured, and killed anyone who opposed the party or the High Chancellor. In addition, after the party established control over the British government, it ensured that citizens continued to comply with the party by setting up a complex surveillance system throughout the country. Spies would drive around in vans and listen in on people's conversations, just to make sure they were not espousing views that were contrary to those of the party. In addition, the party controlled people's thoughts by blacklisting any type of art or media that contradicted the party's views. The party also controlled all the news media so that it would avoid any bad press. This limited the ability of opposition forces to question and to undermine the party's rule. In sum, the Norsefire Party used majoritarian parliamentary institutions to legally undermine the democratic process in the United Kingdom and establish a party dictatorship.[14]

Constitutional Flexibility

Another aspect of majoritarian democracy in the United Kingdom that could give a single party the means to take over government is constitutional flexibility. Constitutional flexibility means that it is very easy to change the constitution. This means that a single party could easily rewrite the constitution to keep the party in power.[15]

The United Kingdom is somewhat unique in that it has an "unwritten constitution" and it is easy to change. Most democracies in the world today have a single, written, legal document that outlines the structure of the political system in the country. This document usually defines how government officials are elected or selected, how they are removed from office, and what they can do while in office. In addition, there is a process by which the constitution can be changed. Usually any changes to the constitution require agreement of a supermajority of political elites and voters. The United Kingdom's constitution is different because democracy in the United Kingdom evolved slowly over time. There was no major event, like a constitutional convention, where founders met together to design political institutions. Instead, political officials slowly introduced democratic principles into the political system over time. Therefore, instead of a single, written document, the British constitution is a compilation of Acts of Parliament (such as the Parliament Acts of 1911 and 1949), common law, customs, and conventions.[16]

Because the constitution in the United Kingdom is "unwritten," a simple majority in Parliament can change it. Hence, if a single party had enough seats in Parliament, and wanted to eliminate opposition parties and take control over government indefinitely, they could simply pass a series of laws to keep themselves in power. This is exactly what the Norsefire Party did in *V for Vendetta.* It won 87 percent of the vote in a national election, giving it enough seats in Parliament to abolish the unwritten constitution. In its place, the party established a totalitarian, party dictatorship where the party would determine who could hold government office and what types of policies the government would pursue. The party also made it illegal for anyone to oppose the government.

Lack of Judicial Review

Another aspect of majoritarian democracy in the United Kingdom that could allow a single party to take over government is lack of judicial review. There is no independent judiciary in the United Kingdom that determines whether Acts of Parliament conform to the "unwritten" constitution. Hence, if a parliamentary party rewrote the constitution to eliminate opposition parties and keep themselves in power indefinitely, there is no independent judiciary to declare that the party is violating democratic principles.[17] In *V for Vendetta*, there was no judicial branch that could have prevented the Norsefire Party from changing the rules, undermining democracy, and taking control over government. If an independent judiciary existed, the Norsefire Party might have had a harder time taking over and establishing a party dictatorship, at least through legal means.

Unitary and Centralized Government

Unitary and centralized government is another aspect of majoritarian democracy in the United Kingdom that could give a single party the means to take over government. In these types of systems, local governments have limited power. The central government in these systems can both create and dissolve a local government. The central government also determines what types of powers a local government has. It can determine whether a local government can collect taxes, what it can collect taxes on, and what it can spend tax revenue on. In other words, the central government can control what types of policies each local government pursues. If a local government tries to shift policy far away from the ruling party's policy preferences, then the central government can cut funding from the local government or dissolve it.[18]

When a central government controls what local governments do, that means that there are no local governments that can challenge Parliament. Therefore, in a country with a centralized, unitary government, if a single political party tries to take over government indefinitely, there are no local government units that can legitimately challenge the party's actions. For example, when the Norsefire Party established a party dictatorship in the United Kingdom, there were no local governments that could legitimately prevent the party from taking control.

Motive: National Interest and Repressing Religious and Ethnic Minorities

Although majoritarian political institutions could give a political party the ability to take over government and establish a dictatorship in the United Kingdom, in order for this to happen, a party would have to exist in Britain that would want to establish a dictatorship. Currently, no viable party exists in the United Kingdom that would want to establish a party dictatorship. However, in *V for Vendetta*, such a party did exist, the Norsefire Party. This made it more likely that democracy could break down in the United Kingdom in the movie.

Publicly, the Norsefire Party took control of the British political system because (1) the country was facing several crises, (2) the existing democratic government was incapable of dealing with these crises, and (3) the Norsefire Party wanted to resolve these crises. Privately, the Norsefire Party wanted to take over the British government because it wanted to establish an extremist right-wing, nationalistic/religious totalitarian dictatorship. Once it took control, it repressed anyone who was not British and not Christian. The party banned any non-Christian religious texts from the country. Furthermore, if an ordinary citizen engaged in "immoral" behavior, the government tortured and killed them; however, it is important to note that high-ranking members of the party often engaged in immoral behavior but were exempt from punishment. Hence, the Norsefire Party's real motive for establishing a party dictatorship was to force citizens of the United Kingdom to adopt the party's political and social views, and eliminate anyone who disagreed with these views.

Opportunity: Consent of Other Elites and Citizens

Even if a political party has the means and motive to undermine democracy and establish a dictatorship, it also needs the consent of both other elites and the masses in order to take over. In the movie *V for Vendetta*, both conditions were met. Economic, social, and military elites in the country allowed the Norsefire Party to take control of government, whereas British citizens agreed that the party should take over.

The economic elites that encouraged the Norsefire Party to establish a dictatorship in *V for Vendetta* were leaders of major pharmaceutical companies. These company heads wanted to create a virus that the United Kingdom could use as a weapon to wipe out an entire civilization while leaving its wealth intact. However, they also wanted to make sure they had a cure for the virus so no other country could use it against the United Kingdom. In order to create this virus, they needed human test subjects to test the virus on and test potential cures. Because many subjects would inevitably die in these trials, such a study would be highly unethical and a democratically elected government that protects civil liberties would be highly unlikely to support such a project. In addition, even if the pharmaceutical companies eventually developed the virus in other ways, the United Kingdom probably would not be able to use the virus as a weapon because it would violate the Biological Weapons Convention, which prohibits the use of biological weapons in warfare. However, the Norsefire Party did not respect civil rights and liberties. It would have had no problem providing test subjects for such a study and would have had no problem using the weapon in warfare. In fact, the party would want those companies to create such a weapon and would pay those companies a substantial amount of money to develop such a deadly weapon. Hence, owners of these major pharmaceutical companies would be strongly in favor of the Norsefire Party coming to power because the party would have paid them to create the deadly virus.

The Norsefire Party also convinced leaders of the Church of England (the established church in England) to support their bid to set up a party dictatorship. The movie only briefly mentions that members of the church supported a party dictatorship. Many leaders of the Church of England probably supported the party because the party supported Christian values. However, some leaders of the Church of England were corrupt, and aligning themselves with the Norsefire Party gave those specific leaders more leeway in being corrupt.

Next, it is important to note that the movie is silent on how military leaders responded to the Norsefire Party's bid to establish a party dictatorship in the United Kingdom. I can only assume that, given the massive war that devastated the world's political and economic systems, the British military was severely weakened or overstretched during the time in which the party was coming to power. Otherwise, the military might have prevented the party from taking over. If this was the case, it made it a lot easier for the party to take over the United Kingdom.

Last, most British citizens gave the Norsefire Party their consent to take over the United Kingdom. (The party executed anyone who did not consent.) The citizens that consented had faced several political, economic, and health crises, and it did not seem as though the democratically elected government could deal with those issues. There was a major world war, people were dying from new diseases and viruses, and terrorists were wreaking havoc across the United Kingdom. People were afraid that the situation was going to continue to get worse. They believed that only a strong, centralized dictatorship could adequately address all of the issues the United Kingdom was facing. As a result, these citizens threw their support behind the Norsefire Party and supported the establishment of a party dictatorship.

Therefore, in sum, the United Kingdom became a party dictatorship in *V for Vendetta* for three reasons. First, majoritarian political institutions in the United Kingdom give a majority party the means to change the constitution to keep themselves in power indefinitely if they want to. Second, a party in the United Kingdom, the Norsefire Party, was willing to take advantage of their majority status to change the rules and keep themselves in power. Last, key players in the United Kingdom (elites and citizens) wanted a centralized political party to change the rules and keep themselves in power.

Would Democracy in the United Kingdom Really Break Down?

Although the scenario portrayed in *V for Vendetta* is something that citizens of majoritarian parliamentary democracies should think more deeply about, it is highly unlikely that such a situation would happen in the real world. The United Kingdom is an older democracy, and older democracies are unlikely to break down, as demonstrated by Figure 13.2. According to data in the POLITY IV dataset,[19] of the eighty-four democracies that broke down in the dataset, the average age of the democracy was 12.5 years old. The United Kingdom has been democratic for 133 years, so this makes it unlikely to break down.

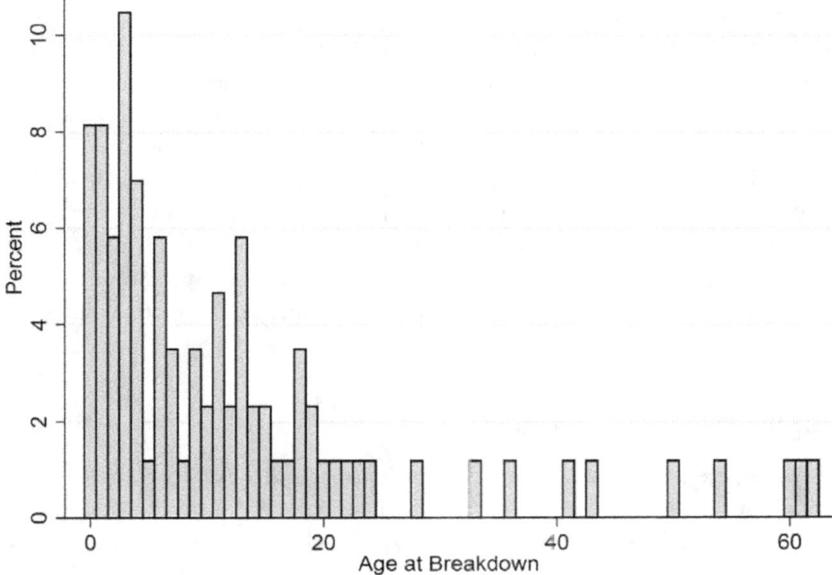

FIGURE 13.2 The Age of Democracies at Breakdown (1800-2013)

It is not surprising that older democracies are less likely to break down. In older democracies, there is a long history of the democratically elected government solving crises. Hence, when a new crisis occurs, citizens have observed their democratically elected officials solving crises in the past, so they are more likely to believe that they can do it again and less likely to think introducing a dictatorship is necessary to resolve the crisis. For example, during World War II, the Conservative Party in the United Kingdom controlled enough seats in Parliament to safely control the executive and keep Prime Minister Winston Churchill in power. But instead of Churchill ruling alone during this crisis, he actually formed a coalition government that included members of both the Labour and Liberal parties. He did this to send a signal to the Germans that the United Kingdom was unified in trying to defeat the Nazi Party. The United Kingdom's ability to adhere to democratic principles and still win World War II is but one in a series of events British citizens can refer to when considering whether the democratically elected British government can handle similar crises in the future (others include World War I, surviving the Great Depression, rebuilding after two world wars, and coming out victorious after the Cold War). Nevertheless, even though democracy is unlikely to break down in the United Kingdom, the scenario presented in *V for Vendetta* is something that should give citizens of majoritarian democracies pause. We currently live in a world that is generally stable when it comes to political, economic, and social conditions. If the world ever experienced major political and economic crises similar to what happened in *V for Vendetta*, a dictatorial political party could emerge in a majoritarian democracy that could easily take over government if it won enough seats.

Although beyond the scope of this chapter, I think it is important to conclude by mentioning that consensus and mixed-type democracies are also capable of breaking down and regressing back into dictatorships. There are historical examples of all different types of democracies that broke down. The reasons behind these breakdowns are complex, just as in the case in *V for Vendetta*. Thus, to further our understanding of the factors that can lead to democratic breakdown in specific countries, we need to identify the specific circumstances and specific actors (be it parties, military leaders, or individuals) that influence breakdown in those countries.

Chapter Discussion Questions

1. Compare and contrast the basic characteristics of democracies and dictatorships.
2. If you could design your own legislature, what kind of rules and systems would you include to make it work? Consider problems like efficiency, representation, and capacity to enforce rules versus concerns over liberty.
3. Do you think democracy is likely to break down in the United Kingdom in the near future? Why or why not?

Notes

1 Linz, Juan J. 1978. *The breakdown of democratic regimes: Crisis, breakdown, & reequilibration*, Baltimore, MD: The Johns Hopkins University Press; Hagopian, Frances and Scott P. Mainwaring. 2005. *The third wave of democratization in Latin America: Advances and setbacks*. Cambridge: Cambridge University Press; Norris, Pippa, 2008. *Driving democracy: Do power-sharing institutions work?* Cambridge: Cambridge University Press.

2 Brooker, Paul. 2000. *Non-democratic regimes: Theory, government, & politics*. New York: Palgrave MacMillan; Ghandi, Jennifer. 2008. *Political institutions under dictatorship*. Cambridge: Cambridge University Press.

3 Marshall, Monty G., Ted Robert Gurr, and Keith Jaggers. 2014. *Polity IV project: Political regime characteristics and transitions: 1800–2013*, Center for Systemic Peace, http://www.systemicpeace.org, accessed April 28, 2015.

4 According to the Polity IV dataset, after 1809, the United States had a more open and competitive political process.

5 Hagopian and Mainwaring, *The third wave*.

6 Marshall et al., *Polity IV project*.

7 A historical example is Brazil in 1964. Brazil experienced a severe economic crisis and the national government was incapable of agreeing on a solution to the problem. The military stepped in to make sure the government could continue to run and established a military dictatorship that lasted twenty years.

8 A historical example is the Third Reich. The Nazi Party wanted to radically reshape German society, while also eliminating the Jewish population from Germany. It could not do so unless it had complete control over the German government, as the other parties would have prevented the Nazi Party from pursing such a radical agenda.

9 Hagopian and Mainwaring, *The third wave*.
10 Brooker, *Non-democratic regimes*; Linz, *The breakdown of democratic regimes*.
11 Lijphart, Arend. 1999. *Patterns of democracy: Government forms and performance in thirty-six countries*. New Haven, CT: Yale University Press.
12 Lijphart, *Patterns of democracy*.
13 Ibid.
14 At the end of the movie, V blows up the Houses of Parliament. This seems likes a symbolic gesture, as parliamentary institutions gave the Norsefire Party the means to take over the United Kingdom.
15 Lijphart, *Patterns of democracy*.
16 Ibid.
17 Ibid.
18 Ibid.
19 Marshall et al., *Polity IV project*.

14

UNDERSTANDING CIVIL WAR THROUGH *STAR WARS*

Michael A. Allen

BOISE STATE UNIVERSITY

The assault on the Death Star seems lost for the rebels: One X-Wing remains in the Death Star trench with active proton torpedoes. Luke Skywalker represents the last hope for the rebellion's assault and Darth Vader has him in his targeting computer's crosshairs. Right before Vader fires, the self-interested Han Solo comes from off-camera and provides the necessary cover to allow Skywalker to take a final shot at the thermal exhaust port. He makes the shot, the Death Star explodes, Darth Vader's ship floats into the vastness of space, and the movie concludes with Luke, Han Solo, and Chewbacca receiving medals from the Rebel Alliance. How did the rebellion convince a farm boy, a smuggler, and a fugitive slave to risk their lives fighting the Empire? The study of civil war in international relations can help us to understand how *A New Hope* has remained a compelling space opera for the past several decades.

The beginning, duration, and conclusion of civil war all contain a multitude of intersecting and crosscutting forces that cause, prolong, and conclude such conflicts. From the end of World War II until the present day, civil wars have become the most common kind of wars states participate in and can be more costly (in both human and economic terms) than wars between countries in the contemporary period. Consequently, it should be no surprise that a space opera that continues to captivate global culture employs an intergalactic civil war as the background for its plot. This chapter explores what *Star Wars Episode IV: A New Hope* can teach us about civil wars, as well as what the research on civil wars can tell us about what is really happening in the *Star Wars* universe.

Mobilization and Recruitment

Conflict between people and their government has been going on for as long as governments have existed; however, the version of these conflicts we see is increasingly more complicated today than it was thousands of years ago. Traditionally, states were less interested in private property protection, the rule of law, and being the exclusive actor that could exercise the legitimate use of force within its territory. Instead, states used to be interested primarily in increasing their power and efficacy internationally, and would often allow competitors for state power, such as mercenaries and private armies, to exist within their borders. Challengers for sovereignty could hire private armies (or use their own) to challenge the state, and the contest for the right to rule would play out on the battlefield. In the modern state system, however, these alternative avenues of power and force are far less prominent, and a potential rival for governance cannot simply hire a standing army; instead, they must go out and actively recruit people to become part of their campaign.

Convincing people to give up their lives in the pursuit of installing you (or your group) as the legitimate government is difficult to do, as they are unlikely to think your goals are worth their life. This is compounded further by having another actor (the state) actively dissuading the same people (the ones you are trying to convince) from taking up arms against them by using techniques of accommodation as well as repression. This twin nature of two actors fighting over similar populations of people has led to a healthy scholarship surrounding mobilization of individuals by both rebel groups and states. Traditionally, scholars debate whether it is grievances, greed, or some combination of the two that convinces individuals to risk their lives for a better political system and a better tomorrow. Below, I discuss each of these concepts in greater detail.

Grievances

Grievances are the category of all the conditions and harms that people are unhappy with in their life that may encourage them to seek change in the status quo.[1] The conditions they experience that bring them unhappiness can vary quite a bit, but the traditional major factors scholars point to are political and economic disparity. In terms of rebellion, grievances are existing costs that an individual thinks may cease to exist if a revolution is successful. Economic and political hardship can come from several sources in an individual's life: they can come from their life choices, missed opportunities, economic change, job loss, lack of opportunity or advancement, political or legal barriers to economic advancement, etc. However, not all hardships are equal and temporary setbacks are not the ones most likely to make someone join an armed resistance against the state. Instead, the more likely conditions that encourage radicalization are structural relationships that foreclose opportunity to an individual.[2] Political and economic exclusion can limit a person's prospects enough that risking one's own life may seem like the best opportunity to escape poverty.

In *Episode IV*, we can see seemingly destitute conditions from the very beginning as we visit Tatooine; people are generally not well off and there is little sign of large infrastructure (i.e., roads, centralized power plants) or development. The main economic hub of the region, Mos Eisley, is a "wretched hive of scum and villainy" according to Obi-Wan Kenobi as he guides Luke Skywalker there to find a pilot.[3] The opportunities for individuals within Tatooine are clear: you can be a farmer, you can join the military (by enrolling in the Imperial Academy), or you can abandon polite society and become part of the criminal underworld. Of note, however: Tatooine does not appear to be a base for rebels. Even though it is a great place to hide from the Empire and it has many black market opportunities, rebels do not appear to be actively recruiting from the planet. This might be partly due to its peripheral location in the galaxy, but it is also because there is a lucrative alternative to rebellion: organized crime. Some scholars argue that the state behaves very similarly to organized crime in how it functions[4] and this comparison is apt for rebel groups (one that we will return to shortly). For now, it is important to note that this offers a third competitor for individuals in regards to violence and social rule: we have the state, the rebels, and organized crime.

Political deprivation works in a similar way to economic deprivation, as it is where people systematically do not have access to make policy decisions. A straightforward means of allowing people access to the political institutions of a state is through democratic institutions (people can vote to have their grievances addressed or they can vote for people they think will address their issues). However, even non-democratic institutions can be politically inclusive and facilitate some level of representation within a government. For example, autocratic government may have appointees for particular groups that are otherwise excluded from the political process and can advocate for their issues. If the autocracy contains decision-making bodies of multiple members, having representative individuals from various societal cleavages in society (i.e., age, gender, ethnic, or religious lines) may enable some level of political inclusion. Notably, for scholars who approach civil war from a grievance-based perspective, the poorest countries in the world are not the most likely to experience a civil war, but relative poverty – how poor people are relative to other people within the same society – is a better predictor for how prone a society is to civil war. Relative metrics can show what can be gained through revolution; if everyone is poor within a society, then war may not make anyone better off and it may be difficult to finance.

Ethnic cleavages represent another important dividing line that societies organize around. Starting in the Cold War, and accelerating after the collapse of the Soviet Union, several civil wars seem to be across ethnic lines. Being in control of the government can give you access to the tools necessary to oppress people politically as well as economically. In terms of recruitment, ethnic civil wars offer a unique dimension as the target pool of recruits to draw from is well defined and victory or defeat for one side is a cost borne by all members of the ethnic group. These wars also tend to be more violent and more likely to end in one side winning. Although the *Star Wars* universe seems to present an ideological civil war between the ideals of the Galactic Empire and the rebellion, there is also a distinct ethnic component to the rule of the Empire: All members of the decision-making bodies are human. In the expanded universe of *Star Wars*, it is much clearer that the Empire has xenophobic tendencies and this is just not a bias of what we saw in the film. This means that the rebellion can offer non-humans quite a bit to gain from joining the rebellion. For example, Mon Mothma tells us in *Episode VI* that "many Bothans died to bring us this information."[5] Whereas the Death Star battle at the end of *Episode IV* primarily showcases the contributions of the human pilots in the X-wings, it is clear throughout the film that the leadership of the rebellion includes many non-humans in addition to humans. However, repression is not always enough to spark a revolution.

Although theories of grievance-based causes for rebellion are powerful, they miss a vital component of explaining human behavior. Larger ideological appeals to better one's life, the lives of others, emotion, and reason may work well to encourage some individuals to join a revolution against an oppressive government. However, such appeals alone are not enough to staff fully a war-capable army against a government. Consequently, we turn to a second theory of mobilization: greed.

Greed

The game-theoretic problem of the prisoner's dilemma exemplifies a fundamental problem in political science: collective action The prisoner's dilemma illustrates a situation where rational self-interest can override what is otherwise collectively good for everyone. The prisoner's dilemma is modeled on a situation where two prisoners, who cannot communicate, are interrogated by the police after an armed robbery and are offered the opportunity to either go against their partner and pin the crime on them (Defect) or stay silent and cooperate with their partner (Cooperate). If both prisoners stay silent, they get a minimal sentence of one year for something minor such as a weapon-possession charge. If they both defect, then they each share the blame for the robbery and spend three years in jail. If one defects and the other stays silent, then the one that defects gets to go free as their partner takes the full sentence for the crime and serves five years in jail; this is true no matter which one defects and which one stays silent. The optimal solution is for the prisoner to defect; no matter what their partner chooses, they are always better off defecting as cooperating carries a higher punishment in each case. Throughout political science scholarship, this is an oft-cited problem for situations where there is a cost to being cooperative and a benefit for non-cooperation. With many actors (more than two), we get into a class of issues called collective action problems.

In regards to rebellion and revolution, Mark Lichbach astutely points out that, even in areas of deprivation, there is a collective action problem that mirrors the prisoner's dilemma: The costs for active participation in revolution are high and the benefits are usually public goods – that is, goods that are distributed to everyone no matter whether they participated in creating or providing them.[6] If a person chooses to help the revolution, they risk their own life by fighting against the state. If the revolution succeeds and they participate, they risk dying, but gain the benefits of revolution if they live (we can think of this as a change in deprivation for those dispossessed previously). If the revolution succeeds and they do not participate, they benefit and risk nothing. If the revolution fails and they participate, they gain nothing and risk their lives. If the revolution fails and they do not participate, they risk nothing and gain nothing. As with any standard prisoner's dilemma, the optimal solution is to defect as, in each case, you are better off not risking your life than risking it for the sake of the greater good. Of course, if everyone thinks as you do, then there would never be a revolution, as everyone knows they are better off staying at home than taking to the battlefield.

Consequently, a solution to overcome the "prisoner's dilemma" (or as Lichbach refers to it, the "Rebel's Dilemma") from the group perspective is to offer selective benefits for participation. That is, you offer a resource that people can only gain by actively participating in your rebellion. Such selective benefits for collective actions exist in many forms such as social standing, symbols (like an "I Voted" sticker given out at election time), monetary payments, future jobs, special access to other kinds of resources, etc. Additionally, you could impose costs for non-participation such as social pressure, economic penalties, or violence. The most straightforward selective benefit you can offer to anyone is to pay him or her. If you participate in the rebellion, the rebel group will pay you for it. Essentially, rebellion becomes a part- or full-time job. This solution to the dilemma presents an extreme possibility for some rebel groups in the greed explanation: rebellion may be an economically beneficial activity to participate in. Rebel groups may be financed through resource extraction, taxation, or through external funding from other actors, and all of these can lead to making warring into a business for the rebels. At the very least, we know people who are asked to risk their lives are far more likely to do so if they are monetarily compensated for taking on personal risk.

In *Star Wars*, we see a clear dynamic of political and economic repression. The Empire did away with democratic governance, as the existing Senate in *Episode IV* is purely a symbolic institution; Grand Moff Tarkin informs us "the Imperial Senate will no longer be of any concern to us. I have just received word that the Emperor has dissolved the council permanently. The last remnants of the Old Republic have been swept away forever."[7] The Empire also indiscriminately uses violence to punish potential sympathizers by using the Death Star to destroy the entire planet of Alderaan. In addition to political disparity, economic disparity is present in various planets and particular in-groups (humans) are privileged politically over out-groups (non-humans). In the classical understanding of why people attempt to fight regimes, this should be enough, but the greed explanation provides particular insight into notable figures in the *Star Wars* universe.

Political and economic repression is not enough for everyone to take up the fight against the Empire. Although it may motivate some actors, perhaps Luke Skywalker is an example of an individual that is willing to pay personal costs to provide a public good, Han Solo clearly is not impressed with such lofty ideals. Solo only becomes hooked into the rebellion with selective incentives through direct monetary payments. A debt over his head notwithstanding, Solo aids Skywalker's and Kenobi's escape with a lucrative payment scheme (so much money that Skywalker is convinced that they could buy their own ship for the amount offered) and, subsequently, only decides to attempt a rescue of Princess Leia Organa after Luke promises him even more monetary incentives:[8]

LUKE: Rich, powerful. Listen, if you were to rescue her, the reward would be…
HAN SOLO: What?
LUKE: Well, more wealth than you can imagine!
HAN SOLO: I don't know, I can imagine quite a bit.

Solo's reward for his active participation in the rebellion becomes a continued sticking point in his interpersonal relationships:

HAN SOLO: It is for me, sister. Look, I ain't in this for your revolution, and I'm not in it for you, Princess. I expect to be well paid. I'm in it for the money.
PRINCESS LEIA: You needn't worry about your reward. If money is all that you love, then that's what you'll receive.

While Organa attempts to guilt Solo and enact social costs on his non-participation in providing a collective good, she initially fails in her attempts. We know that the social costs do work to some degree on him as Solo does come back to aid the revolution in the trenches of the Death Star despite no additional promises of compensation for doing so.

It is worth noting that greed alone is unlikely to fuel a successful revolution. If your group is only fighting for profit and not for other public goods, you are more likely to devolve into a gang or cartel akin to Jabba the Hutt's cartel. Lichbach offers this about groups that only offer monetary reward for participation without resorting to broader public appeals in terms of nationalism or ideology: "To be effective, selective incentives must be tied to ideological appeals. Selective incentives without political ideology are counterproductive. Like everything else, they have a diminishing marginal utility…This principle explains why unorganized peasant upheavals and rural banditry almost always degenerate: participants are too easily attracted to selective incentives."[9] Early on, Solo could have easily worked for the Empire if the reward was high enough. Eventually, he does buy into the greater cause of the rebels.

Government Response and Civil War Duration

While potential and existing rebel groups actively create the incentives necessary to attract supporters and members, another actor is keenly aware of this and attempting to do something similar: the state. The government has a variety of tools at its disposal because, prior to a rebellion, it is the legitimate source of political and military power within a political system. Consequently, the state wants to offer incentives for non-participation in a rebellion and can do so through repression and accommodation.

Repression is the use of coercion to inflict costs upon participants or potential participants in an uprising against the state. Repression has a few distinct goals. First, if possible, states want to use repression to remove rebels from the general population. This can be through imprisonment or through force. Second, it wants to increase the costs of participation or joining with the rebel group through directly and indirectly imposed costs. Naturally, death and imprisonment are direct costs to any individual, but disruption of livelihoods, social networks, and families are also costs that individuals may weigh in considering whether they continue their rebellious activity. Third, the full result of repression should be to decrease rebel activity. This third part is not always guaranteed.

When selecting how to employ repression, a state has multiple options to choose among, but we will treat them as two general categories: discriminate and indiscriminate repression. Discriminate repression targets individuals who are known to be part of or supporters of the rebel group. The benefit of discriminate repression is that it is targeting individuals who are directly involved in acting against the state. However, discriminate repression is difficult to employ, as it requires intense intelligence gathering as to who the targets are, what activities they actually have conducted, and involves finding and/or retrieving the target. This makes discriminate repression costly in terms of both economic and human resources as well as slower than the alternative.

Indiscriminate repression targets a group of people whose members may or may not be actual rebels. Indiscriminate repression is more cost-efficient than discriminate repression as it requires less refined knowledge about the potential targets and it can bring social pressure on the real rebels to limit or stop their actions. The downside of indiscriminate repression is that it harms innocent people. This is a larger issue in counter-insurgency strategy, as you do not want to turn non-supporters or moderates into rebel supporters or active members: If the state's behavior negatively affects individuals, they have more incentive to take up arms against the state. The vast majority of literature suggests indiscriminate repression is more likely to inflame rebellion than squash it, although there is some limited evidence that indiscriminate repression can be successful.[10]

The Galactic Empire uses both. The opening scene of *Episode IV* shows a massive Star Destroyer chase down an Alderaan Cruiser to capture a political target suspected of rebel activity, Princess Leia. The resources required to find information on this activity, track down the ship, overtake the ship, board the ship, and fight the crew for control are immense. The immediate goal of recovering the Death Star plans fails, but Darth Vader goes on to imprison Leia and interrogate her to find information about the rebel base. This targeted search, interrogation, and imprisonment of Leia are all forms of discriminate repression.

When it is clear that Leia is not willing to divulge information about the Rebel Alliance's base, Grand Moff Tarkin and Darth Vader give her the choice to divulge the information or they will use the Death Star to destroy her home planet of Alderaan; this is a threat of indiscriminate repression. She quickly gives up the (purposely bad) information that the rebel base is on Dantooine, and the Galactic Empire decides to destroy Alderaan regardless, an extreme form of discriminate repression at which Leia expresses horror. In response, Tarkin remarks, "You're far too trusting. Dantooine is too remote to make an effective demonstration – but don't worry; we will deal with your rebel friends soon enough."[11] The use of discriminate repression is not only to punish the community for its support of rebels (after all, the Princess of Alderaan is a rebel), but also to send a signal that other planets would pay a similar penalty for their support. Tarkin is clear that this demonstration, destroying a planet, must be visible; the symbol of Alderaan's destruction is important.

The other major tool a state can use to stifle rebellion is accommodation. Instead of increasing the costs of rebellion, a government can increase the benefits of non-rebellion. A government can do this by either addressing the grievances held by the target group or by offering direct payments to groups or individuals to dissuade them from joining the rebel group. Both repression and accommodation are similar games that the rebels and the state are playing, as rebels can just as easily offer targeted costs (punishment or threats of punishment) as well as targeted benefits. In *A New Hope*, we see far more repression than we do accommodation by the Galactic Empire. However, we do not have to look far to find instances where the Empire is willing to meet the needs of would-be rebels and have them help the Empire.

In *Episode V: The Empire Strikes Back*, Lando Calrissian is the Baron Administrator of Cloud City, a place devoted to mining tibanna gas on the planet of Bespin; Cloud City's quasi-legal operations are at the mercy of the Empire as the planet is within their territory and the autocratic regime is not beyond seizing assets or complete operations from individuals within their control. Darth Vader knows, from intelligence gathered by bounty hunters, that high-value rebel targets are headed to Cloud City. Prior to their arrival, he is able to negotiate with Calrissian. Calrissian is aware of his delicate position and openly discusses it with the rebels he is hosting:[12]

LANDO CALRISSIAN: So you see, since we're a small operation, we don't fall into the…uh…jurisdiction of the Empire.

LEIA ORGANA: So you're part of the mining guild then?

LANDO CALRISSIAN: No, not actually. Our operation is small enough not to be noticed…which is advantageous for everybody since our customers are anxious to avoid attracting attention to themselves.

HAN SOLO: Aren't you afraid the Empire's going to find out about this little operation and shut you down?

LANDO CALRISSIAN: That's always been a danger looming like a shadow over everything we've built here. But things have developed that will insure security. I've just made a deal that will keep the Empire out of here forever.

Given this precariousness, the Empire is able to exploit it to their benefit and negotiate terms that allow Calrissian to maintain Cloud City in exchange for handing over the rebels. When the betrayal becomes clear, Calrissian asserts to his rebel friends, "I had no choice. They arrived right before you did. I'm sorry."[13] However, this is not the end of the interactions between the manager of Bespin and the Galactic Empire.

Within scholarship on international relations and conflict, scholars have fruitfully explored war as analogous to a "bargaining model" where war results when two parties cannot agree about their relative power, resolve, prospect for winning a war, and a distribution of goods. Within the bargaining literature, there are two major causes for conflict: information asymmetries and commitment problems.[14] Information asymmetries (i.e. when one party knows information that another party does not) are more likely to make war between actors occur as actors may not know the true power of the opposing party; that is, both actors may think they are stronger than they really are, more likely to win a conflict than they really are, and, consequently, more likely to risk war thinking they can win it. Information asymmetry is not an issue with Bespin; however, there may be one between the Empire and the rebellion.

Commitment problems are issues when, once one side has made a concession, the side that gains from the agreement is unable to commit to not using that concession for further advantage. That is, if one side becomes stronger from an agreement, they can use that new strength to demand more from the now-weaker side of the deal. This issue plays out in the relationship between the Empire and Cloud City, as the Empire, while occupying Bespin, changes the terms of their original agreement not once, but twice. First, when discussing the fate of the captured rebels, Darth Vader and Calrissian argue:[15]

LANDO CALRISSIAN: Lord Vader, what about Leia and the Wookiee?

DARTH VADER: They must never again leave this city.

LANDO CALRISSIAN: That was never a condition of our agreement, nor was giving Han to this bounty hunter!

DARTH VADER: Perhaps you think you're being treated unfairly.

LANDO CALRISSIAN: No.

DARTH VADER: Good. It would be unfortunate if I had to leave a garrison here.

LANDO CALRISSIAN: This deal's getting worse all the time.

The discussion implies an implicit threat of force. Vader suggests that Lando may think he is treated unfairly, but Calrissian is only able to keep his actual grievances to himself; the Empire occupies his city with military forces, and resistance is likely to be crushed. However, this deal that is getting worse all the time reaches a tipping point for Calrissian later:[16]

DARTH VADER: Good. See to it that he finds his way here. Calrissian, take the princess and the Wookiee to my ship.

LANDO CALRISSIAN: You said they'd be left in the city under my supervision.

DARTH VADER: I am altering the deal. Pray I don't alter it any further.

Vader is well aware that he is in a position where he can make additional demands as he unilaterally alters the deal he originally made with the leadership of Bespin. Even though Calrissian initially assumed that he was getting a fair deal by turning in the rebels, he would have been wise to know the Empire could not credibly commit to not making further demands and would do so if it would advantage their prosecution of the war against the rebellion. A credible commitment is one in which one party can make a claim or statement about their behavior in the future and the opposing party can believe that information. Making credible commitments can be very difficult in negotiations between conflictual parties, as both parties have incentives to misrepresent their position, bluff, and lie. Consequently, establishing credibility with your commitments to deals is difficult.

Commitment problems plague parties both prior to the beginning of a war and during the war; however, they have stronger effects on the conclusion of wars as well.

How Do Civil Wars End?

Most civil wars do not end in a negotiated settlement between parties. Instead, they typically end with one side decisively winning the war. This is partly due to the commitment problems I mentioned previously. When a state negotiates a settlement with a rebel group, one of the normal (and reasonable) demands by a state is for the rebel group to disarm and cease their hostility against the state. This demand makes sense as, for there to be a post-conflict stability, the threat of violence from the rebel group needs to recede and allow the state to resume its normal functions. However, this very situation is likely to create instability as opposed to stability.

The greatest threat the rebel group faces is for the state to eliminate the group as a whole. In a post-settlement world, the rebel group would dispose of their capacity to contest the state, which would enhance the state's position relative to the rebel group. This creates a fundamental commitment problem as, pre-settlement, a state cannot credibly commit to not wiping out the group. That is, a state will be tempted to use its powerful position to eliminate a former rebel group to prevent any future uprisings, even after a negotiated peace has led to rebel disarmament.

The type of civil war may also create different settlement opportunities for the state, some more credible than others. In an ethnic-based civil war where a group seeks separation from the state, there can be a settlement that allows a group to have its own country or some level of autonomy. This settlement also allows the group to remain armed or have a standing military and overcomes the inherent commitment problem imposed by disarmament. Even then, if the two forces remain asymmetric, the threat of a renewal of hostilities will remain between the groups. Alternatively, an ideological civil war does not have this luxury, as the civil war is a contest between ideas about how the state should behave. Each settlement that is possible between the state and the rebels, short of a one-sided victory, will be either a policy change or an institutional change. Such changes have a distinct possibility of reversal (i.e., the state can go back on the agreement) and a disarmed revolutionary group will have to rearm just to negotiate back to what it had already earned.

It is appropriate that the original *Star Wars* trilogy ends with the collapse of the Galactic Empire and the victory of the rebels. Whereas there are ethnic components to the civil war, the primary challenge is over how the Empire governed and the rebels wanted a radically different system than the oppressive rule the Empire offered. The post-Empire galactic rule could either lead to a new round of representative democracy such as in the old Republic days, or might lead to several smaller clusters of groups choosing their own governments.

Conclusion

Civil wars are one of the deadliest forms of conflicts in human history and there remains much for scholars to explore in how civil wars begin, endure, and end. However, despite what we do not know, we have a theoretical and empirical grasp on several processes that are common among civil wars. As this chapter shows, it is clear that the same themes we see in reality also exist in the *Star Wars* universe. This iconic franchise remains iconic for several reasons, not least of all because it does reflect our society and our experiences with conflicts in some tangible ways.

Chapter Discussion Questions

1. In *Star Wars*, we see a racially divided society, but neither the Rebels nor the Empire actually mention this. How can ethnicity (and religion) be important to understanding a civil war?
2. Do you expect rebels in civil wars to be more like Luke Skywalker and motivated by ideals or like Han Solo and motivated by their self-interest?
3. Is repression by a state ever justified to maintain security? What is more effective, discriminate or indiscriminate repression? Why do states use either of these tactics?

Notes

1 Gurr, Ted R. 1970. *Why men rebel*. Princeton, NJ: Princeton University Press.
2 Regan, Patrick M. 2009. *Sixteen million one: Understanding civil war*. Boulder, CO: Paradigm Publishers.

3 Lucas, George. 1977. *Star Wars Episode IV: A New Hope*. San Rafael, CA: Lucasfilm.
4 Tilly, Charles, Peter B. Evans, Dietrich Rueschemeyer, and Theda Skocpol. 1985. *War making and state making as organized crime*. Cambridge, MA: Cambridge University Press.
5 Marquand, Richard. 1983. *Star Wars Episode VI – Return of the Jedi*. San Rafael, CA: Luscasfilm.
6 Lichbach, Mark I. 1994. "What makes rational peasants revolutionary? Dilemma, paradox, and irony in peasant collective action." *World Politics*, 46(3): 383–418.
7 Lucas, *Star Wars Episode IV*.
8 Ibid.
9 Lichbach, "What makes rational peasants revolutionary?" 416.
10 For example, Lyall, Jason. 2009. "Does indiscriminate violence incite insurgent attacks? Evidence from Chechnya," *Journal of Conflict Resolution*, 53(3): 331–362.
11 Lucas, *Star Wars Episode IV*.
12 Kershner, Irvin. 1980. *Star Wars Episode V – The Empire Strikes Back*. San Rafael, CA: Lucasfilm
13 Ibid.
14 Fearon, James D. 1995. "Rationalist explanations for war," *International Organization*, 49(3): 379–414.
15 Kershner, *Star Wars Episode V*.
16 Ibid.

PART VI

Inter-state Relations

15

BUGGERS AND ASTRONAUTS

Ethics and Security in *Ender's Game*

Mary Elizabeth Sullivan

UNIVERSITY OF CENTRAL ARKANSAS

This chapter examines the 1977 novel and 2013 film adaption of Orson Scott Card's *Ender's Game*. *Ender's Game* depicts the recruitment and training of a young boy, Ender Wiggin, to serve in a high-tech global military, known as the International Fleet (I.F.). Having been marked as a military prodigy, Ender is removed from his parents' home and trained for combat in an orbiting space station/school. Although his fellow students initially bully Ender, he eventually fights his way to the top of his class. Ender is then moved to a forward command center where he must participate in virtual battles against the Formics, a technologically advanced alien race who have attacked Earth in the past. The climax of the book occurs when Ender and his classmates must engage in a massive simulation of an attack on the Formic main forces. This is presented as a "final exam" that will be observed by high-level political leaders to determine whether Ender should be given command of I.F. forces. Once the simulation is over, Ender, having wiped out all the virtual Formics, learns that the battle was actually real. The commands he and his classmates entered into the computer simulators were actually being carried out in real time. Ender learns he has killed an entire alien species without realizing it. This chapter will ask to what extent the actions taken against the Formics (also referred to derisively as Buggers) by the International Fleet conform to the principles of Just War Theory. Was the decision to destroy the Formic home planet morally justified? Were the restrictions placed on the liberty of Earth's inhabitants just as well?

Card's novel illustrates many of the insecurities of a post-nuclear-age America. Weapons are bigger; the stakes in each encounter are unimaginably high. We face an enemy with the literal capacity to wipe our species off the planet. Yet, Earth's own military resources have also increased. Given the amazing training facilities and weapons shown in the film and the relatively modest civilian home of the

Wiggins family, it seems likely that the I.F. commands an enormous portion of the planet's GDP. This is an extreme example of a military-industrial complex, a system in which military spending has become the heart of the nation's economy. Yet, it is not clear that Card intends to be critical of these developments. In general, he presents the I.F. as facing difficult decisions, especially given that the characters are working with imperfect information.

It is not surprising that the twenty-first century would see a revival of interest in this story as well. The decision to seek and destroy future opponents on their home turf before they have the opportunity to attack has been a hallmark of the United States' "War on Terror." Like the book, the film version wrestles with these decisions, and the difficulty inherent in interpreting the motives of a potential enemy whose ways are literally alien to our own understanding. In the film, the Formics' non-human nature is not used as excuse for their killing directly (i.e., killing them does not count because they are less than human), but rather as an explanation for why diplomatic means are not an option. As in the book, the actions taken by the I.F. are problematic, but not depicted as necessarily unjust.

Political Issues as They Arise in *Ender's Game*

Several different politically relevant questions come up over the course of *Ender's Game*. The movie opens with Earth preparing for an eminent attack from an alien force known as the Formics. They are a large, intelligent, insect-like species that attacked our planet once in the past, resulting in severe devastation. Their first major invasion was repelled through the insight (or blind luck) of a single commander, Mazer Rackham. Hailed as a military genius, he was able to disable the entire Formic fleet by locating and taking out a single key vessel (although how he achieved his victory is kept secret from both the audience and Ender's character for much of the film). Having narrowly escaped annihilation, Earth is in the process of preparing for the (in the minds of the public) inevitable "next war." To achieve this aim, nations have united into a single political entity, under the leadership of the Hegemon, an autocrat, who is never personally encountered, but whose power is felt throughout the story.

Because the First Invasion was repelled through the work of a single "genius," the I.F. military strategy at the opening of *Ender's Game* focuses on finding and grooming the next great genius. The I.F. monitors gifted children on earth, with the more successful ones being sent on to Battle School in an orbiting space station. It is assumed that if Earth is to survive again, it will be through the actions of a naturally gifted and solitary individual, rather than a coordinated effort of many people, the careful management of resources, or the development of new technologies. This particular decision never seems to be questioned. Furthermore (and much more controversially), the I.F. strategy relies heavily on the involvement of children, some as young as six. Much of *Ender's Game*'s emotional resonance depends upon the fact that children are being forced to face potential violence that they are not emotionally capable of dealing with. Once Ender's cohort has received basic training in zero-gravity combat, they are brought to the forward command center of Earth's forces for further training. Although Ender is unaware of it, in his final "simulation" he is actually commanding I.F. forces that are attacking the Formics. A few key issues come up in this battle, beyond Colonel Graff's decision to mislead Ender. One is the development and use of the Molecular Disruption Device, a weapon capable of starting off a chain reaction that will destroy all adjacent matter. It is the mother of all weapons of mass destruction. Furthermore, as the final move in his last battle (again, unaware that he is fighting for real and not in a simulation), Ender makes the decision to aim the MD device at the heart of the Formic home planet, setting off a reaction that destroys their entire globe and species. Thus, humans engage in a war that is both pre-emptive and total in nature. Having learned that he is responsible for both the deaths of thousands of human soldiers that were under his command and the entire Formic population, Ender enters a period of extreme depression. He feels both anger at the I.F. leadership for deceiving him and guilt over his own choices. Colonel Graff defends their decision, claiming this was the only way to defeat the Formics and preserve our own species. According to Graff, the threat posed by the Formics justified the extreme measures taken against them. Questions of when a nation is justified in going to war and what tactics it may use have been addressed in a body of political theory known as Just War Theory. How would Just War scholars evaluate the decisions made by Graff and the I.F.?

Justness and the Decision to Go to War

The Just War tradition contains two important strains: *jus ad bellum* and *jus in bello*. The first refers to the justness of a nation's decision to go to war. The latter strain refers to debates on what actions or tactics can be justly used when fighting a war. *Jus ad bellum* generally allows that war can be waged under several conditions, including defending oneself when one has been attacked, defending neighboring states that have been attacked, and pre-empting an imminent attack by an enemy. In any of these cases, the moral blame for the start of the war falls on the initial aggressor.[1] In the scenario presented in *Ender's Game*, the Buggers had launched the first deadly attack against the planet Earth years prior to the start of the story. According to Earth's political leaders, the Second and Third Invasions (collapsed into a single attack in the film) were justifiable as pre-emptive attempts to prevent destruction by this enemy. Although the later chapters of the book show that these leaders were ultimately mistaken in their belief that the Formics intended to repeat their attack on Earth, was this a reasonable assumption to make? In international politics, leaders often have to make major decisions with incomplete information about other nations and their intentions, capacities, and future reactions. This problem is magnified in *Ender's Game* because Earth's opponent is not even of the same species, making understanding them even more difficult.

Part of the difficulty in assigning moral responsibility for the invasions lies in the fact that, at the time each invasion took place, communication between Formics and humans was not possible. This negated the possibility of a diplomatic solution and made intentions difficult to interpret for both parties. Colonel Graff interprets the massing of Formic ships on their planet as a clear sign that another attack is being planned and that Earth is the intended target. Ender himself questions this interpretation, posing the possibility that these ships could have been intended for defensive purposes. Barring the possibility of an actual conversation with the Formic leadership on their plans, did Earth's military leaders have a moral obligation to wait to see if an attack was actually launched before taking action themselves? Many strict interpreters of Just War Theory would say yes. Under this understanding, the Second/Third Invasion could be considered a preventative action, but not a pre-emptive action.[2] The key difference being that a preventative war stops a *possible* future attack, whereas a pre-emptive war intervenes before *definite* plans of attack are fully carried out. Yet, if Colonel Graff and other members of the I.F. leadership honestly believed a Formic plan to attack Earth's population was already in the works, then humans would have the right to defend themselves, including by possibly striking first in a pre-emptive war.[3]

In addition to the requirement that the aim of the war be defensive rather than aggressive, *jus ad bellum* requires that each military mission have a reasonable chance of success. Not only do political leaders have a duty to refrain from unprovoked attacks against their neighbors, but they also have a duty to their own troops, and should not send them on missions doomed to failure from the start. Should the I.F. have been more cautious in its deployment of human life? Here we see some of the weaknesses in the I.F. plan. It is apparent that their plan depends entirely upon the discovery of an exceptionally gifted child prodigy, such as Ender Wiggin. The I.F. must find (or possibly breed) this child savior and train him/her, and the rest of the military's strategy can be left in his or her hands. As far as a plan for national defense goes, this is utterly daft. There is no evidence of any theological or supernatural prophecy that fed the I.F. hopes of a child savior. Yet, there is no back-up plan in place. Graff's conversations with other I.F. officers indicate all hopes rest on Ender and his exceptional talent for military tactics. If his training did not work out, humanity was doomed. If the I.F. intelligence on Formic war preparations was correct, there would be no time available to train another commander.

Questions about Ender's ability to command I.F. forces aside, it was never clear at any point that he would be *willing* to fight the Formics. The decision to deceive Ender about the "final simulation" was the result of these very doubts. Leaving aside the uncertainty about whether the Formics intended to invade and the moral issues associated with the manipulation of children, the I.F.'s decision to launch a pre-emptive war in which the odds were so strongly stacked against them, such that their only hope was to gamble on the abilities of a child prodigy, was negligent in the extreme. Right up until the last moments of the final battle/simulation, it seems likely Ender will be defeated. Although a more cautious and responsible military strategy would have made for less dramatic storytelling, without a responsible plan that made Earth's victory likely, the I.F. decision to attack first (even if they were legitimately threatened) becomes unjustifiable.[4]

Thus we can see some of the *jus ad bellum* issues that arise in *Ender's Game*. Although the I.F. commanders were likely mistaken in their assumptions, their interpretation of the massing of Formic ships on the planet's surface was not an unreasonable one, given the past behavior of the Formic military. Further, the "language barrier" made diplomacy an impossibility. Given the imperfect information that the I.F. had to use in making their decision, it is *possible* to argue that their decision meets the basic criteria of *jus ad bellum*, primarily by presenting the attack on the Formic home planet as an act of pre-emptive self-defense. However, this still leaves the question of whether the means used to fight the Formics were justifiable.

Justice in War in *Ender's Game*

The second strain of Just War Theory, *jus in bello*, examines the justness of war tactics. Even a war whose overall aims are just may be fought unjustly if methods such as the intentional killing or starving of civilian populations or the torture of prisoners of war are used. The ends do not necessarily justify the means. To determine if the I.F.'s manner of waging war against the Formics was just, we must first ask whether their attack was proportional to the threat posed by the Formic forces. The film is somewhat vague in regard to the damage done in the First Invasion. However the I.F. leadership has gathered intelligence on the Formics' home planet since then, coming to the conclusion that it has been depleted of water and other natural resources. The assumption is then made that their invasion was an attempt to wipe out humans, leaving Earth ripe for colonization. If these suppositions were accurate, then the direct (and total) attack on their home planet would be proportionate to the harm they had intended to inflict on humans. Flashbacks and references to this earlier attack show it to be devastating in nature.[5] If one felt sufficiently certain that the Formics intended to threaten the very existence of humanity and that the decision to go to war in the first place was justified, then it would follow that, given their pattern of past attacks, the decision to launch a major attack near or on the Formic home planet would not violate proportionality.

The second major factor to consider in *jus in bello* is that of discrimination. In a just war, fighters must differentiate between combatants and non-combatants, and between military and civilian targets. As Thomas Nagel has argued in his work, you must remember that you are only fighting the government/military of a nation, not its people as a whole:

> [Justice] requires us to forgo certain potentially useful military measures, such as the slaughter of hostages and prisoners or indiscriminate attempts to reduce the enemy civilian population by starvation, epidemic infectious diseases like anthrax and bubonic plague, or mass incineration. It means that we cannot deliberate on whether such measures are justified by the fact that they will avert still greater evils, for as intentional measures they cannot be justified in terms of any consequences whatsoever.[6]

It is in this measure of justice that *Ender's Game* fails so spectacularly. There are two major ways in which the tactics employed by the I.F. fail standards of discrimination in war. The first is the development of the MD weapon. This device sets off a huge chain reaction that tears apart all connected matter. Its size and scope make it impossible to use in a targeted manner. The second is Ender's decision to aim the MD weapon directly at the home planet of the Formics. Until this point in the battle, military spacecraft from both planets had been fighting in the area near the planet. As these craft are armed and firing on Earth's forces, they can be considered valid military targets. Even the targeting of the Formic queen by Mazer Rackham during the First Invasion fits within this framework. The queen was in a military vehicle in the midst of the fighting, giving orders to the fighters around her. However, the Formic home planet clearly contained a mixture of both military and civilian installations. Many of the individuals living there may have had no direct involvement in the war; some were infants or larva. Furthermore, the I.F. (including Ender) were unaware of Formic political structures. They had no way of knowing whether there was widespread civilian involvement or support in the war effort. Yet, every organism on the planet was destroyed.

It should be noted that Ender did not realize when he ordered weapons to be aimed at the home planet that he was fighting in the real world rather than a simulation. However, military leaders present in the simulation room (including Colonel Graff) *did* know that Ender's commands would be executed in the real world, and could have stopped him.[7] In fact, the ruse of the "simulation" was designed so that Ender would be less likely to hesitate over his destruction of this species. As Ender was able to come to understand how the Formics' minds worked, he also grew to empathize and respect them. The I.F. forces realized that this empathy might make it difficult for Ender to order their destruction and deliberately deceived him. For these reasons, the International Fleet as a whole certainly violated norms of discrimination in warfare, even if Ender personally cannot be blamed. High-level political leaders chose to use Ender as a tool in their annihilation of the Formics.

Realism in *Ender's Game*

However, even if Ender had been aware he was no longer operating in simulation mode, he might not have been intellectually prepared to act any differently.

James Cook has noted that despite the wide range of training given to child soldiers in Battle School, Just War Theory was not part of the curriculum. Cook appears surprised by this, as he notes, "Given all this [the long tradition of Just War Theory] it seems odd that just war theory and the tradition weren't taught to Ender. United States service academies present just war principles and puzzles to all their cadets and midshipmen."[8] Unlike Cook, I do not find this decision by the I.F. to be puzzling. The leadership of the I.F. has already committed themselves to an extreme realist approach to relations with the Formics. Ender's role was not to question the fleet's decisions regarding either *jus ad bellum* or *jus in bello* but to devise battle tactics that would achieve the aims that the command had already chosen.

Realism is a theoretical alternative to Just War Theory. Under a realist approach to politics, there are no limits to what a nation may do in pursuit of its own well-being. In fact, many realists would argue that political leaders have an obligation to put the success of their nation ahead of any other concerns, including ethics. To a realist, the ends, in this case winning a war or other conflict, justify whatever means are necessary. This school of thought is not new; it has been around as long as people have been thinking and writing about politics. The ancient Greek historian Thucydides commented that "the strong do what they can and the weak suffer what they must" after observing the behavior of cities at war during his lifetime.[9] Where a Just War theorist would argue that, even if war is inevitable, there should be limits on how one fights and who ones targets, realists believe that all is fair, or perhaps more accurately, that there is no such thing as fairness when one is discussing international politics.[10]

The I.F. appears to have embraced this realist approach in their encounters with the Formics. When Colonel Graff considers how and when the Formics should be attacked, his only consideration is the well-being of Earth and its people. He dismisses the possibility that the Formics may not actually be planning a second attack; if there is even a *chance* they may harm Earth then actions against them are justified in his view. Furthermore, when developing weapons and battle tactics, issues such as proportionality and discrimination between civilian and military targets are never considered. This is not a mere oversight on the I.F.'s part. In a realist framework, these issues do not matter. The "rightness" of an action is determined solely by how successful it is likely to be. Although some might argue that this stance is immoral, realists would defend it by saying that their obligation to protect their own people outweighs other considerations, including the rights of enemy soldiers and civilians.

The use of children plays into this as well. One of the key "benefits" of child soldiers in the real world is that they are less likely to question the decisions of their commanders, particularly in the realm of ethics. Children, particularly those as young as Ender is in the book, are more likely to accept that whatever a grown-up tells them to do is inherently "right." A military that was interested in developing soldiers with the capacity to make sound individual moral judgments would not be recruiting six-year-olds. However, a military that has already decided to pursue a realist agenda might find it very convenient that its soldiers (children) are unable to question its decisions.

Liberty versus Security at Home

Just as a government dedicated to a realist approach to politics would be willing to use any means necessary to defeat its enemies in war, it might also be willing to use any means necessary against its own people. In the world of *Ender's Game*, major infringements on the liberty of Earth's citizens have been enacted under the justification of promoting planetary security. Are these measures fair? This section looks at the domestic politics on Earth as portrayed in *Ender's Game*, particularly, government surveillance of individuals and family-planning regulations.[11] Ender, as well as his siblings Peter and Valentine, spends a significant portion of his childhood under constant surveillance. Surveillance technology is able to tap directly into one's neurological system, obliterating even the possibility of privacy. A monitor placed at the back of the neck transmits all of the wearer's sensory data to the I.F. and its watchers. Indeed, as the opening lines of the book attest, "I've watched through his eyes, I've listened through his ears" (1). Once the monitor is removed and Ender is sent to Battle School, he still exists in a world without privacy. His use of his computer is monitored; mail from his family is intercepted. Like a prisoner in the Panopticon, Ender is constantly being watched.

Ender's Game deals more with the consequences of the *removal* of Ender's monitor than with the implications of its *presence*. Once the monitor is removed, bullies at school feel they can now attack Ender without possible consequences; it is revealed that the I.F. leadership decided to remove the monitor to see how Ender would handle this exact situation. Ender is able to defend himself, but the scene is still a frightening one for him. The removal of the monitor signals both failure (he is no longer in the running for a position at the Battle School) and vulnerability (he is no longer being watched and/or protected by outside forces). Yet the consequences of having lived under constant surveillance are not dwelt upon, even in the 2013 film version, whose audience, one would think, might be extra attuned to issues of electronic surveillance.

The other vivid example of intrusive government policies in a "private sphere" is the strict family-planning regulations. Earth's families are limited to two children. Ender is the third child in his family, an exception specifically granted because his older brother and sister had shown high potential as military strategists. Ender was bred for his role as a military savior. This position as a third child leaves Ender open to further bullying and contributes to an internal doubt about whether he has a right to exist at all. Furthermore, it is evident that Ender's family, and presumably others as well, bristle under these regulations.[12] Despite organized religion being banned, Ender knows his parents were raised in religious families; his mother is Mormon; his father is Catholic. Both are denominations that generally oppose family planning and would certainly object to it being forced upon a married couple. In fact, his mother wanted to have more children and took the opportunity offered to have a third.[13] The significant reaction others exhibit toward Ender's status as a third child underscores that this is a rare, if not unique, situation. Thus, it seems that the Federation has not only legislated a two-child limit, but is actually able to enforce it, although the means by which they do so is never discussed.

In both the neurological monitoring of children and the strictly enforced reproductive limits, Earth's government under the Hegemon has crossed the ultimate threshold of intervening in the very bodies of its citizens. All of these restrictions have been justified by the threat of Formic invasion. Earth's inhabitants appear to have given up individual freedoms in exchange for greater security. From a utilitarian standpoint, this may be justifiable; as mentioned previously, the First Invasion caused horrific devastation. It is not unreasonable that a democratically governed people might choose to divest themselves of basic privacy rights if they thought doing so might increase their chances of survival as a species. Yet, even a weak liberal would cringe at the extent of the violations we observe. Although Earth's society is not depicted as overtly dystopian, the audience is meant to feel uncomfortable with the extent to which the government has come to control people's lives in the name of greater security.

Conclusion

Ender's Game poses some interesting political questions. Was Earth's decision to attack the Formics morally justifiable? Was Ender's conduct in combat, and that of the International Fleet more broadly, ethical? How did the Hegemon use the Formic threat to enhance government power at the expense of personal liberty? These are not easy questions to answer.

Ender's Game is not anti-war, although it does wrestle with the costs of war. Likewise, Just War Theory does not argue that war should never happen. Theorists, such as Michael Walzer and Thomas Nagel, accept that war is sometimes an unavoidable aspect of the human condition. However, Just War Theory also asks that we look a little closer at *why* we go to war and *how* we choose to fight. In *Ender's Game*, the audience can see the reasoning that leads I.F. commanders to conclude that the destruction of the Formic race as a whole is the only way to ensure human safety. Colonel Graff is not depicted as evil, only calculating. His character truly does believe that the ends, in this case anyway, really do justify the means. Although not as overtly critical of those in power as it might be, *Ender's Game* leaves its readers uncomfortable with their choices. It *may* be the case that the destruction of the Formic home planet was the inevitable tragic outcome of their own earlier expansionist policies; yet, the people of Earth should still be a bit more suspicious of those who rose to power on a wave of fear. Regardless of whether the ends are thought to justify the means, the means themselves are quite ugly. As a result, at the end one does not feel much elation at Earth's victory. Although the presence of a common enemy has united the peoples of Earth, this development is not entirely wholesome. *Ender's Game* raises serious questions about ethics in both war and domestic politics, and Ender himself is left with uncertainty as to whether he is actually the hero or the villain of this tale. So are we.

Chapter Discussion Questions

1. Giving that the I.F. had incomplete information about what the Formics were planning to do, was their assumption that another attack was imminent reasonable? Does this justify the decision to launch a pre-emptive attack?
2. Just War theorists argue that you must differentiate in your treatment of combatants and non-combatants. What difficulties might arise when applying this principle in practice? Did the I.F. follow this principle?
3. Does the threat of Formic invasion justify the restrictions placed on the liberty and privacy of earth's inhabitants? Are there times when values, such as liberty or ethics in warfare, should be compromised in order to ensure our survival?

Notes

1 Walzer, Michael. 2006. *Just and unjust wars: A moral argument with historical examples.* New York: Basic Books.

2 They were not certain that the Formics intended to attack (the book makes it clear that they did not, in fact, plan on launching another attack on Earth; the film leaves things a bit more ambiguous).

3 Cooper, Kody W. 2013. "The unspoken rules of manly warfare: Just war theory in *Ender's Game,*" in *Ender's Game and philosophy: The logic gate is down*, eds. Kevin S. Decker and William Irwin. Chichester: Wiley & Sons, 175–186.

4 Cooper, "The unspoken rules of manly warfare."

5 The book is slightly more detailed in its account of humans' earlier encounters with the Formics, mentioning "the scathing of China" on more than one occasion (25). If the Formics had shown both the capacity and inclination to destroy all (or nearly all) of mainland China on their first foray into our solar system, it again seems that they posed a very serious threat.

6 Nagle, Thomas. 1972. "War and massacre," *Philosophy and Public Affairs*, 1(2): 123–144; 128.

7 For an interesting discussion of the role this technology plays in *Ender's Game* and other works of science fiction, see Hantke, Steffen "Surgical strikes and prosthetic warriors: The soldier's body in contemporary science fiction," *Science Fiction Studies*, 25(3): 495–509.

8 Cook, James L. 2013 "Ender's beginning and the just war," in *Ender's Game and philosophy: The logic gate is down*, eds. Kevin S. Decker and William Irwin. Chichester: Wiley & Sons, 151–162; 137.

9 Thucydides. 2008. *The landmark Thucydides: A comprehensive guide to the Peloponnesian War*, ed. Robert B. Strassler. New York: Simon and Schuster, 352.

10 For a more modern discussion of realism in international politics, see Morgenthau, Hans J. 1993. *Politics among nations: The struggle for power and peace*. Boston, MA: McGraw-Hill.
11 These themes are much more prominent in the book than in the film version.
12 Although there certainly is precedent for government-implemented family-planning policies, to adherents of the liberal tradition, this signals an especially intrusive foray of government policy into the private sphere (and I think it likely Card intended it as such).
13 Card, Orson Scott. 1985. *Ender's Game*, New York: Tor Publishing, 22–23.

16

BATTLESTAR GALACTICA AND FOREIGN POLICY

Michael E. Flynn

KANSAS STATE UNIVERSITY

> Is this what the two of you have been doing for the past six months? Debating the finer points of Colonial law? Well, guess what, we're at war! And we don't have the luxury of academic debate over these issues!
>
> – *Admiral Helena Cain, "Resurrection Ship, Part I," Episode 2.11*

The 2003 remake of *Battlestar Galactica* is one of the most popular science fiction franchises ever.[1] This level of success is certainly warranted. *Battlestar Galactica* does not just use the science fiction genre to provide cheap escapism, rife with exotic locales, spaceships, close calls, reversing polarities, and cool gadgets, but uses the medium to address questions of great social and political importance. Indeed, whereas the series takes place in a distant time and place, it is remarkably grounded, using science fiction as a vehicle for examining how humanity, on the verge of extinction, would react when faced with the most dire of circumstances. It is this combination of the incredible and the ordinary that makes *Battlestar* so worthy of our attention.

Battlestar Galactica addresses a wide range of ideas that are of interest to political scientists, and students of foreign policy in particular. Using a cataclysmic attack on humanity as a starting point, the show touches on several subjects, such as the use of force, the importance of institutions in foreign policymaking, the use of torture, the role of religion and ideas in foreign policymaking, and how policymakers shape grand strategy. In this chapter I explore how *Battlestar* provides insights into the political processes associated with foreign policy decision making. Specifically, I focus on those parts of the show that deal with the role of institutional structures in shaping foreign policy decision making, and take a closer look at one institution in particular – civilian control of the military.

The World of *Battlestar Galactica*

Before delving too deeply into substantive issues, some basic background information is in order. The Cylons, an advanced race of robots, were created sixty years prior to the start of the series by Dr. Daniel Graystone on the planet Caprica, one of the Twelve Colonies (planets) on which humanity resided. Though they were initially created to serve as soldiers in the Caprican military, humans quickly recognized the potential for other applications. Cylons were eventually employed for a wide variety of menial chores.[2] After quickly developing a collective consciousness, the Cylons began to plot the overthrow of their masters. The resulting "Cylon War" spanned twelve years and humanity suffered devastating losses. The war ended suddenly when the Cylons inexplicably expressed their desire to sue for peace with the Colonies. After signing the peace accords the Cylons vanished from colonial space. The Colonies constructed a space station following the end of the war in an effort to maintain some form of diplomatic relations with the Cylons, every year sending a colonial military officer to the station to await the arrival of Cylon delegates. But none ever arrives.

After forty years the peace is abruptly broken when Cylon agents suddenly appear, destroying the space station. With remarkable speed and coordination, the Cylons launch an all-out assault on the Twelve Colonies. Cylon ships appear in orbit over all twelve planets, bombarding their surfaces with nuclear weapons, destroying ships in orbit, and hunting down those who flee. The Cylons' genocidal campaign against humanity is wildly successful – out of billions of people, fewer than 50,000 were able to escape, forming a hodgepodge fleet composed of freighters, tankers, transport ships, luxury craft, and the only remaining military – the *Battlestar Galactica*.

Prior to the Cylon attack, the government of the *Battlestar* universe is comprised of an overarching political unit – the Federal Republic of the Twelve Colonies of Kobol. The Articles of Colonization, drafted forty years prior to the beginning of the series, marked the creation of a unified federal system. The federal government of the colonies is comprised of two primary branches – an executive and legislative branch. The executive branch is headed by a democratically elected president, and supported by an appointed cabinet. These are the officials who oversee the executive bureaucracy and its various departments, such as the Ministry of Defense and the Department of Education. The legislative branch was bicameral, although the only chamber observed in the series is the Quorum of Twelve, which functions as the upper house. Each colony sends one delegate to the Quorum of Twelve.[3] These institutions represent the core of the civilian side of the Colonial government. Under the executive branch is the military of the Twelve Colonies, the Colonial Forces, which is composed of two main branches. The Colonial Fleet is the primary branch of the colonial military. Working with the Fleet are the Colonial Marines.[4] The Colonial military forces are subservient to the civilian side of the government, with the Colonial Ministry of

Defense acting as the civilian bureaucracy that oversees the Colonial Forces. The Ministry's primary mission is to defend the Twelve Colonies from the Cylons, when and if they return to attack.[5]

After the attack on Caprica, Laura Roslin, the Secretary of Education, finds herself the unlikely successor to what is left of the former regime. And with the destruction of the Colonial fleet, Galactica's commander, William Adama becomes the de facto leader of all remaining colonial military forces. To make matters worse, we learn that a number of Cylons who appear human have infiltrated the fleet. Ferreting out these Cylon spies quickly becomes a top priority for Roslin, Adama, and the crew of the *Galactica* as they attempt to lead the survivors toward salvation, while also staving off the Cylons who attempt to snuff out the last remnants of humanity.

Lessons Learned from *Battlestar*

In evaluating the lessons that *Battlestar* holds for students of foreign policy, it is worth discussing the show's starting point. One of the fundamental challenges that the survivors face is organizing themselves after the Cylon attack. Providing order and security in this environment is challenging at best, so it is worth considering how the survivors set about the basic tasks of governing themselves in a world where both security and resources are scarce.

The institutions that the survivors put in place do not spring up out of nowhere, but are largely based on the rules that existed before. Pre-existing rules and norms figured prominently in the survivors' efforts to organize themselves. In political science we refer to this idea as path dependence. Path dependence can be thought of as a kind of momentum; once things start down a certain path it becomes increasingly difficult to make large and significant changes to some alternative. Once particular institutions or policies take hold, we tend to invest more time, effort, and resources into those particular areas, rather than constantly exploring and building new ones. Transitioning to alternatives is possible, but often requires several years of incremental change and reform.

What Are Institutions and Why Do They Matter for Foreign Policy?

Institutions are central to much work in contemporary political science. Although we tend to think of institutions as organizations like universities, corporations, or other complex groups, political scientists usually adopt a slightly different definition. Institutions can be thought of as the "rules of the game."[6] Some of these rules are explicitly laid out in formal documents, like the United States Constitution, which articulates the most general elements of how the government is structured. Other institutional rules might be unwritten, informal norms and expectations that govern behavior. We can also look at institutions with varying levels of specificity. We might consider governmental institutions in the United States with a general sense for understanding larger, more "macro-level" decisions, like how the separation of powers affects decisions to use military force. The Constitution gives Congress the power to tax, raise and support a military, and to declare war. Alternatively, it gives the president the power to command military forces as the commander-in-chief. More narrowly, focusing on institutional structures within the military can be helpful for understanding who gets promoted and when. Knowing exactly what these rules are and where they come from can all help us to better understand how policy decisions are made.

Because institutions establish the rules by which human interactions occur, there is a constant tension between longevity and change. Institutional stability allows individuals to engage in a wide range of activities with others across space and time without having to constantly reassess the terms of every interaction.[7] To facilitate interaction and build trust among participants, institutions must provide some degree of stability for those participants. After all, why invest time and energy into adjusting your behavior to conform to a set of rules if there is little reason to believe that others will do the same? Stability does not preclude change, however. Formal governmental institutions, but also informal rules, such as fairness and justice, tend to persist over time, with individuals making small periodic adjustments as changing circumstances dictate. Sudden and dramatic institutional changes are possible; an invasion by an external power may result in a very dramatic and sudden change in governing institutions. However, even where we see such sudden changes, informal institutions can still potentially curb the effects of otherwise radical changes to formal institutional rules.[8] Accordingly, pre-existing institutions and norms exert a substantial pull on the status quo, or moves away from the status quo.

In foreign policy decision making, institutions not only dictate the rules, they also determine who the key players are, their responsibilities, and their authority. For example, there are several areas in foreign policymaking where the president and Congress have overlapping powers and responsibilities. For instance, the president can negotiate and ratify treaties with congressional consent. Alternatively, Congress has the power to raise and maintain an army and a navy, whereas the president has the power to command the military as commander-in-chief. Although their powers overlap considerably, the rules as outlined in the Constitution determine who matters for specific purposes.

Although the executive and legislative branches have foreign policymaking powers that are directly outlined by the Constitution, there are other actors who also exert a great deal of influence. Although we often think of the president as being synonymous with the executive branch of government, there are thousands of other individuals within the foreign policy bureaucracy who also influence foreign policy decision making. Through their power to make appointments, presidents can exert substantial control over who occupies senior leadership positions within the bureaucracy. The president appoints all positions like secretary of state, secretary of defense, and the national security adviser; these are the individuals who are often tasked with carrying out the day-to-day operations of the government. The military as a whole, and the individual branches (i.e., the Army, Navy, and Air Force), constitute an additional set of actors who influence the policymaking process. Although the military is formally subordinate to the civilian government, this relationship is far from simple and is often intensely political.

Bureaucratic actors are also typically regarded as having their own interests. Whereas elected officials may pursue policies that are desired by the constituents who elect them, the interests of bureaucratic actors arise from different sources. In some cases it may be the specific duties of the office that they occupy.[9] For example, officials within the State Department may prioritize diplomatic solutions to international problems, preferring to exhaust all options before turning to military force. Alternatively, officials within the Department of Defense might focus more on military solutions to international conflicts.

Last, societal interests constitute an essential group in the policymaking process. Although not endowed with formal institutional powers, like the president and Congress, the public can still exert a powerful influence over foreign policy. Democratic institutions give members of the public the opportunity to select the leaders who ultimately craft foreign policy. We typically assume that elected officials make decisions and pursue policies with the goal of retaining office. Pursuing policies that alienate a key constituency is a good way to be removed from office, so leaders should pursue policies favored by their constituents.[10] As with bureaucratic actors, the specific interests of these societal actors may vary. Some might be interested in ideological goals, others in economic goals. Regardless, societal interests can leverage electoral support for politicians into continued support for the policies they prefer.

Institutions determine how these actors relate to one another, and how they are able to affect policy outcomes. One way we can view institutions is as constraints on the ability of any one actor or group of actors to dominate the policymaking process. Democratic institutions, through mechanisms like elections and the separation of powers, impose constraints on political actors, reducing the ability of any one individual or group from exerting undue influence on policy outputs. Due to the large number of actors and interests that can affect decision-making processes, it can be difficult to change policies, and they tend to persist over time.

Examples of Institutional Influences in *Battlestar Galactica*

Institutions play an important role in *Battlestar Galactica*. From the beginning of the series, issues concerning governmental structure, jurisdiction, power, and authority all take center stage. Thinking about these issues in the context of the *Battlestar* universe also provides greater insight into how real-world institutions function, but also how they respond to major shocks, like the Cylon attack.

After the Cylon attack, virtually all of humanity is wiped out, with about 50,000 people left alive. In spite of this enormous shock, we see pre-existing institutions quickly re-emerge. Secretary of Education Laura Roslin fulfills her constitutional obligations by assuming the office of the President of the Twelve Colonies, the legislature is reconstituted, elections are held, and the military continues to provide security to the survivors. Why is this? It would be easy to imagine humanity devolving into several separate bands of survivors. Indeed, other popular science fiction series, like the *Walking Dead*, often depict a world where a cataclysmic event has led to the collapse of organized government and society.

We can think of the persistence of pre-existing institutions as a result of the costs associated with abandoning them. Following the Cylon attack humanity's goal was survival, plain and simple. The Cylon fleet pursued the surviving humans aggressively, attacking every few hours. The *Battlestar Galactica*, as the last military vessel, was the only ship capable of defending the other ships in the fleet. Once the survivors were removed from immediate danger, attention did begin to shift to how to govern their day-to-day lives. Other forms of governance could have been considered, but these options must be viewed against the backdrop of the looming Cylon threat. As far as the humans are initially aware, there is a clear distinction between the Cylons and humanity. The Cylons are large, metallic machines with a giant red "eye." Furthermore, they are organized, and have advanced military capabilities on par with those possessed by the humans. Also, given the environment (deep space) and the fact that the *Galactica* was the only battlestar-class ship to survive the initial Cylon attack, the means of providing security for what was left of humanity were not readily available to all. Denizens of the *Battlestar* universe were also fortunate in that a high-ranking government official and a large military unit survived the initial attacks, preserving some of the most hierarchical and organized entities from before the Cylon attack. Alternatively, in the context of a post-apocalyptic environment like the *Walking Dead*, the enemy is not organized, not strategic, does not possess advanced military capabilities, and does not discriminate between human targets. Under these circumstances, a variety of basic, readily available weapons and tools are sufficient to defend oneself against a zombie or two. Survivors in these environments are also often portrayed as building new organizations, as lone individuals find one another and new groups grow, developing their own organizational rules.

Considering these factors, the transaction costs of forming a new government – i.e., the associated time, energy, risk, and financial costs – would have been quite high, and would have put the survivors at risk. Against this backdrop, pre-existing institutions provided a clear way forward. Laura Roslin, as Secretary of Education, would not necessarily be an obvious choice to lead during what was likely the greatest security crisis that humanity had ever faced. She had no real leadership experience in foreign affairs or any military experience. Yet the Articles of Colonization listed her office (i.e. Secretary of Education) as forty-seventh in the line of succession for the presidency. Accordingly, Roslin's ascension to the presidency was a relatively low-cost decision, and had a relatively high degree of legitimacy, even though she was not democratically elected. That said, her ascension to the presidency did strain her relations with military leaders, and there was some bargaining that took place between Roslin and Commander Adama over their appropriate spheres of authority. Roslin ultimately agreed to cede jurisdiction over security and military matters to Adama, whereas Adama consented to Roslin's authority over the civilian portion of the fleet. Accordingly, we see the re-emergence of institutions that generally resemble those that came before because they represent a familiar set of rules by which the various actors can operate.

Under the circumstances, it is easy to imagine that the civilian government would have collapsed, leaving the military in a position to govern the entire fleet. The military (and by proxy, Commander Adama), with its exclusive control of the *Galactica* and its squadrons of Viper fighters, enjoyed a monopoly on the tools of military force. This would have provided military leaders with a powerful bargaining chip had they wanted to forcibly take control of the government. Although possible, such a move would likely be more difficult than one would initially think. Usurping civilian control of government could lead to challenges to the military's authority and legitimacy. Even in the face of sudden and enormous changes, pre-existing norms and ideas can still exert a powerful influence.[11] Adama himself repeatedly expressed his opinions regarding the proper role of the military in society, as well as his attitudes toward the appropriate norms of democratic governance. Although he possessed the capabilities and the opportunity to do so, forcibly taking over the government was a move that Adama was not willing to make without sufficient motivation.

Furthermore, although such a move would ostensibly increase its power over the affairs of the fleet, even a peaceful and successful takeover would carry costs for the military. Due to shortages in personnel and equipment, the military was already finding it difficult to fulfill its primary role of protecting the survivors; taking on the responsibilities of governing would have likely been beyond the military's capabilities. After all, Adama and his crew were already spending all of their time figuring out how to defend against the Cylon attacks, trying to replenish ammunition and supplies, training new pilots and crew members to replace those lost in combat, and upon the revelation that the Cylons now had units that looked human, trying to figure out how to detect Cylon infiltration of the fleet.

We can also see an element of path dependence in the policies that are adopted by humans toward Cylons. As noted above, we learn that the Cylons have somehow evolved and are able to produce several Cylons that appear to be human, rather than the purely mechanical "toaster" versions that fought during the Cylon War. Debates over the line between humanity and machine animate much of the series. In spite of these Cylons' human appearance and their ability to feel pain and other emotions, humans are slow to change their views. Senior officials continue to approach the Cylons as though they were purely mechanical beings, and their policies reflect the view that Cylons – regardless of appearance – are not human. Even though Roslin and Adama profess their support for democratic institutions and the rights we typically associate with those institutions, they still use torture to gather intelligence from captured humanoid Cylons. Human policy toward the Cylons does change over time, but very slowly. This is partially driven by past experiences. In the case of the military, their job has long been to combat the Cylons, and senior leaders, like Commander Adama, who fought the Cylons in the first Cylon War, have developed attitudes that are not easy to change. Their organizational mission also shapes their views – to provide security for the fleet. Seen in this light, humanoid Cylons are first viewed as threats, which precludes the possibility of viewing them as anything other than machines. These dynamics make top-down policy change difficult at best. The evolution of the relationship between Sharon "Boomer" Valeri, a humanoid Cylon, and the rest of the fleet illustrates the gradual nature of these changes. Upon the revelation that Valeri is a Cylon, she is subject to brutal treatment by other humans. Only through repeated efforts to aid the humans and cooperate with them in evading the other Cylons does it become clear to Roslin, Adama, and others that Valeri is more than just a machine.

The Soldier and the Schoolteacher: Bureaucratic Politics and Civil–Military Relations

One of the most important sets of institutional structures in foreign policy – particularly for democratic states – concerns control of the military. In the United States, the military constitutes the largest group of bureaucratic organizations and actors involved in foreign policymaking. In democratic societies more broadly, the military is viewed as subordinate to the authority of the civilian governments. Civilian officials typically have the final say on when, where, and how military force is used. However, the military remains a powerful and influential actor in the foreign policymaking process, and the reality of civil–military relations is often complex. Military officials can, and often do, use their status and expertise to influence policymaking. Similarly, civilian policymakers may have distinct policy preferences that conflict with military training and goals, leading to conflict between the civilian government and the military.

Bureaucratic Politics and Civil–Military Relations in Theory and Evidence

Whether we are aware of it or not, civilian control of the military presents us with a puzzle. Political scientist Peter Feaver succinctly describes the puzzle, or the central tension, of civil–military relations as follows: "The civil-military challenge is to reconcile a military strong enough to do anything the civilians ask with a military subordinate enough to do only what civilians authorize."[12] If the security of the state depends on the creation of a powerful military force, how can we be sure that this very military force will not be turned on the state it was created to protect? Why do military officials themselves not seize control of government? These issues feature prominently in the *Battlestar* universe as the survivors begin the process of reorganizing themselves.

Political science can offer some insight into how civilian governments relate to the military, as well as where problems and conflict might arise.[13] At its core, the concept of military professionalism consists of the idea that the military officer is a professional – one who specializes in some aspect of the application of violence. This role, however, is one that is necessarily subordinate to the state – to civilian leadership. It is not the duty of the military officer to judge policy, but to provide civilian leaders with a particular type of expertise and advice on how best to employ violence and military force in the pursuit of the state's foreign policy goals. Although these roles might seem clear, military officers may appear to defy civilian control in the course of providing expertise and advice. Such an outcome does not even require the preferences of civilian and military officials to be at odds. For example, Feaver assumes that both the civilian government and the military share the same general goals (i.e., securing the state) but notes that various factors may lead the military to behave in ways that deviate from the civilian government's wishes (i.e. "shirking").[14]

The literature on civil–military relations relates closely to the literature on bureaucratic politics, discussed above. Considering these literatures together can help us to understand the factors that contribute to the level of conflict that exists between the military and civilian government. The idea that military officers should maintain their professionalism and follow civilian orders seems simple, but this can often be a fine line to walk. Bureaucratic politics theory assumes that organizations and the actors within them have distinct preferences, themselves shaped by various aspects of the organization itself. Training and an individual's socialization into the broader organization shape attitudes on the correct ways of carrying out the organization's mission, as well as more narrowly defined tasks. Through extensive training, members of the military become experts in the use of military force. The specifics of this expertise depend on the type of training that individuals receive, on the specific service that they belong to, and also the specific jobs that they have during their careers. The three branches of the United States military (Army, Navy, and Air Force) represent this specialization in its broadest sense. For example, the United States Army's official doctrine emphasizes the importance of its professionalism and expertise in the application of land-based military power, stating that "like other professions, we apply our knowledge using expertise developed through extensive education and training."[15] Within each branch individual officers typically come to focus on and develop skills in very specific areas and activities, such as artillery, infantry, special operations, nuclear weapons, engineering, logistics, intelligence, and more.

Civilian control of the military in democracies is widely perceived as legitimate, even by members of the military. However, this does not mean that the views of civilian policymakers and military officials will be in sync. For example, in Feaver's theory, the first assumption about military officers' preferences is that military actors care about policy goals and how they are pursued.[16] Even where they share more general goals (e.g., the security of the state), this may give rise to divisions between civilian authorities and their military subordinates. Although civilian leaders establish general policy goals, they will generally turn to military officers to provide advice when military force is deemed necessary. The extensive training and experience that military leaders possess implies that they have an objective basis on which to judge the challenges associated with using military force. However, it is possible that their training and experiences will lead them to offer advice that conflicts with civilian goals. For example, policymakers may want to carry out a military operation, but may not like the advice military leaders have to offer regarding the required number of troops, or the expected duration of the operation.

Bureaucratic Politics, Civil–Military Relations, and *Battlestar Galactica*

The question of how a civilian government relates to its military forces pervades much of the *Battlestar* universe. We can easily find examples from the series that help to illustrate some of the basic relationships that scholars of civil–military relations often discuss. Although the basic governmental structure of the Twelve Colonies persisted following the Cylon attack, the incredible circumstances in which the survivors found themselves exerted an incredible strain on these political institutions. Civil–military relations in particular were subjected to extraordinary levels of pressure as the survivors tried to find the best possible strategies for moving forward.

As discussed previously, the structure of the government of the Twelve Colonies of Kobol closely resembles the basic structure of the United States government. Particularly relevant here is the fact that the institutions governing civil–military relations dictated that the civilian government had authority over the military.[17] Laura Roslin became the legal successor to the presidency following the deaths of President Adar and the other members of the president's cabinet, making President Roslin the commander-in-chief of the armed forces. Although technically legitimate, the extreme nature of the security environment following the Cylon attack, and the fact that Roslin's position as secretary of education placed her quite far down on the list of succession, caused many to question the legitimacy of her government, as well as her own individual capacity to govern in a time of extraordinary crisis. Indeed, her status as the 47th in line for the presidency reflected due diligence on the part of the drafters of the Articles of Colonization more than any realistic expectation that a secretary of education would be a likely or desirable leader in a time of crisis.

The tension between the civilian government and the military comes to a head relatively early in the series. Indeed, the precarious reality of President Roslin's position vis-à-vis the military is made apparent by Commander Adama's and Colonel Tigh's derisive remarks that the President is nothing more than a mere "schoolteacher." The initial disdain that military officials show for President Roslin seems to be rooted in the idea that humanity is facing an unprecedented security threat with a president that is woefully under-qualified for the leadership position that she holds. President Roslin and Commander Adama butt heads early on, with Adama demonstrating some reluctance to embrace Roslin's role as president, or to recognize her authority over him. The reluctance of *Galactica*'s senior military officials to immediately submit themselves to the new civilian government may seem reasonable, given the circumstances, but it highlights the fundamental challenges associated with the military's responsibilities to protect the state while also subjecting itself to the orders of a civilian government.

Consider this example: What are senior military leaders to do when their professional military opinion leads them to believe that the policies pursued by civilian officials will expose the military, or even the entire state, to an extraordinary level of risk? Early in the first season, President Roslin embraces a controversial foreign policy aimed at finding the lost planet of Kobol, and eventually planet Earth, which is regarded as nothing more than a fairy tale. Roslin claims to be guided by visions that are seemingly related to ancient religious texts. Increasingly skeptical of her decisions and ability to lead, Commander Adama intervenes, forcing Roslin to resign and imprisoning her in the *Galactica*'s brig. Tensions are exacerbated when a Cylon injures Commander Adama, leading Colonel Tigh to assume command of the *Galactica*. Tigh soon declares martial law and disbands the Quorum of Twelve after Roslin convinced its members to continue supporting her in finding Earth. Captain Lee Adama, President Roslin's military advisor, is imprisoned with Roslin for forcibly resisting the imposition of martial law and attempting to protect Roslin's hold on office.

This represents an extreme case, but it exposes some of the fundamental tensions that military officers confront. If the military is ultimately intended to protect the state and its civilian populace, does there come a point at which the military has a responsibility to use force to check the very government that it is intended to serve? Given that the military is already strained in terms of personnel and resources, pursuing a foreign policy based on vague, ancient religious texts is incredibly risky. At the very least, there is the possibility that the fleet will waste a tremendous amount of resources in search of a planet that may or may not exist. Exploring unknown space would also require the military to provide security with little intelligence of the environment they face. All of this opens the survivors up to a greater risk of annihilation by the Cylons. Alternatively, although he commits a serious act of insubordination by drawing a weapon on Colonel Tigh, a superior officer, Captain Lee Adama is protecting President Roslin and serving his civilian government. The fact that Captain Lee Adama resists Commander

Adama and Colonel Tigh in their efforts to remove President Roslin from power indicates that the appropriate response is far from clear, as both groups believe they are fulfilling their basic responsibilities to protect the survivors. Senior military leaders – Commander Adama and Colonel Tigh – clearly believe that President Roslin's plans represent a significant threat to the survival of the fleet. Alternatively, Lee Adama clearly believes that he has a responsibility to protect Roslin as the rightful head of the government. Neither side wants to see the Cylons win, but the appropriate boundaries for civilian and military leaders are far from clear.

In *Battlestar Galactica* we can see the importance of institutions, especially in the context of civil–military relations. The incredible circumstance in which the survivors find themselves produces a tremendous amount of conflict between the civilian government and the military. Although the traditions and norms associated with democratic governance and the role of the military in a democratic society clearly continue to carry weight, *Battlestar Galactica* illustrates how conflict can arise between the civilian government and its military, even when both groups share common goals.

Conclusion

Battlestar Galactica covers a wide range of topics and themes that are of interest to students of foreign policy. More narrowly, *Battlestar* provides a useful vehicle for understanding the importance of institutional relationships in foreign policy decision making. The basic rules and norms that emerge in the aftermath of the Cylon attack to govern the survivors closely resemble those of the Twelve Colonies that came before. Norms of democratic governance and civilian control of the military continue to carry a great deal of weight. Pre-existing institutional structures provided a clear, low-cost way for the survivors to organize themselves and quickly move forward after the initial attacks. The weight of the past exerted a strong influence on the survivors' policy choices, even as they were forced to re-examine the fundamental nature of the conflict between humanity and the Cylons.

The show also does an exceptional job of highlighting the potential complexities of civil–military relations. Civilian control of the military is just one of the institutions that survives the Cylon attack, but the struggles associated with maintaining the appropriate balance in this relationship figure prominently in driving the *Battlestar* storyline. Despite sharing more general policy goals, we see conflict emerge between the civilian government and the military. Work on civil–military relations and bureaucratic politics can help us to understand how conflict can develop between the military and civilian government under such circumstances.

Ultimately, this discussion only scratches the surface. *Battlestar* is a rich source of relevant and thought-provoking material for students of political science. Although the deep-space setting, complete with robots and spaceships, may seem extraordinary, the issues and questions that the survivors confront are all too real.

Human interactions after the Cylon attack largely resemble those preceding it. How the survivors deal with challenges, the rules they follow, the views they hold, and the policies they pursue are heavily rooted in their past experiences. Remember, all this has happened before, and all of this will happen again.

Chapter Discussion Questions

1. Governments often use security threats as justification for suspending or altering specific institutions – sometimes temporarily, and sometimes permanently. Discuss how the security threat posed by the Cylons is used to justify these sorts of actions by both the military and the civilian government in *Battlestar Galactica*. Think of examples of similar behavior in the real world.
2. The nature of the Cylon threat changes throughout the series. Specifically, the survivors quickly discover that the Cylons have created new "human" Cylons, who look, feel, and act just like "regular" humans. How does this discovery change the nature of the relationship between the humans and the Cylons? How does it change the nature of the relationships amongst the survivors themselves? Ultimately, how do you think these issues influence the survivors' policymaking decisions?
3. In Season 2 we are introduced to Admiral Helena Cain and the *Battlestar Pegasus*. The introduction of Cain, as well as the *Pegasus* and its crew, represents a major shock to the survivors. Discuss how Roslin, Adama, and the crew of the *Galactica* react to Cain's arrival. How does her introduction affect the nature of civil–military relations in the Fleet? What, if any, problems does it create for the survivors in the military and/or in government?

Notes

1 Throughout the article I will use the term *Battlestar* to refer to the entire show and/or universe. When referring to the ship itself, I will refer to it as the *Galactica*.
2 "Cylons," Battlestar Galactica Wiki, http://en.battlestarwiki.org/wiki/Cylons, accessed December 3, 2014.
3 "Government of the Twelve Colonies," Battlestar Galactica Wiki. http://en.battlestarwiki.org/wiki/Government_of_the_Twelve_Colonies, accessed January 5, 2015.
4 "Colonial Fleet (TRS)," Battlestar Galactica Wiki, http://en.battlestarwiki.org/wiki/Colonial_Fleet_%28TRS%29, accessed January 5, 2015.
5 Ibid.
6 North, Douglass C. 1990. *Institutions, institutional change, and economic performance*. New York: Cambridge University Press, 4.
7 North, *Institutions, institutional change, and economic performance*, 83.
8 Ibid., 89–91.
9 Allison, Graham T. 1969. "Conceptual models and the Cuban missile crisis," *American Political Science Review*, 63(3): 689–718; Halperin, Morton, Priscilla Clapp, and Arnold Kanter. 2006. *Bureaucratic politics and foreign policy*. Washington, D.C.: Brookings Institution Press.

10 This is a common assumption in political science. For example, see Bueno de Mesquita, Bruce, Alastair Smith, Randolph Siverson, and James D. Morrow. 1990. *The logic of political survival*. Cambridge, MA: The MIT Press.
11 North, *Institutions, institutional change, and economic performance*.
12 Feaver, Peter. 2005. *Armed servants: Agency, oversight, and civil-military relations*. Cambridge, MA: Harvard University Press, 4.
13 For key works on civil–military relations, see Huntington, Samuel P. 1981. *The soldier and the state: The theory and politics of civil-military relations*. Cambridge, MA: The Belknap Press of Harvard University Press; Feaver, *Armed servants*.
14 Ibid.
15 United States Army. 2012. *Army Doctrine Publication (ADP) 1*, 2–5.
16 Feaver, *Armed servants*, 63.
17 "Government of the Twelve Colonies," Battlestar Galactica Wiki, http://en.battlestarwiki.org/wiki/Government_of_the_Twelve_Colonies, accessed January 5, 2015.

NOTES ON CONTRIBUTORS

Michael A. Allen is an Assistant Professor of Political Science at Boise State University. His research and teaching focus on asymmetric relations between powerful and weak actors in the global economy, inter-state conflict, civil war, insurgency, and terrorism. In addition to working on the above topics using quantitative research and game theory, he enjoys the genres of science fiction and fantasy and is an avid player of competitive games of strategy across trading card games, board games, and video games.

Ted Henry Brown is an Assistant Professor of Political Science at Southwestern Oklahoma State University. He routinely teaches courses in political theory, international relations, and research methods. His research interests are diverse but include studies of rhetoric, political theory, and the analysis of public policy and popular culture. Previously, he has co-authored a book chapter on *Ender's Game* with Christie L. Maloyed.

Zachary Callen attended Illinois State University, where he earned a B.A. in 2001 and an M.S. in 2003. He received an M.A. from the University of Chicago in 2005, followed by his Ph.D. in 2009 and is now an Assistant Professor at Allegheny College. His research focuses on issues of federalism, local politics, public policy, political geography, and transportation infrastructure. In particular, he is interested in antebellum railroad and canal developments, with a particular focus on how previously local internal improvement projects became national issues. His more recent research emphasizes rural economic development and the role of technology in state building. He is a long-time science fiction fan, and cannot help but be excited about the new *Star Wars* movies.

Raymond V. Carman, Jr. is an Assistant Professor of Political Science at State University of New York College at Plattsburgh. His teaching and research focuses on American political institutions (including courts, federalism, intergovernmental relations, and state politics) as well as judicial behavior and politics (including civil rights and liberties, constitutional law, judicial decision making, judicial selection, and the psychology of judging). His most recent research draws from both political science and social psychology in order to explore what causes state high court judges to develop particular role orientations – or beliefs about what should properly be allowed to influence their decisions – and to examine what effect role orientations have on judicial decision making.

Conor M. Dowling is an Assistant Professor in the Department of Political Science at the University of Mississippi. His research and teaching interests are in American Politics, where he studies both mass and elite political behavior with a substantive focus on issues of electoral competition, representation, and public policy, campaign finance law in particular. In terms of science fiction, he currently enjoys watching *Star Wars* and *Harry Potter* with his children.

Jennifer Kelkres Emery directs the Site Relations department at The Washington Center. Her research is published in the *Journal of Policy History*, the *Journal of Political Science Education*, and *PS: Political Science*. As an Assistant Professor at the University of West Florida, she taught courses in American politics, political psychology, the media, and research methods. She is currently completing a book on partisanship in America, with a focus on social identity theory.

Jocelyn Evans is a Professor of Political Science at the University of West Florida where she serves as the Associate Dean of the College of Arts, Social Sciences, and Humanities. She is the author of *Women, Partisanship, and Congress* (Palgrave, 2005) *One Nation Under Siege: Congress, Terrorism, and the Fate of American Democracy* (University of Kentucky Press, 2011), and *Central Ideas in American Government* (Soomo Publishing, 2014, 5th ed.) with Dr. Kristy Michaud. Her work has also appeared in several journals, including *Social Science Quarterly, Journal of Political Science Education*, and *National Social Science Journal*.

Benjamin Farrer is an Assistant Professor in the Environmental Studies Department at Knox College, Illinois. His main interest is in under-represented groups in democratic societies. His research and teaching activities focus on parties and interest groups, environmental policy, and methodology.

Michael E. Flynn is an Assistant Professor of Political Science at Kansas State University. He received his Ph.D. in political science from Binghamton University in 2013. His work focuses on the political economy of state behavior in the areas of foreign policy, conflict, and security. He also focuses on the intersection of foreign policy and human rights issues, with a focus on non-governmental organizations.

Lilly J. Goren is Professor of Political Science and Global Studies at Carroll University in Waukesha, Wisconsin. Her research integrates popular culture, literature, and film as a means to understanding politics. Her published books include *Mad Men and Politics: Nostalgia and the Remaking of Modern America* (Bloomsbury Publishers, 2015, co-edited with Linda Beail); *Women and the White House: Gender, Popular Culture, and Presidential Politics* (University Press of Kentucky, 2012, co-edited with Justin Vaughn) – winner of both the 2014 Susan Koppelman Book Award and the 2014 Peter C. Rollins Book Award; *You've Come a Long Way, Baby: Women, Politics, and Popular Culture* (University Press of Kentucky, 2009); and *Not in My District: The Politics of Military Base Closures* (Peter Lang, 2003), as well as articles in *Political Research Quarterly, White House Studies*, and Berkeley Electronic Press's *The Forum*.

Steve B. Lem is Associate Professor and Chairperson of the Department of Political Science at Kutztown University of Pennsylvania. He obtained his Ph.D. in political science from Binghamton University (SUNY). His research focuses on political representation in Western democracies with a particular emphasis on the link between voters, political parties, and welfare policy. In addition to his interests in political science, he is an avid science fiction and comic book fan.

Christie L. Maloyed is an associate instructor in the Office of the First-Year Experience at University of Louisiana at Lafayette. She teaches courses on theories of democracy, religion and politics, and the history of political thought. Her research focuses on religion in the American founding era and current debates over civic education. She has also worked in the area of politics and pop culture and has published on AMC's show *Mad Men* and co-authored a book chapter with Ted Henry Brown on Orson Scott Card's *Ender's Game*.

Scott E. Robinson is the Bellmon Chair of Public Service at the University of Oklahoma. His research and teaching focus on the management of public service organizations as they cope with various forms of disasters or extreme events. His research has appeared in the *International Journal of Mass Emergencies and Disasters* and the *Journal of Emergency Management* as well as the *American Journal of Political Science* and the *Journal of Public Administration Research and Theory*. His current projects include better models for vulnerability to tornados and public trust in government organizations – especially those that seek to provide advice on public safety issues.

Mary Elizabeth Sullivan is Assistant Professor of Political Science at the University of Central Arkansas. Her research interests include Medieval and

Renaissance political theory, political language, and the transmission of classical political sources. She received her Ph.D. in Political Science from Texas A&M University in 2010.

Joseph E. Uscinski is an Associate Professor of Political Science at University of Miami. He originally hails from New Hampshire. He received his B.A. from Plymouth State University and his M.A. from University of New Hampshire. He earned his Ph.D. in American politics at the University of Arizona. He is the author of *American Conspiracy Theories* (Oxford University Press, 2014) and *The People's News: Media, Politics, and the Demands of Capitalism* (New York University Press, 2014).

Julie VanDusky-Allen is a lecturer in the Department of Political Science at Boise State University. She teaches courses in Comparative Politics, American Politics, and research methods. Her research focuses on how political parties adapt to and overcome institutional limits to their power. She has recently published work in *Comparative Political Studies, Politics and Policy*, and *Foreign Policy Analysis.* With respect to science fiction, she especially enjoys stories about space travel and time travel.

Justin S. Vaughn is an Associate Professor of Political Science at Boise State University. His research focuses on American national politics, especially related to the presidency. He has published five books and more than two dozen scholarly articles and essays, including the award-winning book, *Women and the White House: Gender, Popular Culture, and Presidential Politics* (University Press of Kentucky, 2012, with Lilly Goren).

BIBLIOGRAPHY

Aikau, Hokulani K., Karla A. Erickson, and Jennifer L. Pierce, eds. 2007. *Feminist waves, feminist generations*. Minneapolis, MN: University of Minnesota Press.
Aldrich, John. 1995. *Why parties? The origin and transformation of party politics in America*. Chicago: University of Chicago Press.
Allison, Graham T. 1969. "Conceptual models and the Cuban missile crisis," *American Political Science Review*, 63(3): 689–718.
Almond, Gabriel. 1956. "Comparative political systems," *Journal of Politics*, 18(3): 391–409.
Arrow, V. 2012. *The Panem companion: From Mellark Bakery to Mockingjays*. Dallas: Ben Bella Books.
Asherman, Allan. 1988. *The Star Trek Interview Book*. New York: Pocket Books.
Atkinson, Matthew D., Ryan D. Enos, and Seth J. Hill. 2009. "Candidate faces and election outcomes: Is the face-vote correlation caused by candidate selection," *Quarterly Journal of Political Science*, 4(3): 229–249.
Barbour, Christine and Gerald C. Wright. 2015. *Keeping the Republic: Power and citizens in American politics: The essentials, Edition* 7. Thousand Oaks, CA: CQ Press.
Bellamy, Richard. 2008. *Citizenship: A very short introduction*. Oxford: Oxford University Press.
Benner, Laurence A. 1989. "Requiem for Miranda: The Rehnquist Court's voluntariness doctrine in historical perspective," *Washington University Law Review*, 67(1): 59–163.
Benoit, William L. 2006. "Retrospective versus prospective statements and outcome of presidential elections," *Political Research Quarterly*, 56(2): 331–345.
Best, Robin E. 2011. "The declining electoral relevance of traditional cleavage groups," *European Political Science Review*, 3(2): 279–300.
Bianco, William T. and David T. Canon. 2015. *American politics today, fourth essentials edition*. New York: W. W. Norton & Company.
Borrelli, MaryAnne. 2002, *The President's cabinet: Gender, power, and representation*. Boulder, CO: Lynne Rienner.
Braumoeller, Bear F. 1997. "Deadly doves: Liberal nationalism and the democratic peace in the Soviet successor states," *International Studies Quarterly*, 41(3): 375–402.
Brennan, G. and L. Lomasky. 1993. *Democracy and decision: The pure theory of electoral preference*. Cambridge: Cambridge University Press.
Brin, David and Matthew Woodring Stover. 2006. *Star Wars on trial*. Dallas: Benbella Books, Inc.

Brooker, Paul. 2000. *Non-democratic regimes, theory, government, & politics*. New York: Palgrave MacMillan.

Bueno de Mesquita, Bruce, James D. Morrow, Randolph M. Siverson, and Alastair Smith. 1999. "An institutional explanation of the democratic peace," *American Political Science Review*, 93(4): 791–807.

Bueno de Mesquita, Bruce, Alastair Smith, Randolph Siverson, and James D. Morrow. 1990. *The logic of political survival*. Cambridge, MA: The MIT Press.

Campbell, Angus, Philip Converse, Warren Miller, and Donald Stokes. 1960. *The American voter*. Chicago: University of Chicago Press.

Campbell, Joseph. 2008. *The hero with a thousand faces: The collected works of Joseph Campbell*. Novato, CA: New World Library.

Card, Orson Scott. 1985. *Ender's Game*. New York: Tor Publishing.

Carpini, Michael X. Delli and Scott Keeter. 1996. *What Americans know about politics and why it matters*. New Haven, CT: Yale University Press.

Collins, Suzanne. 2008. *The Hunger Games*. New York: Scholastic Press.

Congressional Research Service. 2014. *The Constitution of the United States of America: Analysis and interpretation*, Centennial ed. Washington: U.S. Government Printing Office.

Converse, Phillip E. 1964. "The nature of belief systems in mass publics." In *Ideology and Discontent*, ed. David E. Apter. New York: Free Press of Glencoe, 206–261.

Cook, James L. 2013 "Ender's beginning and the just war." In *Ender's Game and philosophy: The logic gate is down*, eds. Kevin S. Decker and William Irwin. Chichester: Wiley & Sons, 151–162.

Cooper, Kody W. 2013. "The unspoken rules of manly warfare: Just war theory in Ender's Game." In *Ender's Game and philosophy: The logic gate is down*, eds. Kevin S. Decker and William Irwin. Chichester: Wiley & Sons, 175–186.

Courtois, Stéphane and Mark Kramer, eds. 1999 *The black book of communism: Crimes, terror, repression*. Cambridge, MA: Harvard University Press.

Dahl, Robert A. 1971. *Polyarchy: Participation and opposition*. New Haven, CT: Yale University Press.

Dalton, Russell J. 2014. *Citizen politics: Public opinion and political parties in advanced industrial democracies*, 6th edition. Thousand Oaks, CA: Sage CQ Press.

Dauber, Michele Landis. 2013. *The sympathetic state: Disaster relief and the origins of the American welfare state*. Chicago: The University of Chicago Press.

Dawson, Michael C. 1995. *Behind the mule: Race and class in African-American politics*. Princeton, NJ: Princeton University Press.

Delaney, Tim. 2007. "Pop culture: An overview," *Popular Culture and Philosophy*, 64 (December): 6–7.

DeLeon, Richard E. and Katherine C. Naff. 2004. "Identity politics and local political culture: Some comparative results from the social capital benchmark survey," *Urban Affairs Review*, 39(6): 689–719.

Dicker, Rory and Alison Piepmeier, eds. 2003. *Catching a wave: Reclaiming feminism for the 21st century*. Boston, MA: Northeastern University Press.

Dolman, Everett Carl. 1997. "Military, democracy, and the state in Robert A. Heinlein's Starship Troopers." In *Political Science Fiction*, eds. Donald M. Hassler and Clyde Wilcox. Columbia, SC: University of South Carolina Press, 196–213.

Dovi, Suzanne, 2002. "Preferable descriptive representatives: Will just any woman, black, or Latino do?" *The American Political Science Review*, 96(4): 729–743.

Downs, Anthony. 1957. *An economic theory of democracy*. New York: Harper and Row.

Doyle, Michael W. 1983 "Kant, liberal legacies, and foreign affairs," *Philosophy & Public Affairs*, 12(3): 205–35.

Dunn, John. 2005. *Democracy: A history*. New York: Atlantic Monthly Press.

Edling, Max M. 2008. *A revolution in favor of government: Origins of the U.S. Constitution and the making of the American state*. Oxford: Oxford University Press.

Elazar, Daniel. 1970. *Cities of the prairie: The metropolitan frontiers do American politics*. New York Basic Books.

Elazar, Thomas. 1972. *American Federalism: A view from the states*. 2nd edition. New York: Harper & Row.

Entman, Robert. 1989. *Democracy without citizens*. New York: Oxford University Press.

Epstein, Lee, Jeffrey A. Segal, Harold J. Spaeth, and Thomas G. Walker. 2012. *The Supreme Court compendium: Data, decisions, and developments*, 5th edition. Thousand Oaks, CA: CQ Press.

Fearon, James D. 1995. "Rationalist explanations for war," *International Organization*, 49(3): 379–414.

Feaver, Peter. 2005. *Armed servants: Agency, oversight, and civil-military relations*. Cambridge, MA: Harvard University Press.

Findlen, Barbara. 2001. *Listen up: Voices from the next feminist generation*. Emeryville, CA: Seal Press.

Fiorina, Morris P. 1981. *Retrospective voting in American national elections*. New Haven, CT: Yale University Press.

Franklin, Benjamin. 1756. To Governor Richard Morris on Behalf of the Pennsylvania Assembly, 11 November 1755, in *Votes and proceedings of the House of Representatives, 1755–1756*. Philadelphia: New Printing Office.

Garner, Robert, Peter Ferdinand, and Stephanie Lawson. 2012. *Introduction to politics*. Oxford: Oxford University Press.

Ghandi, Jennifer. 2008. *Political institutions under dictatorship*. Cambridge: Cambridge University Press.

Gillis, Stacy, Gillian Howie, and Rebecca Munford, eds. 2007. *Third wave feminism: A Critical exploration*. New York: Palgrave MacMillan

Gladwell, Malcom. 2000. *The tipping point: How little things can make a big difference*. New York: Little, Brown, and Company.

Gladwell, Malcom. 2005. *Blink: The power of thinking without thinking*. New York: Little, Brown, and Company.

"Global Peace Index: 2014," *Institute for Economics & Peace*, http://www.visionofhumanity.org/sites/default/files/2014%20Global%20Peace%20Index%20REPORT_0.pdf, accessed March 1, 2015.

"Global Study on Homicide," *United Nations Office on Drugs and Crime*, 2015, http://www.unodc.org/gsh, accessed March 1, 2015.

Goren, Lilly J. 2012, "Fact or fiction: The reality of race and gender in reaching the White House." In *Women and the White House: Gender, Popular Culture and Presidential Politics*, eds. Justin S. Vaughn and Lilly J. Goren. Lexington, KY: University Press of Kentucky, 97–120.

Green, Donald and Ian Shapiro. 1994. *Pathologies of rational choice theory*. New Haven, CT: Yale University Press.

Green, Donald, Bradley Palmquist, and Eric Schickler. 2002. *Partisan hearts & minds: Political parties and the social identities of voters*. New Haven, CT: Yale University Press.

Gurr, Ted R. 1970. *Why men rebel*. Princeton, NJ: Princeton University Press.

Hagopian, Frances and Scott P. Mainwaring. 2005. *The third wave of democratization in Latin America: Advances and setbacks*. Cambridge: Cambridge University Press.

Hall, Richard L. and Frank W. Wayman. 1990. "Buying time: Moneyed interests and the mobilization of bias in Congressional committees," *The American Political Science Review*, 84(3): 797–820.

Halperin, Morton, Priscilla Clapp, and Arnold Kanter. 2005. *Bureaucratic politics and foreign policy*. Washington, D.C.: Brookings Institution Press.

Hamilton, Alexander, James Madison, and John Jay. 2003. *The Federalist papers with letters from "Brutus,"* ed. T. Ball. Cambridge: Cambridge University Press.

Hansen, John Mark. 1991. *Gaining access: Congress and the farm lobby 1919–1981*. Chicago: The University of Chicago Press.

Hantke, Steffen. 1998. "Surgical strikes and prosthetic warriors: The soldier's body in contemporary science fiction," *Science Fiction Studies*, 25(3): 495–509.

Haywood, Leslie and Jennifer Drake, eds. 2003. *Third wave agenda: Being feminist, doing feminism*. Minneapolis, MN: University of Minnesota Press.

Heater, Derek Benjamin. 2004. *A brief history of citizenship*. New York: New York University Press.

Heinlein, Robert. 1959. *Starship Troopers*. Reprint, New York: Ace.

Hernandez, Daisy and Bushra Rehman. 2002. eds. *Colonize this! Young women of color on today's feminism*. New York: Seal Press.

Hokulani, K., Karla A. Erickson, and Jennifer L. Pierce, eds. 2007. *Feminist waves, feminist generations*. Minneapolis, MN: University of Minnesota Press.

Holmes, Anna. 2012. "White until proven black: Imagining race in Hunger Games." *The New Yorker*, http://www.newyorker.com/books/page-turner/white-until-proven-black-imagining-race-in-hunger-games, accessed January 12, 2015.

Horwitz, Linda and Holly Swyers. 2010. "Why are all the presidents men?: Televisual presidents and patriarchy." In *You've come a long way, baby: Women, politics, and popular culture*, ed. Lilly J. Goren. Lexington, KY: University Press of Kentucky, 115–134.

Huntington, Samuel P. 1981. *The soldier and the state: The theory and politics of civil-military relations*. Cambridge, MA: The Belknap Press of Harvard University Press.

Huntington, Samuel P. 1996. *The clash of civilizations and the remaking of world order*. New York: Simon and Schuster.

Inglehart, Robert. 1971. "The silent revolution in Europe: Intergenerational change in post-industrial societies," *American Political Science Review* 65(4): 991–1017.

Inglehart, Ronald and Christian Welzel. 2009. "How development leads to democracy: What we know about modernization," *Foreign Affairs* (March/April), http://www.foreignaffairs.com/articles/64821/ronald-inglehart-and-christian-welzel/how-deve lopment- leads-to-democracy, accessed May 18, 2015.

Jackson, Andrew to Andrew Jackson Donelson. 1996. 5 July 1822, in *The papers of Andrew Jackson, 1821–1824*, eds. Harold D. Moser, David R. Hoth, and George H. Hoemann. Knoxville, TN: University of Tennessee Press.

Katz, Richard S. and Peter Mair. 1994. *How parties organize: Change and adaptation in party organizations in Western democracies*. London: Sage.

Kertzer, David I. 1988. *Ritual, politics, and power*. New Haven, CT: Yale University Press.

Key, V. O., Jr. 1942. *Political parties and pressure groups*. New York: Thomas Y. Crowell Company.

Keyssar, Alexander. 2009. *The right to vote: The contested history of democracy in the United States*. New York: Basic Books.

Kitschelt, Herber, Peter Lange, Gary Marks, and John D. Stephens. 1999. *Continuity and change in contemporary capitalism*. Cambridge: Cambridge University Press.

Kohn, Alfie. 2000. *The case against standardized testing: Raising the scores, ruining the schools*. Portsmouth, NH: Heinemann.

Laakso, Markku and Rein Taagepera. 1979. "'Effective' number of parties: A measure with application to West Europe," *Comparative Political Studies*, 12(1): 3–27.

Lanoue, David. J. 1994. "Retrospective and prospective voting in presidential-year elections," *Political Research Quarterly*, 47(1): 193–205.

Larson, John Lauritz. 2001. *Internal improvement: National public works and the promise of popular government in the early United States*. Chapel Hill, NC: The University of North Carolina Press.

Lau, Richard R. and David P. Redlawsk. 2001. "Advantages and disadvantages of cognitive heuristics in political decision making," *American Journal of Political Science*, 45(4): 951–971.

Lawson, Chappell, Gabriel S. Lenz, Andy Baker, Michael Myers. 2010. "Looking like a winner: Candidate appearance and electoral success in new democracies," *World Politics*, 63(4): 561–593.

Lazarfeld, P. F., B. Berelson, H. Gaudet. 1948. *The people's choice: How the voter makes up his mind in a presidential campaign*. New York: Columbia University Press.

Lee, Mordecai and Susan C. Paddock. 2001. "Strange but true tales from Hollywood: The bureaucrat as movie hero," *Public Administration & Management*, 6(4): 166–194.

LeGates, Marlene. 2001. *In their time: A history of feminism in Western society*. New York: Routledge Press.

Lenz, Gabriel S. 2012. *Follow the leader: How voters respond to politicians' policies and performance*. Chicago: University of Chicago Press.

Lenz, Gabriel S. and Chappell Lawson. 2011. "Looking the part: Television leads less informed citizens to vote based on candidates' appearance," *American Journal of Political Science*, 55(3): 574–589.

Lichbach, Mark I. 1994. "What makes rational peasants revolutionary? Dilemma, paradox, and irony in peasant collective action," *World Politics*, 46(3): 383–418.

Lijphart, Arend. 1999. *Patterns of democracy, government forms and performance in thirty-six countries*. New Haven, CT: Yale University Press.

Linz, Juan J. 1978. *The breakdown of democratic regimes: Crisis, breakdown, & reequilibration*. Baltimore, MD: The Johns Hopkins University Press.

Lipset, Seymour and Stein Rokkan. 1967. *Party systems and voter alignments: Cross-national perspectives*. Toronto: The Free Press.

Lupia, Arthur. 1994. "Shortcuts versus encyclopedias: Information and voting behavior in California insurance reform elections," *American Political Science Review*, 88(1): 63–76.

Lyall, Jason. 2009. "Does indiscriminate violence incite insurgent attacks? Evidence from Chechnya," *Journal of Conflict Resolution*, 53(3): 331–362.

McFarland, Daniel A., James Moody, David Diehl, Jeffrey A. Smith, and Reuben J. Thomas. 2014. "Network ecology and adolescent social structure," *American Sociological Review*, 79(6): 1088–1121.

Magstadt, Thomas M. 2015. *Understanding politics: Ideas, institutions, and issues*. Stamford, CT: Cengage Learning.

Mansbridge, Jane. 1999. "Should blacks represent blacks and women represent women? A contingent 'yes,'" *Journal of Politics*, 61(3): 628–657.

Mansbridge, Jane. 2003. "Rethinking representation," *American Political Science Review*, 97(4): 515–528.

Maoz, Zeev and Bruce Russett. 1993. "Normative and structural causes of democratic peace, 1946–1986," *American Political Science Review*, 87(3): 624–638.

Marshall, Monty G., Ted Robert Gurr, and Keith Jaggers. 2014. *Polity IV project: Political regime characteristics and transitions: 1800–2013*, Center for Systemic Peace, http://www.systemicpeace.org, accessed April 28, 2015.

Mason, Amelia. 2014. "The hidden roots of 'Hunger Games' hit song? Murder ballads, civil rights hymns." *The Artery*, http://artery.wbur.org/2014/12/10/hunger-games-mockingjay, accessed January 15, 2015.

Massicotte, Louis, André Blais, and Antonie Yoshinaka. 2004. *Establishing the rules of the game: Election laws in democracies*. Toronto: University of Toronto Press.

Mayhew, David R. 2004. *Congress: The electoral connection*. 2nd edition New Haven, CT: Yale University Press.

Migdalek, Jack. 2014. *The embodied performance of gender*. New York: Routledge Press.

Mill, John Stuart and Harriet Taylor Mill. 1970. *Essays on sex equality: John Stuart Mill and Harriet Taylor Mill*, ed. Alice Rossi. Chicago: University of Chicago Press.

Miller, Ross A. "Domestic structures and the diversionary use of force," *American Journal of Political Science*, 39(3): 760–785.

Montesquieu, Charles de. 2002. *The spirit of the laws*, ed. A. M. Cohler, B. C. Miller, and H. S. Stone. New York: Cambridge University Press.

Morgenthau, Hans J. 1993. *Politics among nations: The struggle for power and peace*. Boston, MA: McGraw-Hill.

Nagle, Thomas. 1972 "War and massacre," *Philosophy and Public Affairs*, 1(2): 123–144.

Norris, Pippa, 2008. *Driving democracy: Do power-sharing institutions work?* Cambridge: Cambridge University Press.

North, Douglass C. 1990. *Institutions, institutional change, and economic performance*. New York: Cambridge University Press.

Novak, William J. 1996. *The people's welfare: Law and regulation in nineteenth-century America*. Chapel Hill, NC: The University of North Carolina Press.

Oneal, John and Bruce Russett. 1999. "Is the liberal peace just an artifact of Cold War interests? Assessing recent critiques," *International Interactions*, 25(3): 213–241.

Phillips, Anne. 1998. "Democracy and representation: Or, why should it matter who our representatives are?" In *Feminism and Politics*, ed. Anne Phillips. Oxford: Oxford University Press, 224–241.

Pitkin, Hanna Fenichel. 1967. *The concept of representation*. Berkeley, CA: University of California Press.

Pocock, J. G. A. 1992. "The ideal of citizenship since classical times," *Queen's Quarterly*, 99(Spring): 35–55.

Popkin, Samuel L. 1991. *The reasoning voter: Communication and persuasion in presidential campaigns*. Chicago: University of Chicago Press.

Popper, Karl. 2002. *The logic of scientific discovery*. New York: Routledge.

Powell, Jr., G. Bingham. 1986. "American voter turnout in comparative perspective," *American Political Science Review*, 80(1): 17–43.

Prilleltensky, Isaac and Lev Gonick. 1996. "Polities change, oppression remains: On the psychology and politics of oppression," *Political Psychology*, 17(1): 127–148.

Putnam, Robert. 1994. *Making democracy work: Civic traditions in modern Italy*. Princeton, NJ: Princeton University Press.

Rao, Gautham. 2008. "Sailors' health and national wealth: Marine hospitals in the early republic," *Common-Place* 9(1), http://www.common-place-archives.org/vol-09/no-01/rao, accessed October 12, 2014.

Regan, Patrick M. 2009. *Sixteen million one: Understanding civil war*. Boulder, CO: Paradigm Publishers.

Riker, William H. 1982. "The two-party system and Duverger's Law: An essay on the history of political science," *American Political Science Review*, 76(4): 753–766.

Riker, William H. and P. C. Ordeshook. 1968. "A theory of the calculus of voting," *American Political Science Review*, 62(1): 25–42.

Rodden, Jonathan A. 2006. *Hamilton's paradox: The promise and peril of fiscal federalism*. Cambridge: Cambridge University Press.

Roth, Veronica. 2001. *Divergent*. New York: HarperCollins Publishers.

Roth, Veronica. 2012. *Insurgent*. New York: Katherine Tegen Books.

Saval, Nikil. 2014. "The secret history of life-hacking." *Pacific Standard*, April 22, 2014, http://www.psmag.com/business, accessed May 15, 2015.

Schuessler, A. A. 2000. *A logic of expressive choice*. Princeton, NJ: Princeton University Press.

Schultz, Kenneth. 1999. "Do democratic institutions constrain or inform?" *International Organization*, 53(2): 233–266.

Schumpeter, Joseph. 1943. *Capitalism, socialism, and democracy*. 1971 reprint. New York: Routledge.

Skowronek, Stephen. 1982. *Building a new American state: The expansion of national administrative capacities 1877–1920*. Cambridge: Cambridge University Press.

Surowiecki, James. 2005. *The wisdom of crowds*. New York: Anchor Books.

Teaford, Jon C. 2002. *The rise of the states: Evolution of American state government*. Baltimore, MD: The Johns Hopkins University Press.

Thucydides. 2008. *The landmark Thucydides: A comprehensive guide to the Peloponnesian War*, ed. Robert B. Strassler. New York: Simon and Schuster.

Tilly, Charles, Peter B. Evans, Dietrich Rueschemeyer, and Theda Skocpol. 1985. *War making and state making as organized crime*. Cambridge, MA: Cambridge University Press.

Todorov, Alexander, Anesu N. Mandisodza, Amir Goren, and Crystal C. Hall. 2005. "Inferences of competence from faces predict election outcomes," *Science*, 308(5728): 1623–1626.

Tooker, Elisabeth, 1978. "The league of the Iroquois: Its history, politics, and ritual." In *Handbook of North American Indians*, ed. William C. Sturtevant. Washington, D.C.: Government Printing Office, 418–441.

United States Army. 2012. *Army Doctrine Publication (ADP) 1*, 2–5.

Vaughn, Justin and Lilly J. Goren, eds. 2012. *Women and the White House: Gender, popular culture and presidential politics*. Lexington, KY: University Press of Kentucky.

Von Neumann, John and Oscar Morgenstern. 1944. *Theory of games and economic behavior*. Princeton, NJ: Princeton University Press.

Walker, David B. 2000. *The rebirth of federalism: Slouching towards Washington*. 2nd edition New York: Chatham House.

Walker, Rebecca. 1995. *To be real: Telling the truth and changing the face of feminism*. New York: Anchor Books.

Walzer, Michael. 2006. *Just and unjust wars: A moral argument with historical examples*. New York: Basic Books.

Watson, Cynthia Ann. 2007. *U.S. Military service: A reference handbook*. Santa Barbara, CA: ABC-CLIO, INC.

Weber, Max. 2009. *From Max Weber: Essays in sociology*, ed. H. H. Gerth and C. Wright Mills. Abingdon, Oxon: Routledge.

Wollstonecraft, Mary. 1967. *A vindication of the rights of women*. New York: W. W. Norton.

INDEX

For Product Safety Concerns and Information please contact our EU representative GPSR@taylorandfrancis.com
Taylor & Francis Verlag GmbH, Kaufingerstraße 24, 80331 München, Germany

www.ingramcontent.com/pod-product-compliance
Lightning Source LLC
Chambersburg PA
CBHW071518110726
47908CB00003B/879

* 9 7 8 1 1 3 8 6 3 9 7 7 5 *